SEED

OF THE

VOLGA

KAREN SCHUTTE

Seed of the Volga ----- Karen Schutte

Scripture quotations are taken from the *Holy Bible, King James Version*, Cambridge, 1769. Permission, all rights reserved.

This novel is a work of fiction because several names and dates have been changed. The novel is based on the lives of real people.

Published by Green Spring Publishing 2015; all rights reserved.

ISBN for printed material: 978-0-9904095-3-3

ISBN for e-book: 978-0-9904095-4-0

© *Cover design by* Thayne Sturdevant, Graphic Design. Cover photograph of Kanton Church, Susannenthal, Russia is property of Karen Schutte

2015 Interior Design: Elizabeth Klenda at Frontier Printing, Fort Collins, CO.

Published in the United States of America by Green Spring Publishing – Fort Collins, CO. 80528

Historical Fiction: Second in the Family Saga Trilogy by Karen Schutte

Books by Karen Schutte

The Ticket – 1st in the Trilogy – 2010 – 2015

Seed of the Volga – 2nd in the Trilogy
First Edition 2013; 2nd Edition 2015

Flesh on the Bone – 3rd in the Trilogy - 2014

Watch for THE TANK COMMANDER - 2016

They came to America with the Bible in one hand and a sugar beet hoe in the other.

— author unknown

Dedication

This book is dedicated to my mother, Beata.

Acknowledgments

The first chapter of this novel was inspired by one particular story, told to me by my grandmother, Raisa in her broken English. It was a no-brainer to select this intriguing story that continued to fascinate me; it was the story about her 'princess' grandmother, who was born in a German castle. After extensive research, it was discovered that the princess was actually her great-grandmother; it was she who fled the castle with an aunt to journey to the Volga River settlements in Russia. Her last name was Hohenzollern—German royalty from Hesse. It is said that, German Prince Frederick Hohenzollern currently lives in the Black Forest family castle. I predict another trip to Germany to perhaps meet with Prince Frederick or in the least, to examine their family tree.

As a longtime student of history, I am highly influenced by historical family tales and the manner in which the actual history is woven into the stories. I am very grateful and proud of the sacrifices these people, especially my family, has made for themselves and for those who followed. Their fascinating lives have compelled and challenged me to tell their story, the story of *Die Wolgadeutschen.* I dedicate this historical novel not only to my mother, but also to the courageous Germans of the Volga, who left behind a life that was becoming unbearable, in hope of finding freedom and opportunity in America. They came to America with a Bible in one hand and a sugar beet hoe in the other. The first, second, and third generations carry on their legacy. I wrote this story so you may read and understand what our forefathers' decisions and sacrifices mean to all of us.

As in my first novel, *The Ticket,* I have changed many of the names of the persons involved in this story, in respect of family privacy. These are real stories about real people and how they lived. There is no sugarcoating, just the pure, unadulterated version of how steep their mountains were.

Thanks to my special angel, Michael, my husband of fifty years. You were my rock, even on days when the writing and the ideas didn't gel; you poured me a glass of wine, we took a break, and we talked things over. I hope you haven't become tired of making dinner reservations, because this isn't the last book I am going to write.

To our four sons, Mark, Todd, Brett, and Erick; to our daughters-in-law and also to our precious grandchildren who continue to encourage and cheer me on—a big thank you. I extend my utmost appreciation to the Volga German families of Theresa Rose Wegner Ennis: thank you for granting access to your own incredible Volga genealogy.

My deepest gratitude I extend to cousin, Kerry Thompson, editor of the Susannenthal Newsletter. Without her help and the deeply researched material she provided concerning Die Wolgadeutschen and our own family genealogy, this book wouldn't be what it is. It was her son, a laboratory technician, who discovered the far eastern markers in our family blood.

I didn't just sit down one day and whip this story out. There were months of extensive research, digging through a mountain of files and notes, which I have collected over the years. This was followed by the organization of my material. After the initial story was written, it took numerous rewrites and a village of people reading and sending their suggestions back to me.

To these people, my readers, I send my deepest gratitude: to my cousins, Pat, Anna, and Andy who loaned me the priceless bundle of letters which their father wrote and saved during World War II. This collection of historical written word put virtual wings on my story. And of course to my mother, Beata Wamhoff, who was there every time I needed verification or answers. I love and cherish you!

Speaking of wings, to the gracious professional people who gave of their time to read and edit my numerous drafts. First, is my German-born neighbor, Ilse DeGranda; longtime friend and retired reading/English teacher, Janie Lewis; retired English teacher, Dorothy Bush - deceased; senior editorial reader/critic, Julia Graham; reader/historical researcher, Kerry Thompson; retired newspaper editor, Pat Schmidt; retired Cheyenne, Wyoming, high school principal and commercial writing/business teacher, Jan Felton.

My heartfelt thanks to Green Spring Publishing—you were great to work with. Just when I thought I had done everything I could with the story, it went to my editors who stuck like glue, guiding and prompting me forward; and I saw it in a whole new light. Elizabeth Klenda, you were a genius when it came to designing the interior layout—you made it look so easy. It's difficult to properly thank everyone who worked on my novel, especially, Thayne Sturdevant, Graphic Designer. Your expertise and patience were classic and inspiring. Simply put, I have a great team!

As with my first historical novel, *The Ticket,* this novel, *Seed of the Volga,* was also a challenging labor of love and curiosity. It goes beyond thrilling to describe the insight I gained as I painted the stories I remembered with my words. I am filled with awe and gratitude as I hold a deeper respect of the emigrant's courage and determination and of the unthinkable sacrifices they made to leave their tight-knit family groups along the Volga to immigrate to America. Because of them, we enjoy living in freedom as Americans. Because of them, I am free to write their story so others have the opportunity to know what I know about the brave and faithful *Die Wolgadeutschen.*

Finally, I know of this story because of my grandmother, Raisa, who shared personal stories of her family history, family secrets, and adventures as she remembered them.

Foreword

"For every thing there is a season and a time

  for every purpose under the heaven:

A time to be born and a time to die;

A time to plant, and a time to pluck up that which is planted;

A time to kill and a time to heal;

A time to break down and a time to build up;

A time to mourn and a time to dance;

A time to cast away stones and a time to gather stones together;

A time to embrace and a time to refrain from embracing;

 A time to get and a time to lose;

A time to keep and a time to cast away;

A time to rend and a time to sew;

A time to keep silence and a time to speak;

A time to love and a time to hate;

A time of war and a time of peace."

Ecclesiastes: 3:1-8 (KJV)

Introduction

Decades of war had left the European region of Germany in a state of devastation. The majority of continent wars were either fought on German soil or battalions of soldiers marched across the borders, raping and pillaging as they went. After the Thirty Years' War, followed by the Seven Years' War, there was nothing left in the fertile Rhine Valley of Southwestern Germany; farms and cities were burned to the ground. The once prosperous and proud farmers and craftsmen of the region had nowhere to turn; they were ripe for change and offers of new beginnings.

German-born Catherine the Great, empress of Russia, issued a generous manifest, inviting these destitute Germans to immigrate to Russia, to the northeastern area along the fertile Volga River. She wanted this area settled, and she knew well the reputation of the Hessen farmers of southwestern Germany. Catherine hoped they would not only settle the area but also teach the Russian peasants more productive methods of tilling the soil.

The first German emigrants to leave Germany journeyed by boat to St. Petersburg and then across the vast area of Russia. Using crude, lightweight boats, they carried them on their backs while crossing the land, and putting them in the water when they came to the numerous lakes and rivers. There were no trains or convenient ferries in which to ride. Everything they did, they accomplished through their own ingenuity, brawn, and determination. When those who endured the eight- to ten-month trek overland finally arrived in the area along the Volga, they found that much of what Catherine the Great had told them was not true. Regardless, over the years they persevered and they prospered, learning to adapt to the harsh Russian winters. They kept to themselves, not integrating into the Russian peasant culture.

When settling along the Volga, *Die Wolgadeutschen* elected to segregate themselves into like villages, according to religion, whether it was Mennonite, Lutheran, or Catholic. They embraced this new life and the fertile area along the Volga River was brought to life. For decades, the Volga Germans flourished and prospered.

Decades later, when the Russian government began to take back promises and opportunities, *Die Wolgadeutschen* immigrated again, this time seeking opportunities of a better life in America. It is rumored they carried with them two things—the Bible in their right hand and a sugar beet hoe in their left. They were hard working, devout, and dedicated Christian family people. They asked for nothing but freedom and opportunity; in return they willingly gave their sweat and loyalty as they spread their way of life, their seed—the *Seed of the Volga*—across this country.

The Volga Germans made a respected and notable name for themselves not only as capable farmers, but also as a people. Their faith and sacraments came first in their lives; it is what sustained them and what they centered their lives around.

Present day farms in America, from Maine to California—from Minnesota to Texas were/are settled and worked by descendants of these industrious '*Rooshian*' immigrants. Their names are found on rural mailboxes, on gravestones, in phone books, and in the census publications across the land they tilled—America!

(*STEINER*) GENEALOGY CHART:

Michael Schutte **& Karen (Wamhoff)** - Lovell, WY
1941 -   ^   1942 –

Arnold Wamhoff & **Beata (*Kessel*)** -Lovell, WY
1914 – 2003   ^   1920 –

Jacob *Kessel* -Surtschin, Hungary & **Theresia (*Steiner*)** -Susannenthal, Russia
1900 – 1989   ^   1900 – 1986

Karl *Kessel* & Katherina Mell, Hungary   **David *Steiner*** & (*Sofie*) Wagner, Russia
"THE TICKET"   ^ 1874 – 1944   1878 – 1952

Johann Phillip *Steiner* & Elisabeth Wasmuth, Russia
^ 1828 -   1844 –

Johann William *Steiner*, Russia & Marie E. Hohenzellern, Germany
^   1801 -   1801 -

Johann Wilhelm *Steiner* & Anna M. Keweno, Russia
^   1776 -1815   1775 -

*First to immigrate to Volga: **Johann Heinrich *Steiner*** & (1) Katherina Rau –died 1770
Born in Kemel, Germany   1740-1823   (2) Catherine – died 1776
(3) Elizabeta Dortman
^   1753 –

Born in Kemel, Germany: **Johann Peter *Steiner*** & Christina Keilman
^ 1721 -   1722 –

Kemel, **Germany**   **Johann Ludwig *Steiner*** & Catherine
1672 – 1723   1797 –

*Records from Lutheran Church in Kemel, Germany dating: 1672

Note: Names in italics indicate fictitious name.
XXXXX

Prologue

Germany 1761: The warm autumn air was thick with acrid smoke and the smell of fresh blood; sensing danger, Heinz Steiner crouched low in the dense thicket. As the crack of gunshots and then screams echoed through the dense woods, his survival instincts took control as he stopped and carefully considered his options. Listening closely, Heinz determined the sounds were coming from near the clearing at the north edge of the woods where the widow Rothnig and her five scrawny, starving spawn lived in a makeshift hovel. Heinz realized he should leave the area and create a healthy distance between himself and the probable killing; yet curiosity overrode caution as he crept in the direction of the expected carnage.

Unarmed, Heinz was no match for the élite French troops who relentlessly terrorized the lower Rhine and upper Danube River Valleys. Their mission was to maraud and plunder the already destitute southwestern German farms and towns. They killed whatever and whomever happened to be in their path, and they enjoyed it.

Heinz edged through the grove of aspen and spruce that skirted the Rothnig hut. Remaining hidden in the shadows of the trees at the edge of the grove, his eyes and ears strained for sounds of danger; his entire body was coiled, ready to flee. More often than he cared to remember in his twenty-one years, he had witnessed unspeakable cruelty and death, yet he froze in utter horror at what now filled his eyes and ears. Diverse hacked and severed body parts of the widow and most of her children were scattered like rocks about the yard. Five slipshod, sweating French soldiers stood waiting in a semicircle with their pants down around their ankles, taking turns with the dead widow's naked thirteen-year-old daughter. Heinz could see she was barely conscious; that was probably a blessing if blessings were to be had on this day. Without warning, her emaciated ten-year-old brother burst from his hiding place. Having only a garden hoe as a weapon and determined to protect his sister, he charged the soldiers. With one swipe of an experienced French sword, his head was severed from his body.

Heinz turned his eyes away from the horrendous sight. He covered his ears with his grimy hands, trying unsuccessfully to escape from the ungodly sights and sounds that filled the woods — the sounds of human suffering. Carefully and silently, he edged back into the dense cover of the trees. As soon as he felt it was safe, he turned and broke into a hard run; his long muscular legs hauled his six-foot frame away from the slaughter. When he could no longer hear or smell the decimation, he stopped. Sweat and grime matted his blond hair and dripped from his chiseled jawline. Heinz closed his blue eyes tightly and bent over as his stomach convulsed, spewing its meager contents across the forest floor. Weakly lifting his head, he spotted a dense thicket; Heinz moved off the path and, dropping to his hands and knees, he wormed his way to the interior of the bramble. His mind was a whirlwind of emotions—shame at his cowardice and yet pride in his hard-earned sense of survival.

Heinz buried his face in the damp leaves. He rolled twice so the musty earth and molding leaves enfolded and camouflaged his stinking body. He didn't know how long he had hidden in the thicket when suddenly he felt the ground vibrate from the hooves of many horses traveling fast through the woods. Heinz wormed his way even farther into the undergrowth and froze. After the thundering hoofs passed, he raised his head and realized tears were washing streaks down his filthy face. With shaking hands he reached to wipe them away.

Heinz wondered if he could or ever would feel clean and live life without this constant controlling fear and wariness; although, instinctively, he knew it was the fear and the wariness that had so far kept him alive. He bowed his head and repeated the all-too familiar prayer that constantly raged through his head. Each time he repeated it, he hoped this time God would hear.

Dear Lord, if you are listening, please put a stop to this senseless killing. Where are you when your people are suffering? Why are you allowing this to happen? Help me to understand, and dear Lord Jesus, help me to survive. I ask this in your name. Amen.

Heinz rested for another minute. There were always stragglers who followed the armies, pillaging what was left behind. They had no qualms or conscience, taking what the dead wouldn't be using as they stripped clothes from slain bodies, leaving them where they fell. Heinz closed his eyes and thought about what life might be like without war. He didn't have any idea what living life in peace and with prosperity would be like, but he dreamed of it just the same. There had to be something better than this living hell. If there was another way to live, he was determined to find it someday.

With relentless emotional pain, twenty-one-year-old Heinz remembered how he came to be there and of that cold autumn day five years ago when he had turned sixteen. His family had gathered for the evening meal in the warmth of their farmhouse kitchen. Standing at the head of the table, Johann Peter Steiner unexpectedly announced that he and oldest son Franz were leaving their farm to fight in the war. They believed it was their duty to *Deutschland* and to God, and besides, they had been paid a goodly sum to join the army. Heinz remembered how his mother Christina screamed and cried for them to stay, for the family to remain together, but his father had made up his mind. He instructed his two youngest sons, Heinz and Phillip, to remain at home with their mother and work the farm as best they could. The family made a pact that, after the war, they would meet in Hamburg at Saint Martin's Lutheran Church; whoever arrived first would post their names on the announcement board.

It was only a few months after her husband and son marched off to war that Christina died from a mysterious stomach illness. Heinz and Phillip dug a grave for their mother under a linden tree. Two weeks later, after their farm was burned to the ground by foreign soldiers, they fled into the forest to fend for themselves. It became their rite of survival, roaming the barren countryside and discovering ingenious ways to stay alive and away from the soldiers or those who would force them to be soldiers.

Germany was still reeling from the devastation of the Thirty Years' War[1], and now the Seven Years' War ravaged the German land. Without opportunity to recover from decades of continuous plundering, destruction, and excessive taxation by wealthy German princes, Hessian and Palatine land and farms along the Rhine River were decimated. War had destroyed all manufacturing, building, craftsmanship, and trade. All that remained of once-prosperous peasant farms was the seared evidence of what was. Resilient as they were, the people continued to struggle to sustain or prolong what life was left, and Heinz was caught in the middle of it all.

~~~~~~

1761: Crouching, Heinz Steiner began to ease out of the thicket; he moved a few inches then waited, listened, and moved again until he felt certain he was alone and safe. He slowly straightened his body until he stood tall. He eased forward, steadily and purposely like a cat, through the dense foliage. Coming to a secluded pool, he didn't bother to pull the stinking and tattered rags from his body as he slipped into the cool, silky water. Allowing his body to sink to the bottom of the natural spring, Heinz felt the water cover him like a baptism. He was careful not to make any sound. In the cover of an overhanging branch, he scooped up a handful of sand and rubbed it through his hair over and over again until it felt clean. He scrubbed his skin with the gritty remnants until it too was pink and fresh.

Heinz was about to pull himself out of the pool when he heard voices and the sound of dry twigs snapping on the trail. Quickly, he slipped soundlessly under the surface of his watery sanctuary. He swam toward the deepest, secluded area of the pool where branches of overgrown currant bushes draped into the water. Surfacing only long enough to inhale a supply of air, Heinz submerged again, moving to the protective camouflage of the low branches. Under the cover of the branches, his face gently broke the surface of the pool as he inched back deeper, merging with the exposed tangle of tree roots and limbs. Heinz remained motionless in his exclusive refuge.

Heinz froze as he felt the water move suddenly. Instinctively, he realized the men had found the pool and were either drinking or bathing in it. It sounded like there were four or five of them. Experience reminded him if they weren't soldiers, then they were either a lone group of men or, even worse, part of the roving Landgraves of Hessen-Kassel. These hated and feared hunters earned their keep from the ruling princes by rounding up stray men to sell as mercenary soldiers to the English. Fighting a revolution of their own in America, the English paid well for German soldiers. Heinz shuddered as he recalled the night the Landgraves chased him and his youngest brother. They captured Phillip after the two brothers had made a quick decision to split up. The Landgraves had chosen to follow Phillip. Heinz escaped into the obscurity of the woods. He never knew what happened to his brother or if he survived. All Heinz knew was *he* was still alive, and he had become proficient at staying that way.

~~~~~

Germany 1763: As all wars do, the Seven Years' War came to an end, leaving over half of the German population dead. The land which remained was nothing more than an incapacitated wasteland where nothing grew and no man flourished. The war had ended because there was simply nothing left to fight over.

Heinz blended in with scores of homeless who wandered from one burned-out village to another, from crumbling house to crumbling house, looking for work and food. His filthy clothes hung on his malnourished body; he looked no worse than the others he met on the road. He cleaned himself when he could, but his main objective was to sustain his life wherever and however that might be. When the opportunity came along, they all helped themselves to copper roofing and stained glass from burned-out cathedrals, looted destroyed shops, and even walked uninvited and uninhibited into once-impressive castles and homes of departed wealthy noblemen. They took what was left behind and what served their purpose of survival; it was theirs because they needed it.

Heinz was slowly working his way north to the port of Hamburg where his family had agreed to meet after the war. He had entertained the idea of getting enough money together for passage on a boat leaving Germany. He wanted nothing more than to get on a ship and leave the hellhole where he struggled daily to survive—a country he no longer felt allegiance to or considered home. Heinz hoped he would be reunited with his father and brothers as they had planned, but he was now a man, and knowing what men know, he seriously doubted they had survived.

A hundred and fifty miles from Hamburg, Heinz stumbled onto what remained of a burned-out barn. Remaining innately vigilant, he stood hidden at the edge of the woods and scanned the destroyed farm. After making sure he was alone and safe, he moved cautiously though the opening where a barn door once hung; Heinz paused as he slowly scanned the interior. He crawled up what was left of a crude ladder, listening and watching for danger as he moved. Once he was up and inside the loft, he relaxed and stretched out on a bit of musty straw that covered the floor. Heinz ran his grimy hands through his oily hair, scratched, and then lay onto his back. He gazed up past the partially destroyed barn roof into the fading blue of the evening sky. As weariness and the feeling of safety relaxed his body, his eyes fluttered with denied sleep.

Suddenly his internal alarm flashed. He sensed movement in the dark corner of the loft. Heinz narrowed his eyes in an attempt to adjust to the dim light. *Nothing there*, he thought. *I must be going crazy. It was probably only a large rat.* Then, he was certain he saw it again. The small form moved slowly out of the dark corner and hesitated just at the edge of the shadows. Heinz was stunned to see it was a young girl. She appeared to be seventeen or eighteen. Like his, her clothes were torn and threadbare. Her blonde hair matted and snarled around a sweet oval face. Heinz noticed her eyes were wide and dark with wary fear. He slowly reached out his hand to her.

"I won't hurt you, Fräulein. Please come closer, I have some old bread crust you can have." He stayed where he was as his hand held out the bread.

She cocked her head to the side as she studied Heinz's face but remained where she was—her eyes wide, cautious, and questioning.

Heinz motioned for her to come closer. "What is your name, Fräulein? Mine is Heinz—Heinz Steiner from Kemel. I am on my way to Hamburg in hope of finding my family and perhaps a ship to take me from this worthless land. Here, please take the bread. You must be hungry."

The girl inched closer and reached for the food. Quickly grabbing the bread from his hand, she wriggled back, out of reach, where she felt safe. He watched intently as she cradled the bit of bread with her hands. She hesitated a moment then held it to her nose and smelled it. Heinz watched as she stuck out her tongue to taste it, savoring the food before she took a bite. The girl took small, careful bites and chewed them slowly, her eyes closed in pure bliss.

"Name is...is Il-sa," she whispered.

Heinz shook his head, not sure he had heard her speak. He bent his face toward her and said gently, "Excuse me, I...I didn't hear what you said."

The girl lifted her face, and it was then that Heinz saw her luminous green eyes. "I...am sorry. I haven't spoken to anyone for weeks. I said my name is Ilsa. It is Ilsa Kechter, and this is my family's farm. The soldiers...they came." She put her head down and moved it side to side in an attempt to wipe the vision from her eyes. "It was about three months ago. They rode into our farm in the early morning. They killed my parents and took my older brothers with them. I think they were Russian because they came from the north, and their words sounded Russian. They...they were so cruel and barbaric. We had not experienced so much war as they have in the southern part of Germany, and so we were not ready for such as we got that day. *Bitte,* please I am sorry for my rude speaking. I haven't asked about you. What is your story, Herr Steiner?"

Heinz smiled at the girl. He told her how he had lived for the last six years and that he had heard of work and safety farther north. He told her of his plan to leave Germany if and when he could.

"Please, Fräulein Ilsa, call me Heinz. I can't help but wonder how did you alone escape from the soldiers?"

Ilsa explained that under the barn, they kept a root cellar. It was where she found food to keep herself alive. "As you can tell, I have not had a piece of bread for a very long time. I would like to offer you some potatoes and carrots if you are hungry also."

Heinz discovered that Ilsa preferred to sleep up in the corner of the barn rather than in the cold, damp cellar. She managed a little smile when she told him she didn't wish to sleep under the earth until she was dead. They talked a while longer before Heinz explained he was very tired.

Ilsa returned to her corner, and the two were soon fast asleep. Sometime in the night, Heinz felt tugging at his sleeve and heard the soft whispering voice of Ilsa. At first he thought he was dreaming until he heard her speak again.

"Heinz, I am so sorry to disturb your slumber, but I am quite cold, and you also must feel the night chill. Would it—could I— could I sleep next to you for the heat of your body?" She bowed her head in embarrassment. "You must know I feel disgrace to ask such a thing of you. I want nothing more than to feel warm, if you do not mind?"

Heinz smiled ear to ear and stretched out his arms to the attractive blonde. "If you don't mind the smell of my unwashed body, I promise I will only keep you warm. I am a gentleman even though I don't look like one."

Ilsa snuggled her back tightly into Heinz's chest as he wrapped his arms around her, resting his chin on top of her head. They melted into each other, both benefiting from shared body heat. Ilsa fell asleep in moments; however, it took Heinz a bit longer to relax. As first light seeped through the broken barn, Heinz awoke to a feeling of wetness on his arm. He snuggled closer to the warm little body that he held tightly in his arms. It felt so good to be close to another human being. He didn't want to move, ever. However, as the wetness on his arm increased, and he felt Ilsa quiver, he shook her gently and asked, "Ilsa, are you having a bad dream? Wake up, wake up."

Ilsa rolled onto her back and looked up at him with a tearstained face. "Heinz, I must thank you for keeping me so warm during the night, but now I am filled with worries about what is to happen to me when you leave."

Ilsa didn't give Heinz a moment to respond as she sat up and turned to face him with a serious expression. "Heinz, take me with you to the north. Please, there is nothing left for me here. My family is dead—all dead, and I am alone. Please, let me come. I promise I will not be a burden. I know the area well. We can pack a bag with the potatoes and vegetables that are left in the cellar, which will keep us alive for a while."

Heinz thought for a moment, considering various situations they might actually experience on the journey to Hamburg if he took her with him. "Ilsa, I am happy to know you feel safe with me, but I was expecting to travel alone." Without thinking he reached to pull a piece of old straw from her matted blond hair.

All along, his instinct had been to travel alone, but now everything had changed. Heinz was quick to rethink his plan as he witnessed the terror in the young girl's eyes. Hastily rethinking his previous plan, he said, "But I—I am most happy to take you with me, if that is what you want. However, we must consider that we are two single people traveling together, and it may put us in more danger. Perhaps to be safer, if you would not object, as soon as we can find a minister, we should be married. You are Lutheran, aren't you?"

Her face flushed, and her green eyes grew wide as she nervously searched for the right answer. Then with a little nervous giggle she declared, "Yes—yes, of course I am Lutheran. Of course I am!" Ilsa agreed it was a practical idea to get married, even though they had only met. "Our marriage will be for survival and of course, the appearance of decency." Ilsa could think of no good reason to tell Heinz she was a baptized Catholic.

They had been walking since dawn; the sun was directly overhead when Heinz stopped beside a pond and sat down under the shade of a linden tree. He patted the ground next to him; Ilsa moved closer and sat. "Ilsa, I have been wondering, why did you stay on the farm? Why didn't you try to find people you know to help you?"

Ilsa put her head down and looked at the grass for a moment. Then lifting her head, she looked up at Heinz. Her green eyes sparkled as a sly smile prompted the dimples in her cheeks to respond, and then she replied, "I was waiting for you, Heinz. I was waiting for you"

~~~~~

Love was not something the young couple had even considered, but two weeks after their marriage ceremony, they consummated their union. In the beginning it was out of mutual need, but as time went by, they fell deeply in love. Ilsa was not strong physically, and her malnourished body suffered two miscarriages during this time.

Along the way, Heinz noticed posters on walls, and he heard men talking in the beer gardens about an incredible offer that Catherine the Great, ruler of Russia, had issued to Germans, enticing them to immigrate to her country. Heinz was curious to learn more about this offer, this manifesto.

It took the couple over a year to make their way on foot to the port of Hamburg. They stayed for a time wherever they could find work along the way, saving as much money as possible as they continued to find a way to leave Germany. The first place they went when they arrived in the city of Hamburg was St. Martin's Lutheran Church. Heinz scanned the announcement board, but there were no messages from his father or brothers. He said a private prayer as he left his own name on the board. Every week, he and Ilsa returned to check the board.

~~~~~~

It had been almost eleven months since Heinz and Ilsa had arrived in Hamburg. During one of their visits to the church, they noticed two shabbily dressed men standing by the corner, watching intently as each person entered the church. As Heinz walked closer, his breath caught in his throat. *No it can't be. My mind is playing tricks on me. The younger man resembles my brother, but his hair is long and unkept. Their eyes are sunken, and the old man's face is covered with a grizzle of gray whiskers. Could it be? No, I cannot hope any longer.*

As he started up the front steps, one of the men called out to him. Heinz froze as he recognized the voice of his brother, Franz. He and Ilsa turned slowly and walked down the steps toward the two men. "Franz? Franz is it truly you?" Heinz embraced both men at the same time, tears streaming down his face. His father and brother were alive; they had been in the city for nearly two weeks.

As they walked down the street, Heinz filled them in on what he knew of the past years. Understandably they were saddened to learn of Christina's death. Heinz told them what had happened to his brother Phillip and that he had no idea where Phillip was or if he was even alive. The four of them agreed to find a modest apartment where they might live together. During the next few months, they worked at anything that came their way. Living frugally, they pooled every spare coin but remained poor and without hope for a better future. In the evenings, sitting in the shadowy light of the lamp, they began to form a plan to leave Germany, to immigrate to someplace, anyplace, where there was work and a future.

They knew of other members of the Steiner family who enjoyed a higher rank of living. Crown Prince Von Steiner lived in an impressive, fortified castle high above the southern portion of the Danube Valley and had been relatively unaffected by the wars that raged in the lowlands and farms. They had survived because they were able to barricade themselves inside the castle walls and were not easy prey for the marauding French troops or the warring bands of renegade soldiers. The farmers and peasants of the Von Steiner's dynasty were the ones who needed to leave the fatherland because there was nothing for which to stay.

Hamburg, Germany, 1767

For less than two years, Heinz and Ilsa had been living in a depressed area of Hamburg with his father and brother, barely making enough money to survive. They continued to yearn to leave Germany, but opportunity had not come their way. They knew many of their countrymen were leaving the land of their birth, going to Poland, Hungary, America, England, and Russia. Every day, as he worked at the docks, Heinz saw the huge ships and the long lines of disheveled people boarding them and leaving—leaving it all behind.

Heinz would never forget the early spring day when, as usual, he walked to work on the docks. By chance or God's plan, two men introduced themselves as agents of Catherine the Great.

As the men began to speak, Heinz forgot about his job and spent the next two hours talking to them. Filled with elation and hope, he rushed home to tell Ilsa the news—the news that would change their life, the news they had been waiting for.

He burst into their meager rooms, grabbed his wife around the waist, and twirled around the room until they were both dizzy. "Frau Steiner, pack what you want to take. We are leaving Germany. We will sail to Russia to our new life, our new future!"

That evening the Steiner family gathered around as Heinz eagerly described the manifesto from the German-born ruler of all Russia. "Catherine the Great has offered any man who will agree to a plan which promises money for clothes to travel, money to buy tickets to Russia, and guides to take us to the Volga River area where rich land lies waiting to be farmed. We are expected to vow allegiance to Russia as long as we live there. We will be free to practice internal self-government, to practice our own religion, and to pay no taxes for thirty years. We will not have to serve in the Russian military. We will be given land to settle and farm, as well as livestock. All this is waiting for us, even grants and advancement of money without interest for houses, animals, and implements to till the soil. It says we are free to leave Russia whenever we want. We will only be required to relinquish a certain percentage of our property back to the government."

It was a dream, come true, and they were all eager to leave. The following day, Heinz, his father, and brother met with the agents and promptly signed the necessary papers. They were aware they had to leave Germany quickly if they were to leave at all. They had overheard the heated discussions in the beer gardens concerning the wealthy princes and rulers of Germany who were proceeding with a ban on emigration from Germany. Over the last four years, the ruling class had lost a considerable number of working Germans who had boarded hundreds of ships, taking them out of Germany.

~~~~~

Heinz turned twenty-six that June, and on August 3, 1767, the Steiner family set sail for Russian soil and a new beginning. They never looked back at the country of their birth; they were leaving all the horrors and calamity of the past behind them. Their future as *Die Wolgadeutschen* or the Volga Germans looked bright and promising. They had no idea what actually awaited them, but it had to be better than what they were leaving behind.

As they sailed out of the port of Hamburg, Heinz and Ilsa stood at the railing with mixed emotions, watching the city and country of their birth vanish from view. Heinz slipped his arm around the thin shoulders of his wife and pulled her close to him. He did not notice all the while that Ilsa stood with one hand protectively covering her belly.

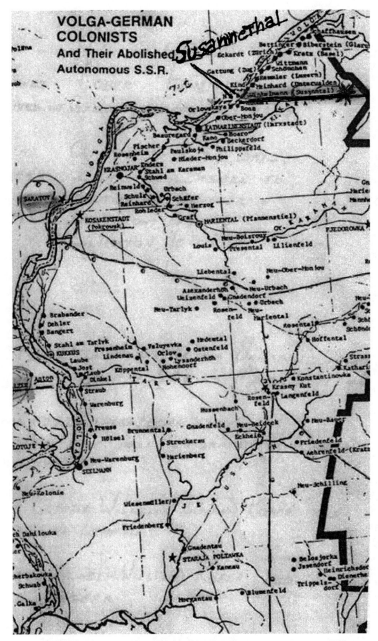

*Map of the German Settlements along the upper
Volga River, Russia*

Chapter One

In the Beginning: September 6, 1873

Violent bolts of white hot lightning rent the inky mid-September night sky, illuminating the earth below. Deafening explosions of thunder echoed from the sheer granite cliffs of Reinstadt Mountain as icy rain drove hard out of the north, bullied by fierce, howling winds. The unexpected, early fall storm pelted freshly harvested fields of golden wheat stubble and drenched the compact shucks of corn, which stood at attention like good German soldiers. With relentless force, the storm continued to blast the formidable granite ramparts of the imposing stone castle as it stood reign on the summit of Reinstadt Mountain high above the sparkling Hessen city of Frankfurt. It was customary late in each day for most castle servants to gather down in the kitchen for a cup of tea and juicy bits of castle gossip.

Reinstadt Mountain Castle

Princess Theraisa Von Steiner felt a shudder of fear surge through her body as the storm raged, but even the turbulent storm was no match for the trepidation that consumed her soul. She stood alone at the window in her chambers, knowing she also stood alone in her world of privilege and rigid tradition. Persistent questions tormented her mind. Foremost was how she would protect her aristocratic parents from the truth. It was true she was educated she was acquainted with the landed gentry of her Hessen state, and she was regarded as a great beauty. However, she couldn't cook. She didn't know how to wash her own clothes or even care for her golden tresses. Confiding in her parents— announcing she was pregnant and unwed —was unthinkable.

Earlier in the week, Princess Amelia and Prince Heinrich Von Steiner had presented their daughter a coveted invitation to the elite Harvest Ball to be held at the summer palace of the prince of Palatine. "We would so enjoy your good company this evening. Please come with us, lovely daughter. The distraction will do you good for a few hours. Consider putting on a ball gown and leaving your room along with all your dismal thoughts. It will be such a gay affair with many of our dear friends in attendance."

Their twenty-year-old daughter tearfully but firmly declined— again. "I am completely shocked that you ask me to dress in a bright silk and forget for one evening that I mourn my betrothed. Do you forget so easily that my love, my life, my David lies cold and freshly buried in the Lutheran cemetery?" Of course, Theraisa understood that her parents simply hoped to distract her from the relentless grief.

Thus, Theraisa stood alone in body and spirit at the narrow stone window of her chamber, watching as her parents' coach wound cautiously down the narrow, rain-slick, cobblestone mountain road. She stood, frozen like a statue, as the cold rain beat relentlessly against the mullioned windowpane. Her pale hand reached slowly to touch the surface of the glass as one slender index finger extended to trace a rivulet of water as it wriggled slowly then quickly down the window. Theraisa's other hand unconsciously moved to cover her abdomen. It rested there only a moment before she felt the warmth of her own flesh. She lowered her head to peer with wonder and apprehension at her belly where a child was growing. David's child formed inside her, never to know his father. There would be no wedding as planned; her betrothed had been killed in another of the endless German wars. The only religious ceremony she and Captain David Ritter would ever experience had been his funeral.

Theraisa Von Steiner was now left alone with the knowledge that she was unmarried and pregnant. She could not and would not entertain the idea of acknowledging such disgrace to her aristocratic parents. Now, this night with her parents absent from the castle, the opportunity she had hoped for presented itself. Theraisa was agonizingly aware of her thickening waist, and time was her ever-present adversary. Silent tears of unbearable bereavement, fueled with fear of the unknown and shame, coursed down Theraisa's flushed face. She realized no time could be wasted. Tonight she would go to her aunt Louisa.

Moving toward the door of her chamber, Theraisa's legs felt as though lead weights were tied to them. She knew this task was going to be unbearably difficult. She loved and respected her aunt, and now she had no other recourse but to admit to her that she was with child, a child conceived in a moment of religious sinfulness. Theraisa was confident she could trust her aunt with her confession, and she prayed the woman would think of some way to help her.

Not wishing to alert any of the servants, Theraisa quietly opened the narrow, wooden door to her chamber. The expected chill of the unheated hallway swirled around her ankles as it rushed to invade the warmth of her rooms. Slowly she closed the heavy door behind her and moved down the deserted hallway, her voluminous silk skirts swishing the cold, damp air around her legs. Cautiously turning the corner, she hurried up the wide stone steps to her aunt's chamber. Pausing a moment to catch her breath, her hand lifted slowly before knocking softly on the carved walnut door. Courage caught in her throat as she heard a familiar lilting voice call from within. "Yes, who is there, please?"

In a hushed voice, she managed to reply, "Auntie Louisa, it is I, Theraisa. May I speak with you for a moment?" Theraisa waited for what seemed an eternity before she heard her aunt's gracious invitation to enter. She pushed down on the iron handle and pressed her body weight against the heavy door.

The golden candlelight from within poured into the hallway, illuminating the figure of Theraisa Von Steiner, standing in the doorway.

The young woman turned to close the heavy door. With her head down, a curtain of golden curls fell forward over her thin shoulders, obscuring her tearstained face. She slowly crossed the room to where her aunt sat at her desk, writing letters. Theraisa's blue silk gown swirled around her legs as she walked, catching the glimmer of candlelight in the luminous fabric. As Theraisa approached her esteemed aunt, Louisa raised her head and looked intently at the delicate face of her favorite niece.

"*Mein Gott in Himmel*, my sweet, what is it? What is causing you such unhappiness? Come, sit here on the settee and talk to me," her aunt said as she moved effortlessly to the small couch and ceremoniously patted the burgundy velvet upholstery beside her.

Theraisa walked with trepidation toward the settee with her head down, hot tears of shame dropping onto the thick French carpet. Then, without warning, her legs and her determination gave way as she fell to the floor in front of her aunt. Raising herself up, Theraisa buried her face in her aunt's lap as wracking sobs poured from deep within her.

"I—I have no other place to go with my truth. I know of no other person who might help me make a decision. I have only you, Auntie Louisa, only you who I believe can help me."

Louisa reached out and pulled her niece to her feet and then onto the French settee beside her. She embraced Theraisa and held the distraught young woman against her aging bosom while the girl's tears subsided. Theraisa shivered with debilitating emotion as she struggled to regain her composure. With her delicate Austrian lace handkerchief, Louisa reached to wipe the tears from the beautiful face of her niece.

"Now there, my Theraisa, what is it? Of course, it is understandable that you grieve for Captain Ritter. Is this causing you distress again tonight? Are your memories tormenting you?"

The young woman took a deep breath, calling upon her German tenacity and courage. "No, no, it—it is not that I am thinking of him tonight. It is much more than that, so much more, auntie! I am—am—" Again the tears came, hot torrents of tears filled with shame and guilt. "Auntie Louisa, I can tell only you. I believe only you can help me. I am—I believe—it is—I am with child!" Once the unspeakable, shameful words were out of her mouth, her slender white hands rose quickly to cover her face and her humiliation, as sobs of disgrace racked her swelling body.

A blush of shock filled Louisa's face as her soft hazel eyes fell to Theraisa's abdomen. Louisa recovered quickly as she reached out to the beloved daughter of her dead husband's brother.

She took a brief moment to gather her words. "Theraisa, my darling, are you very sure you are with child? Sometimes when a woman is in mourning, her monthly time becomes late until she is able to cope with the circumstances and her emotions. Are there obvious reasons you think you carry Captain Ritter's child?"

Theraisa lifted her anguished face toward her aunt. "Yes, oh yes, Auntie, as it shames me to tell you this. There was a day in the woods last summer when David and I were so much in love, and we wanted to be together—and we—we gave in to our desires. We believed it was going to be such a long time before we would see each other. We wanted to be totally together. We were so afraid, Auntie, that we may never have another chance to *know* each other. And, and we—we didn't have another chance, did we?"

Tears rolled uncontrolled down Theraisa's face. She shook her head, trying to clear her mind as she continued. "We did what we should not have done, Auntie, and now he is dead. I am alone, left in this life without him and in unmarried shame as I carry his child. Whatever am I going to do? It is unthinkable that I would confide in my parents. I love them too much to bring this shame to them. I must leave my parents' house. I have to make some excuse that they will accept. Where can I go, Auntie Louisa? I beg you, please, please help me! You are my only hope."

Badly shaken, Louisa Von Steiner rose unsteadily to her feet and walked to stand before her window. With her back to her niece, her right hand rose discreetly to wipe tears of grief and shock from her eyes. She stood at the window, the delicate fingers of her hand touching her aging face; she stood motionless for what seemed an eternity.

Without warning Louisa turned with a radiant smile on her face. She walked quickly across the French carpets to sit on the settee next to her niece. "I have an idea, and I think it is a good— no, a brilliant idea, my dear. We will ask your father for funds to travel to the Volga for a long overdue visit with your cousin, Phillip, and the other relatives who have settled and live along the Russian River. We will tell him you must leave the memories of David and your sorrow. You need a change. A vacation will be very good for you and, of course, you cannot travel alone." Louisa laughed as she was filled with the excitement and genius of her idea.

"Of course, I will suggest we travel at the earliest possible moment because you are wasting away with mourning, and the Russian winter fast approaches." She stood and began walking back and forth across the room, her face animated with excitement as she spoke. "All of your friends and nosey relatives will understand and surely accept that this time away will be a good thing for you." Louisa clapped her hands with glee. "It is perfect. It is so perfect, and I know it will work. I will speak to your father and mother at breakfast in the morning. If your father can arrange passage, I would like to leave by the end of the week!"

Louisa pulled Theraisa to her feet as she cupped the girl's beautiful face in her hands. "Take heart, my darling. We will travel to Russia where you will have your child in private. You may even decide to stay, make a new life, and raise the baby there. I will return to Germany eventually. Of course, we will decide what we will do after the child is born—when the time is right. The immediate thing is to get you out of Germany and away from prying eyes and gossiping tongues."

Theraisa appeared puzzled as she asked, "Auntie, what do we tell the relatives in Russia? I am pregnant and not married."

Louisa's eyes lit mischievously as she smiled. "I have already thought of that. When we arrive in Russia, we will tell the relatives that your husband, Captain David Ritter, was killed on the front, and you needed a change because of your stressful mourning and delicate condition. That should take care of the gossips!" Louisa took the girl by her elbow and guided her toward the door. "Go to your rooms now, my darling, and make plans for our journey. I will be there with you every step of the way. Say your prayers tonight, and ask our Lord to help us with our plan and be with us on our journey. I will come to you in the morning after I speak with your parents. Peace my child, peace now!"

As Theraisa walked slowly out into the hallway, shameful concern no longer consumed her. Now there was hope.

Louisa called after her niece, "Theraisa, remember in your prayers tonight to cast your burdens upon the Lord, and he shall sustain you."

Her aunt shut the heavy door to her chamber as Theraisa hurried to her rooms and closed her own door softly behind her. She pulled her heavy silk dress over her head of long, blonde curls and then carefully hung it in the clothes cabinet. As she slipped quickly out of her undergarments and unwound the binding cloth from around her belly, she immediately felt the cool night air wash over her nakedness. Theraisa's eyes moved slowly, almost shyly, down her body to peer at her expanding waist. The realization enveloped her that it wouldn't be long before she would be unable to conceal her condition with a binding cloth, but now this fact no longer alarmed her.

Theraisa pulled her fine, white wool nightshirt over her head and climbed into the soft featherbed. Her toes reached to the bottom, and she instantly appreciated the heat radiating from the warmed bricks her maid had put under the covers earlier in the evening. She looked up through the darkness of her chamber as she folded her hands and prayed to her father in heaven. *I know you have a way for my life, dear Father in heaven, although I do not know what it is. I thank you for my aunt and her plan to protect me and my parents from shame. Please, dear Lord, help my parents to agree with this plan, and help Auntie Louisa and me to prepare for the journey. Keep us safe in your care, and forgive my sin.*

Emotionally exhausted, Theraisa fell asleep with her hands still folded in prayer. Her dreams were not any different that night. David's face came to her, tempting her with his engaging, dimpled smile and sparkling blue-green eyes. Theraisa dreamed of the warmth of David's breath on her skin, how he slowly took the pins from her hair and watched as it flowed over her shoulders like a golden waterfall. She had loved him with her whole heart and soul, yet now she knew that this memory and the child she carried were all she would ever have of him. As she shifted restlessly in her sleep, she woke momentarily and thought, *Oh my love, my David, you were my whole life, my future. Why did you have to die and leave me so alone to face the consequences of our love?*

Falling back asleep, she returned to the dream; only this time, the dream turned into a nightmare as she witnessed David's death from the sniper's bullet. She had been told his cavalry unit had been ambushed near the Austrian border. David had been in the lead as usual, and he was the first to die as the fatal bullet entered his chest and exploded in his heart. In an instant, he had been taken from her forever.

Awakened once again, Theraisa raised herself up as she wiped the tears from her eyes. Throwing back the warm outer cover, she stumbled to the dressing table and poured water from the cool stone pitcher into a porcelain bowl. Theraisa submerged both hands into the water and splashed it over her burning face. "How can the memory of our love be both good and bad at the same time? All I know is that it disturbs me. I fear the complete beauty of that moment will haunt me for the rest of my days!"

~~~~~

Early the next morning with the help of her maidservant, Louisa Von Steiner dressed in a burgundy, watered-silk morning coat. She left her chamber, holding her head high with confidence; she was ready to execute an utterly convincing performance. She pulled air deep into her lungs and walked confidently down the long, winding staircase to the breakfast room where her brother-in-law and sister-in-law were having their morning coffee and streusel.

Louisa's gentle nature was confronted with the garish wall of murals depicting traditional German hunts: the wild boar, a magnificent stag, a frantic red fox desperately trying to outrun a pack of *Kammerhunds,* and finally the tenacious dachshunds pursuing a badger down his hole. Even though she felt disdain, she never uttered a word of disapproval, knowing the head of household loved such things.

Crown Prince Heinrich Von Steiner, the castle patriarch, stood as Louisa entered the room, his muscular, six-foot frame filling the chamber with a commanding presence. His steel-gray eyes rested on his attractive, raven-haired sister-in-law as she strolled gracefully into the dining hall, the fabric of her morning coat swirling like a cloud around her slim body. A servant pulled a carved walnut chair from the massive banquet table. Prince Heinrich stood waiting as Louisa gracefully took her seat. Reclaiming his chair, he wiped his mustached mouth with his napkin as a fond smile wrinkled his leathered face.

"You are looking lovely this morning, Louisa. I trust you had a restful night in spite of the wretched storm!" He reached down to scruff the neck of his favorite *Kammerhund,* while the chamber dog sat loyally at his feet, patiently waiting for a morsel of food.

Louisa returned his smile and heartfelt greeting as she acknowledged her sister-in-law, Amelia. "JA, thank you, I am in good health this morning. The wind and the rains were not a bother to me. I only snuggled deeper under my eiderdown quilts. I trust you both enjoyed the ball last night and that you, Amelia, were the toast of the palace in your beautiful, bronze brocade gown."

Princess Amelia responded with obvious pleasure, "Oh yes, the dress was perfect for the ball. I have to tell you as well that our good mayor, Burgermeister Roth, was in fine form, very entertaining with his constant stories. It was a grand evening, and we enjoyed ourselves in spite of the absence of you and our daughter."

Louisa's eyes rose to the massive chandelier of Murano crystal as she gathered her thoughts. "I—I have something of concern which I feel compelled to discuss with you this morning. Theraisa came to my chambers last evening, much distraught in her unrelenting grief. I fear she is not recovering from her loss as any of us would like. She confides that she sees reminders of David everywhere her eyes rest, and she can find no peace." Louisa lifted the porcelain cup to her lips and sipped the hot liquid. "I am very worried about her. I have prayed long about what I might do to help her. This morning I awoke with what I consider to be a marvelous solution."

Prince Heinrich and his wife exchanged glances, both conveying concern. Their curiosity was aroused as Heinrich boomed with authority. "Of course, my dear, please tell us what you think would console and comfort our cherished daughter."

"This may come as a surprise to you, but I am confident that after you think and pray about it, you will see the wisdom and necessity in the plan." Louise drew a deep breath into her chest, praying for courage of her own. "I would like to travel with Theraisa to the Volga, to Susannenthal for an extended visit with your cousin, Phillip, and other Steiner relatives who have lived along the Russian river for decades. It would be of great benefit for our dear Theraisa to remove her from the constant memories of Captain Ritter. Of course, I would look forward to a long, leisurely visit with our cousins myself, some of whom I have never met. It would be a lovely adventure for both of us, I am sure."

Louisa pushed back her chair to rise from the table as a servant rushed to assist her. "Please speak in private if you wish, and then tell me of your decision. I think it would be good to secure passage on the next ship, which disembarks from Lubeck, crossing the Baltic Sea to Kronstadt, Russia. I am sure you have the connections to achieve this quickly, Heinrich, as winter weather from the north comes soon."

Prince Heinrich's face was animated as he reached across the table to cover his wife's hand with his own. "Amelia, my dear, I think this is a brilliant idea. We are well aware of how the death of Captain Ritter has affected our daughter and how pale and thin she has become." Heinrich turned to face his sister-in-law. "It is so unselfish of you, dear Louisa, to volunteer to accompany Theraisa on this trip so she may recover from her loss and regain her health and composure. I am very much in favor of the journey." He turned again to his wife, his eyes wide with optimism. "Are you in agreement, my dear?"

Amelia replied with hesitation, "Yes, yes, of course, Heinrich. But it is all so sudden. Selfishly, I am not sure I can be without my daughter for such a length of time. Does it have to be so—so impulsive? Can't we take some time to prepare for such a long and arduous journey? Wouldn't it be wiser to delay the trip until the warmth of spring and the northern snow melt?"

Louisa responded with unexpected urgency. "I realize it is sudden, my dear, but your daughter desperately needs to remove herself from the tormenting memories of her betrothed. As you are aware, the Russian winter will soon be upon the Baltic, and the time to journey is immediate. I believe the sooner the better. I am sure with some effort we can be ready by the end of the week. I am looking forward to the trip and am filled with confidence it is the precise thing that will help Theraisa overcome her anguish. I realize with all my heart how much she means to you, and I know you wish for her life to be filled with happiness."

Prince Heinrich stroked his beard then remarked, "Of course you shall not travel alone, and I think I shall send Otto as your protector. I am confident he is most capable of attending to your safety. I realize you are both used to having a maidservant at your beck and call. However, I doubt that would be acceptable in the frugal villages along the Volga. Perhaps you can hire someone to take care of your menial chores once you arrive."

Heinrich slapped the table with vigor as he stood. "Well then, I shall begin to make the arrangements this very morning. Of course, you will both need traveling permits to leave Germany, and I know just the gentleman whom I shall call upon to obtain those documents quickly. I will tell you of the final plans as soon they are made. I assume you will speak to Theraisa, and the two of you may begin to pack your clothing and other belongings that you wish to take on the journey." Heinrich turned to face his wife. "Also, Amelia, my dear, will you kindly select appropriate gifts for our Volga family so our ambassadors will not arrive empty-handed? Perhaps a letter should be sent immediately to alert Cousin Phillip and his family of their arrival." Heinrich turned again to his brother's widow. "I will take care of everything, Louisa. Please go now and convey the news to our daughter that I have given permission for her to leave on an extended visit to the Volga River and homes of our family!"

Prince Von Steiner pushed back his oversized dining chair, stood, and added with authority, "It goes without saying you will be staying through the winter because of the impossibility of travel in these months. I assume you will need a goodly sum of money to sustain you both for a period of, say, six months or more. Agreed?"

Louisa stood and bowed. "Yes, yes—I think you are covering everything we need, Heinrich. I appreciate your timely connections in making the necessary arrangements. I think your decision to send us to the Volga is a wise and loving one. Let me assure you, I will be at Theraisa's side constantly, and I am confident we will have a wonderful and healing adventure. Thank you, thank you for your trust!" She turned and, lifting her long skirts, she flew up the curving staircase toward Theraisa's chamber.

Practically out of breath, she reached her niece's door and impatiently knocked twice. "Theraisa, my dear, it is Auntie Louisa. May I come in?"

Theraisa was sitting at her brocade-covered dressing table, combing her long hair when she heard her aunt's voice. Quickly, she stood and hurried to open the carved wooden door. Louisa rushed into the room, saying, "Close the door. Please close the door, my dear. I have wonderful news—jubilant news!"

Theraisa led her aunt to the small, curved French sofa where they sat facing each other. "Did you speak to Papa and Mama? Did you, did you?"

With a smile that spread from ear to ear, Louisa announced, "We are leaving for the Volga by the end of the week! Your parents have agreed with my plan to take you away from your memories, so your heart and soul may heal."

Theraisa threw her arms around her aunt. "Oh dear Gott in Himmel, Auntie Louisa, you really convinced them that we should go? I can't believe it. You have solved my problem, and I will love you forever, you dear, dear woman!" She stood and began to twirl her blue silk-twill skirts around and around the spacious room, and then she quickly asked, "What do I pack for such a trip? I have never been out of the state of Hessen. I am sure you will help me in this situation as well, won't you, my godmother?" The two women hugged and laughed with nervous anticipation.

Holding her niece in her arms, Louisa reassured her, "Theraisa, I want you to know that I will be at your side through whatever this journey might bring. The trip may not be easy, but I assume you realize this. It will be very far and perhaps not pleasant when we cross the Baltic Sea to Kronstadt. After we reach the Russian port, we will travel by a series of small riverboats and finally by train over the Russian plains to the headwaters of the Volga. Russia is an extremely huge country with many sparsely populated areas. Toward the end of our journey, we will travel by steamship down the meandering Volga River to Saratov[2]. Our cousin Phillip lives in Susannenthal[3] near the port of Saratov."

Louisa paced back and forth across the floor as she spoke in rapid German. "Your mother will send Cousin Phillip and his wife, Elizabeth, a letter announcing our pending arrival. Oh yes, your father is sending Otto as our protector—I am confident he will serve us well. I will have your personal maid bring up your traveling trunks and assist you in packing appropriate clothing. I assume you realize your fine ball gowns and silks will not be needed or appropriate, as the area is rather primitive. Take your plain Hessen, homespun dresses, wools, and twills. We do not wish to put ourselves above our family with our finery or to flaunt our wealth. Do you understand, my dear? Also, my sweet, remember you are in mourning, so your clothing must be of dark color."

Seeing the disappointment in her niece's face, Louisa took a deep breath and quickly added, "However, you might consider packing your lovely midnight-blue silk gown. You should have *one* nice dress in case a special event should arise. Also, Theraisa, I think wearing your conservative black-twill traveling suit would be most appropriate. I suggest you pack a long wool coat or two and many scarves and covers for your hands. I understand we should take two pair of good, warm boots and an older pair to wear on board the ship. The salt from the seawater destroys leather. I am sure we will be able to purchase more suitable clothing for the climate once we arrive in Susannenthal where Phillip lives."

Theraisa's eyes were wide with wonder and fear of the unknown, but she responded quickly. "Yes, of course, Auntie Louisa." Theraisa then put her face into her soft hands as a torrent of tears rolled uncontrolled down her lovely face. Sobbing softly, she said, "I can't believe you have helped me so and we are actually leaving. I must admit I am excited, relieved, and yet quite frightened. How can I feel all these things at once, Auntie?"

Louisa stood, embraced her niece, and walked slowly to the door before turning with an afterthought. "Theraisa, because of your condition, you may expect your emotions to swing from one extent to the other. However, try your best to control them to protect your—your delicate situation while we are preparing to leave. May I also caution against exposing your fear or concern of leaving to your parents. You must make them believe this is the only thing that will help you recover from losing your captain. Do you understand the circumstances, my dear? Our ultimate goal is to spare your parents' disgrace in the eyes of our Hessian kingdom and the church."

Theraisa lifted her head and drew a deep breath of fresh air into her lungs. Blowing her nose into her handkerchief and exhaling, she forced a smile onto her flushed face. "Of course, Auntie, of course, I will do everything you say. How can I ever in this world thank you?"

Her aunt smiled. "My darling, you can thank me by living the rest of your life in happiness."

"I will see you at dinner, Auntie, and perhaps Papa will have more good news for us. I am in your debt forever!" With that Louisa hurried from her niece's chamber and walked quickly to her own to begin the monumental task of packing for months in the primitive Russian steppe.

Later that day as Louisa was resting on her French bed; she was alarmed by insistent knocking at her door. She lifted her head from the lace-covered pillow. "Yes, who is it, please?"

"Louisa, it is I, Amelia. May I come in to speak with you for a moment?"

Louisa rose stiffly, wiping the sleep from her eyes as she moved to open the heavy door. "My dear, come in, please. Should I ring for tea and a biscuit while we visit?"

"No, no, that is not necessary. I won't be long." Amelia crossed the chamber floor to stand at the center dormer window. She stood for a moment, apparently admiring the garden before turning to face her sister-in-law. You have such a beautiful view from your windows. I suppose you never tire of looking at it, do you?"

Louisa's eyes narrowed. "Why no, my dear, I never tire of looking at the spectacular gardens of the estate, even when they are at rest. Is—is there something on your mind, Amelia? I sense that you did not visit my chamber to speak of my view from the windows."

Princess Amelia flushed and turned again, pretending to inspect the gardens. Clearing her throat and choosing her words carefully, she spoke. "Louisa, you know you are most dear to us and how much we cherish your presence in this castle. I have known you for over twenty years, and I believe I understand you as I would a natural sister!"

Louisa's eyes widened while her body tensed. Amelia spun around to look at her sister-in-law as her face filled with anguish; she took in a long, slow breath. "Louisa, what is the real reason you are taking my daughter away, out of the country so quickly?"

Instantly, Louisa's internal alarms were clanging. She knew she must be very cautious and choose her words with forethought. She was treading on very thin ice. "Amelia, dear Amelia—it is as I have told you. Theraisa is becoming ill with her grief. She needs to be away from incessant wagging tongues and reminders of her unbearable loss. The trip, the change of scenery, will be very good for her, and at the same time it will put your mind at ease, trust me—please trust me!"

A soft, sweet smile spread across Amelia's regal, porcelain face. "Louisa, I *know!*"

With impressive calm, Louisa tipped her aristocratic head in question. "You know what, my dear?"

"I know why you are taking Theraisa away. It is because she is with child; am I not correct?" Amelia turned again to face the window, quickly adding, "You do not have to answer my question, Louisa. I would not ask you to betray my daughter's confidence. But I am a woman who has suffered through five pregnancies. I know well the signs. They are all the symptoms my daughter has tried in vain to conceal. It all makes sense now."

Amelia walked slowly to the doorway. Grasping the iron handle, she paused and turned, facing her sister-in-law. "Thank you, my dear, dear sister. Thank you for protecting Heinrich and me and our daughter as well. You will be richly rewarded for your generosity and your kindness toward our family!"

Louisa did not bother to respond. She knew her answer was written all over her face, and she wasn't fooling anyone, only perhaps Heinrich, who was oblivious to the perils of being a woman.

~~~~~

Prince Heinrich spent the next few days in a fury of activity to secure traveling permits, a coach to drive his sister-in-law and daughter to the port at Lubeck, and passage on a ship sailing for the Russian port of Kronstadt. Even with all of the activity, he had time to muse.

Thinking back, Heinrich remembered that only a month past, he had been tending a sick horse in the stable and happened to walk near the area where the contents of his daughter's night pot was habitually tossed. For some reason, he looked over at the mess and stopped in his tracks as the significance of it exploded in his mind. His daughter was pregnant! Heinrich had felt sick to his stomach with concern, and then rage at the thought that Captain Ritter had taken advantage of his daughter and left her in this shameful condition. *It is a good thing he is dead, because if he were not, I would definitely kill him with my bare hands.*

Prince Heinrich had not shared this information with his wife, hoping to protect what he considered her delicate nature from the truth. He prayed it would take care of itself somehow and spare his noble family's reputation from unthinkable disgrace.

It was Wednesday evening, and dressed for dinner, the four members of the royal family sat at the impressive walnut banquet table, partaking of the sumptuous fare. Suddenly, Heinrich cleared his throat and with authority said, "I have an announcement to make!" He raised his glass of Riesling wine, and addressing his wife, daughter, and his sister-in-law, he said, "You will be happy to hear that plans and reservations are completed for your journey to the headwaters of the Volga River and on to Saratov. You will be leaving this Friday, traveling by coach overland to the ship *Konig-Albert*, which is moored in the port of Lubeck.

"You will be traveling with the well-known Deutschland tenor, Herr Dieter Schultmann. He and his entourage are making a journey to Russia to perform for Catherine the Great and the Russian court." Heinrich smiled with a twinkle in his eye as he twirled his thick mustache before continuing. "I am sure he would be honored to have two beautiful ladies in his company for at least part of the journey. Perhaps he will even sing a song or two in your honor!"

~~~~~

For the remaining part of the week, the Von Steiner castle was frantic with packing and other preparations for the arduous journey. All too soon, Friday dawned to find the black traveling coach waiting patiently in the courtyard. Otto and the castle servants had secured an impressive number of bags onto the roof of the coach, nestling them securely behind the driver. Otto took his seat beside the driver as they waited patiently for the family to say their good-byes.

Visibly shaken with second thoughts, Prince Heinrich and Princess Amelia escorted Louisa and their daughter to the waiting coach. The two women were dressed in comfortable black-twill traveling suits. Louisa wore a beautiful velvet hat trimmed in pheasant feathers while Theraisa had selected a simple, bronze wool eyelet bonnet. Amelia reached out for her daughter, drawing her into her arms.

"I have asked the Lord to keep you safe on your journey so you may be free of the memories which haunt you. Remember to say your morning and evening prayers, and enjoy your visit with our cousins. It is our hope that you will benefit from your great adventure and return safely to our side."

Princess Amelia pulled a gold cross and chain over her perfectly styled blonde hair. "Here, my darling, I want you to wear this gold cross, and remember the love of your Lord and your parents every day. Some days are going to be better than others. Have faith and do what you have to do so you come back to us. God's speed, my darling—my love goes with you."

Theraisa struggled to maintain her self-composure as her father took her briefly into his arms. She stood up on tiptoes to embrace him. Heinrich wrapped his burly arms around her frail form and whispered into her ear, "Travel safe, Theraisa, and be strong as I expect you to be. Remember, you are the daughter of noble birth, and always conduct yourself accordingly." Heinrich turned to Louisa. "We pray for a safe trip, a wonderful reunion with the family along the Volga and a speedy return to Germany. We trust you will watch after our daughter in every instance, Louisa."

Louisa tipped her head in acceptance, thinking it was odd Heinrich would say such a thing—not the expected farewell. She bid good-bye to her brother-in-law and sister-in-law as she climbed into the coach. As soon as the door was secured, Louisa tapped the ceiling to signal the driver to proceed. The four matched roan horses leapt forward, pulling the coach down the winding mountain road. Princess Theraisa leaned out the window and waved to her parents as they stood watching the carriage disappear from view. When she couldn't see them any longer, she pulled her head back inside the coach, covered her face with her hands, and burst into tears.

Louisa put her arm around her niece and pulled her close. "Go ahead now, dear girl. Let the tears go. There is no one here to speculate or gossip. You are safe now." Louisa handed Theraisa her white lace handkerchief.

After they had traveled for an hour or so, Theraisa recovered from her melancholy as Louisa spoke, "I have been thinking for some time, Theraisa, perhaps it is a good idea that you travel as 'Frau Ritter' instead of Fräulein Von Steiner. I believe this change will protect your virtue and honor. You have great cause to begin practicing your new name. Do you think this is a good idea, Frau Ritter?"

Louisa smiled as she continued. "Also, Theraisa, I think it is fitting, as a married woman, you move your engagement ring from your left hand to the ring finger of your right hand, to designate your marriage. I realize you and David were not given the time to be married as you planned. However, we will simply declare you were married months before he was killed. This should satisfy inquiring minds, don't you think, Frau Ritter?"

Theraisa removed the hand covers and looked at the beautiful gold ring David had given to her in promise of marriage. Smiling, she moved the ring from left to right, and she closed her eyes as she laid her hands on her swelling stomach. "Yes, Auntie Louisa, it is a very good idea. It is what I have wanted from the first time David kissed me. Now, I *am* Frau Ritter, widow of Captain David Ritter and, of course, I am still in mourning. Oh, Auntie Louisa, again I thank you for your brilliant plan. I can hardly believe we are safely on our way to Russia and a new beginning." Frau Ritter stuck her head out the window of the coach for a final glimpse of Reinstadt Mountain, the home of her parents' castle. Longingly, she continued to peer out the window until her life as she knew it disappeared from view.

Chapter Two

On Their Way: September 9, 1873

Annoyed, Frau Theraisa Ritter tilted her aristocratic head as she readjusted her perfectly-coiffured mass of golden curls. Each time the coach hit a rut in the road, her body was jolted, and her face contorted in a grimace. After a particularly rough stretch of road, Theraisa was thoroughly irritated, "Auntie Louisa, do you know how long we must endure this dreadfully coarse ride? Is this what the road is to be like the entire way to the port of Lubeck?"

Louisa looked up from her needlework as she tried to hide her irritated amusement. "I know you are quite pampered, Theraisa, and have not traveled abroad, so you have many new experiences ahead. You are going to have to learn to accept some discomfort and appreciate this gift of escaping family humiliation."

Louisa reminded her niece that her father predicted that with good weather and strong horses, their trip on land would take about three days. Of course, this included stopping at inns for meals and staying the night as well. Hoping her explanation would suffice, Louisa returned her attention to the crewel embroidery that lay in her lap.

After several moments she looked up, and with an edge of exasperation, she inquired, "Theraisa, don't you have *something* to occupy your time like needlework or an entertaining book? Truly, it will make the journey go by more quickly than looking out the window every two minutes and complaining about your discomfort."

Theraisa scowled as she reached into her valise for a book. "You know quite well, Auntie, I hate needlework. I always prick my finger and do not enjoy the blood or the pain. It truly bores me to tears." She attempted to read as the coach lurched and bounced over the rut-filled road.

Still annoyed and uncomfortable, Theraisa complained for the fourth time within the hour, asking why the horses would trot for a while then gallop, and then trot. "Do we have a driver controlling them, or are they running loose?" She stuck her head out the open window and attempted to look up onto the driver's seat as her long blonde hair blew over her face obstructing her view, drowning her curiosity, and irritating her even further.

Louisa released a long, petulant sigh. "Oh, Theraisa, my dear—don't be ridiculous. Of course we have a driver. You saw him when we climbed into the coach. Perhaps if you take a nap, you will feel less anxious." Louisa wondered with dread if her niece's negativity and painfully privileged attitude would last the entire trip.

After what seemed like several hours, the coach rolled to a stop. Theraisa peered out the window to see a quaint, shuttered inn set back in a forest of conifer and spruce. Both ladies were relieved when the coach door opened, and the driver assisted them down the steps. They were delighted to discover they would have time for lunch while the driver arranged for a change of horses. Finishing the tasty fare, they took a short walk to relieve their aching muscles, and then their journey continued.

They had been settled inside the coach for only a few moments when, feeling refreshed and suddenly curious, Theraisa voiced an interest in their family history. She asked her aunt if she knew who was first in the Von Steiner family to leave Germany to immigrate to the Volga River. "When did they leave? Do you know any of our family history? Why did the people who left Germany travel to such a remote area like the Volga, in Russia of all places?"

Louisa turned to gaze with wonder at her niece. "I had no idea you might be interested in the Von Steiner family history, but you have asked the right person since it is one of my favorite topics." Louisa smiled smugly as she tilted her intelligent, middle-aged face to the side and ran her tongue over her parched lips. "I do think this traveling does not agree with my skin. It is quite dry, isn't it?"

Then smiling thoughtfully as she gazed intently at her niece's inquisitive expression, Louisa began to reveal what she had learned. "As you are well aware, the Von Steiner family is highly esteemed German royalty. For unknown reasons, the initial family split— perhaps over religion and argument over inheritance. We simply don't know. Regardless, the end result was that a few remained in a life of luxury and power, while others were destined to work the fields and became unfortunate victims of decades of war that devastated the region. Those farmers and merchants of the Steiner family who had nothing left after the wars are the family members who immigrated to the Volga. We are most fortunate and blessed to belong to the branch of the family who inherited the wealth and title. Regardless, we have kept in touch with some of our people who immigrated to Russia." Louisa smiled sweetly as she patted her niece on the knee and then continued.

"Through extensive research into the family history books and diaries, I was able to trace the Volga branch of the family line back to Johann Ludwig Steiner, who was born in 1672 on a small farm outside Kemel, the Hessian state of Germany. His youngest son, Johann Peter Steiner, born 1721, and two of his adult sons were the first to immigrate to the Volga in the year of our Lord, 1776. Johann Peter, Franz Christian, Johann Heinrich, or Heinz, and his wife, Ilsa, left Germany together. Ilsa died from childbirth en route to the Volga area.

"Heinz married again in 1776, and this wife was said to have also died in childbirth. His third marriage in 1777 to Elisabeta was blessed with six children. Peter Wilheim was the eldest, and his only son, Peter William, was the father of our cousin Johann Phillip, whom we will visit on the Volga.

"Your grandfather, Crown Prince Christian Heinrich, never left Germany. He was a firstborn son, as was your father. As you are well aware, your brother Christian Johann will inherit the Von Steiner Castle and the title of crown prince, and so it goes." Louisa rubbed her stiff neck, and then brushed the dust from her traveling suit.

Theraisa's eyes grew bright with understanding. "Now I understand how it is we are related to the Steiner families of Russia. I appreciate the explanation, Auntie, because I was quite confused."

Louisa continued. "Because Johann Heinrich Steiner and his family were the first to immigrate, many of the people with the name of Steiner who live in their area are descendants from him. However, as I mentioned, Johann Peter and his family were not with the first groups of Germans to leave for the Volga. The initial German emigration arrived in St. Petersburg in mid-1774, so our family members were indeed fortunate that they emigrated two years later. When those first surviving Germans laid eyes on the area along the Volga, they expected to see newly constructed homes waiting. They saw nothing but open land, and winter was weeks away!

"It is our understanding that the first ten years were extremely difficult for those early immigrants. If they didn't die from starvation, there was always pestilence, drought, disease, raiding Mongolian tribes, and corruption from the Russian government which decimated their numbers. The early representatives of Catherine the Great had convinced the German people that Russian winters were similar to winters in Germany. The immigrants soon discovered this was only one of many lies told to them.

"The Steiner people settled on the meadow or *Wiesenseite* side of the Volga—and called their village Susannenthal. The people who lived on the meadow side suffered frequent raids because they were closer to the Ural Mountains, which the barbaric Mongol tribesmen claimed as home turf."

"Phillip has written that the German people living there have chosen not to mingle with Russian peasants but prefer to keep to themselves in their own well-established villages. They have learned how to survive the winters by using their own ingenuity and adopting various Russian means of survival. They wish to keep their culture pure, and most speak 'high German,' with a predominating Hessian or Southern German dialect. They refer to themselves as the Volga Germans or *Die Wolgadeutschen.*"

Louisa raised her eyes to her niece, who was yawning. "Do you wish me to continue, dear girl, or are you weary?"

Theraisa smiled. "Oh nein, Auntie Louisa, I merely had a small yawn. I find this fascinating. Please do continue."

Louisa smiled as she went on. "Your great-cousin, Johann Phillip, was the fifth child of Johann William, and he married Marie Elisabeth Wasmuth. A year ago we received a letter from

Phillip and Elisa announcing they had been blessed with their seventh child and were prospering."

Theraisa tipped her head to the side, asking, "How do you know all of these facts about our family? There are so many years and so many people to keep track of—six generations!"

Blushing with pleasure, Louisa explained that since her husband, Theraisa's uncle Peter, passed away, it has been her ambition to learn all she could about his family and to record it for the generations who would live beyond. The Lutheran church in Kemel, Germany, which was not far from the family castle, had graciously provided access to their extensive records.

Louisa took a drink of fresh water from the leather flask. "Do you remember learning about the bitter Thirty Years' War— Lutherans fighting against Catholics? Perhaps it was this war that caused the split in our family. I know it took your grandfather a very long time to rebuild our lands. Nobility and peasants suffered from the war."

Louisa's expression was grim as she continued. "The horrific wars have left thousands of German people in a state of great poverty. It seems there was one battle after another, especially in our area of southwestern Germany, where entire villages were burned and the people slaughtered."[4]

Louisa rubbed the dust from her eyes as she looked out the window. "They were desperate people. Most had lost their homes, farms, and large numbers of family members. There was nothing here for them, only bad memories and no way to make a living or help in starting over! This is what the manifesto and Catherine the Great gave them—opportunity for a new life!"

Theraisa looked thoughtfully out the window. "But why did so many German people decide to leave? It was a desperate act, leaving their German homes and families to move north and east to Russia, of all places."

Removing her laced boots, Theraisa curled her feet under her voluminous skirts. She reached to untie the black ribbons from her wool bonnet, which she removed and laid on the seat next to her. "Now, Auntie Louisa, I do remember studying about the early wars and the devastation, especially where we live in southwestern Germany. I can understand why the people needed a solution to their problems. What did this manifesto say? What did the Empress Catherine offer to do for the German people? Why would she do this for people from our country since she was a Russian empress?"

Louisa looked up from her needlework. "Catherine the Great was born in Germany and continued to favor the country of her birth. She was a smart one and also a wise ruler. She knew her adopted nation was in need of settlers of knowledge in order to educate and influence the outer Russian communities and illiterate peasants.

"Catherine realized the rich riverbed along the Volga River south of Simbirsk was prime farming land. This area had been inhabited for centuries by wild Mongolian tribes, and she planned to push them out of Russia, using German settlers to do her work for her. Catherine had done her homework and understood the intelligence as well as the desperate situation facing the efficient German farmers, especially in our war-torn region of Hesse."

Louisa paused and blotted her face with her white lace handkerchief. "Excuse me, my dear. This dust is beginning to bother me. Now where was I? Oh yes, Catherine the Great made a proposal that many destitute Germans could not ignore. It was a lifeline! Her manifesto offered to clothe them, give them money, and take them to Russia. She gave them all the rights they might want in their own communities. Most impressive was the freedom from taxes and military service.

"At this time you have to understand, these people had nothing, so of course her manifesto was like a dream for them." Louisa crossed her legs and took another drink from the water flask. "At the time they left Germany, there was already a constant stream of immigration to America, Poland, and Hungary. It is obvious the Russians took note of this vulnerability and saw an opportunity to lure German settlers to their country as well."

As the sun began its descent into the western horizon, Louisa looked out the window and exclaimed, "Look, Theraisa, I believe we have arrived at the inn where we will stay this first night! I am quite ready to make my exit of this carriage for a few hours. Where I sit is numb. I look forward to some soap and water to freshen up and then perhaps a hot meal. How about you? Are you ready to stop this bumping and bouncing for a few hours?"

Louisa quickly stored her needlework in her valise as she tidied her hair and smoothed her traveling suit. "Theraisa, dear, do put your boots back on. It would not be acceptable to walk into the inn with bare feet!" She laughed heartily at the thought of her aristocratic niece walking barefoot into the fine German inn.

Once they arrived at the inn, the driver and Otto took the ladies' bags to their rooms and then disappeared for the night. After a wonderful meal of succulent, crispy pigs' knuckles, fluffy white mashed potatoes, and tart heaps of pungent sauerkraut, Louisa ordered a glass of strong sherry to finish her meal. "Theraisa, would you like a small glass of sherry to help you sleep?"

"Oh, Auntie Louisa, I think that may be a good idea, as I am beginning to ache already from all the bouncing in that coach today." Theraisa had not failed to notice that her aunt had consumed over four glasses of the strong drink.

After their meal, the two ladies climbed the stairs to their bed chamber, both looking forward to a comfortable night's sleep in beds heaped with feather quilts. Louisa watched thoughtfully as Theraisa brushed her long, silky hair. "Dear girl, I have just had a thought. Perhaps to make your appearance more like a married woman, you should cut your hair and pull it back into a bun as is customary. What do you think of the idea? I have a small scissors in my valise, and I could trim it so it would be manageable for you."

Theraisa stopped brushing her hair and stared in the mirror at her reflection. Tears filled her soft blue eyes. "Oh, Auntie, my goodness, I had not thought about my long hair. I suppose you are right. My hair is that of a girl, and I am now a widow, expecting a child. So I suppose it is the best thing to do. Go ahead and cut it as you think best."

Theraisa suddenly remembered how many glasses of sherry her aunt had consumed at dinner and silently questioned her ability to wield a scissors. "Shouldn't we perhaps wait until morning?" She hoped a good night's sleep might steady her aunt's hand. "Wait, Auntie. Do you—do you think I will still be pretty, with my hair pulled back so severely?"

Louisa approached her niece, scissors in hand, ready and willing to trim the girl's hair. Reading the concerned expression on Theraisa's face, Louisa said, "I assure you, my dear, I may have had more than one glass of sherry, but I can still cut your hair. Now sit down here, and let's get to work."

After the candles were extinguished, Theraisa lay in her bed thinking about the unknown circumstance of her future. She turned onto her side, snuggling deeper in the goose down bed and listened to the rhythmic snoring of her aunt.

In the darkness, Theraisa reached her hands to her head, running her fingers through her once-glorious hair. Frightened and suddenly nostalgic, tears slowly rolled from her eyes and down her cheeks. *So many things have happened to change my privileged life. It is as though I have lost control of my life as it once was, and now I am being pushed and pulled through a life I don't recognize.*

Early the next morning, Louisa and Theraisa finished preparing for their second day of travel; Louisa reached into her valise and pulled out a square of black Austrian lace. "Here, my dear, this is something I do believe you should wear over your head as a widow in mourning."

Theraisa reached for the large square of delicate black lace and draped it over her sleek new hairstyle, securing it at the top. She smiled at the reflection in the small hand mirror. "There now, I believe this actually completes my appearance as a widow. Thank you, Auntie. It is a beautiful section of lace, and I think it looks rather good, don't you?" She bent forward to admire herself again in the small mirror then stood straight and turned, expecting verbal approval from her aunt.

Attired in simple, black traveling suits of worsted wool twill, the two women exited the inn climbed back into the coach, dreading their second day of travel. Louisa had wrapped a black silk babushka around her hair in an effort to keep the constant invasion of road dust from soiling it. As the coach lurched forward, Louisa addressed her niece in an attempt to divert her attention from her discomfort. "Theraisa, I must say you look elegant and also much older with your hair pulled back into a bun. The black lace head cover is also quite attractive, my dear. How do you like it?"

Theraisa smiled as she replied, "I thought I would not like to cut my hair, as I was very fond of it, and David especially loved it. But I do think it improves my appearance as a woman in mourning and I—I am becoming used to it. Danke, Auntie, Danke!"

They rode without speaking for several minutes. Before long, Louisa was enduring a tedious headache; she laid her head back against the seat and closed her eyes, hoping the pain would subside. Theraisa entertained herself by looking out the open window of the coach as they passed through dense, deciduous woods. "Auntie, do look at these glorious autumn leaves. They are quite marvelous, I must say. They remind me of yellow-and-red butterflies as they fall and spin through the morning air."

Reluctantly, Louisa opened her eyes and lifted her head to peer out the window. Her face lit up with wonder as she too witnessed the miracle of the trees showering the waiting earth with their final glory of the season. "Yes, dear girl, it is a most beautiful sight, I do agree. My dear, do you want to hear more about our family's emigration? I think I am feeling better—that is, if you are still curious."

Theraisa turned quickly and responded. "Oh yes, Auntie. It is fascinating, and I do so want to understand all about the Volga and our people who live there now."

Louisa smoothed her rumpled skirt and began. "Many of the early emigrants left Germany to escape religious persecution: Catholics, Lutherans, Mennonites, Moravians, and Hutterites.[5]

Opening her silver water flask, Louisa took a deep swallow of the cool liquid and continued. "Ahhh, that's what I needed— now I can talk a while longer. When the people finally arrived in Russia, they were told they would *not* be allowed to settle in the cities as they were led to believe. The majority of German emigrants were instructed to travel to the Volga and farm the land, no matter if they were craftsmen or professionals. They were led overland by Russian guides. All immigrants were subjected to grueling journeys over unbelievably inhospitable land, and many simply fell to the frozen Russian soil and died. Actually, I have read accounts of some of the first emigrants who spent the winter in Russian peasant huts along with cattle, sheep, pigs, and inhospitable Russian peasants. It took almost a year for the immigrants to reach the Volga.

"Although we are not certain, I suspect this is when Johann Heinrich's first wife died. It's a wonder all of them didn't die. The people had been told that the land along the Volga was very much like the land they left in Germany. They were told the climate was mild, the ground was fertile, and it was an extremely beautiful area. All were lies, as they discovered upon arrival. It certainly was a fertile area, but it was barren and windswept, and there were no villages or even shelters as they had been told would be waiting for them. In reality, the first settlers spent the first months burrowed in shelters dug into the high riverbanks like animals, and many more died from disease and starvation. I imagine some simply died from hopelessness."

Theraisa's face grew pale. "Auntie, those conditions sound terrible. I can't imagine how they must have suffered. Are these things still going on today? Will we be in danger when we arrive there?"

"Oh, my dear girl, I don't believe things are nearly as difficult as they once were. The letters we receive from your cousin Phillip tell us they are doing well, and most villages are quite safe. There are no more raids from barbaric tribesmen. Also, please do not despair about where we will live. There are now many lovely villages with adequate houses, and I am sure we will find something to live in during our short visit. I don't think we should stay with Phillip, as they already have a large family in their small house."

Louisa tipped her head back; her dark brown eyes gazed in thought at the ceiling of the coach. She knew she would have to suggest her next idea in a most diplomatic manner, and she was searching for the right words. "Theraisa, it has occurred to me that perhaps we should not draw too much attention to our presence when we arrive in Susannenthal. Perhaps it would be best if we were to find a small house, something near to where Phillip and his family live. What do you think?"

"Whatever you think is best, Auntie. I am comfortable leaving it in your hands. I believe I will try to take a short nap. I am feeling rather ill with the constant movement of the coach.

Perhaps if I can fall asleep, I will feel better when I awaken. Do you mind?"

"Good heavens, girl, no, no; please close your eyes and try to rest. I will work on my sewing while you are napping. Go ahead now and close your eyes."

Louisa settled back into the seat and gave her attention to the needlework on her lap. She looked over at her sleeping niece and thought, *"You are so naïve and spoiled, Theraisa. How are we ever going to succeed with this venture? It will be only through the grace of our Lord—yes, only through His grace will we survive this."*

~~~~~

As they neared the inn on their final night in Germany, Louisa grew weary of sitting on the rigid coach seat with little to do than stare out the window. The landscape of northern Germany grew dim with approaching nightfall. The sun was making its departure with a splendid farewell flare, piercing through the darkening sky. Vivid points of copper, mauve, orange, and purple shot through the stratus clouds that rested on the horizon.

Louisa gently shook her niece's shoulder. "Theraisa, oh, Theraisa, do wake up and look at this sky. It is very unusual, is it not? A good omen, I believe!"

Theraisa rubbed the sleep from her eyes and peered out the window of the rolling coach. "Oh my goodness, that is amazing. I am ravenous, quite thirsty, and I ache in every bone." She began to smooth her hair and adjust her clothing in hopeful preparation.

Chapter Three

Escape to Kronstadt: September 12, 1873

Late morning on the third day of traveling, they arrived at the seaport of Lubeck, Germany. Louisa and her niece were eager to experience traveling by ship on the next segment of their journey. Along the Lubeck dock, they noticed crowded rows of shabby barracks where poorer passengers were forced to wait for another ship. The first-class passengers were often provided with lodging at well-appointed rooming houses or with prominent citizens who opened their doors for a price.

~~~~~

Captain Franz Mueller stood at the head of the gangplank, supervising the loading of cargo. He was a large, black bear of a man with a full beard and an impressive head of wild, oily hair. Theraisa felt a shiver of apprehension when she observed the unkept captain.

Beaming with obvious elation, the captain greeted the two aristocratic German women. "Welcome, welcome—to the grand *Konig-Albert*, the finest ship to sail the Baltic Sea. The first mate will show you to your cabin, where I am sure you will be most comfortable. Perhaps you would grace our table with your presence this evening? We dine at seven o'clock. May we expect the pleasure of your company?" He lifted the gloved hand of the older lady to his lips in a chivalrous gesture.

Louisa's face lit up with exaggerated pleasure as she forced a bright smile. "Of course, Captain, we will be honored to join your table at dinner this evening. My niece and I look forward to the pleasure. Thank you!" She withdrew her hand as soon as was acceptable, thinking there was something she didn't like about the captain other than he had a noticeable tendency to sweat.

Louisa and Theraisa followed the first mate to the far end of the upper deck where he opened the door to what seemed to be a cabin designed in miniature. "I hope you will be comfortable here, Frau Von Steiner and Frau Ritter. Please contact me if I may be of further service." He shut the door quickly, leaving Louisa and Theraisa standing practically nose-to-nose in the confined quarters. Neither woman said a word as their eyes scanned the nine-by-ten foot space.

Theraisa's face froze with amazement and disbelief. "Auntie Louisa, is this where we *both* are to sleep, and--and to live, while we cross the sea to Russia? I can't believe they expect both of us to exist in, in *here*. Look, I can barely turn around without bumping into you. Oh, dear God, this is terrible. It is unacceptable. Please go and tell the captain that we can pay more for a larger cabin. Please, Auntie, please, I beg you."

Louisa wrapped her arms around her niece and patted her back as she tried to soothe her. "Theraisa, relax yourself. We will make do with what we have been given. Don't you understand that we are not in a position to demand larger quarters? We are very lucky to be on board. We will make do, my dear, and hopefully, we will have good winds and fair weather so the five-hundred mile journey to Kronstadt will pass quickly." Louisa inspected the room closer. "The space is actually quite clever. Look how the bunks are built on one wall and the other wall has an armoire in which to store our clothing. Of course, only one of us will be able to stand before the armoire at a time." She smiled in an effort to lighten the situation. "Look, there is a dry sink with a bowl and pitcher for washing and even a mirror above. I think it looks to be quite convenient."

"But, Auntie, have you ever slept in a *bunk*? And what in heaven are those railings for? It---it looks like a crib. It appears to be most uncomfortable. Why would they make it like a crib? We are not babies to fall on the floor!"

Louisa couldn't help herself and burst out laughing. "Oh, Theraisa, what a sheltered life you have lived. No, I have never slept in a bunk bed. This will be a first for me as well. And I believe the railings are on the bunks, so if the seas become rough, we will not be tossed out onto the floor!"

Theraisa's face filled with disbelief. "Surely you joke? You expect the water will become so high with waves it will toss us out of the bed? I sincerely hope we do not experience such a thing. That sounds terribly frightening. I swear, Auntie Louisa, if that happens, I will be in your bunk with you! The two women had packed smaller, separate traveling trunks with only those items they would need on a daily basis. They hoped to simplify their needs for the trip across the Baltic and then across land to the Volga. Their other larger trunks were stowed below in the cargo hold. Louisa and Theraisa spent the rest of the afternoon unpacking and getting settled in their berth and then took turns in the cramped space, dressing for dinner.

~~~~~

The *Konig-Albert* was not normally a passenger ship; it was an upscale cargo ship that accepted a limited number of paying passengers. On this particular trip across the Baltic, the German tenor, Dieter Schultmann, and his small traveling orchestra as well as Frau Von Steiner and Frau Ritter were the only human cargo. Captain Mueller was delighted to be able to enjoy the company of the two women on this trip. He stood as the elegant yet simply dressed females entered the makeshift dining room. "Ladies, please allow me to seat you at our table. We are most honored that you've seen fit to join us this evening. I hope what our cook has prepared is to your liking." The two women were successful in hiding their disbelief at what the captain called a dining room and the fact there was only one table.

Theraisa gave a small, frightened squeal as the ship lurched and swayed. Captain Mueller reassured the two women. "No need to worry. As you might have realized, we are underway. The tugboats are pulling us out into open water, away from the port of Lubeck."

Theraisa relaxed when she experienced a more gentle movement of the ship as it slipped through the calm waters of the port. "I am quite ravenous this evening, and the food appears to be very good, Captain Mueller. It is so kind of you to invite us to your table."

Captain Mueller swelled with gratitude and pomp. "Ladies, may I introduce the well-known German tenor, Dieter

Schultmann." Louisa and Theraisa nodded their heads in unison as the portly singer stood and bowed deeply.

Herr Schultmann was adorned in skintight leather breeches and a brown velvet waistcoat. His thick, blond hair was wavy and shoulder length. It was apparent he was expertly barbered from head to toe. The famous tenor's massive shoulders seemed to fill the room, matched only by his expansive waistline. He was known for his magnificent voice, but it was quite obvious he also enjoyed any and all attention that might come his way.

"Herr Schultmann"—Captain Mueller swept his hand toward the two women—"it is my pleasure to introduce Frau Louisa Von Steiner and her niece, Frau Theraisa Ritter, from Frankfurt. Now, please let us begin our meal. May the steward pour you all a glass of splendid German Riesling wine with your dinner this evening?" The steward was a grimy, unshaven common sailor who was noticeably uncomfortable in his newly assigned position.

Theraisa responded quickly, "Nein, thank you, Captain. I do not believe that I care for any wine." Everyone else began with a glass of the sparkling, honey-colored, German nectar of the vine.

Well into the meal, Captain Mueller addressed Louisa. "Frau Von Steiner, please excuse me, but my curiosity overcomes me. Why is it that you have decided to venture out onto the Baltic Sea in late September to travel to Kronstadt? You do realize that we are at risk to encounter angry seas as winter storms approach from the north?"

Louisa smiled slightly at what she considered was a rather rude and personal question; preparing her answer, she adjusted the skirt of her burgundy wool gown. "Actually, Captain, my niece and I are well aware of the possibilities of a storm. However, we have plans to travel farther into Russia once we reach Kronstadt to visit relatives on the Volga. My niece is recently widowed, as I am sure you can tell from her black widow's gown. Her parents were of the opinion that a change of scenery was needed. I trust you will take every caution to see that we enjoy a safe passage to Kronstadt." Louisa added the final sentence as a subtle warning for the captain to mind his manners *and* his own business.

The captain's head snapped up as he acknowledged the obvious implication from the attractive female passenger. "Yes, yes of course, I will do all I am capable of doing to see to any comforts that I might provide so you both enjoy your trip." He turned quickly to address Theraisa. "Frau Ritter, please accept my condolences for your loss. I pray your journey will take your mind from your grief. If there is anything I can do to make your trip more comfortable, please call on me."

"Captain, perhaps you might be able to tell me how long our voyage will be?" Theraisa asked.

"Of course, of course, my dear, I will try to answer your question. If we encounter favorable winds, we should be able to cover the four hundred fifty miles in about nine days. If the winds are not in our favor, it could take weeks."

Theraisa's face grew ashen with shock. "Weeks?" she shrieked. "Weeks?"

Louisa put her hand on her niece's shoulder. "My dear, let's hope for the best. I am sure we are in good hands with the captain, and he will do everything he can to expedite our journey. Am I not correct, Herr Captain?"

The captain's face reddened as he nervously assured his female passengers he would do all within his power to see that they were on Russian soil in days and not weeks. He turned, and with a flamboyant bow to the German tenor, he said, "Herr Schultmann, would you be so kind as to grace us with an aria before we adjourn to our berths for the night?"

The beefy tenor took a sip of wine, rose from his chair, puffed his chest, and moved majestically to position himself near his waiting musicians. He bowed gallantly then cleared his throat as he announced his selection. Herr Schultmann lifted his chin, inhaled deeply, and began to sing. The sound that came from deep in his throat astounded all who listened. Theraisa turned to look at her aunt, and behind a gloved hand, she whispered with admiration, "Auntie, he is marvelous, isn't he? What power, what presence. I have heard this selection before but never such as he performs it." Everyone present was delighted with the short concert from the famed tenor.

Excusing themselves later, Theraisa and Louisa bid good night and retired to their cabin. "Oh, Auntie, I am so very tired tonight. I believe I shall fall directly to sleep with this gentle rocking and the sound of the wind in the sails. Goodnight, dear aunt."

~~~~~

The second day out from the port of Lubeck the *Konig-Albert* sailed head-on into an early winter gale. The bitter northern winds were relentless, causing the turbulent waves to crest at twenty feet. Everyone, except the crew, was instructed to remain inside their cabins, as they would endanger themselves if they ventured out onto the slippery, treacherous deck.

Theraisa remained in her bed with the covers pulled up to her chin. Louisa was alarmed at how extremely pale her niece was. "Here, my dear, the first mate has delivered a pot of savory soup to our cabin. May I spoon a bowl of it for you?"

At the smell and mental vision of food, Theraisa leaned over the side of the bunk and vomited into the chamber pot. She raised her head weakly and replied, "Oh, dear Gott in Himmel, Auntie, can't the captain or someone make the wind and the waves stop? I am so sick. I feel like I am dying."

Without warning Theraisa felt her reserves fall away, as she was consumed with overwhelming self-pity. "Oh, Auntie, I have tried so hard to be strong, to keep my feelings to myself, but—but now, this is all too much. I cannot bear it. I want to go back home, please, Auntie. I don't want to do this! Please do ask the captain to turn the ship around, back to Lubeck." Theraisa rolled into a fetal ball and covered her head with her arms as she sobbed uncontrollably.

Louisa's hands rose to cover her face, and in a fluid motion of frustration, her hands swept back over her forehead. Her own face was bone-white as she strived to calm her niece. "Theraisa— Theraisa, for heaven sake, you have to be realistic. There is no turning back now, and you know better than anyone that we cannot return home. This storm will come to an end eventually. We simply must endure until it blows itself out. Try to sleep now, my dear—sleep." The air in the room was brittle with tension between the two women. As Louisa sat on the narrow edge of Theraisa's bed, she gently stroked her back until the young woman fell asleep.

For the next two days, the ship's bow continued to rise sharply as it scaled each wave and just as suddenly dove with frightening speed into the trough, only to rise again to mount the next towering wave. One monstrous wave after another rose and then fell, seeming never to end. Not concerned with the comfort of their passengers, the crew had all they could manage trying to retain their own footing on the precarious deck while freeing the rigging and sails of crusted ice. The deck was treacherous with multiple, uneven layers of frozen seawater. The crew had been through storms like this before and realized they must persevere to keep the ship afloat until the storm blew itself out.

After thirty-six hours of rough seas, Louisa was becoming concerned with the well-being of her niece. Theraisa had eaten little food, and what she did manage to swallow exited her stomach with a vengeance as she became increasingly weak.

Later that day when the first mate delivered their meal, Louisa inquired, "Excuse me, sir, I know you are very busy, and the captain has better things to do than to deal with seasick passengers, but I hope you might ask him to visit our cabin. My niece is quite ill, and I wonder if he might know of something that can be done to help her. I won't delay you any longer but would appreciate at your earliest convenience your relaying my request to the captain. Thank you, sir."

Early that evening, Captain Mueller knocked at their door. "Frau Von Steiner, I hear your niece is quite ill." As he stepped into the cabin, the offensive order of seasickness assailed his nostrils, eliminating the need for an answer to his question.

"Yes, Captain Mueller, she is very sick with the sea, and I am becoming concerned for her and the child she carries. I wonder if you might know of something that would help settle her stomach. She has not eaten for two days and is becoming quite weak as well."

The captain looked with concern at the young widow. "I had no idea she was with child. I will have the first mate bring some herbs which may help Frau Ritter with her sickness without compromising her—her condition."

The first mate returned about an hour later with an herbal tea of ginger, sassafras, and lemon. He also presented Louisa with a vial of laudanum. "The captain said that perhaps this tea and the medicine will help the lady. The cook also sent up half a loaf of dry, brown rye bread which he thinks might help settle her stomach."

The tea and rye bread did help calm Theraisa's stomach, and the laudanum relaxed her so she was able to sleep. Finally, after two-and-a-half days, the seas calmed, and Theraisa was able to rise weakly from her bunk. She woke in the night realizing that the ship had stopped its erratic tossing and the seas were calm again.

Not able to sleep and suddenly feeling claustrophobic, she decided to leave the cabin and enjoy a breath of fresh sea air. Moving quietly, she pulled on her long wool cape and boots then opened the door to the cabin. Once out in the cool, starry night air, Theraisa breathed deeply. *Oh Mein Gott, it feels so good to breath clean air into my body.*

As Theraisa sat on the bench, she was suddenly aware of soft guitar music drifting through the crisp night air. She pulled her wool cape tighter around her neck as she stood and cautiously moved in the direction of the music. She moved quietly around the corner of the cabins and spotted a lone sailor sitting with his back to the wall, eyes closed, as he strummed soulfully on his well-seasoned guitar. Theraisa approached him with caution. "Excuse me, sir. Do you mind if I sit quietly and listen to your music?"

The pockmarked sailor was startled by the young woman. "Oh, I'm sorry. I didn't notice you standing there. Of course, madam, sit down. You will not disturb me. I hope I play music that you like. I must warn you I am not what you might deem— talented. I am not used to playing for an audience. Is there something in particular you wish to hear?"

"Oh my, let me think. Yes, there is a song very special to me. It is called 'Green Sleeves.' Do you know it?"

The young sailor drew his long, thin fingers across the strings as the evening air was filled with the gentleness and nostalgia of the age-old tune. Theraisa was so consumed and carried away by the music, she was not even aware of the warm tears streaming down her face.

The sailor stopped playing when he saw she was crying. "Oh, miss, I am quite sorry. Is it that my playing is so bad that you cry?" Theraisa was embarrassed as she reached up to wipe the tears from her pale, sunken cheeks. "Oh—nein, nein—it is just that I recently lost my—err, my husband, and this was a special song to us. It reminds me of him. I—I really must go back to my cabin now. Thank you, sir—for your kindness; I enjoyed listening to your music. I bid you a good night!"

The sailor watched as she rose and walked in an unsteady gait along the deck until she disappeared from view.

Chapter Four

On Russian Soil

Kronstadt, the canon-studded port of the Russian Admiralty, appeared in all its glory as the *Konig-Albert* slid into the dock. Before the sun presented itself on the eastern horizon, Theraisa and Louisa had dressed warmly. Packing a few last-minute belongings, they left their cabin. Up on deck, standing together at the rail, Theraisa's face beamed with anticipation as she declared, "Auntie, I can barely contain myself just thinking of walking on solid ground again! I...I feel so worldly and can now refer to myself as having *traveled* outside Germany!"

As the first glow of sunshine bled into the copper-and-peach horizon and began to warm the frosty air, Dieter Schultmann approached the two simply-dressed female travelers. "Well, it does appear that we have survived the crossing of the water, only to have this vast, frigid land lay before us. I trust you have made your arrangements to travel to the Volga?"

Immediately irritated, Louisa turned to face the impertinent tenor. Even though she was impressed with his talent, she had taken a personal dislike to him the first night at dinner. He was quite full of himself and moved about as if he were a rooster strutting through the barnyard. "Oh, Herr Schultmann, I did not expect to see you up so early. I assure you there is no need to concern yourself with our travel plans. Our protector, Otto, is quite proficient in taking care of our safety and travel arrangements. Now, if you will excuse us, we have some last-minute details to attend to before we dock." The massive German tenor moved quickly to take Louisa's gloved hand, which seemed to disappear within his bearlike hands. Putting on his most charming face, he smiled and bid them good travel. Being as gracious as possible, they returned his well-rehearsed salutation.

Louisa and Theraisa couldn't help but snicker into their gloved hands as they made a rather hasty exit toward their cabin.

"Oh, Auntie Louisa, you have such a way with words. I am sure Herr Schultmann didn't even understand what you really meant!"

~~~~~

As arranged by Heinrich Von Steiner, their Kronstadt escort was waiting at the dock, eager to meet the two travelers and their escort from Frankfurt. A gallant, slender Russian greeted the aristocratic German women and settled them inside a weather-worn coach. Otto and he sat up with the driver as they rode a short distance to St. Petersburg, where they left the coach to board what appeared to be a small river craft.

As they walked from the coach to the boat, the weather grew noticeably colder as a sharp wind blew in from the north. It was an uncomfortable but thankfully short forty-five-mile journey down the Neva River to a point where they entered Lake Ladoga, which connected to the Volkhov River. After crossing the lake, they boarded a larger, more comfortable steamship and headed south down river for approximately 140 miles, where they entered Lake Ilmen. As the steamship eased into the lake, ice crystals fell like small white bombs from the frigid air. The bitter north wind blew up the skirts and down the necks of the two women, causing a series of shivers to trickle down both their spines.

On the steamship, Louisa and her niece tried desperately to get warm inside the tiny community cabin. "Oh, Auntie, I am so cold that I feel as though I have icicles hanging from my hair and nose. Is this what the Russian winter is going to be like? I hoped since we are traveling to the south that it would begin to warm up a bit. What do you think?"

All too aware of the bone-chilling cold, Louisa looked up from her needlework. "Theraisa, drape this blanket around your shoulders and put that babushka over your head. Perhaps we might move closer to the charcoal brazier. We should both try to get some sleep. The boat is not very crowded, so we have room right here on the benches to stretch out instead of trying to sleep sitting up." She noticed her niece looking with suspicion at the disheveled crowd of passengers.

Louisa put her arm across her niece's shoulders, "Don't worry, my love, Otto is nearby and won't allow any harm to come to us. He is quite imposing, don't you think?" After they arranged their own sleeping areas, Louisa continued. "Yes, Theraisa, I do believe the winters in Russia are worse than in Germany. You must realize we are much farther north. Perhaps when we reach the end of the water travel and board the train, we will be more comfortable." They endured three more boat changes as they traveled. Finally, after what seemed like weeks, they arrived at the point where they would begin the final portion of their journey, crossing hundreds of miles of vast, inhospitable Russian landscape by train.

~~~~~

Upon disembarking from the steamship, Louisa and her niece climbed quickly into the shelter of a waiting carriage where they buried themselves under a mound of fur robes. In an attempt to reassure her niece, Louisa commented, "We will ride this coach to the train station for the last leg of our overland journey. At that point we will connect with the Volga River, where we will board another boat to Saratov."

Louisa noticed that Theraisa's face was wet with tears. She reached into her valise and pulled out a handkerchief. "Here, my dear, please stop crying, and do wipe your nose. I know you are cold and weary. I too am chilled, but we have to keep moving, or we will freeze into a pillar! Slide over here and allow me to wrap my arms around you. Perhaps we will benefit from each other's body heat and be more comfortable." Theraisa fell asleep immediately.

Late in the day, they arrived at the train station and hurried to their assigned car. Louisa looked up into the leaden-gray sky and noticed snow was falling harder as the howling wind began building crusty drifts of snow onto the track. As Theraisa looked out the window of the train, she saw icy mounds of snow clinging to naked branches in the sparse groves of birch and linden trees.

The two women had looked forward to riding in what they presumed to be the comfort of a Russian train for the next two hundred miles. The train would take them to the mouth of the mother river, the Volga. Conditions at the train station were atrocious. The platform was filled with trampled snow and treacherous ice; hordes of poorly dressed people pushed and shoved to find an advantageous spot out of the wind while they waited for the southbound train. As they waited in the shelter of the station, Louisa noticed several travelers purchasing food, packaged especially for the trip. She turned to her niece and commented, "I am told there is nothing to eat on the train, Theraisa. We are encouraged to choose something here to take with us." Louisa took the initiative and, giving Otto some coins, she asked him to buy several small loaves of rye bread and white cheese sandwiches along with several fresh sausages that a peasant woman was selling from a cart.

Otto arrived shortly with a knapsack filled with incredible aromas. Theraisa held the containers of hot tea with her bare hands. "Oh, Auntie, I don't want to drink the tea yet—I must first warm my hands. Thank you, Otto, this is quite nice." After they had waited for a short time among throngs of peasants, Theraisa's hand rose to cover her nose and mouth. In a hushed voice she implored, "Auntie, I can't bear these offensive smells. They are everywhere!"

Louisa replied in a hushed whisper, "Shhh, Theraisa, I do believe some of these peasants have wiped their unwashed bodies with kerosene to protect against parasites such as fleas and lice. Try not to touch anyone if you can help it, and please don't make such a face when you look at them."

They were relieved to hear the whistle of the train. A portly conductor looked at their tickets and with a forced smile directed them to a special heated coach. The two women were settling inside the reserved coach when a second conductor moved down the aisle. He stopped in the center of the car and loudly announced, first in Russian, then in German, "We will be delayed for a short time while the workers break ice from the train and the wheels of the cars. As soon as this task is complete, we will be on our way."

Theraisa and Louisa moved closer together, sharing their body heat. Desperately seeking any kind of comfort, they tore the sandwich sacks open and enjoyed a cold lunch of rye bread, cheese, and bratwurst.

To distract her niece, Louisa said, "Theraisa, I was thinking about something which I read recently about this part of the journey. It involves a particular hardship that the early settlers had to endure while traveling to the Volga because there were no trains at that time. Can you imagine picking up a small boat and carrying it for two hundred miles to the headwaters of the Volga? Well, that is exactly what some of the early German settlers were forced to do—over the same route we just traveled. I do believe I would have died as Heinrich's first wife did."

Theraisa responded with disbelief. "No, Auntie, I can't even imagine how they did that. It causes me to feel guilty for complaining about riding in a train to the Volga. Those poor people had to suffer through things we can't even imagine."

Both women were reaching the point of exhaustion from the arduous conditions. The pampered life of the privileged they enjoyed in Hessen had not prepared them for *this type of exertion.*

They were obviously edgy and physically displayed signs of their grueling journey. Louisa laid her head back onto the seat then raised it again as a thought occurred to her. "Theraisa, dear, please excuse the interruption, but I feel compelled to speak to you of something else which has come to mind." Her niece turned her head and rolled her eyes as she thought, *"When will she ever quit giving me instructions? One would think I was three years old."*

Louisa sat straighter in her seat as a slight frown formed between her brown eyes, and her voice took on a serious note. "Theraisa, I want to make very sure you realize our relatives who live in Susannenthal do not live in castles. From the letters we have received, it is also evident they elected to drop the prefix from our surname, to simply read as 'Steiner.' I also assume you realize the members of the Steiner family in Russia are simple people, what we might deem peasant farmers."

Theraisa digested her aunt's words. "Well...well, just what kind of house do they live in? Are they peasants like the people who live below our castle?"

Louisa put her head down as a smile crossed her face. "Oh dear me, again, my sweet child, you remind me of your sheltered life." She took a deep, relaxing breath before she continued. "I am not sure what kind of house they live in, but I assume it is not built from stone and fine wood as our castle. It will be simple and small. The settlers most assuredly have built homes in a style which best withstands the harsh Russian climate. Most importantly, Theraisa, they will be clean even with a dirt floor, as German houses are. Also, I am quite certain we will not have anyone to help us. We should feel fortunate if indeed we each have a bedroom to ourselves, and certainly our new circumstances won't compare with the castle chambers." Before Theraisa could complain, Louisa added, "Perhaps we will be able to hire a village girl who would be willing to come in to cook and clean for us. We both may have to learn how to take care of ourselves. You will have many things to learn, because soon you will also have a child to care for."

Theraisa gazed numbly out the train window as she responded, "Of course, Auntie. I will not cause you embarrassment and will try very hard not to expect too much. I am glad we will not have to endure these living conditions forever, only several months. I only hope that wherever we live, we are warm." She exaggerated a shiver as the two women agreed halfheartedly and laughed nervously.

Theraisa was privately horrified when she considered caring for a baby. She didn't know the first thing about children, especially a baby. At that instance she felt the child move inside her, reminding her of all the personal tests and lessons that lay ahead. She rubbed her cold hands together. "Auntie, do Cousin Phillip and his family speak Russian or German?"

Louisa smiled. "Yes, my dear, they speak high German with the Hessian dialect. There may be some words we will have difficulty understanding, as their language has probably evolved to include some Russian terms. In fact, the settlers speak only German in their schools and churches. As I have mentioned, they have not embraced the Russian society or manners. One exception, I understand, is they have become fond of vodka, which they make from fermented potatoes like their Russian neighbors." Louisa smiled as she added, "I do think I may enjoy tasting this drink. It may help warm my insides!"

~~~~~

Louisa spotted Otto walking swiftly toward the train; he had obviously been inside the train station and was now boarding. Enormous chunks of ice lay beside the track as the railway workers finished chopping and breaking the ice from the train. Parts of the engine still appeared to be encased with the brittle hoarfrost as the iron horse huffed and lurched as it built steam and began to roll down the snow-covered track.

Steel-gray clouds of swirling snow blew across the landscape in whirlwinds. The sound of the steam engine chugging and hissing in the frigid air was oddly comforting, and the rhythmic clacking of the iron wheels crossing the breaks between the iron rails was hypnotic. The sway of the cars was gentle at first and then increased to a metrical motion as the train gathered speed. This swaying caused Theraisa to feel an unexpected spasm of nausea. She rose with purpose from her seat. "I am going to open the door at the end of the car and stand outside where I can get a bit of air. Excuse me, Auntie."

Louisa was alarmed as her niece rose from her seat. "Theraisa, do you want me to come with you? Please be careful and hang on to the railing."

Theraisa steadied herself by holding on to each seat as she moved purposefully down the aisle. The other passengers raised their heads in curiosity to watch the aristocratic young woman as she passed their seats. When she reached the end of the car, she grasped the door handle and turned it hard, using her body to push the door open. A gust of icy wind took her breath away as she stepped into the exterior alcove. The bitter wind pulled at her hair, even though it was protected with a black babushka. Theraisa held tightly onto the iron railing that separated her from the speeding ground. She took the frigid air into her lungs, allowing it to settle her stomach and her nerves. The snow swirled upward in spiraling drafts from the speeding train. She drew her wool scarf closer around her face. After a few minutes, feeling better, she turned and reentered the car. Again, she noticed people looking up to stare at her as she passed.

As her niece crossed in front of her and eased back down onto the seat next to the window, Louisa commented, "Oh my goodness, girl, if only you could see yourself. You look like a walking snowman. Here, allow me to at least brush the snow from your coat and hair. Did the frigid air help settle your stomach?"

Theraisa allowed a great sigh to escape her half-frozen and chapped lips. "Auntie, I do feel better. However, I am feeling rather sleepy. If you don't mind, I will lay my head back and take a short nap."

While her niece slept, Louisa occupied her time watching the landscape fly by as the train sped down the track. She could barely see through the window, as ice had built a semi-opaque crust on the inside of the glass. The landscape rolled by in a continuous blur of snow, ice, naked trees, and small collections of humble villages and farms. Soon, she too was overcome by the hypnotic motion of the moving train, and submitting to exhaustion, she snuggled deep into her robes.

~~~~~

Finally, they arrived at the northern headwaters of the Volga and transferred once again onto a large steamship for the final leg of their journey down the impressive Russian river. They had been traveling across the vast country for almost a month and were exhausted. Otto was never far away, tending to their luggage and accommodations. Louisa thought of what a comfort it was to have him near to help with the arduous journey.

They found seats inside a large gathering area in the center of the boat, where other passengers sat like stones on the wooden benches. After they were settled in their seats, Theraisa looked longingly out the window of the steamship. "If it weren't so bitter cold outside, I would enjoy standing at the rail and watching as the land goes by."

She pulled her fur robes up to her chin. "I do wish we could have found a seat closer to the little iron stove down there on the end. Looking at all the people that are crowded into this ship, I suppose we are lucky to have a place to sit. Anyway, Auntie, where is this village of Susannenthal in which our cousins live? Is it far now?"

They shared their remaining rye bread and cheese as Louisa pulled out her map of the area and studied it before responding. "Oh my goodness, it looks as though Susannenthal is about ten kilometers north of Saratov. We should actually pass by the village before arriving at the port of Saratov. We will have to travel back to the north to reach Susannenthal. However, I doubt if we can see anything out of the windows, as they are becoming as icy as the windows on the train. I am hopeful Phillip will be there to meet us. I am feeling very excited that the end of our journey is in sight."

After more than three hours on the river boat, they moved closer to a single window which a deckhand had momentarily scraped clear of ice. Theraisa's eyes squinted as she searched the horizon intently for a sign of the small port city of Saratov, Russia. Her face mirrored her fatigue yet was animated with intrigue as she peered through the icy window. "There it is, Auntie. I believe that is Saratov. See it—over there, all those buildings? We are finally here. We succeeded, Auntie. We have arrived at our destination."

Louisa put a protective arm across her niece's shoulders. "Well done, my dear, well done!"

Chapter Five

Susannenthal

For three consecutive days, Phillip Steiner left his warm bed in the darkness of the early November morning to brave the chilled air of the advancing winter. He harnessed two of his wooly Kalmuck ponies to a gaily painted sleigh and traveled downriver from Susannenthal to Saratov. Waiting for the arrival of the steamship from the north, Phillip spent the days walking the streets and sipping hot tea. He knew from experience that the boat schedules were never to be trusted. Yet he was determined to be on the dock to greet his aristocratic German relatives when they arrived. On the second day, as he stood near the waterfront, he looked at the slow-flowing river, frowning as he thought, *Our German cousins had better arrive soon because the strong river current is running thick and slow with freezing water.*

On the third day, after pacing back and forth on the dock for over two hours, Phillip attempted to sit and rest his legs. He found a wooden bench, brushed the thin layer of fresh snow from the seat, and eased his long-limbed body down. Phillip had a hard time finding a comfortable position for his six-foot frame, and he was growing colder. He stood again and walked the dock. *Got to keep moving— if I sit too long, I will freeze into an ice sculpture!* He smiled at the thought of his relatives arriving only to find him frozen into a lump of ice. Phillip had plenty of time to contemplate why two women would attempt the journey from Frankfurt at this time of year. Instinct told him something was not quite right with the explanation they had written.

Phillip's thick, blond hair stuck out from his wool hat. The ends of his hair and tips of his mustache were white with frost. He pulled his long camel-wool coat closer around his tall frame and wrapped the hand-knit wool scarf tighter around his neck. Phillip thought about the essential clothing the early German colonists had adopted from the Russians, like the traditional knee-high 'Filzstiefel' or laced leather boots he wore.[6]

Phillip smiled as he thought how prolific *Die Wolgadeutschen* population had been. *My own family is considered small with seven children. Most families have ten to twelve children. It must be the long, cold winter that blesses us with so many children.*

He paced and nervously pulled at his frosted handlebar mustache. Finally, his blue-gray eyes caught sight of the slow-moving steamship as it eased around the bend. He flinched as the shrill blast from the horn shattered the freezing air. He rose from his seat as he mumbled, "I pray they are on this ship. I can't take many more days away from my chores."

Invasive ice swathed every part of the wooden steamship as it eased into the crudely built dock at Saratov. Sitting low in the water, the frozen vessel groaned loudly as her side bumped sharply into the rigid platform. Great jagged chunks of ice fell from the flanks of the boat, plunging into the freezing river and onto the wooden dock like ominous knives. People waiting on the dock jumped back in fear of being impaled by the sinister- looking shards of ice.

Phillip stood near the rear of the crowd of people waiting on the dock; his eyes anxiously scanned the passengers. He scrutinized each one as they filed out from the shelter of the enclosed cabin and began crowding onto the open deck. Burly stevedores moved quickly to the side of the ship using long iron rods to knock the remaining ice from her hull. When the captain was satisfied the ice would not inhibit or endanger his passengers when disembarking, the gangplank was uncovered and extended onto the dock. The ship's crew began to unload cargo and luggage as passengers walked stiffly and gingerly down the treacherous gangplank.

Phillip noticed several handsome trunks set to one side on the dock by a burly German fellow. Two well-dressed women were personally escorted by the captain and first mate down the gangplank. Phillip's eyebrows arched with possible recognition, and he cautiously approached them. He stopped about four feet from the older of the two and inquired, "Excuse me, might you be Frau Louisa Steiner?"

Startled, yet relieved, Louisa and Theraisa paused in midstride. Both ladies had to tilt their heads upward to look up at the tall man who addressed them. Louisa graciously extended her hand with a guarded smile. "Yes, yes of course I am, and you, sir, need no introduction. I can tell at first glance that you are a Steiner— Phillip, I presume?"

Louisa hurriedly introduced her niece. "And this is my dear niece, Frau Theraisa Von—umm Ritter. She is the daughter of Heinrich and Amelia and widow of Captain David Ritter. She quickly enlightened him. "I should tell you that our dear young woman wears mourning black for her husband of three months, who was killed recently on the German front. It is the reason we have left Germany, to give her some time away to gather her spirits."

Phillip enfolded Theraisa's gloved hands. "Please accept my condolences for your recent loss. Welcome to the Volga. We hope your visit here will help to heal your heart." Then, letting out a great sigh of relief, he continued, "I am so glad you have finally arrived. I was afraid I might miss you because the riverboat schedules are not to be trusted, especially this late in the fall. As you most surely noticed, the river is beginning to freeze. In another week or so, travel on the river will not be possible."

Louisa took Otto by the arm as she drew him into their circle. "Phillip, this is Otto, our traveling protector and assistant."

Phillip extended his hand to the beefy German. "Welcome, Otto. Will you help me load the luggage onto the Troika? Then you are welcome to sit up on the seat with me as we travel to our village." Being a man of very few words, Otto nodded and bent his back to the task.

Phillip led the two shivering women down a cleared pathway on the dock to where his three harnessed ponies and a large, gaily painted sleigh, the Troika, was waiting. The snow and ice on the dock crunched loudly under their boots as they walked mindfully over the frozen path. "Please, over this way, I believe we should not tarry, as the wind is building. Take my hand if you will and climb up into the backseat in the sleigh. You will find fur robes with which to cover yourselves."

After the two women were snuggly settled and the baggage was secured on the back of the sleigh, Phillip climbed onto the driver's seat. He turned and addressed his passengers. "We need to be on our way to Susannenthal while we still have daylight. It is about ten miles to the north." He pointed east toward the Ural Mountains. "As you can see by the curtain of snow, a larger storm is fast approaching. Forgive me; I won't be speaking to you as we ride. I must pay attention to keep the Troika on the road." He laughed heartily at his attempted humor. "Are you comfortable and ready to travel to Susannenthal?" The two women assured Phillip they were settled and ready.

Phillip wrapped a wool scarf securely around his head then cracked the long snake-like whip through the air above the trio of horses. In unison, the stubby, furry creatures leapt forward, eager to be on their way to the shelter of their cozy barn. Effortlessly, they pulled the loaded Troika over the snow-packed road. The tan leather harnesses all but disappeared in their thick, brown winter coats while an assortment of large metal bells attached to the harnesses sent a melodious tinkling tone through the frigid arctic air.

Smiling to himself under the tightly wrapped scarf, Phillip was amused at visions of what lay in wait for his guests. *I am more than sure they are not prepared for the brutality and isolation of the Russian winter.*

~~~~~

Both women turned in unison, looking at each other with surprise then smiling with pleasure at the familiar sound of the tinkling harness bells. "I can't believe we are here in Saratov, Auntie."

Louisa nodded in agreement as she leaned close to Theraisa. "My dear, are you sure you are comfortable?"

Theraisa wriggled deeper into the fur robes and pulled her wool babushka farther down onto her freezing face. "Oh yes, Auntie, I am quite warm, but that wind is dreadfully sharp. When we were on the dock, I felt it go through my coat and clothing directly to my bones. I believe if it stays cold like this, I will not be going outside very often.

"Oh, look out there, Auntie, at the looming shape of the dark- blue mountains in the distance. See how blue the bitter cold air makes them appear? They look as though they are a painting." She shivered at the arctic landscape that lay before them.

Several miles north of Saratov, both women were startled when Phillip drove the sleigh onto a ferry, which took them back across the river to the meadow or eastern side. Subzero arctic air settled heavily at the base of the Ural mountain chain, like the muck that settled to the bottom of the slow-moving Volga River. Late-afternoon rays of sun escaped through dark storm clouds as swirling streaks of pink and mauve light pierced the frigid air. They watched with wonder as it spilled over the hills and valleys that glittered like crystallized sugar. The distant peaks of the Urals looked like frosted cakes with shimmering sprinkles spilling down the slopes to lie on the exposed patches of the butterscotch-colored Russian steppe below.

Louisa was intrigued by the gentle rise of the land as it began at the banks of the Volga. She noticed the ancient flood plain was extremely wide, indicating it had been forming for centuries. It rose in subtle levels then quickly matured into larger, more abrupt rolling hills that continued to build in height and mass until they bonded with the impressive grandeur of the Russian mountain range.

The village of Susannenthal where Phillip lived had been built about a mile from the banks of the Volga, which the settlers called the river of life. Louisa recalled reading that those who lived on this Wiesenseite or east side of the river constructed their villages a reasonable distance away, hoping they were beyond the reach of the river's spring flood plain. Susannenthal was an original "mother" village settled by early German colonists. It was the village where Johann Heinrich Steiner and his group of immigrants settled and where he married for the third time. It was one of eighteen villages that were strung like strings of glistening gems along the Volga.[7]

"Theraisa, have you noticed how different the land is on either side of the river? This meadow side or Wiesenseite is quite flat compared to the west side or hillside of the river, which is called the Bergseite. It appears that the river once flowed farther to the east side doesn't it? I have read that the reason villages were not constructed out in the open steppe at first was the scarcity of surface water and materials with which to build their houses—which I can now see for myself."[8]

Theraisa snuggled farther under the warmth of the fur robes. "Auntie, what do they heat their homes with if wood is so scarce?" "I have read they make bricks from manure and grass gathered from the steppe, called '*mist holtz*' or manure wood. It is said these bricks are supposed to burn long and hot. It is amazing to me how they figured out the best ways to survive in this inhospitable land."

Louisa put her hand over her heart-shaped mouth as a long yawn escaped. "Oh do excuse me, my dear. I believe I have worn myself out with all my talking. The hypnotic rhythm of the bells and the warmth of the fur robes are making me quite sleepy. Do excuse me while I catch a short nap." She slid deeper into the warmth of the robes and was asleep before Theraisa could respond. She was tired as well, but her curiosity had won the duel between a nap and satisfying her inquisitive nature.

Theraisa gazed at the banks of the Volga, where occasional groves of white-bark birch and stately linden trees grew. Thick clumps of red-twig willows were accented with random collections of alder and spruce trees. Farther out on the steppe, there were fewer groves of trees skirted with thick brambles of thorny scrub brush.

Her eyes sparkled with curiosity as she gazed to the upper branches of a birch tree where she spotted a solitary osprey. The bird seemed to be watching the slow-running river below. Suddenly, the osprey unfolded his tightly closed wings and, giving a leap of faith, lifted gracefully from the treetop. Like an arrow it dropped toward the river, tucking its wings before it dove with purpose into the icy flow. Theraisa sat up straight in the Troika to get a better look as the bird pierced the surface of the river and rose quickly back into the frigid air, with dinner clutched tightly in its talons. The sleek bird climbed higher in the sky and Theraisa was surprised as it dropped the fish onto a jagged rock outcropping below. The osprey dove again to retrieve its meal and then flew to a nearby treetop, perching on the edge of an impressive nest.

Theraisa smiled. Feeling warm and relieved that the long journey was over, she too succumbed to fatigue as her eyelids fluttered closed.

Up on the front seat, Otto inquired, "Herr Steiner, where do these squat Kalmuck horses come from? I have never set eyes on this type of horse flesh. Am I correct in saying they appear to be a cross between the hardy Shetland breed and the thickset French draft horse?"

Phillip smiled as he turned in the seat. "JA, Otto, they come from nomadic tribes who live to the far north and were bred to eat less than the huge draft horses, yet they are strong enough to pull the sleigh through deep snow. Their thick winter coats serve them well against our frigid Russian winter months. Most *Die Wolgadeutschen* owned two or more of these stocky, resilient little horses that were originally issued to the early settlers by the Russian government."

Phillip smiled as he added, "Of course, most of our stables also shelter two to four fine trotters for when the weather and the roads are clear. We delight in our horse flesh and often enjoy races in the warm months and when time permits!"

Theraisa and Louisa woke with a start from their short naps as Phillip turned in the seat to speak loudly. With pride and excitement, he pointed ahead to the large number of white painted buildings near the river. "We are coming to my village. We are coming to Susannenthal!"

The two women strained to get a better look at what lay ahead. Everything was covered with snow, and more was falling from the leaden sky.

The village seemed to be constructed much like their villages in Germany, with house and barn built closely together in the center, surrounded with individual gardens, orchards, and animal pens. The area designated for fields lay on an even plane that extended for miles to the east of the tightly packed collection of cottages. The women were amazed to see most of the small houses were wood with a roof of thatched straw, hand hewn wood shingles, or tin.

Lutheran Church,
Susannenthal, Russia

Seeing the solidly built but modest cottages, Louisa breathed a sigh of relief as she commented to her niece. "As we can see along the road, they have built warm wood houses. I remember in one of the letters that Phillip wrote to us he mentioned the logs were cut in Russian forests to the north and floated down the Volga to build their villages. He wrote that their outbuildings are purposely constructed low to the ground to conserve building materials as well as heat in the long winters; some barns are constructed of mud-straw bricks, which they make themselves. At least they don't live in the same building as their smelly animals during the winter months!"

Out of the village center square, the massive, white wood Lutheran church and enormous bell tower rose in impressive domination. Phillip pointed out that the majority of churches along the Volga were built in this Kantor style dictated by the church fathers in Saratov. He also noted that only a few houses belonging to wealthier people and the parsonage were constructed of brick or river stone. Neither woman had known exactly what to expect, but it certainly wasn't what lay before them.

Phillip drove the wooly horses down *Hintereihe* Street and stopped in front of a small but well-appointed house.

After winding the reins around the brake, Phillip hopped down from his seat and moved quickly to help the two women climb down from their cozy nests. "Come now, my family is expecting you. Welcome to Susannenthal and to the house of the Steiner family."

Chapter Six

The Unexpected: January 1874

The very pregnant, Frau Theraisa Ritter paced the packed-dirt floor of their small rented house, stopping to stand before the narrow window that faced the street. She looked out on the unchanging, unyielding landscape, running her slim fingers nervously through her hair. "I am going to go completely insane if I have to stay in this monotonous place a moment longer. It is like a frigid prison cut off from the world." She began to pull at her blond hair and frantically stroke her pregnant stomach. "Why did I ever leave the comforts of my home? My personal chamber was larger than this...this so-called house! The floors, for heaven's sake, are dirt! In the castle, I only knew of stone floors. I am completely miserable shut up in this hovel, and my once-slim figure grows larger each day until I fear I will pop like a bubble." She looked to the heavens as she continued to pace and berate her circumstances.

Theraisa finally settled onto a crude chair and laid her head on the table as tears poured from her eyes. "It is because of you, Captain David Ritter; you left me to bear your child alone in the most terrible place in the world."

At that moment, Louisa burst through the door with a blast of icy air and swirling gusts of snow. She removed her coat and scarf, hanging them on the peg beside the door. "Theraisa, are you here?" Louisa turned and noticed her niece—her head down on the table. Rushing to Theraisa's side, Louisa cried, "Oh dear Gott, what has happened to you? Are you ill?"

Theraisa pushed her aunt away. "I want to leave here. I hate it here, and I want to go back to Germany. I am going to go insane if I have to stay here until this baby comes. All these people do is go to church and isolate themselves in their miniature houses, spinning, cooking, weaving, knitting, singing, and talking. They have no social life, no opera, no theater, and no parties. Never in my life did I dream people actually lived like this. It is the worst kind of torture."

Louisa stood, stunned and speechless, as she desperately searched her mind for something sensible to say. "Theraisa, obviously you are having a bad day. Please calm yourself. Let me make a nice pot of hot tea, and we will talk about what is upsetting you."

Louisa sat patiently as her niece poured her heart out to her. "You know, Theraisa, I think we need a day outdoors, perhaps a ride in a sleigh? If it is clear weather tomorrow, I will ask Phillip if he can take us for a short ride out onto the steppe."

~~~~~

Thankfully, the next day, dawned bright and clear as the sun climbed higher and did what it could to warm the frigid atmosphere. The sky was dotted with fluffy clouds that looked like mounds of downy white feathers. Even the fickle temperature had climbed to above freezing. Phillip harnessed three Kalmuck ponies and drove down the street to pick up the two women. "I have brought the wide Troika today so I may sit between you on the seat and explain about the short route we will travel. I want to take you to the outer steppe to where our fields lay."

Theraisa looked to the side and rolled her eyes with utter disinterest and boredom. *Oh surely it will be of interest to him and Auntie Louisa. At least I am out of that repulsive dwelling they call a house!*

With pride in his voice, Phillip began. "I hope you remain in Susannenthal into the summer so you can see the beauty of our courtyards. As you can see, we have almost two hundred homes in our village." Phillip went on to explain that the houses were built in straight rows separated by four main streets and six cross streets. Each family had equal property; most had a fenced courtyard separated from the neighboring house. "Although you can't see it now with all the snow covering the ground, the front portion of each home includes a small flower garden with lilacs, tulips, rosebushes, and perhaps a fruit tree. And in the rear, there is room for a sizeable personal garden. Of course, the village has huge communal gardens at the edge of town. We all take turns working and harvesting the village gardens."

Phillip pointed to the north edge of the village. "Over there you can see the vast orchards which have cherry, plum, pear, and apple trees, with many bushes of berries such as raspberry, red and black currant, gooseberry, and, of course, Yagada berries for my favorite cake."

Theraisa hid a wicked smile as she thought, *Oh my, how will I ever contain my enthusiastic interest? Should I take notes?*

Phillip urged the horses into a fast trot; the Troika hopped and swayed across the rut-filled snow as he worked to keep it from turning over. "I am not sure if you know that when Johann Heinrich and his sons settled this village, each family was given thirty *Desyatiny*—fifteen to plow, five to hay, five left to woods, and five for the house and farm. This was a system full of problems, and they complained loudly to the Russian government. So, after forty years, we were changed to the Russian 'Mir' system of land distribution. The youngest male now inherits his father's share of land. When the older male children come of age and marry, they receive their own share of land. In fact, when our oldest son

Solomon marries in the summer; he and his wife will build a house of their own on land the government will grant him."

Phillip continued. "Under the Mir system, we have a community church, schoolhouse, meetinghouse, and buildings for our factories. We use in common any source of water, grazing areas, and quarries. All animals are owned by individuals, and there is no limit to how many we may have. I have these three ponies, three trotters, four camels, five cattle, ten pigs, around fifty geese, and many chickens. We live very close for mutual protection from occasional raiding Mongols and from ravenous packs of wolves that roam the steppe looking for food, especially when they are starving in the Russian winter." At the mention of wolves, Theresa's eyes grew wide; she scanned the surrounding woods and hills.

After traveling in silence for a few minutes, Louisa asked, "Phillip, what kind of plants do you raise on this land?"

Phillip rubbed his clean-shaven jaw. "You cannot see our soil under the winter bed of snow, but it is the color of the rye bread. It is very fertile from thousands of years of flooding and rich deposits from the Volga."

"We have tried many crops but have found the best are tobacco, sugar beets for their sweet syrup, sunflowers for the seed and oil, wheat, and rye. We keep the rye for ourselves and sell the wheat to the Russians. You have seen our mills and factories from which we process the rye flour, sunflowers, and tanneries for leather goods. Whatever is left over from the sunflower and tobacco plants is chopped, salted, and fed to the cattle. We waste nothing.

"We also have many fruits from our orchards, which we eat all the days of summer; the rest are dried for use in the winter. Of course we have our vegetable gardens where we grow much cabbage, cucumbers, potatoes, and beets. We even grow small watermelons. Some are pickled, and some are covered with oats to eat during the early winter months." He turned to the two women and laughed heartily. "JA, we eat the watermelons, and the horses and cows eat the oats! It works very well for us."

Theraisa turned to face Phillip. "What do you do for entertainment during the long winters? I must admit I am becoming quite restless."

Phillip smiled. "The women are always busy during the winter with carding the camel's wool and spinning. Then they make the yarn into clothing. We enjoy singing and telling stories while we work indoors during the winter.

Enthusiastically, Phillip added, "We are known for our fine willow baskets, which we all weave during the months we are compelled to spend indoors. Even our children work with the baskets. If you would like to learn to weave baskets, I am sure Eliza would be happy to teach you."

Theraisa rolled her eyes as the thought of spending her evenings sitting and weaving common baskets.

The weather was becoming colder as Phillip expertly turned the sleigh around, and they headed back to Susannenthal. Louisa pointed out onto the steepe where she saw several dogs. "Phillip, what are those dogs doing so far from the village. I noticed they have been traveling along with us, keeping a distance?

Phillip nodded his head. "Yes, Louisa, I too noticed the animals. Unfortunately they are not dogs. They are wolves. If they come closer to the sleigh, I will fire my pistol into the pack. If it was evening, I would be more alarmed. Wolves usually do not attack during the day. We are safe, I will protect you."

Louisa and Theraisa both continued to keep one on the pack of wolves as they kept pace with the sleigh. Phillip kept the pace of the horses up as he tried to distract the two women. "We have done well for ourselves compared to what the first German colonists lived through. Most of the early immigrants settle below Saratov and out into the *Bergseite* (west) of the Volga. The first Steiner people settled across the Volga, above Saratov to the Wiesenseite or east side of the Volga. Around 1800, the first logs were brought down river from the northern woods. The wood available along the Volga is not suitable for building. We needed large logs so we might build better homes. The first building we built from the cherished wood was our church and the bell tower. For us, our lives—our very existence—is centered in our church and religion. Our faith has helped us survive in this foreign land. It gives us courage and reason for our life here."

Louisa pointed to the tall bell tower of the church that pierced the horizon. "Phillip, may I ask why the bell tower seems to be so prominent and important here on the Russian steppe?"

Phillip responded quickly, "JA that is a good question because the bell tower is not such an important part of Deutschland; am I correct? Our bell tower has many assignments in our daily lives and our survival." Phillip flipped the reins along the backs of the horses. "You are well acquainted with the nightly Angelus that rings sweetly from the tower. Whenever a person in our village dies, the bell is also rung in a particular manner designating whether it is for a man, a woman, or a child. Then the bell tolls the age of the deceased. Also, if there is a fire, it calls the villagers to aid in putting it out. Most important, when a blinding blizzard rages over the steppe, the bells ring in a steady cadence to aid travelers to find our village and shelter."

Glancing around, Phillip noticed the wolves had left them, and he offered a quick prayer; the situation had been far more serious than he had let on. Remembering his wife's instructions as he left the house that morning, Phillip added, "Eliza and I would appreciate your company this evening for dinner if you so desire. We can drive directly to our home; I will take you back to your house after we eat. I think she was preparing roast pork ribs and making *Schnitzsuppe* when I left this morning."

Louisa and Theraisa looked at each other with approval, and Louisa quickly accepted the invitation. At least it would be one meal they would not have to attempt to fix for themselves.

"Phillip, please excuse one more question, but I have been wondering if you know how many Germans now live here on the Volga? We have noticed many villages and realize people have been immigrating and living here for over a hundred and fifty years."

"JA, Louisa, according to the recent census that was posted in Saratov, there are over one million immigrants." Phillip smiled broadly as he pulled on the reins and slowed the Troika in front of the Steiner house. "We are here, and I hope you bring your appetites."

~~~~~

As the Steiner family and their two guests sat down to supper, Phillip raised his hand for silence. "We shall bow our heads in prayer. *Segne Vater Does Speise, Uns zur Kraft und Dir zum Preise.*"

Theraisa squealed with delight when she recognized the soup. "Oh, Aunt Eliza, the *Schnitzsuppe* is my favorite." Eliza had prepared the traditional Sunday meal called *Kraut und Brei,* which consisted of roasted pork ribs, mashed potatoes, and the staple dish of sauerkraut, along with a scrumptious berry cake called Yagada-Kuchen. After the meal, the children were excused as the adults sat around the kitchen table and talked as they sipped small glasses of flavored vodka.

Theraisa took the opportunity to study her great-aunt, Eliza. She was, by German standards, rather plump but carried herself with a simple, elegant dignity. Her round face was highlighted with rosy cheeks and heavy eyebrows. Eliza had been blessed with a head of thick, luxurious raven-colored hair, which she parted down the middle and combed back into an enormous bun.

With every opportunity that presented itself, Theraisa observed Eliza interacting with affection to each of her children. She was in complete control, and she ran her small house with efficiency and discipline. When the hour grew late and the conversation slowed, Phillip excused himself momentarily to check on the horses.

Eliza seized the opportunity to pick up her baby and, cradling the child in the crook of her arm; she opened her dress and put the babe to her breast. Without breaking stride she turned to her niece. "Theraisa, I have been thinking about you for the past week and have been wondering about your health and well-being. How are you feeling with your pregnancy? You appear to be quite healthy, and I am happy to see that you do not wear a corset. Wearing the tight garment around your baby's temporary home can do great harm. Have you made arrangements with a midwife to assist in the birth?"

Blushing, Theraisa looked at her extended stomach. "JA thank you, I am feeling well except for the fact I become larger each day. I don't believe either my aunt Louisa or I have spoken to a midwife. We don't know of any such person in the village. I suppose it is time to make arrangements for my confinement."

Eliza looked with compassion at the innocence of the young mother-to-be. "My dear, did you not know that I am a midwife? I will be happy to come to your side when your time comes. I have much experience in giving birth, as you can see by the number of children we have. I have helped many women in our village through their time of labor and even afterward."

Louisa responded quickly, "Oh, Eliza that would be quite wonderful, especially since you are family. I am sure it would help our young mother to be more comfortable. You must counsel us about preparations, as neither of us has experience with such matters."

Eliza responded with enthusiasm, "Of course, I will be honored to act as your midwife. I think perhaps I should come to your house at a time that is convenient to you, so I may check to see how the baby lies inside and if it is turning yet for the time of birth. I will explain everything to you, Theraisa, when I come for the visit. It is good that you understand what is happening to your body and to your baby when he decides to come."

Theraisa's eyes widened with surprise. "Aunt Eliza, you say the word 'he'—do you mean you know I carry a son?"

Eliza moved near to Theraisa and laid her hands on the young woman's protruding belly. "JA, I am right most of the time. I have had much practice in birthing. It is my experience that a girl child spreads the mother's hips wider, and she lays closer to the back. But the boys most often curl up in a ball, high in the mother's cavity, and cause her belly to look like a watermelon. Regardless, when your time comes close, you will feel the baby's body rest lower inside you. Your baby has not yet dropped into position, but I think it will be soon. Should I visit your house next Wednesday?"

Louisa spoke, "Yes, my dear, that would be fine."

Phillip walked back into the house, stomping the snow from his boots at the door, and then took his seat at the table. "Louisa, you asked me earlier today about the current living conditions of Die Wolgadeutschen. It is interesting you should ask these questions because since the time when Catherine the Great died, we have begun to have serious troubles with the Russian government, which alarms all of us."

Phillip moved his chair back from the table and lit his pipe. After taking a long draw of the tobacco, he continued to explain recent developments. He told them that for the last twenty- five years, the czars had passed laws withdrawing many of the original privileges of self-government, such as forcing Die Wolgadeutschen to accept a Russian teacher in their schools. They then passed a major law that forced the young men into compulsory military training.

"We never did, nor do we now, want our German sons to fight Russian wars. We are feeling the Russians breathe hot down our necks with their changes and the endless threats to our livelihood. Many peoples are leaving or talking of leaving— perhaps back to Germany or across the ocean to freedom in America. There are over a million Germans who live in Russia. Seventy-six percent are Lutheran."

Phillip was noticeably agitated as he continued to describe the situation. A deep frown formed between his eyes as they narrowed, and his jaw tightened. "Our family has not yet decided what we are going to do. This is our home, and we don't want to leave, but the attitude of the Russian government is becoming hostile, and some day we may have no choice. Every day they take back more promises made by Catherine the Great. Every day our lives become more difficult; so far we have been able to adjust. We have reliable reports of armed political groups who clash in the streets of Moscow and St. Petersburg. Time will tell what our fate will be."

~~~~~

Later that evening as Theraisa and Louisa lay in their own beds in their small house, Theraisa's head was buzzing with the events and things they learned that day. "Auntie Louisa, this was a most wonderful day, and it did my spirit much good to go on the sleigh ride. The dinner at Cousin Phillip and Eliza's home was so tasty. It made me rather homesick, I must admit."

Louisa smiled into the darkness of the room. "Yes, Theraisa, it comforted me to see the German-style furniture, lace curtains at the windows, wall decoration, and dishes. I especially admired their very high bed with the mound of feather quilts. I expect Eliza crocheted the beautiful cover on their bed and pillow slips—also the *Vorhang*[9] which hung from the cross bars above their bed. I have never laid my eyes on anything so exquisite."

Theraisa replied wistfully, "Did you know that Cousin Phillip told me the benches we saw sitting on their front porch are used often in the warmer months? He told me families sit outside to breathe the fresh air and discuss business and friendly gossip with passing friends and visitors. Doesn't that sound wonderful? I wonder if we will still be here on the Volga when the warm weather comes, or if we will be on our way traveling back to Germany."

The two women had retired early that night and were snuggled deep in their feather beds as a severe blizzard began to build. Louisa woke with a start when the bell tower began to toll. She climbed out of bed to add more *mischt bricks* to the fire. Wrapping her robes tighter around her body, she went to the window to look out. She could barely see a thing in the night as the heavy snow swirled this way and that. It was beginning to find its way through the cracks, and she laid a rag rug in front of the inner door. Suddenly, the frigid night air was filled with incessant howling, snarling, and yelling. Theraisa sat straight up in bed, her eyes wild with fright. "Auntie, are you awake? Do you hear those horrible sounds? What is happening—will you please light the lamp?

The relentless howling and snarling caused the hair on the back of Louisa's neck to bristle as she put her nose to the glass. "It is so dark outside I can't see a thing, Theraisa, but I do see men running with guns and lamps. They are all going in the same direction." At that instant the two women were startled by gunshots. Then all was quiet. Not knowing what else to do, they both snuggled deeper into their warm beds. Louisa rose a second time to make sure the door was bolted tightly.

~~~~~

Early the next morning, they were surprised by a rare visit from Phillip. "I assume you both heard the ruckus last night? Here, sit at the table with me, for I have some disturbing news for you. Last night a pack of wolves surrounded a man who walked alone near the edge of our village. That is where they attacked him. I am sad to tell you that it was, Otto, and he no longer lives. We were too late with our guns to save him, and we have buried what was left of his body. I warned Otto myself about walking about, alone at night, especially during the winter when the wolves are ravenously hungry and not afraid to attack."

After Phillip left their small house, Louisa and Theraisa sat, frozen in shock at the death of their trusted servant. Louisa sat at the table, struggling with writing a letter to her brother and sister-in-law to explain Otto's death.

~~~~~

The following Wednesday, as the late February sun was shining brightly, Eliza walked across the village to the house where Louisa and Theraisa lived. "*Gute Morgan,* my ladies, and how are you doing on this fine winter day?"

After a cup of hot chamomile tea and a slice of dried fruit bread, Eliza got down to business. "Theraisa, I ask you now to remove your upper dress so I may examine your stomach. Please, lie down on your bed."

Although she blushed profusely, Theraisa did as she was asked. She was fascinated and watched carefully as the midwife ran her experienced and gentle hands over her large belly. Eliza poked and prodded the rigid mound, feeling for the baby within. Her brow wrinkled into a frown as she examined the width of Theraisa's hips, and then she measured them again.

"Cousin Eliza, is there something wrong? Why is there a frown on your face?" Theraisa felt cold fear crawl up her spine as she lay inert on the bed.

Not wishing to alarm the young mother-to-be, Eliza reassured her nothing was out of the ordinary. "I think it would be good for you to walk as much as you are able. Exercise will help the bones and muscles of your body to become stronger for the birth. Your life in the castle did not prepare you with the muscles for birthing as our farm women are; I want you to exercise more. Can you tell me when was your last bleeding time?"

Theraisa gave the approximate time to the midwife and watched as Eliza computed the time the baby should arrive. "Theraisa, I think your son could arrive anytime. He has definitely dropped, and his head is positioned in the birth canal. I want to show you what is happening inside your body and what will happen as his birth begins to take place."

Eliza reached inside her valise and withdrew an undersized drawstring bag with a small watermelon inside. "Here, suppose this bag is the sack in which your baby is growing inside your body, and then pretend the watermelon is your son. When the birth pains begin, the bottom of the sack will begin to open, like this. Every pain you experience will open the neck of the sack larger until the baby can fit through and come out. You can expect your time to begin with some light pain and perhaps some blood. Often the water inside the sack breaks and spills out of your body between your legs as the labor time begins. You cannot control it; the baby will not come out at that moment, so do not be worried. This is when you must send for me. I will give your aunt a list of the things I will need."

Louisa walked their cousin to the door. When they were out of earshot, Eliza confided, "Louisa, I am somewhat worried that Theraisa will not have an easy time. Her hips are quite narrow, as are her pelvic bones. The baby is growing large—I think he will weigh between seven and eight pounds. I will do everything I can to ease her pain. I am very good with herbs and creams. I also use massage to help the baby come out. Please call me when our dear girl goes into labor, and I will come at once. Also, Louisa, pray and pray often that our Lord delivers her and her son in good health."

~~~~~

On the tenth of March, Theraisa was taking a slow stroll along the snowy streets of Susannenthal. She was wrapped in a long, black wool coat and wore traditional knee-high leather boots; her babushka was pulled low. She had insisted on going out alone. Theraisa felt she looked rather like a small moving house as she made her way carefully down the street. As she stepped down, her feet slipped, and her swollen body was jolted awkwardly.

Suddenly, Theraisa felt a gush of warm liquid burst from her undergarments and run down her legs onto the snowy street. She looked down in horror and saw that the snow was stained a pale red. Her gloved hand flew to cover her face as panic erupted in her chest. "Oh *Mein Gott in Himmel*—the waters, it's the waters that have broken. I must hurry home, or my clothes will freeze to my body."

Theraisa burst through the door. She began to remove her clothing as the first pain hit her, causing the blood to leave her face. She paced the room looking out one window and then the other. *Where is Auntie Louisa? I need her. I need Eliza, I need—* her thoughts were caught in midsentence as another contraction took the breath from her chest.

At that moment, Louisa strolled through the door and casually began to remove her coat and boots, not noticing her niece who stood with her back to her, gripping the back of the chair. Theraisa turned slowly; with controlled urgency in her voice, she instructed, "Auntie, do not take your coat off, please. You must hurry to get Eliza. I–I–the waters have broken, and I have pains in my stomach. Hurry, Auntie, please hurry and bring her to me. I am so afraid I cannot do this, Auntie."

Louisa rushed to her niece's side. "Oh, my dear girl, my sweet—I will not leave your side. I will find a boy in the street to run to Phillip's house to fetch Eliza. Here, allow me to make you more comfortable. We must get you into your nightdress."

It was only thirty minutes later when Eliza knocked at the door, and then without waiting she rushed into the house. She removed her coat and winter clothes and moved quickly to the bed where Theraisa lay. "Louisa, we must remove the feather mattress from Theraisa's bed and put the horsehair mattress under her. The horsehair is more absorbing and easier to dispose of after the birth." She busied herself with her birthing herbs and creams, and then she asked, "Have you started the water to boil? I will need water, boiling hot water, to keep clean everything that touches our young mother and the baby. Where have you stored the washed strips of white cloth?"

Eliza was a whirlwind of efficient action as she readied the patient and the room for the birth. She was certain, however, that it would be quite some time before the baby would come. She closed her eyes and bowed her head as she prayed silently for guidance.

Eliza handed Theraisa a cup of hot tea laced with Vandel root, an herbal sedative. As soon as the young mother was calmed, Eliza spoke softly to her. "Theraisa, you must lie back, I am going to check on the progress of the birth. This I must do often. It is the only way I can know what is happening. I will use one hand on your belly to feel the position of the baby. At the same time, you will feel as I probe inside your body to check how opened the neck of sack is. Please remain calm, and do not struggle. I will be gentle and quick."

Theraisa lay on her back with her knees apart as the midwife checked the progression of her labor. She pressed her eyes tightly as her face flushed with humiliation and warm tears rolled over her prominent cheekbones. She bit her lower lip with the indignity of the examination and fear of what was yet to come. She offered a silent prayer as she clutched her mother's gold cross in her hands.

Louisa paced, prayed, boiled water, and made ready the white strips of cloth as Eliza instructed. The hours crawled by, pierced with numerous and mounting labor pains. It had been eight hours, yet there was no baby. Theraisa tried to nap, but her distress and worried nature would not allow her to relax.

Eliza confided in the girl's aunt. "Louisa, the labor goes very slowly. It is taking a long time for her to open enough for the child to come." Theraisa cried out as a stronger pain ripped through her young flesh. She thrashed and fought the pain as perspiration began to bead on her forehead. "Here, Louisa, let me show you how to rub her lower back with this herbal cream when the pain comes. It will help her to relax and allow the pain to work for her instead of against her."

When darkness fell, Louisa lit the lamps and fixed a light meal for Eliza and herself. They heard a soft knock on the door, and Louisa moved quickly to open the outer door. Phillip hurried through the outer room to where his wife was standing beside Theraisa. "How does the laboring proceed? Are you coming home for the night?"

Eliza turned to her husband and in a hushed voice said, "Nein, Phillip, this is not going quickly. I will spend the night here. I must be at her side, or she will not live when the moment comes. I have asked Sofie Laubin to bring the evening meal to you and our children. I will return home after Theraisa delivers her child. Thank you for stopping by. Please go now and take care of our children."

After Phillip left, Eliza spoke to Louisa. "Theraisa is what we call a *prim para* or first-time mother. She does not have the wide hips we hope for, nor does she have the physical stamina of a peasant woman. I am going to use every method I know of to help her bear her child. She is beginning to open but is only halfway there. I am not certain how much longer it will be. I have much hope that it will be over before the morning light. As she opens wider, I will take the oil and, with my fingers, oil and stretch, oil and stretch her opening so she doesn't tear at the moment of birth."

Louisa's face grew pale, and she swallowed twice. The two women worked in shifts, with Theraisa massaging her back with the medicinal creams and applying warm cloths and oil to her private parts to relax the skin so it would stretch easily.

It was after midnight when Eliza wiped the sleep from her eyes and tried to engage in conversation with Louisa in order to stay awake. "I am glad you are here, Louisa. Have you delivered a child of your own? Do you know what to expect?"

Louisa blushed. "Nein, Eliza, I am barren, and I have never even been witness to this...this delicate situation. I hope I can be of help to you. I must be honest with you; I am quite frightened and shocked."

Eliza shook her head, and an amused smile curved over her full mouth. "My dear, you have seen nothing yet. When this child is born, if you feel ill, please put your head between your knees, because I cannot take care of you should you faint."

Their conversation was interrupted by thrashing and moaning from the bed. Theraisa bit down on the rag Eliza had given her as she began to wail in protest, "Oh dear Gott, not another pain, no, no. Auggghhh." She cried openly as she pleaded with Eliza. "Please make the baby come. Make him come out. It hurts so badly and I cannot bear it. Where is Auntie? Auntie, help me, you must help me!" Theraisa grabbed hold of the pulling rags, which Eliza had tied to the bed.

Eliza moved to the bed; she was working feverishly now and called for Louisa to assist her. She spoke softly to Theraisa, "We are going to turn you on your side, child. When the next pain comes, I want you to concentrate on breathing in and out, in and out; breathe from the chest, not from the belly."

"Louisa, will you come around and rub her lower back with the herbal cream like I showed you? When the pain comes, rub in a downward motion to help the womb to push the child farther down the birth canal. She is becoming weak, and I fear she cannot bear the child with her own strength."

Eliza moved around to the front and put her ear against the young mother's protruding belly. She listened and heard a strong, loud, steady heartbeat. "This baby is a strong one. He is not tired, and he is fighting to come out." She reached to bathe the perspiration from Theraisa's face. "Theraisa, listen to me. You have to help me. We need to get you up on your hands and knees.

When the next pain comes, I want you to relax your belly. Take a deep breath, and pant like this: 'Hah, hah, hah, hah,' and then,

'Woo, woo, woo,' until the pain relaxes. When you are doing this, I will put my hand on the part that is the baby's bottom, and I will give him a gentle push. You are doing well, my girl. It won't be long now."

Theraisa was only able to stay on her hands and knees for a few moments when weakness caused her to fall back onto the bed. The next pain ripped through her with a vengeance. Theraisa arched her back and held hard to the rag pulls as her belly mounded and held the contraction. She tried to concentrate, to do what Eliza had instructed. When the pain was over, Theraisa's head flopped back on the horsehair bed; her eyes were shut, and her lips were pinched tightly. She was quivering with fear and exhaustion.

Another pain and then another ripped through her as Mother Nature opened the birth canal. Eliza knew Theraisa was beyond understanding any explanations as another hard contraction pushed the baby into the birth canal. "I can feel the baby's head— it is coming! Theraisa, listen to me. Listen now, we are almost there. When the next pain comes, Theraisa pant like a puppy. Remember, 'Oft, oft, oft' then push—push hard when I tell you to."

Eliza was working furiously now. Louisa, more hot cloths and oil, hurry. We have to help the skin around the opening to relax so it won't tear." She massaged warm oils into the skin, pulling and stretching it gently. Her experience told her this would help, but the baby was big, and Theraisa's opening was small. Eliza knew Theraisa would tear when the baby was born; there was nothing more she could do to alleviate that fact. "Louisa, please remove the rag rugs from around the bed. The floor is easier to wash than the rugs."

Eliza saw Theraisa's stomach mound tight and hard as the contraction built. Theraisa was frantically panting and pushing, fighting her body rather than giving in to it. The midwife reached up and with one hand pushed down on the baby's bottom as she and the contraction worked together to push the baby out.

Still semiconscious, Theraisa screamed again as the head and then the body of her son ripped its way out of her body and into the world. Quickly, Eliza moved to the end of the bed and took the baby's head, gently turning him face up as he emerged from the birth canal. She heard a thud on the floor behind her and instinctively knew Louisa had fainted. "I can't attend to you now. I have my hands full, and eventually you will revive yourself," she mumbled.

Theraisa gave one last loud shriek as the child slipped from her body, then fell back onto the bed exhausted. A few minutes later, a final contraction rippled through her body as the afterbirth slid out into the waiting bowl.

Eliza wiped the mucus from the baby's mouth and eyes as he loudly protested his difficult birth and the shock of oxygen entering his lungs. She gently wiped the blood and afterbirth from the child, leaving the protective white coating to be absorbed into his skin. Before she swaddled him in a soft cloth, she inspected his newborn pink body. He was a perfect, healthy boy who weighed close to eight pounds. She noticed he had a long torso and the round Steiner face. Eliza predicted he would be a tall, fine-looking man. She carried the baby to the head of the bed and laid him in Theraisa's arms. Then she walked over to where Louisa lay unconscious on the wood floor. Eliza smiled as she splashed cool water over the woman's face. "Okay, my helper, it is over. You can wake up now and help me clean up."

Louisa struggled to her feet, her face burning with shame. "I am so sorry, Eliza. It's just that I have never witnessed such a thing. How is Theraisa? Is she still living after that? And—and the baby, oh—let me see the baby." She hurried to the bed, where Theraisa weakly held her perfect newborn son in the curve of her arm, tears of exhaustion and joy streaming down her face.

Eliza showed Louisa how to fix a sugar tit for the baby until Theraisa's milk came in. "Do you think you can care for the baby and Theraisa by yourself, or shall I send someone over to help for a few days?"

"I am ashamed to say that I know nothing of caring for an infant or for my dear niece, so I would appreciate having help for several days if that is not a problem." Eliza assured her she would find someone to help out.

Eliza prepared a mixture of fennel and wild thistle to help bring the new mother's milk down, to make it rich and creamy. She also instructed Louisa to prepare a tea using butcher's broom herb to help shrink the womb. Eliza left instructions with Louisa for the care of mother and baby. Exhausted herself, Eliza squeezed into her worn sheepskin coat and went out into the frigid air as the waning light of late winter began to cast shadows on her path home.

~~~~~

Over the next few days, Eliza checked on Theraisa almost daily. She didn't like what she saw; the young mother was not responding as she should. Her new son cried and was unnaturally fretful because her milk was thin and sparse, and Theraisa cried with pain each time the infant took her breast to nurse. Finally, with Louisa's blessing, and much to her relief, Eliza bundled the baby against the icy air and took him to her own home. She had plenty of milk and agreed to nurse and care for him along with her own two-year-old daughter, Louise. Her own baby was almost weaned, leaving Eliza with more than enough milk in her ample breasts. Theraisa's baby was satisfied at last and began to thrive.

Louisa stayed with her niece, caring for her day and night. Time passed slowly, and there was no improvement. On the twelfth day, Louisa urged her niece to sit up in the bed, hoping to stimulate her with decisions. "Theraisa, you must choose a name for your son. The pastor and Phillip's family are pressing to have him baptized. We have other decisions to make as well. You must also think about when we leave the Volga. Do you plan on taking your son with us, or have you considered leaving him here?"

Theraisa opened her eyes and weakly attempted a response. "Oh, Auntie, I decided before he was born that his name would be David after his father. My son's second name will be Heinrich, after my father. It is what he should be called. I—oh dear Gott, I cannot take him back to Germany. If I did, then all would know of my shame, especially my parents. I cannot bear to stay in this wretched country. I want to go home, and I want to see my parents.

You told me that my son grows strong with the milk from Cousin Eliza."

Theraisa wiped the tears from her eyes and took a small sip of water. She swallowed hard and drew a deep breath into her lungs. "Do you—do you think Cousin Phillip and Eliza would want to take my son as their own? They have a good Christian family, and he would be raised strong, as a Steiner. Would you ask them, Aunt Louisa? I cannot bear to do such a thing. I...I suppose that you will have to tell them why I can't take him back to Germany. Would you do this for me, Auntie, yet another favor for me? I can't go on. I feel like something other than my heart is broken inside my body. I don't know what to do or where to turn. My life seems too hard and it seems I have lost all that I love."

Louisa leaned down and kissed the feverish forehead of her niece and then put on her heavy wool coat. Before she left, she assured Theraisa she would take care of everything. "If you need anything, my dear, Sara is right here. I shall return in a couple of hours. Try to take some liquid and nourishment. You must try hard, Theraisa, to rebuild your strength for the journey back to Germany." Louisa wrapped the babushka tightly around her head and then pulled the knee-high boots over her double stockings.

~~~~~

Louisa walked quickly along the snowy street toward Phillip's home. The melting snow caused for a slippery walk as she made her way on the rut-filled road. She pulled the scarf across her mouth because the air was still cold, even though spring was upon them. When Louisa reached Phillip's house, she knocked once, she stamped the slush from her boots and, not waiting for an answer, and she opened the door and slipped into the inner hall. She leaned against the wall; out of breath and exhausted, she removed her boots and hung her coat on a peg.

Phillip heard the outer door open and went to investigate. "Gott in Himmel, woman, what brings you walking on a day like this? The streets are slippery with melting snow and mud. You will *not* walk back to your house. I will hitch up the pony to the wagon. Come now, Louisa, sit at the table. Eliza has just made a pot of tea."

Eliza carried the steaming teapot to the table and poured Louisa a cup. The three of them sat at the table while the children busied themselves weaving baskets. Louisa picked up the cup with shaking and stiff fingers and brought it to her lips, sipping the steaming liquid. She smiled weakly as she felt the warming tea travel down her throat. Suddenly, she sat the cup on the table as her hands covered her face.

Eliza rose quickly from her chair and rushed to Louisa's side. "Oh Mein Gott, Louisa, what is it? Has something happened to Theraisa?

Louisa turned to face the woman she had grown to love. "Nein, nein—it's just I—we want to thank you, Eliza, for doing all you could to help Theraisa during her confinement. This is very difficult for me, but I have come with a request from my niece." Trying desperately to control herself, she took a sip of tea, gathering her thoughts. Then, with great difficulty, Louisa made Theraisa's request known after divulging the uncomfortable truth about why they couldn't take the child back to Germany.

Phillip and Eliza were not entirely surprised. "Of course, we will do whatever you think is best. Eliza and I will be honored to accept Theraisa's son as our own. He will be raised in our home with the knowledge and love of God. We will do all we can to make sure he is a happy child—he *is* a Steiner!"

~~~~~

When Louisa returned to the small house, Sara met her at the door in obvious distress. Louisa rushed to the bedside where her niece lay motionless and burning with fever. She sent Sara for the doctor, but there was nothing he could do for her. He explained in the best way he could that Theraisa suffered from what they called the "birthing fever." Her weakened physical and mental state was complicated by a raging infection and high fever. Over the next several days, nothing Eliza or the doctor did helped cure the growing infection, as each day Theraisa grew weaker.

April 13th had been an especially difficult day and, as it was coming to a close, Louisa managed to spoon some broth down Theraisa's throat. As she sat in a chair near the bed, Theraisa opened her eyes and weakly reached her hand toward her aunt. "Auntie, pl–please don't leave me." She gasped for breath as Louisa stood and wiped her niece's burning brow. "Auntie, I–I am afraid. Who are all these people in the room? And–and there is my David. Why didn't you tell me he was coming? I–I must comb my hair! Where is my brush?"

Louisa's eyes opened wide with recognition. She knew that often when people were at the door of death, they saw others who had passed before. It was said that they gathered to escort the dying one to heaven. Louisa picked up Theraisa's limp hand and encompassed it within her own, holding it firmly. "Oh, my darling, I am sorry. I–I did not realize we were having company. Please don't worry about your hair. You look lovely as always." Louisa reached to touch and caress her niece's beautiful face. "I promised not to leave you, and I will not leave you now. I am right here beside you, my sweet, right here. Hold onto my hand!"

Tears coursed down Louisa's face and dropped onto her bodice as she sat on the horsehair bed where her niece had given birth to Captain David Ritter's son. Louisa sat for what seemed an eternity, holding Theraisa's hand, even after it turned cold and lifeless.

As morning light flooded the room, Louisa woke with a start, realizing that she had fallen asleep with her head resting on the side of the bed where her niece lay motionless and dead. She stood quickly and covered her mouth with her hands as heaving sobs convulsed her body. Louisa managed to cover Theraisa's face with lace before she crossed the room to the washstand to rinse the night from her own face.

Without thinking she moved to stand at the front window looking out into the street. The winter snow was beginning to melt, leaving the streets a mire of mud. The April morning sky was a vivid lapis-blue, and the wakening earth was warmed by the intense sunshine.

Unreasonable thoughts coursed through her mind. *How dare life continue as though nothing has happened! The light has gone out in my life.* Louisa's thoughts were a kaleidoscope of events in her mind. Rationally, she knew she had decisions to make, some very hard decisions. But first she had to tell Phillip and Eliza; they would know what to do. She walked to the bed and pulled the bedcover over Theraisa's face; she put on her coat and walked out the door and down the muddy street.

~~~~~

In the days that followed Theraisa's death, Louisa was inconsolable and bore the guilt of her niece's death entirely on her own shoulders. Members of Phillip's family stayed with Louisa. Theraisa had been washed and dressed in the one good, midnight-blue silk gown her aunt had urged her to take to the Volga for a special occasion. As was custom, Theraisa Ritter was prepared for burial by her family, who also dug her grave. They had no morticians or funeral homes.

The morning of the funeral, Louisa took the golden chain and cross Theraisa's mother had given her the day they left Hessen.

She approached the bed and wrapped the chain around her niece's rigid fingers so the cross of her Lord lay across the back of her hand. At that moment, the events of the past several days descended with a vengeance on Louisa as she slumped to the floor in a faint.

The next thing she knew, she was sitting at the table. Phillip was spooning vodka into her mouth as Eliza wiped her forehead with a cool cloth. Louisa's hand rose, and with one vicious swipe, she cleared the table then laid her head on the smooth wood and sobbed inconsolably.

Phillip and Eliza allowed her a few moments. Then because they were not accustomed to this show of emotion when a fellow Lutheran was called home, Phillip pulled Louisa to her feet. "Louisa, stop this nonsense. We should praise the Lord that Theraisa has been called. She is with the father of her child and all the saints at the feet of the Lord's throne in heaven. Do not be so vain as to think it was your fault that the woman has died and leaves her son and all of us. It was God's will, and only God's. Just as we all have a birth day, we all have a death day."

~~~~~

It was a bright, sparkling spring morning when the Steiner family gathered to carry the open coffin and body of Frau Theraisa Ritter to the Susannenthal Lutheran Church for her burial service. After the service, the pastor closed the casket, and six men in black nailed the lid shut. Each time a hammer hit the wood, driving a nail deep into the lid of the coffin; Louisa flinched and bit her lips until they bled.

When the service was finished, the burial procession began its way to the Lutheran *Gottesacker* near the edge of the village. As the bells began to toll, Louisa's head lifted, remembering the day Phillip had explained one of the purposes of the bell tower. He had told them of the traditional *Die Wolgadeutschen* funeral procession, which was accompanied by the village bell ringing from the lofty bell tower. The bells rang loud and clear in the spring air. They tolled without stopping until Theraisa's age was reached.

At the head of the procession, Phillip and Eliza's thirteen-year-old son Solomon carried a handcrafted black wooden cross on a long pole. He was followed by the pallbearers who carried Theraisa's coffin on their shoulders. Behind the pallbearers, the black-clad family and faithful mourners walked slowly, choosing their path through the slippery, muddy street. Phillip Steiner held tight to Louisa's elbow as she struggled to maintain her composure.

As family and friends sang the final hymn, Louisa watched numbly. More men came forward, and together they lowered Theraisa's coffin into the foreign soil. Raising her eyes, Louisa looked out onto the Russian steppe that was bursting with new life. There were already fields of golden daffodils waving gently in the spring breeze, which smelled of melted snow and wet earth. *How am I supposed to live with this guilt? It was my idea to travel to this country. I took her away from her family and the wonderful life she knew and loved. How am I going to tell her parents?*

After the friends and family walked from the cemetery, Louisa continued to sit near the fresh grave of her niece, inert with self-blame and consuming grief. She looked up through red, puffy eyes at the budding grove of linden trees. Their spreading branches bore the weight of lime-green leaf buds, swollen and ready to burst with shiny new life. It seemed that everywhere she looked there was new life—fresh and beautiful.

Falling to her knees, she looked to the heavens. *Why, dear Gott in Himmel, did you take the dear girl? She was a sinner as we all are, but she deserved to live her life. Oh, why did I ever suggest this trip to the Volga? Watch over her, dear Lord, and forgive me for the misery I brought to her life and now the lives of Heinrich and Amelia.*

At last, Louisa willed her body to rise from the edge of the fresh grave as the departing glow of warm spring sun bled red, gold, and pink into the broad expanse of Russian sky. The rays of the setting sun crowned an ominous gathering of thunderheads with a silver lining just before disappearing in the finality of darkness, behind the mountainous horizon of the Volga River.

Emptied of tears and senseless words of self-recrimination, Louisa turned away from the grave and walked robotically alone down the dark streets of Susannenthal. When she reached the door of her rented cottage, she pushed it open then closed and bolted it behind her. She sat on the edge of her bed in the darkening room, not bothering to light a lamp or remove her mourning clothes. She preferred to be alone with her dark thoughts as she stared with desperation at the four walls, the ceiling, the floor— hoping against hope to find some inspiration and courage to do what she must. In utter exhaustion, she laid back onto the bed. Then almost immediately and against her will, her eyelids closed. Her final thought was of the unthinkable letter she would write to those who waited at the castle in Frankfurt.

Before daybreak Louisa rose from her bed, washed, and dressed in the privacy of the darkened room. She moved as if in a trance across the cold floor to the stove where she stoked the embers and carefully added more wood. After the coffee came to a boil, she poured a cup and moved reluctantly toward the wooden table. The old wood chair scraped against the well-scrubbed floor as Louisa sat down with pen and paper and began. For a long time, she simply sat and stared at the empty paper.

April 29, 1874
My Beloved Heinrich and Amelia:

There is no manner of ease with what I must tell you about the devastating events that have occurred in Susannenthal during the past months. Even though it was not spoken, I am certain you were both aware of Theraisa's condition before we journeyed to the privacy of the Volga. We had hoped to conceal and protect you from the truth, but I recognized the knowledge in your eyes as well as your unspoken words. I do not think Theraisa was aware you knew of her condition, and for that I am thankful.

The trip to the Volga was grueling and took its toll on both of us, but as you know, we arrived eventually and settled in. We were quite comfortable and after a period of adjustment enjoyed our time in Susannenthal. It was a wonderful and enlightening adventure. Phillip and Eliza and the other Steiner relatives were gracious and included us in every instance with their love and hospitality. The winter months were extremely hard; you would have been quite proud of your daughter as she grew into a responsible and lovely woman during her confinement.

She carried the baby to term and gave birth to a healthy son whom she named David Heinrich Steiner. Theraisa had a very difficult and lengthy birth, losing much blood and strength. Eliza is a midwife of much experience and attended to your daughter but to no avail. Eliza was concerned from the beginning that Theraisa would have trouble giving birth. Our Theraisa lost her life from exhaustion and infection in mid-April. She was buried with a Lutheran service and rests in eternal peace in the Susannenthal cemetery.

Before Theraisa died, she asked Phillip and Eliza to adopt her son as their own child. They assured her the child would be raised with love and strong German Lutheran discipline. David is the youngest of their eight children; I am confident he will have a happy and secure childhood. I hope you are in agreement with Theraisa's final request. She realized that it may compromise your position if I were to arrive home with an infant.

I am inconsolable, and I blame myself completely. It was, after all, my idea to take your daughter away from the castle, to protect her and the family name from scandal. I wish with all of my heart it had turned out differently; Phillip and Eliza have tried in vain to relieve my heart and guilt, telling me it was God's will to take Theraisa from this vale of tears.

I booked passage to begin my journey back to Germany on the fifth of May. I hope to arrive in Lubeck near the middle to end of June. My heart shrinks with dread when I think of facing you both, and I wish with all my heart this bitter cup would be taken from me. You are my family. You have been so generous and have taken me into your home after my dear Peter's death. This is not how I hoped to repay my gratitude. My life will never be the same knowing I was partly responsible for the death of your only daughter.

In humble supplication I am yours, Louisa

~~~~~

On the fifth of May, Louisa bid an emotional good-bye to Eliza and Phillip and then asked, "May I hold David one last time?" Eliza handed the infant to Louisa as she and Phillip watched the baby's aunt murmur her good-bye and gently kiss the wiggling infant. Tears rolled down Louisa's face as she handed the baby back to Eliza. "I know he will have a wonderful life with you and your family. It is what Theraisa wanted. It is for the best—for everyone! How will we ever thank you for all you have done for us? There is no way to tell you what is in my heart. God bless you and your family—thank you!"

Then it was time for Louisa to board the steamship in Saratov and begin her journey back to Germany, alone. Ominous dread would not leave her; she was continually tormented with the unthinkable moment when she would face Heinrich and Amelia.

~~~~~

Weeks later, standing at the ship's rail, Louisa watched the Russian landscape disappear as the German-bound ship slipped out of the Kronstadt harbor. She turned her back on Russia and the sad events of the past year as she returned to sequester herself in her assigned cabin.

Exhausted, Louisa lay down on the bed without removing her traveling clothes or unpacking her bags. Feeling drained and empty, she felt the ship move away from the port and out into the

Baltic Sea, destination: Germany. The blackness of the night and a mounting storm enveloped the ship as it bobbed like a toy on the storm- tossed sea.

Louisa refused dinner that evening, choosing to remain alone in her cabin. She laid inert, listening to the escalating wind and building force of the waves as the ship rose and plunged into the black, stormy sea. She folded her hands in prayer, beginning and ending her prayer in the same way she had since Theraisa died—in pleading supplication. Again, Louisa prayed the Lord would take this unbearable cup of shame from her. As she lay in her bunk after praying, unexplainable peace coursed through her body.

Almost at that moment, she felt the ship roll sharply to the right. Instinctively, she grabbed onto the bunk railing as the chairs and luggage crashed toward the opposite wall. She heard the frantic shouts of passengers and crew. The ship was rocked even farther by the thunderous cracking and ominous crashing of the ship's main sail as it fell to the surface of the upper deck. Refusing to answer the frantic knocking at her door, Louisa remained in her bunk, waiting. Without concern or emotion, she turned her head to the side and observed seawater seeping under the door of her cabin. She felt the ship list to the left, tilt, and then roll over onto its side.

Louisa closed her eyes and ears to the sounds of the dying ship and screams of panic from the crew as the sea began to swallow the ship. She lay, waiting. She did not scream; she did not cry, and she was not afraid as the pressure of the seawater burst her cabin door from its hinges. As if in a trance, she closed her eyes as water quickly filled her cabin and then covered her body in an eternal blanket.

PART TWO

Chapter Seven

The Boy, David

David, Phillip and Eliza Steiner's son, was almost nine months old when they received a letter from the child's natural grandfather, Prince Heinrich Von Steiner. The letter informed Phillip and Eliza that the ship Louisa had boarded in Kronstadt, Russia, had gone down in an unexpected, massive spring storm in the Baltic Sea. All aboard were lost.

~~~~~

Johann Phillip Steiner was forty-six years old and his wife, Elizabeth Maria Hardt, was thirty-two when their family was blessed with the adoption of their eighth child and fifth son, David. Their oldest son, Solomon, had been born in 1861, and nearly every two years since, they had been blessed with another child. Their second child, Dobias, was followed by Carl, who died as an infant, following complications from the measles. Johann Wilheim, born two years later, was joined by their first daughter, Mollie, in 1868. In 1870 another son was born, and following German custom, he was named for the infant son who had died before he was born—Carl. Their second daughter, Louise, was born in 1872. She was newly weaned from her mother's breast when their new son, David, vigorously accepted the duties. He was the youngest son and would inherit his father's land, per *Die Wolgadeutschen* custom.

~~~~~

Ten years later, David cocked his blond head and narrowed his deep-set, blue-gray eyes against the glare of the sun as he questioned, "Papa, why do I have to go to school, and Louise is allowed to stay home and cook and sew with Mama?"

Phillip turned to his youngest son with a frown on his face. "Is that what you want---to stay home, with Mama and your sisters and cook and sew all day? Would you also wear an apron?" Phillip laughed as David hastily renounced the idea. Growing serious, Phillip continued. "JA, David, it is more important that you go to school longer than your sister because you are a boy. You must learn more—also to read and write the Russian language. It is now the law of the czars, so when you are called to military service in the Russian army, you will know what they command.

"You have a special gift, my son. The schoolmaster tells me you are his prize student. He has told me how you already know by heart the Lutheran catechism as well as all of the doctrines and creeds. Herr Ertel tells me he is compelled to give you much more difficult work than the other children. God gives you many gifts, my son, and you must use them to his honor. Do you understand?"

David kicked the loose dirt with his foot and shoved his hands angrily in his pants pockets. "Yes, Papa, I understand. I do like going to school and the learning. However, I do not like to learn the Russian words. Also, I never want to serve in the Russian army or to fight in a Russian war. *I am* German. Why do we have to do what the Russian czar tells us to do?"

Phillip reached down and, taking the boy's hand in his own, he began walking up the road toward their home. "David, we live in their country. It is true we are German, and we have our own ways, but the Russian czar has commanded us to send our young men to help fight their wars. I do not agree with this either, but as long as we live in Russia, we are compelled to live by their rules. Do you understand this?"

David kicked another round stone down the road, watching as it skipped and hopped. He stopped and thought for a moment before he turned his face up to his father. "JA, Papa, I understand, but I still do not like it. Someday I will move away from Russia to a place where I don't have to follow Russian laws. I want to live as a German, not a Russian. Their rules are unjust, and they have taken back many promises they made to our people. I don't trust what they say or do."

Phillip took a long, thoughtful look at his son. They walked in silence as he thought to himself, *a fire for justice builds inside him already. When he grows into a man, I wonder what he will do with his life. I think his grandfather Heinrich would be proud of him. He is a handsome lad with deep-set, intelligent eyes and the high cheekbones of our ancestors. His body promises to be tall and straight as a rod. He is a good thinker and a compassionate, God-fearing young man. I wish him to be in my life for a very long time. I know the time draws near when I must tell him of the death of his natural parents and of the generous inheritance from his grandfather.*

~~~~~

Everybody in the Steiner family worked. Phillip often reminded them, "In my house, if you want to eat from my table, then you will work in the gardens, the orchards, and the fields. We all work, we all go to church, and we all pray and read daily from the Bible." Morning and evening prayers were an expected and welcomed part of their daily life.

Each morning after breakfast, except for Sunday, Phillip and Eliza gathered their children and assigned daily chores. It was a beautiful spring morning as the rising sun shot beams of gold, mauve, and copper into the morning sky. The children were awakened from their slumbers by Phillip's voice thundering through the house, "Time to get up—there is work to be done today!"

After they had dressed and eaten a hot breakfast, Phillip announced, "All the boys will come with me to the far fields. It is time to plow the ground and plant the red wheat. Solomon and Dobias, you hook the plow to one camel and the harrow to another, then drive them to the east fields. Carl, you and your brother gather the shovels and rakes. You will do the handwork today. David, you come with me. We will lead the other camels to the field behind the wagon."[10]

German settlers on field camels, Susannenthal, Russia
(Photo courtesy of: AHSGR)

David jumped and skipped alongside his father as they walked to the camel pens. "I love the camels, Papa. They are funny. Did you know that they can spit, Papa?"

Phillip smiled at the innocence of his son. "JA, my son, I know they can spit. Many times I find their spit on my clothes, but they are good workers, and they can eat anything that grows, so I do not have to feed them the good hay and oats that I must give to my horses."

"Papa, Papa—is it possible for me to ride on the back of the camels like I ride on the ponies? Papa, where did the camels come from?"

Phillip cleared his throat as he walked into the corral. "Well, my boy, about ten years ago I bought five camels from a Turkish trader who came to our village. He had both horses and camels for sale. He boasted that camels could survive on thistles and weeds and work for twelve to eighteen hours a day. That is much longer than horses can work.

"It is necessary to keep our camels in the barn during the cold of the winter because they can't take the bitter cold temperatures. They also give us their wool in the spring, which is good to make into scarves, coats, and warm quilts." David smiled at the thought of riding a camel. "And, my son, no, I do not think you would like to ride a camel. I also do not think my camels would welcome you to ride because we have never ridden them. These are working camels, and it is not something a boy like you could do."

David's blue eyes grew larger. "Okay, Papa, but I have one more question. Why do some camels have only one hump and some have two? Do boy camels have one hump and girls two? Is that why?"

Phillip slapped his leg and laughed with glee. "No, no my, son, the humps mean they come from different countries, yet they are cousins. The camel with one hump is called a dromedary camel, and they come from Arabia where there are great deserts. The two-humped camels are from Asian countries. And you may have noticed that they are shorter, have heavy wool hides, and are used to living in colder weather than the camels from the desert. The humps store water, so the camels can work the entire day in the fields without drinking."

Phillip harnessed two squatty Kalmuck ponies to a small wooden wagon and threw in sleeping quilts and enough food for several days out on the *Kelga*. "David, come here. Would you like to drive the pony cart to the fields while I ride my horse and lead the camels?"

~~~~~~

The farming fields of Susannenthal began about twenty miles from the village and continued, far toward the foothills of the Ural Mountains on the Wiesenseite of the Volga River. It was customary for the farmers to plant the fields and leave one or two family members to tend the fields and watch over the crop. Phillip had assigned this task to his two oldest sons, Solomon and Dobias. Next year when Solomon married, he and his wife would live in a

Soddy house out on the *Kelga* during the summer months. When it was harvest time, the entire family would migrate to the outer fields to help bring in the crop.

That afternoon when his father and brothers were busy preparing their fields, David grew bored and slipped away unnoticed. He spotted a double hump camel bedded down on a grassy slope under the shade of a linden tree. David watched closely as the camel chewed its cud and appeared to be sleeping. Daring thoughts raced through his mind. Slowly and quietly, he crept near the camel.

David moved closer until he stood next to the camel, it continued to sleep. Carefully and slowly, he lifted one leg over the hump of the camel. With fluid ease, he settled himself in the natural saddle, between the fuzzy humps.

At first nothing happened. He gently rubbed his hands over the animal's hump and, feeling the softness of the coat, he then stroked the long neck of the camel. Suddenly, the startled, furry beast leapt awkwardly to its feet and took off at an ungainly trot. David's mouth flew open with surprise. His eyes were large with shock and fear. "Whoa, you nasty camel whoa!", The boy grabbed onto the long, shaggy hair that hung from the front hump; he hung on for dear life as the camel's long legs gathered speed over the freshly worked field.

Phillip and his sons looked up from their field task when they heard shouting. To their amazement, they saw young David bouncing up and down and slipping precariously side to side on the back of the quick-trotting camel. The boy had a death grip on the camel's long wool with one hand. He was yelling and waving with the other arm, which only frightened the camel more.

Phillip and Solomon ran one direction while the other three sons ran the other, hoping to surround the terrified camel and equally terrified rider. Finally, after several attempts at corralling the beast, they were successful in grabbing the lead rope.

At the end of the day, David wasn't sure if his bottom hurt worse from bouncing around on the camel's back or the whipping his father had given him.

~~~~~~

At the end of the week, when the Steiner men finished with the spring fieldwork, Solomon, Wilheim, and Dobias were left behind to live in the *Soddy* on the *Kelga*. Phillip gave detailed instructions of what he expected the three young men to accomplish in the fields over the next several months. Leaving two camels and one horse in a corral on the *Kelga*, Phillip hitched the other horse to a wagon where his younger sons, Carl and David, had made a comfy nest in a pile of empty burlap grain-seed sacks. Phillip snapped the reins over the back of the horses and headed back to Susannenthal.

On their way back to the village, Phillip and his two youngest sons met a filthy, disheveled man walking along the dusty road. He hailed for them to stop. Phillip pulled back on the reins. "Whoa there whoa." Phillip stayed in the driver's seat as he addressed the man. "Hello, friend, where are you going on this warm day?"

The man looked up at Phillip with obvious defeat in his slumping posture as his eyes radiated internal despair. The man's hair was matted with grunge, and his face was covered with at least ten days' growth of beard and questionable grime. When he opened his mouth to speak, Phillip noticed the man's remaining teeth were covered with thick, yellow gunk and were black with decay.

With his filthy hat clutched in his hand, he replied, "My name is Hezal Kuzzah. I am going to the next village looking for work, sir. I am a good cow and pig herder. Would you know of any owner who needs his animals taken to the *Kelga* for the summer months? I would be willing to stay and tend to them as well."

Phillip unconsciously rubbed his jaw as he did a quick visual survey of the man. "Well now, Herr Kazzah, I tell you it so happens I am looking for someone to take my cows and also my pigs to the *Kelga* where my sons are staying. They will tend to them, but it would help me out if you would drive them up for me. Are you willing to take the job for a good hot meal and a few coins in your pocket?"

The two men made their agreement, and the pig herder was invited to climb onto the rear of the wagon for the ride back to Susannenthal. David quickly assessed the situation and scrambled up on the seat beside his father. Carl moved as far as possible from the terrible odor of the pig man, who rode happily with his feet dangling off the end of the wagon.

Eliza was less than thrilled to have the smelly man sit at her table. She hoped the savory aromas of her prepared dinner would rise above the disgusting odor that seemed to circulate like flies around Herr Kazzah.

Their temporary dinner guest devoured the food as if he hadn't eaten for two weeks. Phillip and his family were astonished at how much food and drink the man was able to put away. Even more amazing were the numerous ways in which he asked for more food. "Pardon me, Herr Steiner, but I am afraid I have extra butter and jelly, so please pass me the bread that the other will not go to waste." Or he would look at his plate and declare, "Oh my, see there, I have one last piece of bread and find I have need of more butter and jelly." After that day, whenever the Steiner children would ask for extras or eat more than normal, they were teased of being "Hezal Kazzah."

Phillip wasted no time in gathering the herd of cows and pigs for Herr Kazzah to drive out to the *Kelga*. He paid the man, and that was the last they saw of him. Eliza spent the rest of the day down on her hands and knees, scrubbing her house with a bucket of hot water and apple cider vinegar.

~~~~~

Later that fall, Phillip and Eliza experienced a troubling visit from the schoolmaster, Herr Karl Ertel, concerning their second son, Dobias. When Dobias returned from school that day, Phillip took him to the woodshed.

David had been feeding the chickens when he saw his father drag Dobias to the woodshed. When David returned to the house, Phillip invited him to take a walk. As they left the house, David was noticeably shaken and fearful. Phillip walked in silence with his youngest son at his side. David kicked a stone with the tip of his shoe with nervous anticipation. He knew he had done nothing wrong, yet he could tell by the serious expression on his father's face that he was in for a talking to. Unable to bear the suspense any longer, David spoke to his father. "Papa, where are we going? Are you angry with me also?"

Phillip stopped and sat down in a shaded spot beside the fast-flowing Volga River. He patted the ground, signaling David to sit beside him. "David, you are aware of the visit from the *Shoolmahster* today?"

Frantic to defend himself against anything the fearsome schoolmaster might have said, David replied with a quiver in his voice. "Yes, Papa, I saw him, and I saw you take Dobias to the woodshed. I didn't do anything to bring dishonor to you. I would not do that, Papa."

Phillip smiled, and with a reassuring pat on the boy's back, he said, "David, this is not about your doing anything wrong. The schoolmaster tells me that Dobias has been a continual source of trouble in school. He also tells me that a day does not pass that he is not compelled to discipline your brother with the rod. The master explained that no amount of face-slapping, palm- whacking, or flogging with the switch or rod seems to deter Dobias from his lazy inattention and indifference to his lessons. Yet, David—you have said nothing about this disobedience of your brother in school. Why is that, David?"

The blood left David's face; the corners of his mouth grew tight as he clenched his hands into fists and jumped to his feet. "Papa, yes, it is true I know of the troubles Dobias has with the schoolmaster. I must be honest, as God is my witness. This new schoolmaster looks for any small thing my brother does each and every day. He even smiles sometimes as he punishes him. He is cruel, Papa, and he makes Dobias his target even when he does nothing to be punished for.

"He has much trouble with the learning, and I cannot bear that he is punished so cruelly. I did not tell you because I know the rule—if we are punished at school, we will be punished again at home. Papa, please understand. I don't wish to see my brother suffer more. I do not agree causing Dobias daily pain because he has much trouble learning. He really tries to learn, but he just can't. And—and beside that, the other kids tease him and call him 'Dobi the *Dummkopf*'! When this happens, I try to chase them off. I have prayed often on this, Papa— every night."

That evening after the children had gone to bed, Phillip and Eliza spoke of their second son. They were aware he had trouble learning and decided to take him out of school, teaching him only lessons of farming. Phillip lay on his back long after prayers and thought about how David had tried to protect his older, less capable brother, and he smiled with pride.

~~~~~

When David turned fourteen, he was confirmed in the Lutheran Church. Phillip and Eliza also agreed he was at the age of understanding and should be told of his natural parents. Early the next morning, Phillip invited his youngest son to travel to the *Kelga* in pretense of checking the crops. They sat, side by side, on the seat of the painted pony cart as they traveled east along the dusty field road. Phillip offered up a prayer for strength and for finding the right words to deliver this unexpected news to his young son.

"David, the real reason I asked you to accompany me is that I have something very serious to tell you." Phillip pulled on the horse's reins and drove the cart to the edge of the road, stopping in the shade of a grove of linden trees. His father wrapped the reins around the brake pole and stared at the floor of the cart as David's intense blue green eyes never left his face.

Turning to face the boy, Phillip put his arm across the back of the seat. "David, you know how much your mother and I love you, as well as your brothers and sisters. You are a special part of our family, not only because you are the youngest, but also because there was something else that happened fourteen years ago. I want you to listen very carefully to everything I have to say, and then if you have questions, I will answer them."

Phillip's stomach was as hard as a river stone, and sweat skittered down his spine. He wiped his damp palms on the legs of his pants. "You are a Steiner, but you were not born to our house. Your natural mother, Theraisa Von Steiner," Phillip paused to choose his words, "was married to Captain David Ritter. She lived in a castle near Frankfurt, Germany with her parents while your father was at war. Your grandparents, Crown Prince Heinrich and

Crown Princess Amelia Von Steiner, are very important people, David—German royalty. Your father was killed in the war, leaving your mother alone and pregnant with you. She was very distraught and asked her aunt Louisa to help her leave the castle to give her time away from her memories. They decided to travel to Susannenthal to meet and visit the Steiner relatives here."

Phillip noted that David hadn't moved. In fact, he wasn't sure the boy was breathing. "David, I am telling you this because your mother Eliza and I believe you are old enough and intelligent enough to hear the truth and understand. The mother who gave life to you, who birthed you, was very beautiful. She was tall with lovely blonde hair and blue-green eyes, just like yours. You have the dark brown hair of your father."   David shifted ever so slightly in the seat and looked away. "Papa, what happened to my mother? Where is she?"

Phillip licked his lips and swallowed hard. "David, son, your mother died after she gave birth to you. Before she died, she asked if your mother Eliza and I would raise you as our own. You came into our lives and our home as a tiny infant. We always considered you to be a gift from God. After your mother died, your aunt Louisa was inconsolable, and she traveled back to Germany. We heard later that her ship was lost in a terrible storm when crossing the Baltic Sea. She died before she could return to Germany."

David turned and looked at his father, "So I am really an orphan?"

Phillip's face grew red as he exclaimed, "David, never—do you hear me—never have you been an orphan. Your parents of birth are with the Lord, and you were given to our love and care by your dying mother. You know how much we all love you, and that will never change. Even after the day I go to meet my Lord Jesus, you will remain my son."

In a rare display of emotion, Phillip took the boy into his arms and held him tight against his throbbing chest. David didn't move for a few minutes, and then Phillip felt his son's arms move around his back to embrace him as tears of shock, bewilderment, and relief flowed freely down both their faces.

David sat up and wiped his tears. "Papa, why didn't my mother send me back to Germany to live with my grandparents?"

Phillip looked down at his worn boots. "Because, my son, they were quite old and not well, and she thought you would have a better life with us as part of our large family. Besides, you were a tiny baby, and that would have been a very long trip for you."

David's penetrating blue-green eyes bore into his father. "I want to know where my mother is buried."

Phillip turned the pony cart around and drove back into Susannenthal directly to the Lutheran cemetery. Walking the perimeter of the cemetery, he looked for the spot where he remembered Theraisa had been buried. *Die Wolgadeutschen* did not tend the graves of the deceased. They believed that when a person died, their souls went directly to the Lord. What was buried was only the body, which turned to dust and needed no further earthly attention. The crude, wooden cross Solomon had shoved into the grave fourteen years before had long since rotted and fallen to the ground.

Phillip finally came to stand at a particular spot; he turned this way and that, looking at the landscape. He finally walked several feet to the west. "I think her grave is here, David. See how the ground is slightly depressed? I remember this spot and looking at the mountains the day she was buried. I am certain this is where her grave is."

Later that month, the Steiner family attended the funeral of a fellow member of the church. As they were standing at the gravesite, Phillip looked to the far edge of the cemetery and was surprised to see uniform river rocks encircling the spot where he had told David his mother was buried. There was a small wooden plaque at the head of the grave. As he moved closer, he read the crude inscription, "Theraisa Von Steiner Ritter – 1854 -1874."

Phillip looked up to see his son David watching him. He paused and then walked back to where the boy stood. He laid his forearm affectionately across the shoulders of his son.

~~~~~

It was after midnight when Phillip felt Eliza pull hard on his nightshirt, waking him from a sound sleep. "Phillip, listen—out in the street, horses and a wagon coming fast with much noise."

Phillip crawled from his warm bed and hurried to the front door, grabbing his coat from the peg as he went. He opened the door just as the horses and wagon stopped at his front gate. Solomon, his oldest son, leaped from his sorrel horse as his brother Carl strained to pull his horses to a stop. Solomon jumped the gate and was at his father's side in but a moment. He bent over to try and get his breath, his face ashen and dripping sweat.

"Papa, oh mein, Gott—it's terrible—a terrible thing has happened out on the *Kelga*. Wait, I have to help Carl with Liesel— she is in the wagon and in a bad way. Go, Papa, get Mama— hurry!"

Phillip and Eliza hurried down the walk to the wagon. Liesel was lying on her side on a mound of quilts; blood matted her blonde hair, and her plain work dress was torn to shreds. Carefully the two younger men lifted her from the wagon as Phillip and Eliza went ahead with the lantern. They carried the unconscious young woman into the bedroom and laid her on the still warm bed of Phillip and Eliza.

Eliza immediately set a pot of water to boil on the stove and gathered her satchel of herbs and salves. As Eliza worked with Liesel, the men gathered in the kitchen as Solomon described with difficulty what had happened. He was shaking so that Phillip first gave him a glass of vodka to calm his nerves.

Solomon flung the vodka back in one gulp, allowing it to calm him before he began to tell what had happened out on the *Kelga*. "Carl and I had been tending the crops and animals which Herr Hezal Kazzah had driven out. W-W-We thought he was long gone because we hadn't seen him. We had been working out in the fields all that day as Liesel and her helper remained at the *Soddy*. I finished my fieldwork early and decided to muck out the barn before supper.

"As I neared the house, I heard screams and sounds of fighting. I ran, and as I rounded the corner of the hut, I saw the helper girl lying in the yard, bleeding from her mouth. She looked to be dead.

"I again heard screaming come from inside of the house, so I ran and flung open the door. Herr Kazzah was on top of Liesel, beating her and trying to pull her skirts up. She was screaming and fighting for all she was worth."

Solomon began to pace his parents' bedroom as he continued the story. He told how he had grabbed Herr Kazzah off his wife, throwing him to the floor. "Kazzah quickly got to his feet and pulled a long blade knife from his belt and lunged at me. I jumped back and reached for my pistol. Without a moment's hesitation or thought, I shot Herr Kazzah point-blank." Solomon covered his own face with his hands then regained his composure, "Papa, I will never forget the look of utter shock on his face before he fell forward. He gasped and gurgled as blood came from his nose and mouth.

"After making sure he was dead, I rushed to the bed where Liesel was curled up in a tight ball, out of her head with fear. It was only moments later I heard the sound of Carl returning with the camels from the field. Seeing the body of the girl lying in the yard, Carl ran into the house and almost tripped over Herr Kazzah's body. I called for him to come to the bed where I was trying in vain to administer to Liesel. We decided to load Liesel and her helper into the wagon and bring them into Susannenthal—here, to Mother, so she might tend to them.

"It was then that we knew we had another problem—the pig herder's body. Of course, the killing had been self-defense, but we were both frantic and not thinking clearly. It was growing dark when we also loaded his body in the back of the wagon. We covered him with a tarp and set out for the village.

"When we came close to a spot where the road ran parallel to the Volga, we turned off and stopped in the cover of a grove of trees. It was dark now and we were sure nobody was on the road. We pulled Herr Kazzah's body from the wagon bed and slid it into the river. After that, I led my horse to the road, tied him, and motioned for Carl to drive the wagon onto the hard bed of the road. Then, Carl and I broke branches from nearby trees and swept away the wagon wheel and horseshoe prints. We tossed the branches into the Volga."

Carl slumped in a chair as Solomon squatted on the floor with his head in his hands. "We didn't think—we couldn't think of anything better to do with him. Perhaps this way his body may never be found. All we could think of was getting Liesel and the girl to you, but the girl has died." Solomon stood as tears coursed down his face, "Papa, I killed a man—I killed him! I broke one of our Lord's commandments. And what are we going to do with the girl's body? She was an orphan girl without family."

His face a mask of concern, Phillip assured his sons that what was done was done, and they must speak of this to no one. The deed was committed in attempt to save the life of Liesel, his wife; it was justified. Phillip assured both sons that the knowledge of this deed would remain as dead as Herr Kazzah. After discussing their options, Carl and Solomon drove the wagon back to the *Kelga,* arriving about an hour before the sun rose. They buried the orphan girl under a tree at the edge of their property.

The Steiner family contrived a story about why the two sons had ridden wildly into the village in the middle of the night: Liesel had fallen and was seriously hurt. Eliza did what she could for her daughter-in-law, and within days she was back on her feet and ready to return to their home on the *Kelga.* No one ever spoke of Herr Hezal Kazzah again.

Chapter Eight

David and Sofie: Spring 1889

The 'bread basket' of Russia lay along the Volga River, between the provinces of Samara and Saratov. For four years, a consuming and devastating drought and famine covered the land. The life-giving rains came at the wrong time, followed by searing summer winds, which pulled the very life from the soil; the winters were no better—unbearably cold and long. David watched as people scoured the muddy banks of the low-flowing Volga for any sort of edible green or animal. They emptied their granaries; they ate their livestock or what was left of them. Despite meager efforts by the government and private charities, the people were utterly destitute and starving to death. Steamers carrying flour, rice, and other food staples arrived from America, but were near to empty by the time they reached the German settlements. Relatives of *Die Wolgadeutschen,* already settled in America, did what they could, sending money and aid in an effort to sustain the survival of those who remained on the Volga.

Phillip and David often walked the streets of Susannenthal in an effort to help those in need. The two men were shocked by what they saw—people with flesh hanging on their bones, hollow, vacant eyes, and little hope; they gave them what they could. Even the wealthiest of the Volga villages found it impossible to find or buy food.

The Steiner house was filled to the rafters with their entire family. Phillip and Eliza's eight children, wives, husbands, and grandchildren all lived in one house in an effort to conserve fuel. Phillip and his sons built extra sleeping lofts in the rafters and the storage attic. They built bunk-type beds, and their bodies were stacked like cords of wood, but they were warm and when there was food, they ate.

During the long winter months, the older sons removed the straw thatching from their own cottages in the village and out on the *Kelga*; they fed it to the starving livestock. Even with that, they lost nearly half their animals. They watched each animal closely; if it appeared to be losing its battle to live, it was slaughtered and eaten. The family survived another month or two on the food it gave. Phillip could hardly bear the sight of his once-prized trotters barely able to stand, and he finally killed them too, so his family might survive.

Living in such cramped quarters, sickness became rampant. The Steiner family lost one daughter-in-law and three grandchildren. Eliza did all she could with her herbs and salves, but often the illness was beyond what she was capable of curing, and the doctor from Saratov was too busy to travel far. Before the famine, all of the villages had emergency storehouses or granaries to see them through an especially hard winter and to provide seed to plant in the spring. Soon those granaries were emptied. Even if the weather had cooperated, there was no seed left to plant.

Packages and letters from relatives and friends in America told of a virtual Eden where food and jobs were abundant. As a result of this tempting information, there was a large exodus of *Die Wolgadeutschen* to America. Because so many left the Volga, it eased the demand for food; still, those left behind continued to starve and die.

Finally, in the spring of 1894, weather patterns changed. Once again, prosperity returned to the Volga. Phillip and Eliza's sons moved back to their homes and began to reconstruct them. Fields were planted with seed "loaned" by the Russian government.

Long days in the fields filled out David's six-foot two-inch, bony young frame with ropy muscles and sinews. His thick auburn hair spilled in soft waves onto his forehead. Deep-set hazel eyes accented his prominent jawline. As David celebrated his twentieth birthday, he looked eagerly to his future as a man.

One evening as the sun began to set beyond the shores of the Volga River, Phillip invited his youngest son to join him on the front porch of their house for a smoke. "David, you have seen your twentieth birthday, and now that you are an adult, there are some serious issues I have been waiting to discuss with you."

David's curiosity was piqued. They both lit their pipes. "Papa what is it that weighs on your mind?"

Phillip took a long, slow pull on his carved bowl pipe and exhaled the smoke in a frustrated puff. His face mirrored his intense thoughts as he turned slightly on the bench to face his son. "David, you have known for many years that your grandfather, Heinrich Von Steiner, was aware of your birth. Before he died, he wrote me a letter, sending along with it a good deal of money as your rightful inheritance. Upon his request, I have kept the money in safekeeping until you were of age and could make mature decisions regarding your inheritance."

Before David could respond, Phillip continued. "I have something else to tell you, and I'm quite sure you are not going to be as happy with this news." He reached into the breast pocket of his brown vest and pulled out an official-looking envelope. He hesitated and then handed it to David. "It is from the Russian government, David. They want you to carry a rifle for them. They expect you to be in Moscow by the end of the month."[11]

The smile immediately left David's face, and his eyes narrowed. "Papa, I've told you that I don't want to serve in the Russian army. It was my understanding when our family came here over a hundred years ago that one of the stipulations as Germans was we were free from serving in the Russian military." He slapped the envelope down on the seat then stood and spit over the porch railing.

Pursing his lips, Phillip put his large work-worn hand firmly on David's sinewy forearm. "David, we already had this discussion. You know you have no choice. When the czar informed the German government that the *ukaz* with us no longer applied, the Russian government was at liberty to repudiate all promises.

"My son, it is Russian law that we're now forced to live by. You have no choice. If you leave or do not report, they can throw you in one of their prisons, or they may send you to Siberia! Think about your choices. I know you will make the best one. Sometimes, my son, we have to make hard decisions. We do what we have to do. Our life is what it is!"

The young man scowled. "How long do I have to serve? Does the letter say?"

Biting onto the stem of his pipe, David looked off into the distant landscape. "Three, maybe four years, depending if they are at war or not." Phillip bent forward with his hands folded between his knees. His blue eyes were focused on the porch floor as he struggled to give his son reassuring words of wisdom. "I want you to remember something, my son. Courage is not the absence of fear. It is a decision—a decision to do something you must—in spite of your doubt and fear. You must have courage, David.

"You know the Lord walks with you, and only He knows where the road will lead. Have faith, have courage, go with our love. We know you will make us proud as you always have. May our Lord be with you and bring you back to us, safely."

~~~~~

In 1894, David looked out of the window of the moving train as it carried him west to Moscow. He watched with interest as the train sped past poor villages and ragged Russian serfs working their fields with crude implements. He was filled with bitterness that he, a German, was forced to serve the czar because the original *ukaz* no longer existed. He had heard stories of the brutality rained on soldiers of German descent by the Russian military. He was disturbed by the number of crippled soldiers, begging in the train stations along the way. After serving their czar and being maimed, they were forced to beg in order to live.

The first year David served in the military was spent in Moscow, patrolling the streets, against peasants and serfs who gathered against the czar. He made few friends among the Russians and for the most part stayed to himself.

During the second and third years of his internment, David's unit was sent east to the Turkish border. There had been persistent conflict since the 1877-78 war with Turkey where nothing had actually been settled. Issues were again at a boiling point.

Because he sat a horse better than most and was expert in his knowledge of the care and handling of animals, David was chosen by a unit of Cossacks to look after their horses for a time.

Like all soldiers, he was not a stranger to the Cossack's reputation. He remembered hearing in school that during the Thirty Years' War in Germany, brigades of Cossacks had crossed borders and actually fought on both sides. As their own governing force, when they weren't called to battle for the state or a well-paying private cause, most returned to their individual lives. With obvious pride, they considered themselves the elite Russian military! When it came to horsemanship and daring bravery in combat, there were few who could hold a candle to the ruthless and highly skilled Cossack soldiers. At the end of their years of service, they received grants of land from the Russian government and numerous favors from grateful citizens.[12]

~~~~~~

One frosty fall morning as David was working in the horse barns using the curry brush on several Cossack horses, he heard heavy footsteps behind him. Turning, he came face-to-face with an enormous black-bearded Cossack whose breath could have brought an elephant to its knees. The man smelled of sweat and blood, but his impressive uniform was spotless. "You there— soldier, you like the horses, do you? I have watched you and believe you have ability. Would you like to come with us and take care of my horses when we leave here and travel into Turkey?"

Shock flooded over David's face as he struggled to regain his composure and give an answer that might agree with the intimidating Cossack. He saluted as expected then responded in the deepest voice he could muster, speaking flawless Russian. "I am flattered you have noticed my knowledge and respect of fine horse flesh. It is true I have years of experience with horses, and it is the one thing I particularly enjoy in this army."

As David spoke, the Cossack took a step backward then in a voice that made the pigeons take wing. "What accent do I hear with your Russian words? Are you a 'Kraut'?"

David squared his shoulders as he clicked his boots in respect then lied through his clenched teeth. "I am *Die Wolgadeutschen* heritage, but I serve the czar as a Russian soldier.

I am happy to do the bid of the czar and the famous Cossack warriors!"

The Cossack spit his distaste onto the straw then turned on his heel and stalked out of the barn. Relieved he was still breathing; David deflated his chest and remained rooted to the spot with thanksgiving that he had escaped retribution from the Cossack soldier. The Cossack brigade rode out early the next morning with chosen horse-keepers trailing at the rear. David was surprised that even though the burly Cossack had not liked his heritage, he had been invited to join the keepers as they traveled.

David rode and worked with the Cossack soldiers for a couple of months, gaining their respect for his knowledge of horses. As he worked late one night, shoeing three of the horses, he was startled by another tall, lean Cossack who strode confidently into the barn. "That is one of my horses you are working on. Make sure you do a good job!"

David stood up and ran his hand across the back of the roan warhorse. "He's a fine piece of horse flesh. It must be incredible to ride him and feel his power, right?"

The Cossack smiled as he affectionately rubbed the nose of the muscular steed. "Oh, yes, he has carried me faithfully and courageously through many battles. Once he was even wounded in battle. He is not afraid when I use my whip either." The Cossack looked over his shoulder at David. "Do you have knowledge of the Cossack whip?"

Shuffling his feet, David nervously replied, "No, sir, but your reputation with the whip fascinates me. It is something I would like very much to learn one day." The battle-hardened soldier slapped David on the back as he turned to leave the barn.

"Okay then—be here tomorrow at ten a.m., and I will begin to teach you a few moves."

David arrived early the next morning. He was a fast learner and in no time became skilled with a Cossack whip, taking pride in his ability to curl the long piece of leather through the air, cracking it at every turn.

~~~~~

David's service to the czar took a turn for the worse during the summer of 1896. One sultry night, David and fellow German Helmut Mueller were on guard duty at the front gate of their barracks. The night was hot and boring. Helmut slyly glanced around, producing a flask of vodka, which he offered first to David. They had both taken several swigs from the flask when an officer rounded the corner of the guard station and saw them.

They were immediately arrested and thrown into the prison barrack to await certain punishment. Their entire night was filled with thoughts of what the following day would hold for them. They knew from their own participation that it was a punishment that was not easily forgotten. Helmut was nearly hysterical thinking about the consequences. David spent the night deep in prayer. He was determined to endure the flogging punishment through physical and mental strength.

The sun announced the new day with a splendid splash of color as the two soldiers were marched out to face the gauntlet. They were roughly stripped to the waist as their fellow soldiers were handed a leather strip knotted at the ends. The Russian officers stood to the rear, making crude jokes concerning the two German soldiers, who stood with bayonets at their backs. Much to the amusement of his superiors, the officer in charge prolonged the torturous wait.

It was impossible to ignore Helmut's sniveling as he wiped the tears from his eyes and snot from his nose. Ignoring his friend, David clenched his jaws so hard he thought his teeth would break. In his head, he vowed to not give the soldiers the satisfaction of seeing him break. *Never will I break—never!*

First to go was Helmut. He screamed as the first soldier whipped the knotted leather as hard as he could across Helmut's naked back, drawing first blood. He began running as fast as he could; however, by mid-gauntlet, he was stumbling and falling to the ground. Helmut never made it to the end.

David took a deep breath and became empowered by the mature muscles in his strong German thighs and calves; he released a primeval scream and began the gauntlet. As he ran, he threw his arms forward in an attempt to divert a number of the ripping blows away from his face. He screamed German obscenities as he ran; words most Russians didn't understand.

Once he stumbled but caught himself and powered on, concentrating on the end of the line. The flesh on his back and forearms were sliced to ribbons. Blood ran freely and thickly down his body to soak into packed snow. The last Russian soldier swung his knotted leather strip high, intending to hit David's face. Holding his forearm up in protection, David lowered his head and drove for the finish line as the thong opened the flesh on his upper right shoulder, missing the intended target.

David willed himself to heal, but his friend Helmut did not, as infection swiftly took his life. David's back and arms were totally healed by the time his service ended. The physical scars along with an eternal hatred of the Russian military were all that remained.

As the winter snow began to melt on the Turkish border, David boarded a train heading away from the military outpost.

Somewhere in the wilds of central Russia, shortly after two in the morning, he carefully lowered the train window. Quickly scanning the sleeping passengers, David knotted his Russian uniform into a tight ball and threw it out the open window, to fall and rot in Russian dirt beside the tracks where it belonged.

~~~~~

1898: Home Again

Eliza reached up to tenderly touch her youngest son's unshaven, bristly face. She was grateful her prayers had been answered. David had returned safely from serving his time in the Russian army, a mature and worldly twenty-four-year-old adult.

"I can see your mother in your face, my David."

David smiled as he wrapped his long arms around her in a rare moment of affection, releasing her quickly. "It's good to be home, Ma, but I need to leave now. I promised Pa I would help out in the fields today."

She stood watching from the front porch as David swung his long legs over the saddle and galloped off in a cloud of dust out to the *Kelga*. A slow smile spread across her face. She reached up, and with her apron she wiped a tear from her eye as she headed to the chicken coop to gather the eggs.

~~~~~

Sweat bathed David's body. His hardened muscles rippled and strained as he swung the heavy scythe rhythmically through the field of ripened grain. His suspenders held his sweat-soaked shirt in place as it molded to his powerful body. He appreciated the occasional cool breeze from the Urals that washed over his body, giving him brief relief from his task. After cutting the long stems of grain, David worked quickly and skillfully, raking them into bundles, leaving the mounds to be tied with longer strands of straw or grass by his older sisters, Mollie and Louise.

As the swallows began to sweep and dive through the evening air, he untied his horse, leapt into the saddle, and urged the black stallion onto the open road. David felt the pull and push of the powerful animal as they flew down the road toward the village. When the horse began to lather up, he pulled back on the reins until they slowed to a quick trot. David affectionately patted the horse's wet neck. "That's my boy! There is nothing I love more than to feel your strength and power beneath me."

Early the next morning, David walked to the barn behind his father's house. He leaned against the corral fence and watched the camels chew their cud. Since the day he had survived his first and last camel ride, David had not been interested in working with the shaggy beasts. David's long legs stretched into eager, lengthy strides as he rounded the corral and entered the barn where his father kept the prize horses. Working with the splendid horse flesh had always been David's favored pastime until recently when a certain Susannenthal beauty, Sofie Wagner, caught his attention.

Discreetly, Eliza followed her son to the corral that morning. As she gathered the eggs, she watched out of the corner of her eye as he combed and curried three of the horses. "So, David," she teased, "Are you going to hitch a trotter and a pacer or two trotters to the buggy today?"

Her youngest son whirled with surprise. "Oh, Ma, I did not know you were gathering eggs. You are so quiet." He smiled proudly as he ran his hand over the shiny coat of one of the ebony mares. "Aren't they magnificent? They run like the wind!" He turned back to the horse; making his decision, he harnessed two black trotters and led them to the buggy where he expertly hitched them to the tongue.

"I am taking them out for a run today. I finished my chores, and Pa has given me the day off from the field." His eyes lit up with expectation as he continued, "I have asked Sofie to take a ride with me. Perhaps we will even take a picnic to the mountains. This is a day to enjoy, and I intend to do that very thing with the most beautiful girl in the region."

Eliza couldn't help but smile as she teased him further. "And, David Steiner, how do you know she is the most beautiful girl?"

David climbed onto the driver's seat with a mischievous twinkle in his eye. "Because, Ma, I have looked at all the girls for miles in both directions along the Volga, and Sofie *is* the most beautiful. There is no doubt."

Shaking her head, Eliza's unrestrained laughter rippled through the morning air. Standing by the fence with the basket of brown eggs hanging from her arm, she watched David skillfully drive the buggy down the packed dirt road in the direction of the community orchard. She turned and walked slowly across the yard as thoughts of her youngest son and Sofie filled her mind.

~~~~~

David tied his team to a tree and then moved stealthily through the secluded orchard until he stood behind Sofie Wagner as she picked ruby red apples beside the slow-flowing Volga River. Slowly, he slid his large, field-hardened hands around her tiny waist. Without turning to identify who, touched her, an exquisite smile of recognition spread across her face, and her deep-set eyes crinkled with happiness. She spun to face him.

Upper Volga River, Russia

"Sofie, how can I convince you we should marry soon? We have known each other for our entire lives. I have served my time with the Russian army and am now free to continue with my life. I am twenty-four years old, and you are twenty. It is time for to be married. I am in love with you, woman, and more than anything in the world, I want to spend my life with you. What are we waiting for? This fall after the harvest will be the perfect time. We need to begin with our church bans soon."

Sofie turned and walked nearer to the meandering Volga. Stopping on the grassy bank, her hand rose to rest against the rough bark of a linden tree as she pretended to think about David's words.

David remained standing where she left him, waiting with baited breath for her reply. He knew Sofie was teasing him and was aware of his eyes on her as she stood watching the river water swirl in deep eddies and then continue downstream. David gazed with wonder at Sofie's slender figure, the way her skirt blossomed gently over the curve of her hips. His eyes followed the wisps of auburn curls as they escaped from her upswept hair, and he silently admired how they clung possessively to the soft, white dampness of her graceful neck.

Sofie turned her face away from the river and moved back up the bank toward David, where he stood in a secluded part of a grove of alder and linden trees. She could feel the throb of her heart and blood as it raced through every vein in her body, especially in the hollow of her neck. She reached out to him, and he quickly drew her into his arms. As she stood on her tiptoes and slid her left arm around his neck, her right hand caressed the clean-shaven shape of his angular jaw. She looked deeply into his eyes and smiled. "David, I will marry you. I want nothing more than to be your wife and to live the rest of our lives as one."

David was ecstatic as he lifted her into the air and whirled her around. With a twinkle in his eye, he looked down on her upturned face as he gently kissed her full lips. "I love you, woman.

I will love you until the day I die and even after that!" Sofie took his face in her hands and returned his kiss.

Suddenly Sofie pushed him away. His face flushed, David walked quickly to the river. He squatted on the bank where he splashed his face with cool water. He stood for a moment, giving himself time to regain his composure. Sofie walked up behind him and wrapped her arms around him, holding him close to her. Her voice quivered with emotion as she swallowed hard. "Come here, turn around, and look at me. Let's make plans for our marriage."

He turned with a smile on his face. "Oh, my love, it is you who should forgive me for losing myself in you." David picked Sofie up and swung her around as she laughed and squealed. He held her to him for a moment longer; slowly he lowered her to the ground and kissed her tenderly.

They walked a short distance and settled under an apple tree. David stretched his long legs out, his back resting against the trunk. Sofie turned and leaned back against his chest as he said, "Sofie, my father has already given his consent to our marriage. Now, according to tradition, I must arrange for three of my family's friends to call on your father. I will speak to Papa, and he will arrange for the men to visit your house on our behalf." Sofie turned to face him as he took her tiny hand in his. A wicked smile crossed his generous mouth. "Now that you are going to be my wife, I will not have to fight my way through the line of men waiting to dance with you at celebrations." He reached up and ran his fingers through her long auburn hair and pulled her into to his arms.

~~~~~

Late in August, David's godfather and two friends of the Steiner family walked down the dusty village street toward the Wagner home.

Herr Wagner put on his best act, pretending to be surprised by the visit. The procedure was accepted as a rite of passage, and everyone had a part to play. After a casual conversation, the romantic emissaries revealed their true mission. Herr Wagner's eyes grew wide with playful surprise, and he clapped his hands in merry agreement. "This David Steiner who wants to marry my daughter—he is a good man, you say. Does he wish to marry in the church?"

The godfather and friends of the Steiner family replied in unison, "JA, Herr Wagner, he is a fine German Lutheran man, strong of faith and character. He has promised me personally that he loves your daughter and will be a faithful husband to her, giving you many grandchildren."

Herr Wagner stood and with a loud voice said, "Frau Wagner, come into the parlor and bring our daughter Sofie with you. There are men here who say that David Steiner intends to make her his wife." The two women bustled into the room; they had been waiting impatiently behind the kitchen door. Hurrying into the room, their faces beamed with happiness.

Herr Wagner spoke with a booming and boisterous voice. "Sofie, I am told by these friends that you and David Steiner wish to marry. Is this the truth, my daughter?"

Sofie could hardly contain her mirth as she played her part and hastily replied, "JA, my papa, I do wish to become the wife of David and join him in the house of his father."

"Well then, we shall not waste another moment. We must drink to the happiness of my daughter Sofie." He turned to his wife. "Mama, bring out the vodka and perhaps some tea with your special Yagada Kugah."

One of David's family friends rushed out the Wagner front door, jumped on the back of his pony, and raced to the house of Phillip Steiner. Understanding the ritual, the Steiner family had been waiting for Herr Wagner's consent. One and all rushed posthaste to the home of the bride-to-be. In anticipation of the celebration, Eliza had baked a huge pan of *Krimmel Kuchen* to take with them. When the two families came together, the details of the wedding and the bride's dowry were discussed in depth. As the vodka flowed, tensions relaxed and savory food was devoured.

The next day, David and Sofie made an appointment with the pastor of the Lutheran church. Pastor Obermeyer welcomed the couple and proceeded to question them regarding their qualifications for marriage. "I know you are both confirmed in the church. Now each of you must recite from memory the Apostles' Creed, the Ten Commandments, and our Lord's Prayer. Then I need to hear from your own mouths your explanation of your faith and how you expect it to affect your married life together."

After passing the examination by the pastor, they were officially engaged. The pastor posted the church bans, which announced to everyone that in the eyes of the church, the couple was ready to wed.

A week before the wedding, the women related to the betrothed couple discussed the menu. Eliza offered a traditional menu of German favorites. "It is expected we serve a roast pig, fluffy white mashed potatoes, pickled sauerkraut, *kraut kugah* [13], *karduffle*[14] swimming in sour cream and hot browned butter glaze. The menu included all types of sausage like bloodwurst and bratwurst, as well as the favorite, *Yagada Kugah* [15], and a variety of cheese and rye breads. Of course, we will have barrels of vodka, German beer, and sweet white wine." Tomatoes in any form were not on the menu, as they were considered to be poison; corn also was not present on Die Wolgadeutschen table—this particular vegetable was fed only to the pigs.

~~~~~

David and Sofie were married on a clear, crisp day near the end of October 1898. Sofie was a vision of loveliness in her pale mauve gauze wedding dress, finely embroidered with delicate patterns of gold thread. Her thick mass of auburn hair was curled, swept up, and piled on her head. Sofie's mother placed a woven wreath of baby's breath, picked fresh from the Russian steppe, on her daughter's head. As Sofie walked down the aisle of the church, an innocent blush covered her cheeks when she observed the reaction her appearance had on David.

After their vows were consecrated at the village church, a band of merry and boisterous German musicians led the wedding party down the main street of Susannenthal to the home of Phillip and Eliza Steiner, where the *hockzeit* began.

David's older brother, Dobias loved attention, and even more, he loved celebrations. As tradition warranted, he and several of the young, unmarried swanks poured a cup of vodka down the throats of their horses, saving a nip or two for themselves. They lined up at the end of the street, and with great whooping and hollering, the inebriated steeds and riders raced down the street. Dobias and his friends yelled and swatted the flanks of their horses with their hats as they raced, coming to a screeching halt in front of their destination: the wedding *hockzeit*. It was obvious they had a head start on the wedding celebration. From this point, the festivities grew to significant proportions, which many of the guests would not remember the next day—and nor could they remember exactly when the celebration came to an end!

The celebration of the union of David and Sofie lasted for two days. The polka was played nonstop as dancers and revelers skipped, hopped, and twirled, as they shouted, *"Hey Ho Hockzeit."*

At the wedding celebration, David's gaze and smile never left his new wife's face. His deep hazel eyes danced with happiness. "Sofie, my love, I will never forget this day. You are, without doubt, the most beautiful bride in the whole world—and you are mine." Gently, David reached to wind a coppery curl around his finger. He watched with awe as the sun seemed to ignite the glowing color of her hair. He bent closer, burying his nose in the heady lavender scent of her hair, allowing the soft fragrance to fill his senses. With a low groan, David pulled her into his arms. "I think we have stayed here with our wedding guests long enough, come with me."

Finding seclusion, far from the celebration, in the house they had been given, David closed and bolted the door. Sofie reached to unbutton David's shirt. She pulled it from his body and slid her hands gently up the skin of his back. Instantly she pulled back as she turned him around. "David, what is it that I feel on your back?"

David turned slowly not wishing to see what he feared would be Sofie's reaction. He felt her fingertips gently trace the ripples of scarred skin on his back. "Oh, mein Gott; David who did this to you and when? Why didn't you ever tell me?"

"My *Liebchen,* it was something that happened during my service to the czar. I was flogged with leather thongs. We had to run a gauntlet. I have put it behind me, but I must admit I have worried what you would think."

Sofie walked slowly around to face him. Standing on her tiptoes, she reached up and wrapped her hand around the back of his neck, pulling his mouth to hers. "That, my husband, is what I think. I love all of you, including the scars on your back. Never doubt that my love would stop because of something like that. I said my vows today, promising to be your wife. Don't keep me waiting."

~~~~~

The newlyweds set up housekeeping in a small home near that of his parents. Eliza welcomed her son's new wife with open arms. The two women soon developed a mutual bond; they spent months together working side by side in their gardens and houses.

Now that they were married and hoping to start their family, David's mind went back in time to a particular day before they were married. Until now, he had not given any thought about the possibility their children might exhibit Far Eastern physical features, which flowed in the Wagner blood.

He had first learned of this situation earlier in the spring when he and Sofie had gone on a picnic at the foot of the Ural Mountains. David remembered how they had nibbled at their picnic lunch as they rested on a blanket in the shade of linden and aspen trees.

He remembered how Sofie had laid her head in the crook of his arm as they looked up through the canopy of trees. "Oh, David, look how the leaves of the aspen tree dance in the breeze, almost like a thousand silvery green circles quivering and fluttering in the wind." She rolled over and sat up; a serious expression suddenly spread across her face. "David, it has been on my mind and before we become serious about a future together, I must tell you about something terrible, something which happened to my great-grandmother many years ago. It is something that often happened to our people, especially here on the Wiesenseite of the river."

David remembered becoming alarmed because Sofie was so serious. A kaleidoscope of acute maladies blazed through his mind in whirling confusion and alarm, but he held his tongue and allowed her to continue. He pushed himself to a sitting position on the blanket, barely aware of the twitter of orioles high in the trees above them. David took Sofie's delicate hand in his and gave his complete attention to her as she began to tell her grandmother's story, as it was told to her.

"It was a warm summer day when I was a young married woman. Your *Grossvater* and I were living in his family's *Soddy* out on the *Kelga,* tending to our crops. Their land was very near the mountains, and we had all been warned about the occasional brutal attacks by Kirgiz tribesmen from Mongolia. There had been no attacks for a long time, and so we were not as guarded as we should have been.

"I had been working with the hoe in the fields, along with my young, unmarried sister and two other women. Our husbands were driving the camels, farming about a half mile away in another field. We were laughing and working in the rippling afternoon heat. It was a beautiful summer day, and the grain was waving and tossing in the wind like waves on the water. We had tied scarves around our heads, knotting them tightly at the nape of our necks to protect our hair from the sweat and dirt. Suddenly, we were alarmed to feel the ground vibrate under our feet as flocks of birds took flight above our heads. Then we heard the terrifying sound of galloping hooves. Many horses were coming fast and hard, coming from the east. We knew it could only be one thing: a raid from the Ural Mountains, a raid from the fearsome Kirgiz.

"We knew the Kirgiz tribesmen, especially the notorious Kirgiz raiders, were far more dangerous than the Gageezer raiders who came from Siberia to the north of the Volga. The Gageezers only stole from our villages, even though they sometimes also stole women. When the Gageezers raided, we could see them coming across the flat plains and so had time to escape or arm ourselves and fight. But the Kirgiz raiders used surprise, ambush, and the speed of their magnificent horses to attack and do damage to our people. They often emerged suddenly out of the cover of the mountain forests and canyons to raid our villages, kill our men, and rape Die Wolgadeutschen women who worked unaware in the remote fields of the *Kelga*. In the end they stole and did what they came for then rode back, deep into their secluded, nomadic mountain camps.

"Our reaction of fright and fear was immediate; everything seemed to be happening in slow motion as we began to run across the uneven ground of the field to the safe cover of the nearby woods. We could hear the wild whinnying and snorting of the Kirgiz horses as they drew even closer. The rhythmic hammering of the horses' hooves on the packed road seemed to match the pounding of our terrified hearts as we ran. In our panic, we guessed there were twenty or more raiders as the thunderous sound of the horses and screams of the riders entered our field.

"In crazed desperation, we ran from the fields to the cover of the woods and the deep crystal stream that ran down from the snow melt in the mountains. As we reached the edge of the woods, we turned around to see how close they were. We saw the lead rider as his muscular mount reared up and pawed the air.

The leader's appearance was fierce—something out of our worst nightmare. He was riding an immense ebony stallion, and his long hair was flying as black and wild as the mane and tail of the horse. The raider viciously sliced the air with his horrifying, long saber as he and the others spotted us and rode in our direction. He was screaming and screaming. It took me years to forget the sound of his screaming.

"We were deep in the woods, near the stream, as I shouted to my little sister, 'Helga, run, run fast, and jump there into the stream. Make your body sink, and hide in the reeds and willows that grow along the side. Keep your body under the water—only leave your mouth on the surface to breathe. Stay along the cover of the banks. Stay under the water until they are gone.'

"I knew this was her only chance to escape harm. I purposely shrieked loudly as I ran in the opposite direction, hoping to draw the riders away from her. The horses were so close now. I could smell the lather, and I imagined I felt their breath on my neck. I ran and ran, weaving this way and that through the woods, hoping the horsemen couldn't follow through the close-growing trees. My legs felt like lead, and my lungs burned from lack of air; my heart felt like it would burst from terror alone. Somewhere along the way, my head scarf came loose and was lost; my long hair fell down my back and snagged in the branches as I ran through the woods.

"I heard horses directly behind me, running in the soft mud along the stream; some were splashing across the water, looking for the other women. I glanced back over my shoulder as the black stallion bore down on me. Suddenly, the leader of the raiders leapt from his horse, throwing me to the ground. His body pinned me into the soft loam of the alder grove. The breath was knocked from my body, and I remember feeling like I could barely breathe.

"I had no opportunity to fight him. He was too strong, and he glared arrogantly at me as I lay helpless beneath him. I remember thinking his violent-looking, eyes looked like hot, black coals.

Malicious laughter rolled from his snarling mouth as he pulled an evil-looking curved knife from his waist and cut my field dress from my body. With his other hand, he violently seized me by my loose hair. I remember my head falling back, exposing my neck. I feared he was going to cut my throat. Instead, he threw me to the ground. The last thing I knew, he was on top of me. Thankfully, I must have hit my head and fainted.

"The next thing I was aware of was lying on my back. Slowly, I opened my eyes, not believing I was actually alive. I remember looking up through the trees as sunlight filtered down through the branches and soft green leaves, with fingers of silver and gold sunlight. I saw white tufts of clouds floating in a beautiful blue sky. I thought I had died and was looking into heaven.

"Then I tasted blood and felt it running down the corner of my mouth. As I moved to wipe it away, the rest of my body screamed with pain. I felt more blood, warm and slippery on my thighs. I knew I had been raped. The pain that throbbed between my legs was terrible. It took the breath from my chest. I lay very still, hoping that everything would stop hurting. I tried to pull my shredded dress up to cover myself. My violated body throbbed with pain. It was so bad when I moved that I fainted once more.

"I remember opening my eyes again and seeing my little sister Helga standing over me, sobbing and wringing her hands. Her dress and her hair were dripping wet from hiding in the stream. When she saw my eyes open, she ran to my side and stayed there until my husband and the other men were alerted by another woman who survived.

"They came running with their hoes and shovels, but the damage had been done. They found the other two women near the edge of the field. They were dead. Their throats were slashed, and they too had been raped. My husband and the other men never forgave themselves for not hearing the raiders and trying to save us.

"Nine months later, I gave birth. It was my third child and my first daughter. Her head was covered with glossy black hair. Her skin was the color of lightly browned butter, and her eyes were brown with a very slight slant to the outer corners. My husband and I went on with our lives. We tried to forget the past. It was over and done. Nothing could or would be done to erase it. Our daughter was accepted with our love as a child of God and a fact of our life on the Russian steppe."

David remembered when Sofie finished telling her great-grandmother's story that she sat very still with her hands folded in her lap. Her head was bent, and her eyes were cast to the ground as she took a deep breath and then continued speaking. "It is important that you know, David. I carry Kirgiz blood, inherited from my mother as she did from her mother. It is where my brother gets his black hair and exotic eyes. Some of our children may bear their features. The features will not be strong because they have been diluted by three generations. Is this a problem to you?"

He reached to wipe the tears from the beautiful face of the woman he loved. "Oh, Sofie, my love, of course it does not matter to me. We will be blessed by any and all children our Lord gives to our union. We know each child will carry the blood of many generations before them. Perhaps that is where you inherited your beautiful auburn hair—a mixture of the German blonde and the Far Eastern black. It will not worry us, and we will speak of it no more."

He stood and laughed then extended a question of his own. "Sofie, if you think you bring a problem to our union, what about my eye? I have only one good eye."

Sofie's mouth opened with shock, and her hand flew to stroke his right cheek. "Oh mein, Gott in Himmel, David, do not be so foolish. I love you for you, not for the eye that is missing. Was I not by your side when your eye became infected with the grain beard? Even when the doctor had to remove it and you experienced days of discomfort adjusting to the glass eye, I did not leave your side."

Remembering how brave and comforting she had been, David smiled as he stood and pulled Sofie into his arms. "Well, then it is settled. Neither of us is perfect, yet we love each other, and someday we shall be married." They never spoke of that day or had the discussion again.

~~~~~~

Several months after David and Sofie were married; Phillip asked them to move out on the *Kelga*, to tend to the summer crops and livestock. It proved to be a wonderful time. They spent their days working side by side in the fields, and their nights were consumed with uninterrupted love. When they came back to Susannenthal in the fall, they were expecting a child.

David had been thinking seriously about what he wanted to do to make a living. He was not fond of farming. He had found a store for sale on the main street, Landstrasse. It had living quarters in the back.

David bought the storefront with a portion of his grandfather's inheritance and opened it as a bakery. He wasn't a baker, but he was an astute businessman. He hired his sisters Mollie and Louise to do the kitchen work. They were known for their superb baking skills. After a few months, David noticed that his wife was becoming discontented with little to do, being pregnant, and living in the back of the bakery.

"Sofie, I have been thinking about another way to make more money. I would like to sell other things in the bakery. We need special containers for people to take large quantities of baked goods home with them. The customers would buy and reuse the containers or buy new ones each time they come to the bakery. I want you to make your superbly woven baskets as the containers. It is so perfect. No woman in Susannenthal weaves as fine a basket as you, and I would even offer for sale some of the straw field hats you have designed and woven."

A bright smile spread across Sofie's face as she digested her husband's idea. "Oh, David, I love the idea. Weaving with straw and reeds is a relaxation to me. It is something I look forward to doing whenever I have a chance. To be able to sell my hats and baskets is even better. Even after the baby comes, I can still weave. Yes, of course, I will be very happy to weave baskets and hats for your store."

Their combined ideas and talent proved to be a big moneymaking venture for the bakery. Sofie's baskets became famous, and her field hats were especially good sellers. They kept sun and rain off the heads they covered yet allowed a cooling breeze to enter. Sofie was happy to contribute to her husband's business; she often daydreamed about making beautiful hats for fashionable city ladies. In her spare time, Sofie worked on sketches of her ideas but kept them secluded in a drawer.

~~~~~

As the ice began to crack and move in the Volga, their first daughter entered their lives in March of 1900. David named her after his natural mother, Theraisa. When he first laid eyes on her, tears rolled down his high cheekbones, "Ahhh, Sofie, she is a beautiful child. She looks like her mother and already has sun-kissed hair like yours."

Cradling her daughter in the bend of her arm, Sofie gazed down at Theraisa in wonder. "JA, and Raisa has your eyes, my David—deep-set hazel eyes."

Picking her up and lifting his daughter over his head in offering to the heavens, David turned to Sofie with a twinkle in his eye. "Sure, she has the color of my eyes, but she has *two* of them instead of one, like her papa!"

In the next four years, they were blessed with two more daughters. Their second daughter they named Maria, after Sofie's grandmother, and two years later, Elizabeth or Lizzie, was named after David's adopted mother.

~~~~~

Each fall, when it came time to cut the red wheat, it was tradition for Philip and his sons to walk the fields in staggered lines, each swinging his own sharpened scythe. Women or girls usually followed behind, gathering and tying the long shafts of wheat into bundles. After the bundled wheat was loaded into the wagons, they drove them to their village *neft*.

The enormous Dutch-type windmills could be seen for miles away as they rose majestically from the banks of the river. The windmills were used primarily to crush the grain or rye with huge stones.

David enjoyed raising sunflowers. It was also a good crop for Die Wolgadeutschen. When it came time to crush the seeds, the farmers took them to a special mill built for sunflower seeds only, where they harvested the seed into oil, which most Volga women preferred to use when cooking.

Every fall, Sofie drove the wagon by herself out to the *Kelga* during the wheat harvest to search for extra-long shafts of grain and river grass. She filled her wagon with the special shafts as the men wielded their scythes. After Sofie returned with her treasure of long straw stalks and grass reeds, she stored them on a high shelf in the barn until she was ready to use them. When she was ready to weave, she soaked the stalks of straw or grass in water for a day or overnight to soften them. When they were pliable, she removed them and braided or wove them into sturdy field hats as well as different sizes and styles of baskets. The cut or short straw that wasn't used in some way was stuffed into mattress ticking or fed to the animals. Nothing went to waste.

~~~~~

One winter evening when David sat in his chair reading his Bible by lantern light, Sofie finished weaving a hat, stood, and crossed the room to where he sat. "David, excuse me a moment. I wish to speak to you. I would like to train with your mother and learn the trade as a midwife. Since I have given birth to three children of my own and have assisted several times in other births, it is something that interests me and that I would like to do. Besides, I have been told I have a special talent with the birthing herbs. Would you object to this?" Looking up from his Bible, David took a moment to consider his wife's request. "No, Sofie, of course I have no objection. The only question is who will take care of the children if I am busy in the store, and you need to attend to a birthing mother?"

"I have it all arranged with my younger sister. She has agreed to come to our home and care for our daughters if I need her."

Rising from his chair, David embraced his wife. "This idea is fine with me, and I am sure you will be a much sought-after midwife. I must also tell you, Sofie, your baskets and hats are becoming so famous, I am now referred to as 'the hat maker's husband.' Have you heard this gossip in the village?"

Her eyes wide with wonder, Sofie laughed and replied, "Oh no, I have not heard this gossip, and I laugh because you are so much more than that. On the other hand, perhaps you should not forget this particular title in times when you are feeling full of yourself."

David had a unique method of disciplining his daughters without raising his voice or his hand. Whenever they misbehaved, he would close his good eye and stare unblinking with the glass eye at the disobedient child, causing her to cringe and seek a hiding place.

The next evening as David was preparing for bed, his oldest daughter, Theraisa, stood watching him as he removed the glass eye and put it in a cup of salt water. "Papa, were you born with one glass eye and one real eye?"

Laughing at the inquisitive nature of his daughter, David affectionately ran his hand over her silky, blonde hair. "Oh, my Raisa, you ask so many questions. No, I was not born with the glass eye. I was born with two real eyes like your own, but one got hurt when I was a young man, and the doctor had to remove it." Raisa looked intently at her father and then at the glass eye that lay soaking in the cup of salt water. "Papa, where do you keep your real eye? Can you see with that glass eye? Why do you take it out at night? Can I hold it sometime, Papa? Can I?"

"My little Raisa, we had to throw the real eye away because it was sick and didn't work anymore. I take the glass eye out at night to clean it and to rest the eyehole. No, I cannot see out of the glass eye, but God is great because I have one good eye left to see your pretty face."

~~~~~

In early December 1904, the villages along the Volga were mildly alarmed with news of growing political unrest and inner conflict in the larger Russian cities. There was talk of a man, Lenin and his work with an antagonist group called the Communists. *Die Wolgadeutschen* heard frequent and disturbing news regarding the rising number of clashes between the czar's military and small groups of anarchists who roamed the country, bombing trains and government establishments. The czar sent his Cossacks after the bands of revolutionaries, hoping to destroy their efforts, but the violence and political unrest only increased.

News traveled slowly to the outer steppes of the Volga, but more *Die Wolgadeutschen* made arrangements to leave their homes after hearing of "Bloody Sunday." In the city of St. Petersburg on January 22, 1905, an Orthodox priest led 150,000 citizens toward the palace in protest of the czar. Their intention was to present their petition of reform; however, the czar's troops panicked and opened fire on the marchers. When the smoke settled, ninety- two citizens lay bleeding and dead on the snow-packed streets of the city. Normally, protestors were arrested and shipped off to Siberia or another such place from which they would not return.

"Bloody Sunday" would later be recognized as the day from which a revolution was born.

One evening after the children were in bed, Sofie broached the subject. "David, I do not understand why the people are protesting, and now we hear that Czar Nicholas II and the Empress Alexandra are becoming more intolerable of the unrest. The new laws are harsh and seem to make the people even angrier than before."[16]

David put down his Bible and looked up with unmistakable concern. "Sofie, all of these political games are beyond what I understand." He stood, stretched his arms, and began to pace the floor. Sofie was shocked by the serious tone his voice had taken. "Sofie, I am more concerned that the war with Japan is growing in intensity, and since I am yet in the reserves, the czar may call me to serve again. I have been giving our options much thought. Also, there is talk that units of Cossacks have been seen crossing the Volga on their way to attack the back door of Japan. We would be wise to be on guard, as there is talk of several run-ins on both sides of the Volga with marauding Cossacks looking for food and good horses."

Two nights later, David and Sofie had gone to bed at the usual time, Sofie fell asleep quickly, but David was troubled. He laid on his back watching as their bedroom was illuminated briefly by blazing flashes of lightning, followed by the sharp claps of thunder as it rolled across the moonless sky. Suddenly, there was a different sound! It was closer and more immediate—the sound of glass breaking at the front of their bakery. Both David and Sofie sat up in bed as angry shouts of men and gunshots filled the night air, integrating with the lightning and thunder.

In a flash, they jumped from bed and hastily threw on their clothes. Sofie reached into the baby's cradle and scooped the sleeping infant up into her arms. They moved quickly through the dark room, to where their older daughters slept. "Raisa, wake up. Hurry, sweetheart, the storm is so loud outside; we are going to sleep in the cellar." David took Raisa and Maria by their hands as they soundlessly crossed the room to where the trapdoor was hidden under a rug.

David said, "Raisa, can you pull the rug away so I can open the door." With a powerful pull, David opened the trapdoor. Sofie quickly climbed down the steps followed by Raisa, who held onto Maria's little hand, leading her down the stairs.

David instructed them: "Now I want you to be very quiet and play hide down here in the cellar. Mama will light a candle when I close the door. Remember, no crying—no talking. I love you!"

"Papa, don't go. Don't leave us down here. I'm afraid, Papa!" Raisa tried to follow her father up the narrow steps. David turned and kissed her quickly. "Raisa, stop it now; be a brave girl. You are the big sister, and you must be strong so your sisters don't cry. You can do that, can't you? Pretend that Mama, your sisters, and you are playing hide. I will be back in a few minutes."

Closing the trapdoor quickly, David covered the area with the rag rug. He struck a light to a lantern and moved cautiously across the room. Slowly, he unlocked the heavy wooden door between the bakery and his house. Holding the lantern in one hand, he stood in the doorway. He could see several filthy, uniformed men hastily filling sacks with bread and rolls from the shelves. They took everything they could carry as they shouted threatening words into the darkness. The men appeared to be ravenous as they stuffed as much bread down their throats as was crammed into their bags.

The next thing David saw was an impressive whip hanging from one of the looter's waist. Reality exploded in his mind. Cossacks! Without a moment's hesitation, David knew what he had to do and do quickly.

He had not forgotten the possessive, even brutal mindset of the Cossack soldier. Hiding his own fear as best he could and using a strong and confident voice, David addressed the soldiers. "Friends, please take what you need. There is no need to break the glass or the cases. What I have is yours, for the cause of the greatest soldiers in all of Russia. I assume you are on your way to an important battle and have need of my food. My bread is the best you will find on the Volga. Take what you need!" For good measure he quickly added, "I served with a unit of Cossack soldiers as a horse tender in 1896 on the Turkish border."

A brutal-looking, unshaven Cossack glanced up momentarily as David spoke and then raised his whip in the air as he bellowed, "Your bread will do good this day, as we make ready to cross the Urals to teach the Japanese infidels a Russian lesson!" Just as quickly, they were gone, out into the street and on to the next store and the next.

Walking with caution, David crossed the floor of his bakery and closed what was left of the front door. He attempted to repair and secure it for the night, thankful the storm and band of Cossacks had passed. Carrying his lantern, he stepped over the smashed shelves as he hurried back into their living quarters, closing and bolting the inner door behind him.

He sank heavily onto a wood chair and bent forward, covering his face with trembling hands. David's shoulders shook, but no sound came from his mouth. Almost as quickly, he stood again. Throwing the rag rug to the side, David lifted the trapdoor. The first thing he saw ripped through his heart: the terrified, tearstained faces of his wife and little daughters. As soon as Raisa saw her father, she broke from her mother's arms and scurried up the ladder. She flung her trembling little body into his strong embrace. David wrapped his arms around her and buried his face in the soft fragrance of her blonde hair.

~~~~~

Sleep was slow to return as David lay awake, staring into the darkness. He knew he had a life-changing decision to make. It was something that had been on his mind for several months.

He had listened to other men, some who had left the villages of their birth, some who were thinking about emigration out of Russia. After the incident tonight, there was only one recourse, to keep themselves and their daughters safe—*leave Russia!* Recently, David had heard there were over 1,790,000 Germans living in Russia, and 76 percent were Lutheran. Many were leaving the Volga for the same reasons that continued to haunt David. Now was the time to make the arrangements—now, while they still had time to legally leave Russia and the unpredictable future.

The next afternoon as the children were napping, Sofie was busy weaving her baskets at the table when David approached her. "Sofie, after what occurred last night, I have a serious decision to speak to you about. I believe living here is going to become unbearable, and many people will die, regardless whether they are with one side of the revolution or the other. Do you realize that even our own people and villages along the Volga are not going to be spared?"

David knelt before her, taking her delicate hand in his. "My *Liebchen*, we will only be safe, our daughters will only be safe, if we leave Susannenthal and get out of Russia!" Sofie started to speak, and David held his finger against her trembling lips. "Let me finish, Sofie. I am considering emigration to America. Many people from our village, from the Volga, have already left. Several families have written, urging us all to leave within the next year while the borders are yet open. Carl is thinking strongly about it as well. Your brother-in-law, Karl Klinger, is already living in America, in Michigan. It would be easy to put his name down as our sponsor."

David paused long enough to glance at Sofie. Her face was like translucent white stone, and her eyes were wide with fear. David stood and paced the floor; his own face was pale and somber as he spoke quickly and forcefully. "I know this is the only home we have ever known, Sofie, and our parents live here with much family. But I also know in my heart, it is no longer safe. We must escape with our daughters while we can.

"The Russian government is taking back more and more of the things they promised to us. They are taking over our schools and discouraging our religion. We have not had good harvests for ten years, and the government is beginning to take even more of our harvests and animals too. There seems to be no end to it all, and it only becomes worse year after year. Do you understand how dangerous it is becoming? And besides, I am still in the reserves, and with this war with Japan, I could be called back for military service. That is the last thing I ever want to do!"

Her eyes were wide with disbelief. Sofie shook with trepidation as she rose unsteadily to her feet. "Nein, David, nein. You ask too much. Surely there is another way to stay safe without leaving all we have ever known. I can't believe you would even consider this. Oh, nein!

"I love my family too much to take their grandchildren from them. The thought that I would never feel their embrace or look upon their faces again is too much to ask of me—too much."

David tried to take her into his arms, but she pounded on his chest and pushed him away. Sofie turned and blindly ran from their house and down the street in the direction of her parents' home.

Turning toward the window, David watched as Sofie half-walked, half-ran down the packed-dirt street. Filled with guilt and foreboding, not knowing what else to do, he fell to his knees and, lifting his face to the heavens, he began to pray. *Dear Gott in Himmel—hear my cry, hear my need. Please, soften Sofie's heart so she sees the wisdom and the need of my request. I believe with my whole heart that you are speaking to me through your word. I believe that what I ask of my wife is the only way to keep our family safe from certain harm. Give me strength to do what I must. This I ask in the name of your Son, Jesus. Amen!*

When he finished praying, he felt his own tears running down his face and falling to the floor Sofie scrubbed every morning. He didn't know how long he had been on his knees, but rising, he realized he needed his work to occupy his mind with other thoughts. As he moved toward the bakery door, he was startled to hear the rear door to their house open. David turned as Sofie walked slowly, hesitantly into the room. She stood with her head down as her shoulders shook with silent sobs. Her face was pale, and her eyes were red and swollen from crying.

They stood in silence, facing each other from across the small room. Finally, eyes cast down to the floor and her throat tight with emotion, Sofie's words came in choking spasms. "JA, David, my father tells me to return to my husband and do what he asks. You are the head of our house, and I must obey your decision. But, David, he also was crying as he told me this. My mother was not even able to look at me. My father tells me that what you say is probably true." Sofie took a moment to wipe the tears from her eyes and blow her nose.

"But dear *Gott in Himmel,* David, I still don't know if I can do what you ask! How can you do this? You love your parents as much as I do." She put her hands over her face again as her body convulsed with hiccupping sobs.

Crossing the room, David enfolded his wife in his arms. They stood together until she stopped crying, and then David tried again to reason with her. "Sofie, my love, of course I don't want to leave our families either, but the events which have happened and the threats of what is to come are making this decision for us. Of course I love my parents, but I love you and our daughters more, and I am responsible for keeping you safe and happy. It is not only for ourselves that we must leave."

Pulling away from her husband and with eyes wide, Sofie asked, "I don't even know where this America is—is it far? How will we travel there? Why this America? Why not go to Germany?"

Sofie moved to stare out the window. Turning back to face her husband, she implored, "David, oh David, isn't there some other way? It is true that we may be safer, but will we be happier? I truly do not think I will ever completely understand what you say and what this means, but I am putting my trust in God and in you my husband as I should!"

The next morning after they had finished eating breakfast and their daughters were busy playing, Sofie waited to speak in private to David. There were deep shadows under her swollen eyes, and she trembled as she fought to control her emotions. Their two older daughters left the apartment to go into the bakery to help their aunts. Sofie remained at the table, cradling her cup of tea in her hands, her face grim and full of hurt. "David, I have thought of nothing more throughout the night than what you told me yesterday. It is not what I want to do. It is not how I want to live the rest of my life—without the love and security of my family. I have no other choice. I will follow wherever you go my husband, but it is with uncertainty and a heavy heart that I do what you ask." It pained David to see the concern and dread written all over her face. He felt the heavy weight of responsibility for his decision, which he knew would be with him until he drew his final breath.

"How do we get money to travel? We cannot sell the bakery because it is now part of the Russian Mir system. We have personal things we can sell, but will it be enough?" Sofie stood from the table and moved again to look out the window at the familiar village scene.

His eyes were bright with faith and confidence as David replied, "Sofie, I know we will need money and that we cannot sell the bakery. However, I have half of my grandfather's inheritance left. We will sell what we can and use that money to buy our tickets for the train and the ship passage to America. With my inheritance, we will have the means to begin in America. We also will have eighteen dollars, which the Volga Relief Society gives to each family who is leaving the village. I do not think money will be a problem to us, my darling. However, we will have to be frugal and careful in how we spend our money."

Opening his Bible David cleared his throat and said, "I know we are right because for the last three days, I have opened my Bible for morning reading, and these passages have first met my eyes. Listen to the Word of our Lord. I believe He is telling us what we need to do. The first day I read this passage: *'I have set before you, life and death, blessing and cursing; therefore choose life; that you may live.'*

"Still feeling doubt, the second morning, this was the second verse I read: *'I know your works. See, I have before you an open door, and no one can shut it.'*

David turned the pages, and with a smile he said, "This is the verse I read this morning, and it *is* a sign: *'I will go before you and make the crooked places straight.'* We are compelled to walk the path of faith and courage, my Sofie. Our lives will not change unless we make the decision, unless we have the faith and courage to take the first step."

Sofie's face was a rigid mask of compliance as she spoke, desperate to change the subject, if only for a time. "David, do you realize it is almost Christmas? I do not want to tell our children about leaving until after Christmas. I want this to be a Christmas they will remember—or least Raisa will remember. The babies are too young, I know. I don't even think Raisa will totally understand she will never see her grandparents again. Can we do this—have this one last Christmas with our families before we leave?"

David nodded his head in agreement. "JA, Sofie, I do agree with you. I had almost forgotten it is the season of *Weihnachten.* I think we should tell both of our families of our plans so we can all have a special Christmas before we leave. We will go together to tell our parents of our decision tomorrow. It will be hard for all of us, but I pray they will understand and send us off with their blessings."

Suddenly his face lit up with a possibility. "Sofie, perhaps we can convince them to come with us. Also, I am told we have to go through much government papers first to get permission to leave. So I believe it will not be until the spring when we leave Susannenthal—at least not until travel is possible. That would give everyone time to make arrangements, JA?"

They invited both parents to their home for supper the next evening. After they were finished with the meal, David wiped his hands on his napkin and pushed back from the table as he rose from his chair. He stated firmly, "Sofie and I have asked you to supper this night because we have made an important decision, and we believe you should know of it. We hope you will understand our reasons and give us your blessing." David looked at Sofie for emotional reinforcement. His eyes scanned those sitting at his table; every face was ashen.

Bowing his head, David closed his eyes as he offered a silent and brief prayer for strength and then explained their reasons for leaving. David knew if he stopped now, he wouldn't have the fortitude to continue. "We have decided to leave in the spring with two other families from Susannenthal. Please consider coming with us to freedom and safety. I can secure all the necessary papers on your behalf."

Phillip closed his eyes for a moment. "My son, we are too old to leave our home. We will stay, and with the help of the Lord, we will survive whatever is coming."

Sofie wiped the tears from her swollen eyes. "This will be our last Christmas together, and we want to make it very special. With your help, we will make it a *Weihnachten* to remember. Will you help us do this?"

Herr Wagner stood; his face was flushed red with emotion. "You are our children, and we want for you what you think is best. You are both adults, able to make good decisions. We are most sad you will be leaving. It is almost unthinkable we will not see our grandchildren grow up. You realize that for us, your leaving is like a death." He hastily added, "But we give you our blessing, and it will give us peace to know you are safe in America. We promise to keep in touch through letters over the years to come."

The next day David traveled with Solomon Klinger and Friedrich Weber to Saratov with the personal papers needed to secure permission from the *Gemeinde* for them to leave the country. They discovered it would take approximately three months to secure passports from the Russian provincial government.

~~~~~

Christmas on the Volga was the most joyous of all traditional German holidays. Children and parents alike anticipated and planned for the special event with particular elation. Sofie spent many days with her mother and sisters, preparing an assortment of special *Weihnachten* baked goods. Frau Wagner's kitchen was filled with the aroma of baking *Kuchen—Ebbel Kucha, Yaketa Kucha, Rivvel Kucha, Kringel,* along with beet sugar cookie bells and angels.

Raisa sat with her cousins on the braided rag rug that covered the wood floor. They were busy making silver-and-gold paper and woven grass ornaments for their big family Christmas tree. Her older cousin teased Raisa and asked, "Do you think *Belsnickel* will visit our house on Christmas Eve with his pack of willow switches? Will he have one especially for you?"

Raisa's eyes opened wide as she quickly replied, "I have been very good this year, and I think it is you who should fear his visit!" The children all laughed with glee that was laced with a healthy dose of fear of *Belsnickle*. They knew stories by heart of the fearful old man who always arrived at the door on Christmas Eve, dressed in a shaggy cap and a worn sheepskin coat turned inside out.

Finally, after many days of preparation and whispered secrets, it was Christmas Eve. Everybody dressed in their best clothes for the traditional church service. David and the male relatives wore their finest *Filzstiffle* boots and *Bollschupkas* or heavy wool coats topped off with their best *Carduces* or Russian caps. Sofie and the older women wore black babushkas while the younger girls wore white. They all wore long wool skirts and their warmest winter coats, with long, black stockings and leather boots.

Raisa held tightly to her father's hand as they entered the church. Her little feet had to move twice as fast to keep up with his long strides. Raisa's eyes opened wide at the sight of the twelve-foot Christmas tree at the base of the altar. "Oh, Papa, look how beautiful it is. The candles are all different colors and are burning so brightly." She tugged on David's sleeve and began pulling him to the glorious tree to get a closer look at the special gold carousel ornament, with five glistening candles burning underneath. "Papa, why does the carousel turn around? Is it magic?"

David smiled as he bent down to look at the amazing sight. "No, Raisa, it is not magic. The heat from the burning candles makes the carousel turn slowly. It is a beautiful thing, is it not?"

After they were seated, Raisa pulled her father's face down closer to hers as she whispered, "Papa, why is Uncle Carl standing by the tree with that long pole?"

David quickly answered in a low voice, "Raisa, see the wet cloth on the end? He will put out a fire if one starts from a candle. Now hush and listen to the *Schulemeister* as he is ready to begin the program." The schoolmaster read the story of Christ's birth. When he finished, he motioned to the older children. They rose from their seats and marched up the aisle to stand in front of the altar. One by one, they recited assigned and memorized Bible verses. When they were finished, the organ began to play, and the congregation joined in singing the beloved "Silent Night, Holy Night" and "Oh, Tannenbaum." After the service, all of the people hurried to their waiting sleighs. The crisp night sky rang with church bells and whips cracking through the frosty air as teams of wooly Kalmuck horses raced over snowy streets. Everyone was in a rush to get home because they were all expecting two special guests that evening.

As the sleighs arrived at their destinations, the women and girls piled out and hurried into the warmth of the house. The men and boys drove the hard-breathing horses to the barn to secure them for the night. They worked quickly, as they too looked forward to the warmth of the house and the tables filled with steaming festive food. Another inspiring thought was that of retrieving the vodka that had been buried in the snow earlier that day.

David and his family went to the home of Phillip and Eliza Steiner, where the Wagner family joined them. The festive house was brimming over with people and the air was fragrant with baked Kuchen, cookies, and fresh-cut evergreens. Frau Wagner sat out cups of hot apple cider and cinnamon for the children.

Phillip motioned for Herr Wagner and David to come with him. "JA, I need much help to dig our bottles of vodka from the snow drift." Excited laughter rang through the cozy house as the men eagerly hurried outside. David commented, "JA, it is the best when it is cold as the ice." After digging the vodka from the snow, the three men scurried back inside the warmth of the house with their frosty treasure.

Eliza carefully arranged the special gold-rimmed glasses for the Christmas vodka. "Who would like to have raspberry flavor added to their vodka?" All of the women raised their hands.

The men were enjoying their second or third glass of the icy-cold liquor as the women cautiously sipped theirs. Laughter and good cheer filled the house, but there was a strong undertone of sadness, on this, their last Christmas together. Oblivious, Raisa and her cousins sat on the floor, happily eating Christmas cookies; suddenly they were startled by a loud knock at the door. Eliza rushed to the door with a sly smile on her face and opened it wide.

There stood the fearsome *Belsnickle*. The youngest children ran to hide behind their mother's skirts; the older children's eyes grew wide with concern. They remembered that he was there to question children about their disobedience over the past year. The older ones also knew that the bag of willow switches was used on occasion to punish a particularly naughty child.

Belsnickle questioned several children before coming to Raisa. He peered down at her, his bushy eyebrows almost covering the black beads that were his eyes. Raisa felt her hands tremble. She was too scared to look up into his intimidating face as his raspy voice questioned her. "Child, I understand that you do not like to drink your milk."

Raisa was horrified as a single tear trickled down her silky cheek. She bravely lifted her face to the man. "Nein Herr *Belsnickel*—but...but sometimes I do drink it. I promise I will do better." He smiled and patted her on the head. After a brief visit, the *Belsnickle* bid them all *"Frohe Weihnachten"* (Merry Christmas)—and he was gone out the door.

Raisa's Opa Wagner appeared soon after *Belsnickel* left. She rushed to his side all aglow. "Oh, Opa, you missed *Belsnickel*. He was very scary, and he asked me why I did not like to drink my milk. How does he know what each child does that is not good?" Herr Wagner just smiled and shook his head as he walked away, eager for another cup of icy vodka.

~~~~~

Suddenly they heard a sharp rap at the window. David crossed the room in long strides, reached the door, and opened it wide. As if borne on the winter breeze, a beautiful, young woman gracefully swept into the cozy home filled with Christmas spirit and love to last a lifetime.

Raisa's eyes were large with wonder as she whispered shyly into her mother's ear, "Oh, Mama, *Khristkindye* looks like a magic fairy in her long, white gown and veil."

Raisa's large hazel eyes were bright as *Khristkindye* finally moved in front of her. Smiling, she bent down and handed Raisa a fruit-filled candy, a cherished red apple, and cookies that looked vaguely familiar. She reached into her bag and pulled out another gift for the child—a beautiful, handmade leather doll with real hair. She gently placed the doll in Raisa's uplifted hands. The child was speechless as she clutched the doll to her chest. Raisa noticed that every child was given a handmade toy crafted from wood or leather. Before she departed, *Kristkindye* asked each child to recite a short prayer, and then she floated out the open door.

Sofie's mother drew her aside. "Sofie, I want you to have my carved Linden wood box filled with lavender powder. I know how much you like the powder, and I want you to have it." Emotions weighed Sofie's words of acceptance as tears filled her green eyes. She didn't trust herself to speak as she held her mother in her arms.

Eliza Steiner gave Sofie a specially prepared bag of birthing herbs to take with her to America. Sofie put her arms around her mother-in-law. "Thank you for your thoughtful gift. I will think of you each time I use them to help a mother in her time."

Phillip Steiner clapped his hands for attention. Then he raised his glass of vodka. "I make a toast to my son and his wife: *Frohe Weihnachten und eis Guten Rutsch ins 1905.*" Every adult lifted their glass and through many tears wished David and Sofie a Merry Christmas and a good slide into 1905.

The hour grew late, and David and Sofie scooped their little ones up in their arms and carried them out into the cold Russian night.

Sofie waited until they were home in bed before she allowed her emotions to overcome her. With her face hidden in her hands, she sobbed. "Oh, David, it is much harder than I ever dreamed. I'm sorry to cry, but I am afraid. I am afraid to leave my home, and I am afraid of what will happen to us. I know my faith should sustain me and my love and confidence in you as well, but I am weak. Please forgive me, my husband."

She cried herself to sleep that night and the next as well. David did his best to assure and console her, but he had to admit he was not having an easy time of it either. There were questions in his mind—questions for which he had no answers.

~~~~~

Sofie was kept busy for weeks, going through all that they owned and making decisions on what to take and what to leave. She packed four trunks, secretly stowing away a few irreplaceable family heirlooms. Before she closed the trunks, she added one final thing: the handmade box filled with her mother's lavender powder. Sofie's delicate fingers traced the intricate carvings of the Christmas gift from her mother.

It was not easy for Sofie and David to make the many hard, sensible decisions about taking, leaving, or selling their possessions. They made the difficult choices and finally packed only what clothing and personal items they would need to sustain them for a year.

The young couple wasn't surprised to learn their parents had made a final decision not to leave the land of their birth. This was their home, and they preferred to ride the waves of whatever might be on the political and military horizon. This was usually the case along the Volga. The young left and the old stayed behind unable to break with their heritage and memories.

The moment of their final good-bye came all too soon. David and Sofie visited her parents and family the day before they planned to leave. Trying desperately to hold back his emotion, Herr Wagner shook David's hand and slapped him on the back. "David, take care of my daughter and our beautiful granddaughters. May God go with you on your journey and bless your destiny. You will always be in our hearts and our prayers."

Holding their thirteen-month-old baby in her arms, Sofie's porcelain complexion was blotchy from relentless tears that drizzled down her face. She did nothing to stop them. There were too many emotions to control. The incessant knowledge that she probably would never see her parents again in this life constantly tormented her mind and heart. She buried her face in the handkerchief as great gasping sobs poured from deep inside. *As long as I live, I will never forget this scene here today, with everybody crying the cries of the final good-bye.*

David took Sofie in his arms and held her tight as he murmured in her ear, "Sweet wife, please try and calm yourself. You are frightening our daughters, and I know I cannot deal with four crying females."

Back in the wagon, they rode in silence down the street to Phillip and Eliza Steiner's home. There were no more tears because they were all emotionally drained. Raisa stood straight and tall in the wagon behind her father with her soft, little hand resting on his shoulder, a grim expression never leaving her little face. Her younger sister Maria was bundled onto the seat, oblivious to the significance of the wagon ride.

The Steiner family sat waiting on their front porch, waiting with palpable dread for their son's wagon to turn the corner and pull up in front of their home. When that moment came, Phillip rose from his seat and walked down the path to meet his son and daughter-in-law. Eliza remained in her chair. She wasn't sure her legs would support her. David and Sofie climbed down, lifting their daughters from the wagon bed, and internally braced themselves to say good-bye.

Phillip embraced him as if it were their last embrace. After kissing Sofie and his granddaughters, Phillip whispered huskily into David's ear, "Godspeed, my son. Know that you were the light of our life, a wonderful gift from God to our house and our lives. Stay safe, prosper, and live happily with your family. Keep them in the straight path of our Lord, and remember to give thanks as He watches over you. I will see you again in our heavenly home. I have this bag of our hearty red wheat for you to take with you to your new land. Sow the 'seed of the Volga,' and remember your homeland." Phillip turned quickly as tears of heartbreak and doubt rolled down his weathered face. He had said all he could manage. His throat tightened, and with an anguished sob, he stumbled up the path and into the quiet sanctuary of his home. David put the bag of seed inside his coat as his own throat constricted.

~~~~~

Early the next morning just before the sun climbed over the mountains to the east, David opened his Bible for his daily reading and felt a warm, secure peace course through him as he read: "Whether you turn to the right or to the left, your ears will hear a voice behind you, saying; *'This is the way, walk in it.'*" He closed the Bible and folded his hands in prayer. When he finished, he turned to his wife and daughters. "It is time to go to the church for our last communion and the farewell blessing of our pastor and the congregation."

After an emotional final communion, they returned home and waited for David's brother Carl to drive them to the Saratov train depot. He arrived moments later, and David began to pack their traveling trunks into the wagon bed. David turned, taking one last look at the village where he was born and grew up. He felt an innate need to record the final visual reminders of his life. He looked past the roof lines of the village. Far in the distance lay the massive blue ridge of the Ural Mountains. The last thing David thought of was the cemetery where his mother was buried. He said a silent good-bye to her.

Carl and David sat in the front seat as Carl took the reins and drove the lead wagon toward the central village courtyard. It was their *Die Wolgadeutschen* tradition to gather, to say good-bye to the *Ausziehende*, to those who were leaving forever.[17]

In all, three families were leaving Susannenthal that day; they drove their wagons slowly through the gathered mass of weeping people. Even grown men cried with breaking hearts.

Solomon and Emilie Klinger, as well as Friedrich and Esther Weber were in the last two wagons. They were all hoping for a better life in America.

Sofie looked wistfully up the sides of the street at the courtyards and front flower gardens that were bursting in full spring bloom. She thought, *I have never witnessed such beauty of the flowers, especially the lilacs. They all seem to put forth their best fragrance, especially for our leaving. I will never forget this scene. Each street we pass is bordered with splashes of fragrant spring flowers and the people standing along the way dressed in mourning clothes, their tears falling to the dirt.*

Through their own tears and forced smiles, they all waved good-bye to their families, neighbors, and friends as their three wagons turned south, toward the Saratov railway station and away from Susannenthal. Only two of the travelers in the Steiner wagon turned for a final glimpse of their home.

Chapter Nine

No Other Choice

The Steiner family rode in silence as the horses confidently trotted down the rut-filled road to Saratov—knowing the way from memory. Sofie and the girls sat in the second seat while David sat in front with Carl. The two smaller girls slept for most of the journey; Raisa stubbornly remained standing behind her father with her tiny hand gripping the fabric of his coat.

Steiner Family – 1906; Sofie, Lizzie, David, Maria, Raisa Steiner

His nerves on edge, David turned sharply in the seat. "Raisa, please sit down and relax yourself. It is a long way to Saratov and the train. Do not fear, child. Where I go, you will go also. Now, sit in the seat before you fall out of the wagon."

"I know you are sad because we had to say good-bye to Grossmuter and Grossvater—to our life here. But, we will have a wonderful adventure and make a new life together in another country." David smiled and tried to make light of the situation but noticed the sober darkness that filled his oldest daughter's eyes and knew in an instant that he hadn't convinced her of anything.

"Where is another country, Papa? Is it far away? Will I be able to visit *Grossmuter* and *Grossvater?*" Raisa couldn't understand why her grandparents didn't leave with them. David knew if he told her the truth, it would be more than she could understand.

As they bounced along the winding road, Sofie opened her travel case and pulled out a copy of the photograph they had taken before leaving—a memory photo for their parents. Try as they may, she and David had not been able to encourage Raisa to smile, even a little. It was almost like she understood the gravity of what was to come. It was obvious she only felt secure standing next to her father or holding onto his shoulder.

After an hour or so of riding in the wagon, Sofie tapped David on his shoulder. "David, I have been thinking about our journey. I have never been farther from home than Saratov. I am feeling fear and uncertainty. Do you realize I have never ridden the train or even seen a large ship like you say will take us across the ocean? How big is this ocean? How long will it take to cross the ocean to America? What are the people like in America? Do they speak German?"

Looking down at the passing road, Sofie continued, "I'm worried about many things including that I might not like the food where we are going. I know there are many foods I have not tasted as you did when you served in the Russian army. I haven't seen tall buildings or large bridges either. I am afraid of what is ahead of us, David. I go only with the faith that you will be at my side and that our Lord will guide us and keep us from harm. It is what I cling to."

Deep in his own thoughts and concerns, David was slightly irritated with Sofie's insecurities but turned to speak reassuringly to his wife. "You are right, my love. There are many things you and I also have not experienced in this world. We have made our decision, and we have asked the Lord to be with us. Think on the verse: *'Now this is the confidence that we have in Him, that if we ask anything according to His will, He hears us.'*

"We believe this is what we must do to survive, Sofie. We have the required faith, and we know we will have the opportunity to work hard wherever we live in this new country. The Lord gives us the courage to make this journey. That does not mean we go to our future without fear. We all have our moments of doubt. It will be all right, Sofie. We go with God, and he goes with us."

Sofie smiled back at her husband. "Well, I hope it won't take forty years for us to arrive at our destination as it did the Israelites!" Sofie turned her face to the side so Raisa couldn't see, as the tears trickled yet again over her cheeks. *I will never feel my mother's or father's arms around me again in my life, and my little daughters will grow up without grandparents to love them. How can we do this to them? Will it be worth everything we are leaving behind?*

Soon they arrived at the narrows of the Volga, several miles above the city of Saratov, where they would board the ferry to cross the river. Raisa's eyes grew wide with fright as both David and Carl hopped down from the wagon and grabbed the horses' reins, urging the skittish horses to step onto the bobbing ferry. The muddy waters of the Volga pushed and pulled at the ferry.

Raisa stood up in the wagon and began to scream as the ferry swayed with the current, and the horses whinnied in fear. Sofie reached for her daughter and pulled her down on the seat next to her. "Raisa, stop this minute. You are scaring the horses as well as your sisters. You are the oldest, and I expect you to be quiet. Be brave and watch how Papa and Uncle Carl work with the horses. The ferry master will tie the wagon to the boat, and we will not fall into the river. It will be fun. Now hush and do not be silly. Soon we will be on our way to the Saratov train station. Are you excited to ride on the big black train, my sweet?"

Initially, Raisa was calmed by her mother's reassurance. However, when she spotted river water leaking onto the boat, she began to scream even louder and tried to get out of the wagon. David grabbed his daughter and iron-folded her with his free arm so she couldn't move. "Stop it this minute, Raisa. Behave yourself, and sit here beside me."

Feeling the strength of her father's arm around her, Raisa had no choice, and she knew she would receive a whipping if she didn't behave. She settled into the seat beside her father. She alternated between hiding her eyes in the fabric of his coat and keeping a sharp eye on the swirling waters of the river. After they reached the other side and disembarked safely, Raisa laughed and looked back at the ferry, greatly relieved she would not have to ride all the way to America on that wobbly, leaky boat. Sofie smiled as she noticed Raisa looking back at the boat, giving it the evil eye.

When the loaded wagon finally rumbled into Saratov, Carl drove directly to the train station. It was bustling with travelers and stone-faced people who waited near their assorted mounds of trunks and boxes. David and Carl were quick to notice the alarming presence of a large number of aggressive Russian Cossacks patrolling the station.

After the brothers unloaded the traveling trunks, Carl prepared to take the wagon back to Susannenthal. He wrapped his strong arms around the shoulders of his younger brother. "It is my hope to see you in about a year, David. By then I expect you will have a good house for me to live in. I will pray that you have a safe journey and arrive in America without mishap. God be with you and your family." Suddenly aware of the massive lump that had grown in his throat, Carl turned swiftly and leapt up onto the wagon; turning in the seat, he touched the tip of his black wool cap with his finger in a good-bye salute. With a quick snap of the reins, he headed back to Susannenthal with an empty wagon.

The daily train was not scheduled to arrive for another hour, so the families from Susannenthal settled with their luggage along the wooden platform and prepared to wait for the train. Sofie gave the two older girls some dried fruit to suck on while they waited, hoping the food would keep them quiet. The Saratov waiting area was filled with many other emigrants from all along the Volga River; some had waited days for the train. David pulled a favorite pipe from his pocket and lit the rich tobacco. He drew the fragrant smoke deep into his lungs as his thoughts drifted to his previous train rides.

At last the impatient passengers heard the sharp whistle of the smoking black train as it rounded the curve at the edge of town. The engineer applied the brakes; metal on metal screeched as the train slowed then rolled to a stop at the station. Plumes of hot steam whistled and blew from the steam engine as it sat at the depot, waiting for passengers and luggage to board. David glanced over at Raisa. She was holding her hands over her ears, blue-green eyes wide with wonder.

The two older girls were initially frightened by the size of the train and the foreign sounds and the smells it made. David held Maria in his arms while Sofie carried Lizzie. He felt Raisa's hands as she desperately clutched the hem of his coat.

"Raisa, it is all right. Did it scare you when you felt the ground rumble as the train rolled on the tracks? These are just the noises and smells that trains make. The men in the engine shovel coal into the firebox, and the steam from the fire makes the wheels go around.

"Look over there. The men are loading our trunks, and soon we will climb aboard. We will ride it for five or six days and nights across Russia, and then we shall travel through several other countries, and finally we will cross into Germany. It is the country where our family first lived many years ago. It is called the fatherland.

"We will not only sit in our seats for the long ride but also sleep right here. Now, look out of the windows, and see if you can count all the small towns we pass. We may even play our favorite games once in a while if you are a good girl!"

The doting father looked down into his oldest daughter's gleaming eyes, eyes filled with such innocent trust and love. Once they were settled in their seats and the train began to pull away from the station, everybody relaxed.

Raisa was glued to the window. There were too many new sights and sounds for her to sleep. Her bright eyes followed the conductor as he walked down the aisle collecting passengers' tickets. He stopped when he saw the three little girls nestled in the seat.

Raisa looked up at him with frightened, questioning eyes. He smiled as he reached into his pocket and pulled out a round orange and handed it to David. "This is for your little daughters to share. Perhaps the sweet taste will take the fear from their minds for a while." He turned to Raisa. "Have you ever eaten an orange before, little girl? I will be back down the aisle in a while to see how you liked it. It is my favorite fruit."

Raisa thanked the conductor. Then she forgot all about him and turned to her father who held the orange. "Papa, have you ever eaten an orange before?" David replied that he had never had the opportunity, and Raisa interrupted with impatience. "Please, can I hold it for a little while so I can feel the bumpy skin?" Raisa took the orange from her father's hand and held it to her nose. "Oh, Mama, do smell this fruit! I hope it tastes as good on the inside as it smells on the outside. Do we eat the outside too?" She continued to rub her fingers over the rutty texture of the orange and put it to her nose again and again to smell the heady fragrance.

After a few moments, David began to peel the orange. Dividing the orange into sections, David handed them one at a time to his daughters. He saved the final two sections for himself and Sofie so they might also enjoy the rare treat.

The tart orange juice ran from the corners of Raisa's mouth and dripped onto her gray poplin frock. Her eyes opened wide, and her face beamed. "Mama, these oranges are ever so good, and I also like this 'click-ety, clack-ity' train ride too!"

Sofie turned her attention to her hungry baby. She settled the infant into the crook of her arm as she discreetly covered her shoulder with a shawl and cradled Lizzie beneath. Not long afterward, all three daughters took a nap, giving David and Sofie an opportunity to close their eyes as well.

~~~~~

Crossing West across central and then lower Russia, they witnessed hordes of filthy, desperate peasants crowding the roads and train stations. Staring out the window as the train sped over Russian soil, David was reassured he and Sofie had made the right decision. On the second day, it was nearly dusk when their train pulled into the impressive station in Moscow. It continued moving slowly through the station without stopping. David gently woke Sofie so she could witness what he was seeing out the window. Shock filled their faces as they watched the cruelty of Russian Cossacks toward hundreds of defenseless peasants who waited for a train—any train out of Moscow.

Sofie couldn't make herself turn away as she stared out the window of the train. "Oh, my heaven, David, look over there by the water tower. A soldier is beating that defenseless old man with the stock of his gun. But why would he do that? This is too terrible. Times are even worse here than in Saratov."

David and Sofie were thankful their daughters were sleeping. Both breathed an audible sigh of relief as the train began to pick up speed, never stopping to load or unload passengers.

"David, why didn't the train stop? There were so many souls waiting to board. Look back. Some of them are running after the train trying to get on."

David glanced nervously out the window. "They didn't stop, my love, because it was obviously too dangerous. Frankly, I am glad the train is picking up speed."

Trembling, Sofie laid her head on her husband's shoulder. "David, I have never witnessed such desperation and cruelty. I think we are blessed to be leaving this country, but now I am concerned of what shall become of our families in Susannenthal."

David stared out the window, not willing to admit the alarm and fear that filled his own mind. "I don't know what the future holds, Sofie. All we can do is hope we have seen the worst."

During the next three days and nights it took to cross the vast expanse of Russian land, the scenes outside their train window did not change. They never left the safety of the train until they were across the border in Poland. Until then, they made do with what provisions they had brought with them. During the next two days, crossing Polish countryside, they took advantage of every stop, getting off to stretch their legs and allow the children to run and exercise.

Sofie gazed out the window. "David, I am amazed by how far we have already traveled! I had no idea of how big everything is. If we have traveled this far already, and we are not even in Germany, it makes me to wonder how far America is?"

David smiled as he slid his arm around Sofie's shoulders. "Don't be afraid or apologize. There is much that I do not know either. We will learn of it all together. Now I think we should sleep while our daughters are doing the same." Their seats leaned back only a short distance so they had to attempt to sleep sitting up. The little ones were able to sleep lying flat on a seat or the floor.

The train crossed the German border sometime during the night. Early the next morning, it pulled into the German capital city of Berlin. David gazed out the grimy window as the wheels of the train noisily ground to a stop. Everyone was instructed to remain in their assigned seats as more passengers boarded the train, and additional cars were added to accommodate the large number of passengers heading west.

He turned to speak to Sofie. "We are now in the country of our heritage, yet it all is so strange, even the way these people speak German. I never realized there was such a difference between our 'high' German and what I believe is their 'low' German pronunciation. It is most curious, is it not?"

David spent a good deal of time reading about the ship that would carry his family to America. When the opportunity presented itself, he and Sofie practiced their English words on each other. More often than not, they collapsed with laughter at their attempts to speak their new language correctly. But each day they were encouraged with some improvement.

~~~~~

As the train rattled through the German countryside, David was fascinated by the country of his heritage; he couldn't help but notice how regulated the towns and farms looked. Taking in a large breath, he exhaled and thought to himself, *Oh, the simple joy of freedom, of breathing this free, uninhibited air.*

Taking care not to disturb his family, David rose from his seat and walked down the aisle to the rear of the train, where men were allowed to light a pipe. He struck up a conversation with several German men who were also enjoying a smoke. David was full of questions about the current German economic and political situation, as well as the farmland that rushed past their train.

"Excuse me; do you understand my poor spoken word? I am from the settlements along the Volga."

The three men smiled politely and nodded their heads. David yearned for answers to his many questions. "I hope you will pardon my impertinent curiosity, but at every stop I see so many people getting on the train with piles of luggage such as ours. Are all these people leaving the country? Are they all bound for Bremerhaven and the ships to America?"

An older man tapped his pipe to settle the tobacco. "JA, but I suppose we leave for different reasons than why you are leaving Russia. If I have heard correctly, you leave because of constant threat of war and the rising dissention. We leave Germany because of bad harvests, oppression, and famines. We have suffered, and now we hear of '*Amerika*' and a better life—a life of *liberty* and opportunity for material and physical wellbeing. So, yes—we also leave to find something, somewhere, some government to believe in again."

A tall, poorly dressed, middle-aged man turned to David. "I would like to introduce myself. I am Heinrich Richter. I travel with my family for all the reasons Herr Mohr has mentioned. We all weep and realize there is no salvation, no future for us, even though we work hard. Here the system is that the fruits of our labors go to others who own the land. Our government has the people in a stranglehold—not even a talented craftsman has a chance to improve his life. It is all controlled by the few! We are their paupers. We are their slaves, and they intend on keeping us right in this place as long as we lay down like dogs."

David looked at the men as they talked amongst themselves while thoughts and questions raged through his mind. "Please excuse another of my questions, but we have heard that there remains dissention between the Catholics and Lutherans. Is this word true, Herr Richter?"

"JA, JA, it does go on and probably will for generations to come. Unjust and bitter prejudices last a long time, carried from generation to generation. Some people have long memories. Not only is this a problem, but secular persecution of others like Mennonites, Moravian Brothers, and *Valdenslans,* prevents them also from practicing their faith. So, of course, many are leaving in vast numbers for religious reasons."

Herr Richter was extremely interesting and well-versed. He explained that as long as Germany remained under the many feudal rulers and the unjust class system of the old days, the people would rebel. Things had to change, and how that would happen, only the Lord knew. It was a festering sore. The common people hated the rigid hierarchical order that promoted and protected aristocratic privilege. The way it was, they worked and they slaved—only to put meager bread on their tables and rags on their backs while the landowners and princes lived in luxury, wore silk and satin clothes, and ate rich food. The people have said, "No more—we are leaving to find a country where we work for ourselves. We see many brochures and hear salespeople from America and other countries which promise a better life—so we leave to find it!

David nodded his head in acknowledgement. "I was born along the Volga in the German settlements. When my people first came into the region, we were allowed to speak our own language and worship and farm as we wished, without government interference. We did not have to serve in the Russian armies. We were a nation unto ourselves, and it worked well for several decades—or at least until Catherine the Great died. Then change began slowly at first, and now the threat of persecution is rampant and frightening. The war between the czarist troops and the new revolutionary troops is escalating and involving the German settlements and those of the Jews as well."

He and the men talked for a time, but then David noticed his family was awake and looking for him. "I must return to my seat. It has been good to speak with you. You have helped me understand we are perhaps all on this train for the same reason—leaving the old life for a better one filled with opportunity and hope in America. Good day, gentlemen." He hurried back down the aisle to their seats.

~~~~~

David learned it would take perhaps only another day to reach the embarkation city of Bremerhaven in northwest Germany. From there they would assemble in dormitory buildings and wait for the ship that would take them to America. He noticed on his passport that their ship was already assigned. The Steiner family would board the *S.S. Main,* a single-funnel, four-mast ship that would take them across the Atlantic Ocean to their new life.[18]

As the smoking, belching steam train puffed its way across the German countryside, Raisa climbed onto David's lap. "Papa, I would like to play our game of 'Imagine.' I am getting so very tired of riding on the train—forever, it seems."

A broad smile crossed his mouth as he cuddled his firstborn and caressed her golden strands of silky hair. "All right, *Liebchen.* Let's look out the window, and you tell me what you see and what it makes you think of."

Raisa peered out at the passing countryside and pointed to the willow trees along the river. "See, Papa, the wind blows the long, hanging branches of the willow trees, like it blows and tosses my hair. There—see that? It is just the same, I know it is. And, and—those bushes are all short and curly like the hair that grows on baby Lizzie's head!" Raisa continued without taking a breath. "I so love this game, Papa—what do you see? Don't you want to play too?"

"You are a very smart girl, my *Liebchen*. I see how the wind blows the willow branches. You have a very good eye and an even better imagination. Why don't you sit here and look out the window while I speak to your mama. I will return in a short time."

"But, Papa, what is imagination? I don't understand what you mean."

David smiled down at his inquisitive little girl. "That word means that you can see pictures in your head without seeing them with your eyes. Do you understand this?" Raisa nodded her head as she continued to look out the window.

David and Sofie began to assemble their belongings as the train neared their German destination of Bremen, near the huge international port of Bremerhaven. They were told they would have to wait only three days in the passenger dormitories; then they would be able to board their ship. They discovered they were very lucky because some passengers had been waiting for the ship for weeks.

~~~~~~

All three families from Susannenthal had purchased final tickets to board the *S.S. Main* on May 25, 1905; its destination was Baltimore, Maryland. From the beginning, they had vowed to stay together for the duration of the trip for emotional and physical support. The Klingers and Webers joined David and Sofie Steiner on the train platform; all in all, their group from the Volga, numbered twenty. When they arrived at the Emigrants House in Bremen, they passed, one by one, through a visual inspection. The small group from Susannenthal appeared well dressed, groomed, and clean. The officer in charge motioned for them to move to the next line—the area of questioning. As they moved down the line,

David closed his eyes and drew in a deep breath. Sofie turned and asked, "Are you all right, David?"

David smiled and then leaned in to whisper into his wife's ear. "If we had been detained at the last station, we would have been told to take our clothing off and take an antiseptic bath. They would have cut our hair short. After that, we would have been vaccinated and quarantined for several days. Also, our luggage would have been fumigated."

All Sofie heard was the part about cutting their hair. "Why on earth would they want to do all of that to the people?"

"Sofie, have you not seen some of the people in the lines? They are destitute and filthy. They are crawling with vermin. The ship's crew cannot allow them to infest the rest of us, so these problems have to be taken care of before they are allowed on board. I am glad we had our vaccinations before be left Saratov."

The group from Susannenthal had no problems giving the necessary information required for the ship's manifest and the landing in America.

David showed the officers his tickets, and they were directed toward the exit.

Two days after the group from Susannenthal passed the inspection, filled out the columns of the manifest, and signed the necessary paper, they were transported by wagon to the port at Bremerhaven. When they arrived at the dock, David gathered his family and they stood for a moment, looking up at the gigantic ship that would carry them to America. He reached down and took Sofie's hand in his own and squeezed it. "I love you, Sofie. I'm glad you are at my side as we begin this journey."

Sofie looked up at her husband and managed a weak smile. "I love you, too, my David—I love you, too." Neither David nor Sofie knew what awaited them once they boarded the huge ship to America, but whatever it was, they would face it together.

David led them up the wooden gangplank, off German soil, and onto the ship that would carry them to a new life in America. He carried three-year-old Maria while Raisa walked beside him, tightly gripping the tail of his coat.

Suddenly terrified, Sofie struggled to control herself as she mechanically put one foot in front of the other and walked stoically up the gangplank and onto the ship. She held her squirming baby securely in her arms as she dutifully followed her husband's lead.

Once on board, the passengers were directed according to their ticket. The three families from Susannenthal with steerage-class tickets were directed to the iron staircase that descended into the depths of the ship's hold. When they approached the opening, an overwhelming scent of disinfectant assaulted Sofie's keen sense of smell. She stepped back, momentarily stunned by the impact of the overwhelming odor. "David, David, do we have to go down in there in that, that hole where the terrible smell is coming from?"

David tried to be positive as he turned and smiled at his wife. "JA, Sofie that is where our steerage berth is located. Don't worry—you will get used to the smell of disinfectant. We should be happy they have killed all the lice, bedbugs, and bad smells from the previous passengers."

Sofie walked down the iron staircase, pausing at each step; her eyes were wide with disbelief as she covered her mouth and nose with her free hand. Descending the staircase, the damp, dead air closed in around her, and she found it difficult to breathe. Reluctantly, she followed her husband as he led them down the dimly lit aisle to their assigned berth. Gently she laid Lizzie down on the canvas, hay-stuffed mattress. The baby immediately sat up, crawled a short way, and sat back on her round bottom. She smiled at her mother, happy to be free to move on her own. Sofie pushed aside the five soiled life preservers intended to double as their pillows and began to unpack their suitcases. Three-year- old Maria and her eleven-month-old sister curled up together in a corner of their berth and immediately fell asleep as Sofie hummed a soft tune while she worked.

Sorting through their assigned bag of eating utensils, David counted five metal covered dishes divided into compartments, along with forks and spoons. He remembered hearing that their meals would be served from a large heated tank up on deck. They would be notified each day when meals were ready; the passengers were expected to assemble in lines with their eating utensils.

David was eager to leave all the hustle and bustle, so he bent down to whisper in Raisa's ear. "Raisa, would you like to go back up on deck with me to have a look around?" Raisa jumped up and down with glee and grabbed her father's hand as she led him up the iron stairway into the fresh air.

David moved over to the railing that faced the dock. "Raisa, hold on to the wooden rail while I light my pipe. Look at all the people down on the dock lined up to come on board the ship. Just think, they are like us—all leaving their lives here to make new homes in America." He inhaled the fragrant smoke into his lungs.

He could see the long dock where many ships were tied waiting for their passengers. *These ships are all going different places, most across the Atlantic and some across the Baltic Sea.* He stopped in mid-thought, stunned as the next concept exploded in his mind. *My pregnant mother stood on a German dock much like this many years ago with her aunt, waiting to board the ship that would take them to Russia, to Susannenthal.*

Raisa remained silent for a few moments, fascinated by the throbbing throng of people as they moved up the gangplank onto the ship. She tugged on the corner of her father's coat and turned her innocent little face up to his. "Papa, I thought this place *was* America. I don't want to ride on this big boat. I don't like boats. Don't you remember that I don't like boats? I have changed my mind. I do not want to go to—to this place, America. I want to go back to our house and my Oma and Opa in Susannenthal."

Her blue-green eyes were bright with tears. Suddenly she could not hold them back; they began to roll down over her rosy cheeks one after another. Embarrassed, she quickly wiped them away with the back of her tiny hand. "I mean it, Papa. I am not happy here. I do not like the big boat or all these people I do not know. I want to go back to our house behind the bakery. Let's go back down in the hole and get Mama and my sisters and leave. Come on, Papa, come on."

David squatted on his haunches and gathered his daughter in his arms. "Raisa, Raisa, you are old enough to understand we cannot go back to Susannenthal. We have made our decision to leave, we have paid the money, and there is no going back. Do you remember how frightened you were the night the soldiers came to our bakery and broke in to rob our store? We were very lucky they did not hurt us. You are old enough to understand this situation, my *Liebling*, JA?"

Blinking her eyes faster, Raisa tried in vain to keep the tears at bay as her upper lip quivered. "Yes, Papa, but why didn't all my grandparents come with us—and, and—our aunts and uncles and cousins too? I don't want to leave them there where they can be hurt."

Releasing his daughter from his embrace, David took a long, slow draw on his pipe, searching for the right words. "Raisa, we asked them to come with us, but for now they decided to wait, for many reasons. They are all grown people and have the right to make their own decisions. Did you know Uncle Wilheim is preparing to leave in three months and also Uncle Carl and their families? I cannot make everybody do what I think is best now, can I? All we can do is to ask our Lord to protect them and also us on our journey to our new home in America."

They stayed up on deck until David noticed the deckhands gathering to prepare the ship to sail. He turned, and taking his daughter firmly by the hand, he walked back down the iron stairs into the depths of steerage to the assigned berth they would call home for the next two weeks.

~~~~~

Sofie noticed several women down in steerage that appeared to be far along in their pregnancies. *Perhaps I can be of help to the women when their time comes.* She finished storing their personal clothing and food items in their berth then stepped back and looked at the cramped quarters where they would all sleep together.

Feeling the ship move slightly with the rising tide as it prepared to leave the dock, Sofie thought, *Oh, oh— the movement makes me dizzy in the head and sick in my stomach, almost like I am pregnant. I am now glad I packed herbs to settle the stomach. I may need them sooner then I planned.*

She looked up to see David and Raisa move down the aisle toward her.

~~~~~

As instructed, all passengers had settled in their berths as the ship was tugged away from the bustling international dock at Bremerhaven. The single-funnel, four-mast vessel slipped through the black inky water and out into open sea as the sun sank in the west, leaving the shore of Germany behind in the cover of night. The *S.S. Main's* course was set to sail briefly out into the North Sea and then back to the continent. They were scheduled for a brief stop in Antwerp, Belgium, the next morning to pick up additional passengers, fresh produce, and commercial cargo. Then the ship would set its course directly toward the United States of America, where all on board hoped a new life and opportunity awaited them.

Chapter Ten

A New Life

Once down inside steerage, Sofie tried to shake the relentless fear and heartache of leaving her home. She busied herself with arranging their new living quarters while David took their daughters up on deck. Sofie stared with distaste at the stained straw-stuffed mattress. She pulled two thin quilts from one of their bags and tucked them tightly around the soiled mattress. Next, she used their five life preservers to separate the sleeping area.

Sofie recoiled at the thought of laying her face on the filthy life preservers. Suddenly, she got an idea; digging down into her traveling bag, she pulled out an extra petticoat. Unfolding it, Sofie slid the life preservers inside the spacious folds of the slip, tucking it around the sides until she had clean "pillows." Satisfied with her solution to the problem, Sofie decided as time passed, she would fill small bags with soiled laundry, and they could also use them as pillows.

~~~~~

David returned with the girls and handed Lizzie over to her mother. "Whew, I think it is time for a diaper change and something to eat for this little one. There was a food line up on deck so we have all eaten, and I brought a sandwich back for you." David looked around their berth. "I like what you have done to make it nice. You are so clever!" He leaned down and planted a quick kiss on her cheek.

After Sofie ate her sandwich, she changed the baby's diaper and leaned back against the berth to nurse her. David removed the older girls' shoes and began to prepare them for bed. When Sofie finished nursing, David picked Lizzie up to burp her and walk the aisle until she fell asleep. Keeping their nightly ritual, Sofie combed each daughter's hair with long, slow strokes until they were relaxed and ready for sleep.

Reaching down in the dried-food bag, she handed the two older girls a piece of dried apple for a snack. Wisely, she had packed a special bag filled with dried fruit, zwieback, and toast tossing in several cupsful of raw rice to absorb any moisture which might mold the dried food.

Soon, David handed over their sleeping baby to Sofie. With a long sigh, he leaned over the edge of their berth and took his shoes off, storing them in a large drawstring bag.

Awkwardly, David crawled over to where he would sleep. He flopped onto his back and stretched his arms out as a sign of exhaustion escaped his mouth. Not being able to resist, he reached out to stroke his wife's shoulder as she brushed her own hair. Teasing, he inquired, "I don't suppose you would comb my hair and sing sweetly to me too?"

Sofie turned and smiled at her husband. "You get yourself ready for bed, and if you are a good boy, I may sing sweetly to you later."

Not yet asleep, Raisa whispered, "Mama, Papa is not a boy. He's Papa. That is so silly!" Sofie smiled in the dim light of steerage and leaned over to kiss her oldest daughter good night. "Close your eyes now, my sweet. We've all had a very long day. In the morning you can go back up on deck with Papa, okay?"

Closing the curtain of their berth, Sofie crawled under their blanket and nestled into the curve of her husband's arm. David and Sofie decided that tomorrow they would try taking turns in the communal wash room, one staying with the girls in their berth. "We don't know how crowded the washrooms are going to be, so I suppose we will have to wait and see what works best."

David agreed with all that Sofie suggested; he felt his eyes growing heavy. "We have survived our first day, *Liebling*. It's time to close our eyes now and get some sleep." Laughing softly, he added, "My feet are touching the end of the berth. There doesn't seem to be room for *all* of me. I may have to curl up to sleep. And frankly, I don't think there is going to be opportunity for any privacy with us all packed in here like sardines! I don't know how that is going to work with you lying so close to me—a very tempting situation, don't you think?" David smiled as he kissed Sofie good night.

"Oh, also—I would like to continue with my daily prayers tomorrow. I plan to rise early and go up on deck in the quiet of the morning to read my Bible before you and our daughters wake."

After several moments of silence, David thought of something else. "I think I like the rocking of the ship. It is almost like rocking in a giant cradle—ahhh. In the morning while you are getting the children ready for the day, I will take Raisa up on deck to get our breakfast. Would you like to come up to eat and get some fresh air, or do you want to stay down here?"

Sofie propped herself up on one elbow with an amused smile. "I don't know, David. I will tell you in the morning. Good night now, my love. Please stop talking and go to sleep. I am having a harder time getting you settled to sleep than our three daughters!" In the darkness she heard him say under his breath, "That's because you didn't sing softly to me!"

Sofie lay awake a long time that night, listening to the foreign sound of the sea slapping the sides of the ship as it gently rocked and rolled on its course through the North Sea. The rhythmic and incessant pounding of the ship's engine only muffled the sounds of men snoring and the variety of other noises that a thousand or more people make in the bowels of steerage at night. At some point Sofie finally fell into an exhausted sleep.

David woke just before dawn, pulled his shoes on, tucked in his shirt, and ran a comb through his hair. Putting his familiar newsboy cap on his head, he made a quick stop in the men's lavatory. With his Bible tucked under his arm, he headed up the iron stairway and onto the deck. The wood of the deck was slippery with dew as he moved toward a secluded area next to the lifeboats.

He found a spot he liked, and reaching into his pocket, he pulled out his pipe, lit it, and took a deep draw of the fragrant tobacco. After inhaling a couple of puffs, David paused and watched as the sun began climbing higher over the horizon. He prayed silently.

Passengers in steerage woke early that first morning, and it took most people a moment or two to realize where they were. As David made his way back down the aisle, he noticed that lines for the men's and women's bathrooms were already forming. As he neared his own berth, he heard the soft murmur of his family stirring inside the curtained box.

"Papa—I am so glad to see you. I have to go potty. Can you take me to the special room?" Raisa was wiggling around, and it was obvious she needed to go to the bathroom immediately.

"Sofie, where is the chamber pot? When I came down the stairs, I noticed the lines are long for the washroom, and our oldest daughter needs to go now."

Sofie handed David the chamber pot then changed the diapers of the two little ones, storing them in a tin can until she could rinse them out. Drying them was going to be a problem, but David promised to take them up on deck and attempt to dry them in the wind.

The ship provided a public clothesline on the lower deck, but it was usually filled with clothing, which might or might not be there when the owner returned to claim them. Thieves were abundant, especially in steerage. If a person wanted to retain ownership of something, constant vigilance was necessary. The short line outside their berth would have to suffice for anything they needed to hang dry.

~~~~~

David took Raisa up on deck for breakfast as Sofie remained below dressing and nursing Lizzie. When she finished, she nestled the baby against her chest by wrapping her in a fabric sling and tying it securely around both their bodies. She knotted the fabric over her opposite shoulder and adjusted it until both she and her baby were comfortable. Then, taking Maria by the hand, Sofie walked down the dimly lit aisle and climbed up the iron staircase into the brilliant sunlight. She still felt wobbly with the movement of the ship and hoped the sensation would soon stop. She hesitated at the top of the stairway for a moment and filled her lungs with fresh, clean ocean air. Glad to be out of their dusky, dank quarters, Sofie found David and Raisa at a table. When they all had their food, they bowed their heads as David prepared to lead his family in a private prayer of thanksgiving.

"Papa, can I say the prayer this morning? May I, please?" Raisa begged sweetly.

David smiled as he consented, instructing her to speak quietly. She bowed her blonde head, folded her little hands, and whispered, "Come, Lord Jesus, be our guest, and let these gifts to us be blessed. A—men!" She raised her face to look at her parents with a beaming smile. "Did I do good, did I?" With an amused smile, David assured her that it was perfect.

The Steiner family spent most of their first morning up on the deck, soaking up the warmth of the sunshine. After lunch Sofie took the two little ones down to their berth for their naps while David and Raisa remained up on deck. "Papa, let's go over to the railing. I see people over there pointing down in the water. I want to see what is happening."

They maneuvered themselves through the throng of passengers and peered over the side. "Oh, Papa, look at those big fish that are jumping out of the water. Are those what the people called whales, Papa, are they?"

David looked down into the ocean and saw large blue-gray fish leaping out of the water as if they were playing some sort of game. He spoke to another German standing next to him at the rail. "Excuse me, sir. Do you know what kind of fish those are?"

The man turned and smiled. "JA, I have been told they are dolphins, and they often swim along with a ship like this, hoping to eat some small fish which they find in the ship's wake. They are very large fish, JA. I like to fish, but I do not know if I could land one of those."

That evening Sofie insisted on washing the children before they went to sleep. She sat a small bucket of warm water between her legs to steady it as she moistened the cloth; using the bar of soap she brought with her, she worked up a good lather before wiping each daughter's face and hands. "David, there is no place to bathe in private, and I don't feel comfortable taking my clothes off in front of strangers. There are no tubs for bathing, only water from the wall that splashes down. I am concerned with how we are to remain clean. I do not know what the men's washroom is like, but in our women's room, only the first in line benefits from hot water. We do have privacy stalls surrounding holes into which we do our business, and there are about ten washing basins with only tepid water. I hope to do my best to keep our little girls clean, but it will be a challenge."

David smiled fondly at his wife. "JA, Sofie, it is good to try and stay as clean as we can. Our men's facilities are disgusting, I must admit. We also have ten wash basins but only one long trough with sea water running through it all day long where we are to pee. For our bowels there is a row of benches with holes where everything falls into the trough and I expect eventually runs out into the ocean. I do not like the situation, but we have to make do with what we have."

He ran his hand over his whiskered face. "The water that sprays from the wall is good, but I agree it is usually not hot or even warm. I may try it tonight when there isn't a line. Think I will take my razor along—I am feeling scruffy!"

David watched Sofie gently wash the baby's bottom. "I suspect it is different for men than for women with the privacy issue. I took showers with other soldiers when I was in the army, so I am used to the naked sights!" David laughed. "And believe me—there *are* some sights I would rather not see! I guess conditions could be worse. We have to work with what we have." That night they fell asleep listening to the soft crooning of an old German lullaby, coming from someone in steerage who was feeling homesick.

Just after midnight, David and Sofie heard a light tapping on the wood panel outside their berth. A voice whispered through the dim, dank night air. "Frau Steiner, please, oh please excuse me for waking you. Frau Weitzel has gone into labor, and she needs you, if you will please come with me."

Sofie sat up in bed, startled and not knowing where she was for a moment. Sticking her head out of the curtain, she recognized one of her Susannenthal neighbors. "Oh, Emilie, it is you. You say someone has gone into labor? One moment, let me put on my shoes, and I need to find my birthing bag. Then I will come with you."

She turned to whisper into her husband's ear. "David, I am called to help with a birth. Please, can you take care of our daughters until I return? I am sure our friends from home will help you with our daughters in the morning if I have not returned."

With her husband's blessing, Sofie scooted quietly out of the berth and followed Emilie Klinger down the dimly lit aisle and around the corner to the berth where Frau Weitzel lay. Several people were gathered outside. Sofie could hear the moaning of a woman in the throes of labor coming from inside the curtain. She pulled back the curtain and eased inside.

"Frau Weitzel, I am Sofie Steiner. I am a midwife. I am here to help you deliver your baby. First, I need to pull   your nightshirt up so I may examine your belly to feel how the baby lays." Placing her ear to the woman's protruding stomach, Sofie listened to the sound of the baby's heartbeat. "Your baby's heart beats strong. That is a good sign." Sofie then placed her knowledgeable hands over the contracting belly of her patient, sliding them slowly over the protruding mass. Her experience told her the delivery was in the last stages.

A frown crossed Sofie's face as she felt the void above the woman's pelvic bone where the baby's head should have presented a solid area. "Frau Weitzel, is this your first child?" Sofie reached out and again slid her hands over the lower belly to be sure of her diagnosis. "The baby's head is not down in the birth position. Your baby is lying in the breech position. Do you know what this means?"

The women propped herself up on her elbows. Beads of sweat glistened on the expectant mother's forehead. Taking a deep breath, she replied, "Nein, Frau Steiner. This is my third baby. I have two healthy sons. I only know I am having more trouble with this one. I did not have troubles with the first two babies. They came very easy and fast. What does this mean, this breech position?" Another pain began to build, and her stomach tightened into a rock-hard mound as she began to pant and breathe her way through the contraction. Her eyes squeezed tight, and her face scrunched up as her mouth formed an audible "ohm."

Sofie crawled out of the berth and addressed the woman's husband and Solomon Klinger, who were standing nearby. "We need to get Frau Weitzel up to the infirmary where the doctor is." Herr Wetzel's eyes were wide with concern. "I don't know if she will go to a doctor. She wanted you to be with her."

"Herr Weitzel, I will stay with your wife until her baby is born, and I will help her to have the baby. But we may need to have the doctor's help with the birth as well. The baby's head is not down for the birth—its bottom is where the head should be, and the doctor may have to try and turn the baby around. I have done this before, but it can be difficult. To be safe, she should be up in the infirmary. Can the two of you lift her and carry her under the arms up the stairs to the second deck?"

It took considerable effort on the part of the two burly men to carry and drag Frau Weitzel up the iron staircase to the infirmary. Dr. Hauzt was just returning from attending another case when the group from steerage stumbled into the infirmary. The doctor looked up in surprise. "Vas ist das?"

"Herr Doctor, I am Frau Steiner from third class. I introduced myself to you the first day of the voyage. I am a midwife and have a patient here with a problem. This is her third baby, and she is delivering bottom first."

"Do you know what to do in this situation, Frau Steiner?"
"JA, Doctor, I do have experience with turning the baby."
The doctor looked over his glasses at Sofie and questioned,
"What is the procedure you recommend in this situation?"
"I would have her up on her hands and knees then massage her belly and back. I would attempt to move the baby from the outside first. If that doesn't work, I will reach up inside and try to turn the child. It is a large baby, and I do not think she can deliver breech. If the fetus is small enough, I know it is possible to deliver a baby which is breech."

The doctor stood up and walked around his desk to begin washing his hands. "I will examine the patient to verify your diagnosis." Thoughtfully and slowly he moved his hands over the extended belly of Frau Weitzel. When he finished, he nodded his head in agreement. "It is as you said, and I am confident your approach to this problem is sound. I would advise you to go ahead with your techniques and see if you are successful in turning the child since your hands are smaller than my own. If not, I will be nearby to assist you with a forceps delivery, a Caesarean procedure, or whatever is necessary."

Frau Wetzel's face was ashen as another pain tore through her. In spite of herself, tears rolled unchecked down her cheeks. Sofie gently wiped the sweat from her patient's forehead and advised her of the problem. "Frau Weitzel, I want you to turn over and get up on your hands and knees. I will rub and push on particular parts of your lower back and your belly to try to help the baby move so the head is down in the birth canal. You must listen and work with me. I want you to trust that I can help you."

After less than an hour, Sofie felt the baby move until it was sideways in her patient's belly, but it seemed to be stuck sideways and would move no further. "Frau Weitzel, I must reach up inside your opening, and at the same time I must push on the baby's bottom to move him around so his head is down. Then, God willing, he will be ready to be born. Take a deep breath now, and relax so I can help you."

Sofie washed her hands several times. Then she reached up inside the dilated opening until her small hand touched what felt like the baby's bottom. To be sure, she moved to the right and felt the head. Moving back to the left, Sofie began a steady pressure on the baby until the bottom end slipped toward the mother's chest and the head moved down into the birth canal.

"With the next pain, Frau Weitzel, I want you to push." A minute or two passed; then the woman's belly began to mound with another labor contraction. "Now, Frau Weitzel, push now!" The baby's head crowned, and with the next push, the child slid into the waiting hands of the midwife. The doctor approached and congratulated Sofie on a job well done.

"You have delivered a healthy and boisterous baby girl. I will sew the patient up while you care for the infant."

Sofie gently wiped the blood from the baby's skin, taking care not to disturb the sticky white substance that protected the new skin from the drying air. She swaddled the baby firmly and walked to the head of the bed.

"Frau Weitzel, you have a beautiful and healthy daughter who seems happy to be born." She laid the baby in the exhausted mother's arms. "I am very sorry it was so difficult for you, but it is over now, and you have a wonderful gift from God in your arms." Then with a smile, she added, "I thought the baby was another son before it was born, but I was wrong. You now have a daughter who has a mind of her own."

Frau Weitzel looked up at Sofie through a veil of tears. "Frau Steiner, I owe the life of my daughter and myself to you.

You are a gifted midwife, and I would like your permission to name my child after you. I would like to name her Sofie Alexandra."

Sofie smiled and reached to gently caress the face of her patient. "I would be honored to have a child named after me, very honored indeed. You were a good patient. I know it was not easy to do the things I asked you to do when your pain was intense. The doctor and I think it wise that you stay in the infirmary for a day or two so he can watch over you as you regain your strength. Will you do this?"

Exhausted, Sofie turned and walked out the door of the ship's infirmary just as the sun was peaking over the horizon to the east. Stopping for a moment as her eyes rose to the morning sky; she inhaled deeply and absorbed the beauty of the new day as orange, salmon, and mauve rays of morning light shot through the low- hanging clouds. She was deeply moved by the beautiful sight. "A new day and a new child, both are gifts from God."

Sofie closed her eyes and folding her hands in prayer, she whispered, *"Thank you, Lord God, for giving me the knowledge to help Frau Weitzel in her time. Keep mother and child safe. Keep David and my family safe on this journey. I offer up my thanks to you, Lord Jesus, for this wondrous new day."*

Sofie shivered as a cold breeze flowed over her skin. She noticed more clouds gathering to the west. She hurried to the iron staircase and descended into steerage, hoping to get a couple hours of sleep before her own daughters woke.

Several hours later, Sofie woke to an empty berth. David had washed and dressed the children and taken them on deck for their breakfast, leaving her to catch up on her sleep. Herr Weitzel arrived at their berth about the same time David returned with their daughters.

"Frau Steiner, please excuse me. I do not want to disturb your rest, but I see you are awake now. I want to thank you for helping my wife and bringing our daughter safely to us. Please accept this small amount of money in payment. I do not have much, but I want to pay you for your assistance."

Sofie tried to resist the payment because she knew all of the emigrants needed every penny they had with them, but the new

father would not hear of it. He insisted on paying her for what she
did for his family. She thanked him and quickly hid the money
inside her coat.

~~~~~

As David and their little ones climbed inside the berth to
wish her good morning, Sofie laughed as she was covered with
kisses and hugs from her daughters. She suddenly became aware of
the sound of waves hitting the sides of the ship; the rocking motion
seemed to be getting worse. "David, when you were up on deck,
did you see a storm coming? I am feeling so dizzy."

Before noon, slanted streaks of icy rain, driven by building
gusts of wind, began beating down on the decks of the *S.S. Main* as
she moved into the turbulent waters of the North Atlantic.

When the ship's steward announced the coming storm and
that the door to the deck would be secured during the storm, a cry
went up from the passengers. "It must be a very bad storm if they
lock us down in this hole. How are we to get out if we begin to
sink?"

The steward assured the passengers that locking the door to
the deck was for their safety and also to prevent any water from
leaking down into the hold of the ship. "You must relax and roll
with the ship. Do not worry. We will not sink, but you must
cooperate with us. We will bring your meals down to you at the
appropriate time if at all possible."

Many passengers screamed and cried with fear when the
bow of the ship rose then plunged into the deep trough between
waves. Almost immediately, the seasickness attacked many of the
passengers. Before the storm, they had been allowed up on deck
and could vomit over the rail when they felt queasy; now they were
locked down in the hole with no escape. After several hours of
rough seas, smelly vomit puddled in the aisles; people were simply
too sick and dizzy to get up and run for the washroom. Even if they
had been able to make it to the washroom to be sick, there was not
enough room in the cramped quarters for the hundreds of ill
passengers.

Sofie didn't remember ever being this sick. She couldn't
even lift her head from the small pillow without the contents of her

stomach coming up. David tried to put the chamber pot under her mouth, but often he didn't make it in time. "Oh, David, I feel as if am going to die. I cannot stand this. My head and my stomach are spinning, and I have no control. Look in my birthing valise for ginger and sassafras tea. Perhaps that will help settle my stomach."

Desperate, Sofie begged, "Please, David, can you do something to make the ship stop rolling?" David bathed her face with a cool cloth and wiped the mucus from her mouth.

"Nein, Sofie, you know I cannot make the storm stop. I will pray for our Lord to do what you ask and to comfort your stomach and dizziness. Now close your eyes, and try not to think about it."

When Sofie found no relief, she became even more agitated and weakly muttered, "I cannot close my eyes nor stop thinking about this hell we are in. Just listen, David, to the people as they cry and scream. There is no escape from the hideous smells and sounds. I cannot imagine living through this. It is a like a nightmare."

~~~~~

The storm raged for two days and nights. Some passengers were so exhausted from being sick that they defecated where they lay, too weak to rise and walk to the washrooms. David was thankful he and their daughters were not badly affected by the horrible circumstances they were forced to endure. Raisa kept a scarf tightly bound around her mouth and nose. All three children were becoming restless from being kept inside, but there was no place for them to go.

David spent the next two days trying to care for their daughters while keeping his wife as clean as possible. Sometime during the second night, the ship ceased rising and rolling as the violent ocean waves and storm subsided. The ship seemed to quiver within itself as it settled back to glide across a calmer surface. Finally, with first morning light, the ship's crew opened the hatch to steerage. The horrible odor that spilled from the hellhole sent more than one sailor to the ship's rail to empty his own belly.

With cloths covering their mouths, the crew descended the iron stairway with mops and buckets. "All passengers who are able, are required to ascend the stairs onto the deck where you will be served breakfast. We will attempt to clean the area, and when we are finished, you may come back down. Perhaps you will want to make your first stop the washroom. We apologize for your discomfort, but your safety was the most important consideration. Come now, go up on the deck, and breathe the fresh air."

Sofie remained in her berth, too weak to move. David straightened his children's clothing and changed Lizzie's diaper. "Sofie, I will take our daughters up on deck and feed them. Perhaps Emilie or someone from our Susannenthal group will watch the girls so I can come back down to help you. Try to sleep now and I will return as soon as I can. I love you, my darling. Sleep now." He looked down at her, gently stroking her face as she closed her eyes.

Sofie's pallor was ghastly pale; her red-rimmed eyes were sunken in her face, and her hair was plastered to her head. David covered her with a quilt and turned to take his daughters up and out of the unbelievable stench. He carried the two little ones while Raisa followed, holding onto his coat as they climbed the iron stairway onto the deck and out into the fresh ocean air.

The young German father and his children simply stood for a moment, soaking up the warmth of the morning sun and taking the wonderful, fresh air into their lungs. Reaching into his coat, David pulled out a small comb. He combed the two little ones' hair first then attempted to draw the comb through Raisa's thick, tangled tresses. "Ow Papa, that hurts! Do not pull my hair so. Give the comb to me, and I will comb my own hair. I am a big girl, and I can do it myself." David willingly gave up the comb to his oldest daughter and was amused watching her pull through the snarls and snags of her thick auburn hair.

At a water spigot next to the cabin wall, people formed lines to wash up before eating. David instructed his daughters, "Before we eat our breakfast, let's stand here in this line so we can wash our hands and faces." The children didn't object.

David became concerned about their eleven-month-old baby since she had only nursed occasionally during the storm because Sofie had been too sick. In desperation to stop her crying, he had put a cup of warm milk to her tiny mouth. She eagerly sucked at the milk and quickly learned how to drink from the cup. He mashed some of their food and fed her what he could. David heard that several elderly people, babies, and small children died during the storm. He tried to forget the disturbing cries and screams of fear and misery that had echoed throughout the belly of the ship.

Sitting at a makeshift table with his children, David noticed several crewmen emerge from steerage carrying large, heavy canvas bags, which they stacked against a far wall. He estimated there were close to a dozen bags when it suddenly occurred to him what they contained—bodies of those who died down in steerage during the storm.

Later that morning, mourners gathered around the captain who offered a short prayer for the deceased. The weighted bodies were then pushed over the side of the ship one by one, hitting the ocean water with a splash. David tried to distract Raisa from the troubling scene, but it was to no avail. "Papa, what are they throwing over the ship into the waters? Why are peoples crying so? What is happening? Tell me, Papa!"

David caressed his daughter's face. "*Liebchen*, during the storm, some people died because they were old or very sick. They are inside the bags, and they are being buried in the ocean because there is no ground to put them in."

Raisa's eyes opened wide with the horror. "I want to go back down and see Mama. Come on, Papa, come on. We must make sure she is all right. Hurry, Papa, hurry."

David left the two babies with Emilie Klinger before he and Raisa descended the iron staircase. Remnants of the stench lingered in the air in spite of the cleaning attempts by the ship's crew. Covering her mouth and nose with her small hand, Raisa rushed ahead of him and in her distress tore back the curtain of their berth. Sofie's eyes were closed in sleep. "Mama, Mama— please wake up. Are you all right still? Wake up, Mama?" The child shook her mother relentlessly until Sofie wearily opened her eyes.

"Oh, Raisa, do not move me so. Please calm yourself." She raised her eyes to her husband. "David, I do feel somewhat stronger now. Perhaps you can help me to the washroom first. I want to be clean more than I want to eat anything. I am going to the washroom and stand naked under the shower of water to wash my hair and body. At this point I don't care who looks at me. I only want to be clean again!"

The next day conditions were much improved. The passengers in steerage felt they had passed through the jaws of hell and survived. Happily, the remaining trip across the Atlantic was on calm seas, with glistening spring sunshine and moonlight reflecting from the water.

The final morning aboard the ship, David was up on deck, smoking his earth-clay pipe, waiting for the sun to rise so he could read his Bible. Bowing his head, David prayed.

When he opened his eyes, he blinked and then rubbed them, thinking he was seeing a mirage; it was no mirage. Far away on the horizon, he saw land—America. A shutter of first relief then alarm ran the length of his body as he stared at the horizon. David rose and descended into steerage to take Raisa up on deck while Sofie and the babies slept.

An hour later, the morning calm was shattered by three blasts from the ship's horn as boisterous cheering was heard coming from the upper decks. Sofie and her two little ones woke with a start. She hurried to dress the children and comb their hair; then she noticed her husband walking with Raisa gleefully skipping down the shadowy aisle.

"Sofie, it's—America! Raisa and I have seen the land!"

Everyone on board was excited with the news. Even the children felt the excitement and were scampering up and down the aisles. Directions were shouted as suitcases and traveling bags were readied. Most passengers donned their best clothing in honor of this momentous occasion.

Later that morning, as they rounded the southernmost tip of Maryland, the first mate descended into steerage, and using a bull horn, he gave the passengers instructions regarding the Emigration Hall at the port of Baltimore. After learning what lay ahead and what was expected of them, many passengers hurried up to the deck, even though they would not arrive at the actual port of Baltimore for several hours. As the ship entered Chesapeake Bay, eager passengers pushed and shoved to reach the railing. They all yearned for that first look of their new home, America.

David and Raisa stood at the rail for a long time and watched as the lush, green landscape drifted past. Sofie decided to take the two little ones back to their berth to catch a quick nap before they actually docked.

The *S.S. Main* sailed up the Chesapeake Bay to the largest inland port in the United States of America—Baltimore, Maryland. Once the seasoned sailors maneuvered the passenger ship full of immigrants into the assigned slip on the dock, experienced crewmen dropped anchors and threw thick ropes to waiting dock workers as the ship's engines shuddered to a stop. David watched with interest as everyone on board seemed consumed with preparation for debarkation in America.

David and Sofie had taken great pains first thing that morning to remove their smelly clothing and wash and dress in clean clothes—all in preparation to disembark. They wanted to look their best for this most important day. Sofie had quickly stored their dirty clothes in a bag, vowing to wash them the first chance she got.

Sofie exclaimed, "It feels so good, David, to be clean and to know that I don't smell!" She took special pains in pinning her shining hair up and then turned again to her husband. "David, why is it that we sail into this city of Baltimore and not to New York City and the place they call Ellis Island, like I have heard so many other people do?"

David looked up from his packing. "First, it is the choice of the ship we are on where they will take us. I think it is a good thing because it will be much faster getting through the processing here than Ellis Island. Baltimore does not have to process as many immigrants as does the port in New York, nor are the rules as strict." He looked down at her and smiled. "Have I told you today that you are beautiful and that I love you, *Liebchen?*" Sofie blushed and, standing on her tiptoes, gave him a quick peck on the cheek.

Assembling their belongings, the family climbed the iron stairway out of steerage for the last time. David picked up Maria while Raisa possessively clutched the hem of his coat. Sofie secured Lizzie to her chest and carried a soft cloth satchel. Patiently they stood waiting in the disembarkation line as it formed on deck. As their turn came, they stepped from the deck of the ship onto the gangplank. Sofie shrieked and grabbed onto the railing. "Oh, David, I am dizzy again. My legs feel like noodles."

David laughed as he tried to reassure her. "JA, Sofie, my legs feel funny as well. I heard the crew talk about this. It is called 'sea legs.' Do not worry, *Liebchen*. It will go away as soon as your body realizes it is on land and not on the ship anymore." With a low chuckle, David said, "We must look funny to those who wait on the dock. We all walk like we drank too much vodka." Raisa was reassured and smiled brightly when her father reached down and took hold of her hand as they left the *S.S. Main* and walked onto American soil.

Her eyes wide with wonder, excitement, and fear, Raisa held tightly to her father's coattail as the family was herded into a long line. They looked ahead to see that the snaking line led to a large brick building. Here, they understood, they would be either accepted or rejected for entry into America. When they finally arrived inside the large building, David and Sofie were both alarmed by the occasional cries of distress which rang over the buzz of hundreds of immigrants speaking many languages.

The entry system in Baltimore wasn't as stringent as that of Ellis Island, but still they had their rules, and there were doctors to check the immigrants for a number of aliments. Just like Ellis Island, interpreters stood next to the doctors and examiners to help when needed. A man in front of David told them the inspectors were looking for criminals and insane or ill people. If the inspector marked your coat with a letter, that meant you would be detained for perhaps a short time or a long time, or you would be sent back across the Atlantic.

When it came time for David to step forward to be examined by the doctors, he did so with trepidation. The first doctor looked at David's papers and began the visual exam. He drew a quick breath when he noticed David's glass eye. "Sir, I think perhaps we have a problem here. It is your eye—or may I say the lack of an eye!"

David felt the flush of fear as another doctor was called over to examine David's eye. He tried to remain calm and let them examine him closely. "When did you lose your eye, Mr. Steiner?"

David cleared his throat, took a deep breath, and conjured up as much confidence as possible. "Doctor, I lost my eye when I was ten years old due to an infection from a barley beard. I served four years in the Russian army with this affliction, and it was never a problem. I am diligent in caring for the eye, and I assure you it does not affect me or how I conduct my work."

The doctors merged into a white cocoon to deliberate for what seemed like hours. Then with a flash of his hand, the first doctor stamped David's exam papers with the word "approved."

PART THREE

Chapter Eleven

The Early Years in America

As they walked away from the Immigration Building, Sofie clutched David's coat sleeve, tears streaming from her eyes. "Oh, David, David, that frightened me to my bones, and you acted so calm. How did you do that when they could have sent us back because of your eye?"

Unabated, David brushed a tear from her cheek with his finger. "My dear, I realized if I had appeared worried about my eye, they would have thought it was worth the worry. I assume they concluded I had lived without it for so long that the lack of one eye was not a threat or a problem. Relax, Sofie. It is all fine now; I think there are several more lines to pass through before we are able to call this place home!"

Both the Steiner and Klinger families, who had traveled together from Susannenthal, had no trouble clearing inspection. They reunited outside the Immigration Building and waited in a nearby park for the Weber family to clear inspection. Waiting under the shade, David said, "Sofie, Solomon and I need to change some of our money for American dollars so we are able to buy train tickets to Michigan. We were told not to change it all here on the docks because there are many who cheat the ignorant immigrant such as us."

He pointed down the street, "We were directed to a shop just a block away where the owner is German and will not cheat us. We will return shortly. Relax and watch the people—it's entertaining. You might keep your eye out for the Weber's."

Raisa tugged on her father's coat; he ignored her until she pulled so hard he almost fell over. "Raisa, *what* is it? Can't you see I am busy?"

Raisa looked up at her father with large tear-filled eyes. "But Papa, I just wanted to ask one question."

David's heart melted. "Okay, one question and then I have errands to do."

Smiling, Raisa tipped her head to the side as she asked, "Papa, how do they make the streets covered with round rocks and bricks?"

David scooped her up in his arms. "I suppose they have workmen who know how to do that sort of thing. Now you be a good girl, and go sit quietly beside your mother. I will be right back."

Cautiously, David and Solomon approached the money changer's booth in the small German shop and stood in yet another line. They listened closely to the process as other people handed over their foreign money in exchange for American dollars. David had been told on board what his money was worth in United States dollars, and he was prepared to defend his request.

When it was his turn, David walked up to the window. "I give you my money that is worth one hundred American dollars. I have been told by the ship's authorities this is the correct exchange."

The money exchanger looked up at the tall immigrant with the tweed newsboy cap and baggy wool coat. "And, sir, did the 'ship's authorities' also tell you that all money changers charge a fee for this service? My fee for exchanging your money will be one percent. So for the money you give to me, I give you ninety- nine American dollars, and I keep one for my fee. I hope this is satisfactory. Is there anything else I can help you with today?"

Smiling, David folded the money into his wallet and tucked it securely inside the front of his coat, safe from the roaming hands of a would-be street thief. When the two men were finished, they crossed the area to where their families waited. As they drew close, David's eyes widened, and his face paled with alarm. Sofie and Emilie were talking and gesturing wildly, and some of the children were crying and obviously quite distraught.

"What is it? Why are you all shouting? David put his arms around his wife. "Sofie, speak to me—what is the problem?"

"Oh, David, it is the worst. It is the thing we all feared. It's the, Weber's. They were denied entry because their baby is almost two and cannot walk or talk. For this the authorities refuse them to enter America and have sent them back to—to the old country!"

David turned to his friend. "Solomon, what are they going to do? Does anybody know what we can do with this problem? They have nothing to go back to—how can we help? We can't just go on. They are our friends!"

David and Solomon made their way back to the register's office. In respect, they both removed their wool newsboy hats as David knocked on a closed door marked "Rejections." They heard an authoritative voice inviting them to enter. In broken English, David said, "Please, please excuse us, but we believe our friends are in trouble and have a problem being accepted to America. We would appreciate it if you might tell us where they have been taken and what is happening to them. The names are Frederick and Esther Weber, and they have three children with them."

The man behind the desk rolled his eyes as he thumbed through the rejection files. His nose-clip glasses sat on the very end of his bulbous nose, which David found rather amusing. Finally, the man paused, pulled a file out, laid it on his desk, and flipped it open. After reading it for a few moments, he removed his glasses and with a voice of authority explained, "I am afraid what you have heard is correct. The Weber's were denied admission because of their son's inability to function. We have strict rules which weed out any persons who might at some time become a ward of the state or who might bring a communicable disease into the country."

David put his hands on the desk. "Can you tell us where they are so we may speak to them?" Nonchalantly, he gestured to the left where there was a holding room. David and Solomon hurried over, and after being admitted to visit, they found the Weber family huddled in a corner. Their eyes were red and swollen, and Esther tightly clutched her youngest son to her bosom to comfort him. When they saw their two friends moving through the crowd of rejected passengers, Frederick stood and hurried toward them.

"Thank God you found us! Is there anything you can do to change the authorities' minds? Our baby is not ill. He is just a little slow in development—and for this they are sending us back! Well, I tell you this—we are not going back! I have heard there is a freighter going to South America, and I have money to buy tickets for my family. We are told by the officials in the German embassy there are no restrictions on entry in that country. There are steerage tickets available for us. It will be ready for us to board after they herd the cattle on. We have decided to sail on the freighter and wait in South America until our baby can walk and talk. Then we will return to America and become citizens."

David and Solomon stood with their hands shoved deep into their pants pockets. David spoke first. "Frederick, this sounds like a good plan to us, much better than going back to all that we left behind. You will send us letters when you arrive in this South America? We don't know where we are going to be for the present, so send your letters to Sofie's brother-in-law in Michigan—you have the address. If we aren't there, he can get word to us. We will not lose track of you, dear friends."

David wrapped his arms around the beefy torso of his friend, followed by Solomon. "God speed to you and your family. Take heart, for He has a plan for us all, and we will pray for your protection and timely return to America. Good-bye and safe travels!"

David and Solomon left the Immigration Building with heavy hearts. Solomon shook his head. "It wasn't supposed to be like this, David. We were all supposed to set out together in America. I never expected something like this to happen to our group. But now it has, and we have to go on our own way."

~~~~~

David and Solomon returned to their families. David spoke first. "We are sorry to have taken so long, but we wanted to see that the Weber's had a plan of what they were going to do. We can tell you later what happened. We have taken care of the trunks and now should make one more stop at the train station to buy our tickets and then find someplace to spend the night." The children were ready to leave the shade of the oak tree and the grassy park; they wanted to explore and walk down the city street like all of the other people.

Everyone thought it was a fine plan. They chatted eagerly as they walked toward the station. Raisa and Elise, Solomon's youngest daughter, held hands and skipped behind their parents, feeling very grown-up and special. Raisa was indignant as she noticed some people pointing fingers at them and laughing behind their hands when they passed by.

They passed throngs of humanity, some pressing toward them and some pushing them along. The wide board sidewalk of Baltimore seemed more like a busy Berlin street. Everything was so new, so different.

Raisa was overwhelmed with the buzz of conversation and words she couldn't understand; she tugged on her father's coattail. "Papa, I do not know what these people say. I cannot understand their talk. Does anyone here speak like we do—in German?" After a while, she and Elise lagged behind, their faces turned up as their eyes scaled the tall buildings that towered into the blue morning sky, so high above their heads it made them dizzy. Her eyes bright with excitement, Raisa hurried ahead and again tugged on David's coat. "Look over there at that. It looks like a house on wheels, and it is riding on a track like a train except it doesn't have an engine to pull it. Papa, vas ist das?"

David smiled and explained to his daughter that the vehicle was called a trolley car and perhaps someday they might pay to ride on one. "But for now, we have to hurry to the train station to check on trains to Michigan where your uncle, aunt, and cousin live."

Raisa's eyes were wide with wonder and excitement as she tried in vain to take in all the new sights. She put her hands over her ears. "Papa, there is so much noise. Those trolley cars make loud clanking, there are men driving horses pulling wagons, and the peoples are all talking at once. I also smell many smells— some are not good, Papa! Look over there. That boy is selling pickles. I am so hungry for a sour pickle. Can I have one, can I?"

David took her by the hand and pulled her down the sidewalk as she looked back over her shoulder with longing at the pickle vendor. "Nein, Raisa, we do not have time to eat pickles now. We have to buy tickets for the train. Come along now, and watch where you walk. You certainly don't want to step in some man's tobacco juice!"

~~~~~

Sofie couldn't help but take notice of the fashionable women who passed by with their crisply starched white blouses tucked into long, straight flannel skirts. Their shining hair was pinned up, and many wore stylish straw hats attached to their hair with a sinfully long hat pin. Suddenly self-conscious, she reached up and pulled the black babushka off her head and quickly tucked it into her bag. Sofie proudly lifted her chin, tilting her head slightly to the left as she slipped her arm through David's as they walked down the cobblestone sidewalk.

As she walked, Sofie felt as though she was in another world. She was very aware of the din of English-speaking voices, of babies crying, of distinguished gentlemen in high hats, strolling down the street as if they owned it. Trolley cars clanked through intersections with people jumping on and off; young boys were hawking newspapers on every corner, and numerous food vendors skillfully tempted those who passed.

Sofie watched as Raisa left her friend Elise up ahead. Waiting for her parents, the little girl fell into step with them and deftly slipped her hand into her father's. David smiled as he looked down at her. "Papa, I have only one more question for today. What are those things tied around the horses back ends? They look so funny, and I have noticed that all of the horses in this town have them on."

David laughed. "Oh, Raisa, only you would notice that. It is a bag that catches the horse's poop, so they don't do their business onto the streets. Now go ahead and walk with Elise. We are almost to the station."

David and Solomon approached the ticket booth at the Baltimore and Ohio railroad station. Thankfully, the aging ticket master spoke enough German to be understood. David asked to purchase two adult and three children tickets to Sandusky, Michigan. The ticket master looked at his schedule. "For five seats to Sandusky, Michigan"—his finger traced down the schedule— "that will cost you twenty dollars for coach. Train leaves tomorrow at four p.m. The cost is higher because you have to change trains several times. Sandusky is off the beaten path, as we say—it is not a large city."

David blinked once and then stammered in shock as he replied, "You say twenty dollars for four tickets and our luggage— to ride the train from here to Michigan? How far is it? I—I did not expect to pay that much."

"The B & O Railway line ends in Cleveland, Ohio. That's about a two-day ride on the train. There are a large number of German people living in Cleveland. Perhaps you can go that far, find work, and save enough for a ticket to Sandusky, which would be another two-day ride. You will have to change to a different train line out of Cleveland anyway. Now there is a Sandusky, Ohio, as well as a Sandusky, Michigan. Are you sure which one you want to go to? It's up to you, friend. Make up your mind."

David took off his cap and rubbed his head. He didn't understand what the agent was trying to tell him, and he felt the eyes of the man behind of him, boring into his back. David had never felt as flustered and ill prepared in his life; and to make matters worse, the agent was becoming short-tempered with him. *I have to make a decision!* David's voice shook with pressure and indecision. "We have—we have relatives in this place – Sandusky, in Michigan. They are expecting us, but perhaps what you suggest might be the best way. I will buy five tickets to Cleveland—and thank you for your information." He turned and looked blankly at Solomon. They had planned to travel together to Sandusky, and now it was all changed.

Beads of perspiration stood out on David's forehead as he explained to his friend. "The trainmaster tells me it will cost twenty dollars for my family to ride the train to Sandusky, Michigan. I have made the decision to go only to Cleveland, where I will find a place to live and work for a short time. The trainmaster also tells me there are many Volga Germans living in Cleveland in a particular area. Perhaps it is better this way. I know many of our people go to Johann's house, and there will not be room for all of us to stay. If Sofie and I do not like Cleveland, then we will travel to Michigan. You and your family go ahead and travel on if that is what you want, Solomon. Perhaps we will join you in a few months."

He walked back to where Sofie and his daughters waited on the bench. David said, "Sofie, I have made a decision not to go to your sister's house right now, but instead we go to a city called

Cleveland. I want to see what this city is and am told there are many Germans from the Volga there for us to feel comfortable. Solomon and Emilie have decided to go on to Sandusky. We will find a place to stay tonight, and tomorrow we will transfer our trunks to the train."

Sofie stared dumbfounded at her husband. "David, you make such an important decision without speaking to me first. I travel all this way across the ocean with your promise I will see my sister soon, and now you have made plans to go to another place that I do not know? Where we don't know anybody?"

David took a deep breath to calm himself. "Sofie, it is what works best for us right now. I did not want to spend twenty dollars of our money for a train journey so far away. I think it best we learn of how this country works, and then we will know more information when we travel on to Michigan. How far is this Michigan state? I do not know. There is much I do not know, but I will learn—I need time and opportunity to study everything. I would appreciate more cooperation and patience from you. Yes—I have made the decision. Now we shall find a room to spend the night, and perhaps some food would be good as well."

~~~~~~

The next morning the Steiner and Klinger families walked back to the train station and ordered their trunks to be delivered to the platform for their respective trains. The Klinger's took the train to Michigan, and the Steiner family waited another hour for their train to Cleveland.

When they were settled on the northbound train to Cleveland, Sofie decided to speak to her husband again about his sole decision. Before she could speak, tears of bitter disappointment filled her eyes. She turned her face toward the window, attempting to calm down. As the miles slipped past the window, however, she felt more distressed and deceived. Finally there was no stopping her words.

"David, I wish to speak to you about this decision you made. You know that for months I looked forward to seeing my sister and her family. It's what gave me hope. Now you changed our plans without a thought for me?"

David's eyes were bloodshot and had dark circles underneath; his face flushed as he turned and looked at Sofie in dismay. Shocking them both, he slapped his cap against his knee in a rare display of emotion. "Woman, I am tired, I am frustrated, and I am confused in this new place. I was forced to make a quick decision! People were waiting behind me in line, and there was no time to run to my wife and ask her permission to buy a ticket or not to buy a ticket. The ticket man was shouting at me to hurry and make a decision, and a decision I made—and that is that! I am trying to save money and not spend it carelessly. I believe we should take things slow until we learn of the opportunities and the ways of this country. We will go to Michigan, and you will see your sister when I have figured it all out. Until then I do not want or need to hear bad talk from you! That is not like you, Sofie, not at all."

Sofie's face mirrored her embarrassment and dismay as she felt the blush of humiliation flood over her face. David had never talked to her in such a way before, which only added to her fear and disappointment. She continued to stare out the window, barely breathing as David pulled his cap back over his face and pretended to nap.

She stared out the window as the lush landscape flew by. *I must forgive my husband and try to understand. He only did what he thought was best. But—what is going to happen to us? I am so frightened and at this moment feel so far from the only home I have ever known.* Protectively, her right hand slid to cover her stomach.

Thankful to be off the ship and on land again, the family slept well, even if it was on a moving train. In the morning when they stopped briefly at a small town, David bought coffee, milk, and hard rolls for their breakfast.

Sofie played games with the older two girls, telling them to look for cows, pigs, and horses. Raisa especially liked it when the engineer blew the whistle as the speeding train crossed bridges and roads and also when they thundered through small towns without stopping. She was fascinated by the number of cozy farms and the miles of thick, green woods that flew by. The little girls' eyes opened wide when they passed through Pittsburgh. "Papa, look at all those big buildings and tall chimneys with much smoke coming from them! What makes the smoke, Papa, huh?"

David's mind was elsewhere when he looked out the window as miles of cityscape flew past in a blur. Billboards advertising women's hats, aftershave, and hair tonic were a dime a dozen. The train clattered over a steel bridge as he felt a shiver run up his back. He physically and mentally felt his fear grow and gnaw at his gut and torment his mind. He opened his Bible and read.

The two-day train trip across Maryland, Pennsylvania, and Ohio ended when their train pulled into the impressive, modern station in Cleveland. David looked out the window of the train and thought, *now, what?*

Gathering their baggage, David and Sofie stood stunned and immobile as they tried to digest the new world. David shook his head and instructed Sofie and the children to wait for him while he found directions. He began to walk toward the station where he hoped to find someone who spoke German. David whirled as he felt someone tap him on the shoulder. A middle-aged man stood behind him, smiling as he spoke in German. "Sir, pardon me, but may I be of help to you? I saw you get off the train with your family, and you look lost." David exhaled with relief.

"JA, Ja—we were told there is a large community of German- speaking peoples in this city. A gentleman told me it was close to a lake called 'M-erie'—or something."

The man smiled and in perfect German explained, "There is such a community, and it is close to Lake Erie. Look for the area called Tremont, or Ohio City. That is where most Germans and Russian-Germans live. I would suggest that you avoid neighborhoods where your kind of people, haven't settled. That is where trouble waits."

"Yes, my friend, Cleveland is a giant mixture of new and old emigrants. You'll find pockets of Jewish, Slavic, German, Greek, Italian, Polish, Irish, Chinese, Slovak, Ukrainian, and even Negroes who are freed slaves. You will find an affordable wagon over there to take you, your family, and your trunks to the area of your choice. Good luck to you, sir, and to your family. May you find peace and prosperity in America!"

~~~~~

Cleveland: Summer 1907

Her fingernails scraped across the secondhand table in sequence to the escalating pains that tore through her contracting uterus. Sofie reached down and frantically massaged her small belly as the second pain struck like lightning and brought her to her knees. It was then she felt the warm, sticky blood slide down her thighs and saw it begin to pool onto the freshly scrubbed linoleum of her kitchen floor.

Sofie lifted her face to the heavens as tears of realization rolled down her porcelain face. "Dear Lord in heaven, it's too soon. Please not again—do not take another baby from my arms."

It had been only months ago that she had miscarried their first son. Too soon after she lost the last baby, she realized she was pregnant again. Her body had no opportunity to strengthen and restore itself. *I can't seem to function properly living in Cleveland, with the unending noise and the hordes of people who fight and talk loudly at all hours. There is no peace to be had in these crowded tenements or on the streets below. Our children have no safe place to play or to live in this foul stew of humanity.*

As another pain seized her body, Sofie was glad their daughters were sleeping and unaware of what was happening to her. Suddenly, she remembered that before he left that morning, David had told her he was working the late shift at the bakery and wouldn't be home until around midnight. *I'm all alone; I have to do this alone.*

Silently, Sofie willed herself to remain conscious as the next pain prompted her to bear down and push. After the pain passed, Sofie grabbed onto the doorframe. With her free hand, she swept the beads of perspiration and sticky strands of hair away from her face. She gritted her teeth as another pain began to build, and this time, she involuntarily pushed.

Staggering to the alcove where they stored the chamber pot, Sofie quickly lifted her skirts and removed her bloody underwear and stockings. Too weak to squat, she kneeled over the chipped, secondhand pot as nature expelled the unhealthy fetus from her body with a final ripping contraction. More tears rolled down

Sofie's face as she felt her tiny baby slip from her body into the chamber pot. A final contraction gripped her empty womb, and Sofie felt the afterbirth slide from her body just as the blackness closed in around her. Soundlessly, she slid onto the worn linoleum.

~~~~~~

David had put in a long, hot, and busy day at the bakery; he was tired to the bone as he pulled down the shop window shades, went out and locked the door. Wearily, he decided to splurge and take the trolley home. While he waited for his ride, he removed his coat, throwing it across his shoulder. *I can't get used to this heat and constant sweating.* Off to the side of the street, he spotted a pickle vendor and on a whim bought a giant dill pickle for Raisa and stuffed the wrapped pickle into his pocket. The trolley rolled to a stop, and the doors opened. David paid for the ticket and settled back onto a wooden seat. Normally, he walked the two miles to their flat in order to breathe fresh air and relax after work, but for some reason, tonight he felt anxious about working so late. Reaching their tenement building, David took the dimly lit stairs two at a time, eager to see his wife and young daughters.

He reached the unpainted door to their two-room apartment and pulled the heavy key from his front pocket. Once inside the dimly lit room, David hung his coat and hat on the rusty wall hook beside the door. Even though the kerosene lamp on the table was tuned low, as he turned around, David spotted Sofie lying on the floor. Shock and fear sucked the breath from his lungs as he crossed the room in three long strides.

"Oh, dear, Lord Jesus---Sofie. Sofie, talk to me. Please wake up." Then he spotted the bloody chamber pot. Tears rolled down his face as the realization hit him hard. She had been pregnant again and had not told him. David hurried to the dry sink and poured water from the pitcher. He dampened a cloth with the tepid water and gently wiped it over Sofie's face. "Oh please, my love, wake up. Oh, Sofie, I am so sorry. I am so sorry this happened again and while you were alone. Why didn't you tell me?"

Her eyelids blinked once and then opened slowly. Sofie recognized David and weakly squeezed his hand as she tried to sit up. "David, I am so glad you are home. I am sorry I didn't tell you, but I didn't want you to worry. I know how hard you have been working. Now I have lost yet another child in this godforsaken place.

"I can't live here anymore, I mean it. We have lived here for two years—*two* years, David, in this squalor and this—this din of humanity. I miss the calm and serenity of our home in Susannenthal. This is no place to raise our children. They can't grow and be happy in this place. Everything is too much, too fast, too loud, too different. I want to go to Michigan to my sister's house. Please, David, please."

Gently lifting Sofie to her feet, David helped her to stand. Weak from the miscarriage, Sofie moved slowly to the window. Hanging on to the window frame, Sofie looked out through the thick grime on the glass, to the street below. "Where is all the easy life? We were told this was a wonderful country—like a Garden of Eden. Look down there, David. Look at the street, crowded with trolley cars, horse-drawn wagons, buggies, and the filth they leave behind. There are so many peoples, they can't move. This is an evil place. Why don't you see that? We might have freedom and safety in this country from the Cossacks, but living in the big city is not where we belong. Too many peoples all speaking languages I don't understand, and the noise, heat, and odor are unbearable. I want to go to the country. It is what we know."

David moved across the floor and wrapped his arms around his wife as he too looked down onto the street teeming with humanity and congestion. "I know what you say is true, my love. This is not for me either. It is all so different here compared to how we lived in the old country. There are so many new ways and things to learn. I can now understand it is not going to be easy for us to make our way. All we can do is our best and pray it will be better for our children."

As they moved away from the window, Sofie wrinkled up her nose. "What is that I smell? You smell like pickles, David!" Laughing, he reached into his pocket and pulled out the fat dill pickle he had bought for Raisa.

~~~~

In 1909, on the outskirts of Cleveland, David signed on to help a couple of area farmers with their fall harvest. As soon as the work fell off and Sofie had regained her strength, David bought tickets on the train to Sandusky, Michigan. He had saved a fair amount of money in hope of finding a farm or even a team of horses and a wagon. Now some of it would be used for train tickets north. As they were packing up their few belongings, David came across the bag of Turkey Red Wheat seed that his father had given him. "Perhaps now in Michigan, I will have the opportunity to plant this seed—this seed of the Volga!"

Raisa heard what her father had said. "Papa, are we like the red wheat—'seed of the Volga'? I know we are going to live and grow here in America, so that makes us like the seed of the Volga, right?" David simply smiled at her and nodded his head.

Raisa kept her little nose pressed against the window of the train almost the entire way. They were all happy to be leaving Cleveland and enjoyed the train trip as they crossed the Ohio River then skirted the shore of Lake Erie; finally they reached the large city of Toledo on the western tip of the lake. Here they changed trains, crossed the Maumee River, and then headed north into Michigan. The railroad tracks hugged the coast of Lake Erie and ran along Lake St. Clair until they reached Port Huron. Again, they changed to a smaller local train that traveled along the shore of Lake Huron to Port Sanilac in Sanilac County, Michigan.

~~~~~~

Sofie's brother-in-law, Johann, met them at the train with his wagon. It had been six years since Sofie had seen her younger sister and brother-in-law; they spent most of the trip west to Sandusky catching up on family news. Once they arrived at the Kober house, her sister handed her a letter from South America, from the Weber's, which she had saved. Sofie stuck it deep in her pocket to read later that night after they had tucked their daughters in bed. When she and David were alone, they opened the letter and read it together.

September 1906

Dear David and Sofie: Our accommodations in the freighter to South America were quite unpleasant, as we had cattle and sheep in pens next to where we slept. They kept us awake during the first night, but later we got used to hearing them move around, bellow, and do their business! The country here is most beautiful, and we found an area where German peoples live. Frederick found work on the docks, and we found a small but clean house to live in until we are ready to leave.

Houses here are not good. They are built poorly of mud bricks and stamped dirt floors. This is very hot weathers here and much large bugs. We must put the legs of our chairs and beds in cans of oil to keep cockroaches, scorpions, and most large black spiders from crawling onto our furniture. Also before putting on clothes or shoes, we learn to shake them. There are no Cossacks here, but they do have raiders who ride horses at night to rob the people.

I do not know how long we will have to live here. Carl is doing good—he talks and walks now; we expect another baby in five months. We will continue to send letters to your sister's house so if you move, you can always ask her for letters from us. God willing we will see you again someday.
Your friends, Frederick and Esther

Sofie noticed there was not a return address on the letter. Nevertheless, it had been written some time ago, and who knew where they were now.

~~~~~

With help from Sofie's sister and husband, David and Sofie found a small farmhouse to rent, and David got a job hauling freight to Port Sanilac. In no time at all, Sofie and the girls settled in the little house. David was relieved to see the color come back to their cheeks.

Anytime he could work with horses, David was happy. He instinctively knew how to get the most from a team, and it wasn't by working them to death. The other haulers noticed David seemed to make more trips than they did with only one team, and they wondered why. "Where did you get those sleek horses?

How do you make so many trips with horses that are the same as ours? Yet they stay strong and don't break down like ours?"

Pleased with his team and work record, David replied, "Well, I tell you, it's pretty simple—I

David Steiner's
Percheron draft horses

take good care of my horses. I feed them the best hay and rest them whenever I can. Also, I give them a good rubdown each night before I go home to eat my own supper. They like that. JA, they sure do!"

They stayed there until early March. Sofie quickly regained her strength in the country. With spring coming, David tried to find a farm to rent, but there were none. The area had a large population of Germans, and they already occupied most of the available farms. Over the past few months, the area welcomed ten new immigrant families of *Die Wolgadeutschen* who were also looking for a place of their own. They had all worked the sugar beet fields diligently and had caught the attention of the beet factory officials.

~~~~~~

March, 1910
Dear Mama and Papa:

We have lived here in Michigan for over a year. The area is beautiful and very green; it is close to a group of large lakes where we go for the picnic on Sundays. I have a big garden and have built my chicken coop which houses egg-laying hens and fancy roosters whose feathers I use to decorate the hats I make. I enjoy seeing the styles of hats in America and am working on several creations of my own.

Raisa has started school, as she was very bored at home. She learns her lessons quickly and enjoys coming home and teaching Maria and Lizzie new English words. This new language comes slow to David and me. We have learnt enough words to get by but are more comfortable speaking German at home. This upsets Raisa, who asks how we expect to learn English if we don't practice—she is our teacher!

We were happy to see David's brother, Wilhelm, and his family for a short visit before they traveled to Colorado to find farm work. We don't hear from them except on Christmas; they seem to be doing good.

David tells me we are moving again, to a state called Wyoming where several Susannenthal peoples have settled. He already has work with a sugar beet grower doing contract fieldwork.

I am feeling well, with no more miscarriages. The good healthy country air has restored my health, and so if the Lord blesses us with another child, I am sure my body is ready. I would like to give David a son, although he adores his little daughters, and they give us much joy and very little troubles.

We hope you are well and problems with the government are better.

Our love and prayers, Sofie and David

~~~~~

Early that spring the Great Western Sugar Beet Company offered most of the immigrant *Die Wolgadeutschen* families train tickets to travel to a place called Lovell, Wyoming, to work in the beet fields. It seemed a gift from heaven, so they packed their meager belongings and made arrangements to travel by train to the rural area of the Big Horn Basin in Wyoming. Neither David nor Sofie had any idea of how far away this place was, but they were soon to find out.

David had heard there were successful farms and small communities of *Die Wolgadeutschen* already established in the area. Both David and Sofie felt positive about this move, believing and hoping that this was going to be where they would find a home. Before they left Michigan, Sofie wrote a letter to her mother.

Chapter Twelve

Moving On

They left Michigan with two extra trunks of clothing and an odd assortment of household goods that they had acquired over the past three years. Ten families from the area traveled together. They didn't know anything about this new area, except it was west of where they were and other Volga Germans from Susannenthal were living there. So, with high hopes, they moved on. They took the train from Port Sanilac across Michigan through Flint and Lansing and around the tip of Lake Michigan to Chicago where they changed trains. They boarded a train called the Chicago and Northwestern.

Subconsciously, David was nagged by a relentless quest for what he considered "the chosen land"—someplace, anyplace, where he and his family felt comfortable and where they fit in. Because of faith, hope, and promises, the Steiner family was back on a train headed somewhere new. They traveled through Madison, Wisconsin, and Brainerd, Minnesota, and then onto Minneapolis/St. Paul where they changed trains to a Burlington & Missouri line.

When the train stopped for a change of engines, David and Sofie gathered their daughters and got off to stretch their legs. They looked for a grassy spot or a park nearby where the girls could run and play for a few minutes. In Minneapolis/St. Paul, they enjoyed a layover of three hours as well as a dish of ice cream. It seemed they had just settled beneath a shade tree when all too soon they heard the train's warning whistle, and they hurried back to board. "Papa, I think we should stay here—I like it, and I even heard some people over there talking German!" Raisa pleaded with her father, but their tickets were bought and paid for, and promises had been made to travel to Wyoming.

The Burlington & Missouri steam engine pulled the passenger cars west out of Minnesota, crossing the northern point of the Red River close to Fargo, North Dakota. David watched in wonder as the landscape changed from lush vegetation to butterscotch- colored rolling hills, and dotted with sagebrush and greasewood. For the last two hundred miles, the prairie rose and then dipped, forming gentle rolling hills. David noticed many farmers out in the fields with their teams of horses and plows, opening the sleeping earth in preparation for spring planting. His hands itched to hold the reins of eager teams of horses and to smell the pungent odor of the earth as the plow turned it over, in preparation for planting. He watched until the darkness swallowed the daylight and his view of the prosperous farms. David sighed as he closed his eyes in supplication, praying he had made the right choice. A particular peace came over him as he leaned back onto the train seat and fell into a sound sleep.

The sun was just beginning to creep over the far eastern horizon when they crossed the Yellowstone River Valley just south of Glendive, Montana, and pulled into Miles City. They stayed on the train until it arrived at the small station at Huntley, about twenty miles east of Billings. This was where they were told to disembark from the Burlington and Missouri train and wait for the CB&Q local line that would take them close to the rural area of Wyoming where they were headed.

Raisa couldn't sit still; she marched up and down the platform, holding her hand up to shield her eyes against the afternoon sun, looking for some sign of the train or even life. She returned to sit on the bench ever so briefly and then was up again. They were all hot and tired of traveling.

Minutes later, when the train pulled into the station, David saw that it was definitely a no-frills passenger train. With some hesitation, they boarded the weather-beaten, wooden passenger car. David almost had to laugh when the engine began to move away from the station. "I have never heard a train engine make so much noise in an effort to move. Let's hope for the best!" Slowly it headed south for Toluca, Montana.

It was close to noon when the train pulled into Pryor, Montana, just north of the Wyoming state line; the engine hadn't even come to a complete stop when David and his family were startled by a group of about thirty Indians who rushed up to the train. They started whooping and hollering so loud that the two littlest girls began to cry. Raisa pressed her nose to the window, and when David wasn't looking, she stuck out her tongue at the rowdy bunch. David couldn't figure out why one moment she was looking out the window and the next she was crouching on the floor.

David had been occupied, looking out the window at the passing prairie since they crossed into Wyoming. He was not impressed. There were certainly several prosperous-looking farms, but there were more shacks and obviously poor farms and ranches. His heart sank in his chest as questions fired through his brain. Reminiscing, he thought, *Decisions were so much simpler—life was simpler, along the Volga.*

Sofie noticed the expression on her husband's face as he stared out the window at the bleak landscape. She instinctively knew what he was thinking because it was exactly what she was thinking.

~~~~~~

About forty miles northeast of Cody, the train pulled into the tiny town of Frannie, Wyoming, where David and Sofie made preparations to disembark. After they collected their trunks and suitcases, David found a man with a wagon who agreed to take them south to the town of Lovell. It was only about ten miles away, and the man charged four bits for five people and their luggage. When they crossed the Shoshone River and rounded the bend into the town of Lovell, their spirits lifted. David saw a number of prosperous-looking farms near the river, and the town was laid out in an efficient grid. There were a few small shops and two dry goods stores, along with a couple of churches and, of course, the expected saloons and pool halls.

The little family quickly gathered their belongings after the wagon pulled up near a hotel. David paid the man and then arranged to store their large trunks in a spare room at the hotel. He carried their three-year-old daughter while Raisa and her sister Maria followed along, hand in hand carrying their own little bundles. Sofie had her own large satchel, which she flung over one shoulder.

Even though the sun was shining, an unexpected bitter wind chilled them as they walked. They all stopped and pulled their coats from the bundles. The board sidewalk turned into a packed dirt path as they continued, searching for the address written on the paper David carried.

"Papa, Papa—when are we going to find the house where your friends live? I am very tired of walking so far, Papa. I'm cold, and my feet are hurting a lot! And, and—look at Maria. She is so pokey!" Raisa continued to chatter. "It is starting to get dark, and I don't want to be out here in the night—it is too scary!" To make matters worse, Maria began to bawl.

After walking nine city blocks, they came to the modest house at the far end of Shoshone Avenue. Sofie couldn't help but notice the siding was painted white and the scrolling trim a pale green. The yard was beginning to awaken from a long winter's nap, as daffodils were in full bloom and the lilac bush was loaded with fat buds. David pushed open the sturdy picket gate and motioned for his family to enter the yard. They waited as he walked ahead up the wooden steps and rapped soundly on the front door.

A stout man with a full beard answered the door. An expression of both relief and happiness covered his face as his arms flew out to embrace David. "Aww—Steiner—finally, you arrive in our town. Come in, come in and sit down." Upon hearing the commotion, Hermann Miller's wife, Emma, hurried into the room; she immediately embraced Sofie and then smothered each of the girls in her ample bosom. "You are just in time for dinner. You haven't stopped to eat, I hope?"

After a hot meal, the two older girls were given a small pillow and a blanket and shown to the corner of the living room next to the potbelly stove where they were to make their bed. David and Sofie were given the spare bedroom. Their heads barely hit the pillow before they all fell into an exhausted sleep.

The following day David found a small, unpainted wood house across the tracks to the north of town which they rented on the spot. That afternoon, when David took Sofie to look at the house, they cringed when they found bed bugs under the mattresses. "Sofie, I don't think this is a good house. Those bedbugs get in the walls and under the floors. We know they aren't just in the mattress and cushions. It looks to me like if we are going to live here, we will have to fumigate the house first."

As they rode back into Lovell, Sofie commented, "Oh, David, those things just give me gooseflesh. There is nothing I hate worse than to think about something crawling on me and my children during the night, and the bites itch so. Let's go to the general store. I am sure they have the sulfur cans we need to fumigate with. We can return to the house today and get the job done. We should buy about four of them, one for each room. We will have to close the house up tight; because once we light them and they send out that terrible sulfur smoke, we can't go in there for a day or so. Do you think we could stay awhile longer with the Millers?"

~~~~~

Once they got the little house in shape, it didn't take David long to find work on a farm, but he didn't have the money to buy any equipment or horses of his own. His reputation and ability with a team of horses soon spread, and he had more offers to work than he could handle. In the spring the entire family went into the fields to thin and block the young beet plants; in the fall they all helped again with the harvest. It was backbreaking work, and the only time Sofie was excused from the field work was when she was pregnant. Near the end of March 1909, their fourth daughter, Emilie was born. She was healthy, and Sofie had no trouble with the pregnancy or birth.

~~~~~

They had made enough profit that fall for David to buy a wagon and team of his own. David and Sofie joined the Lutheran church in town, and things were beginning to settle; they were happy living at the edge of Lovell. They made friends quickly with the other people from the Volga; even some from Susannenthal had settled there.

David built a small lean-to shed and a fenced yard where Sofie raised her prize chickens. She also had access to straw from the fields and reed grass from the Shoshone River bank for the hats she began to make again.

Later in the month, Sofie made a trip to town; she wore one of her natural straw fedoras. To accent the hat, she had fashioned a white rose from gossamer gauze fabric and tastefully accented it with brown, bronze, and gold chicken feathers. Sofie walked confidently into the dry goods store and headed to where bolts of fabric were stacked. She spent ten minutes looking through the fabric until she found what she wanted to make curtains for the kitchen. As Sofie approached the cash register, the store owner lifted his head and came around the counter to stand beside her. He peered curiously at her hat. "Good day, Ms. Steiner. Did you find what you need? Do you mind if I ask where you purchased your lovely hat?"

Sofie's hand rose self-consciously to touch the straw hat as a smile broke across her face. "Why, Mr. Roth, I—I made this hat myself. I learned to weave with straw and river grasses in the old country. It was a favorite pastime of mine to make hats for the field and also for dressing up. I am flattered that you find it pleasing."

The store owner asked her if she had ever considered making them for profit, and if so, would she make several for his store. Sofie left the store floating on a cloud. She was thrilled to have a way to make a little money of her own and especially doing something that she loved. That evening when she told David, he too was enthusiastic about her good fortune. Every nickel mattered.

That next afternoon, Sofie walked down the dusty lane to the road where their mail box was anchored with sizeable rocks tossed into an old rusty milk can. She pulled open the tin door of the box and pulled out several bills and a letter—a letter from Russia. It was not often that she and her mother wrote, and even less often did they hear from David's parents. Her hands shook as she felt a foreboding chill sweep through her. She hurried back up the lane to the shade of the old cottonwood tree that grew beside the house. Sofie gathered her skirts and sat down beneath it; she carefully opened the letter from her mother.

October, 1909
Dear David and Sofie:

We have enjoyed your letters about your settling in this place called Lovell. It sounds good that you are with other Die Wolgadeutschen families, which makes living better. Of course, we are sad to hear David is having a hard time finding a farm of his own and life is uneven for you all.

It is with great difficulty that I must be the one to tell you of the sadness that has come to our village. Since none of David's brothers or sisters live here anymore, it is I who must tell you of this.

David, in August, your father, Philip, had an illness which left him paralyzed on the right side, unable to speak or walk. He was in bed for a month before he passed away. Shortly after, your mother came down with the flu, and she too has passed into heaven. They were getting on in years and did not have the strength to keep living. We are very sorry to have to tell you of this news, but you know they are at peace now.

Life here is getting harder every day. Political unrest is very bad, and we are feeling the power and resentment of the Russian government as they take more of our crops and more of our way of living. We do not know where it will all stop. We pray for you and for ourselves as well. May God watch over you and our precious grandchildren.

Our love and prayers, Mama and Papa

~~~~~

When David rode his horse up the lane that evening, Sofie met him at the barn. She had news to tell him that she did not want their daughters to hear yet. David was startled to see Sofie in the barn; then he noticed the letter in her hand.

That evening after supper and the dishes were put away, Sofie told their daughters about the deaths of their Oma and Opa back in the old country. David sat in solitude at the kitchen table with his large, calloused hands resting on his open Bible. There were no words, only a jumble of thoughts and memories that churned inside his head. He desperately wanted to read his Bible and feel the comfort from the words but could not bring himself to concentrate. The loss of his parents—of the people who had taken him in and raised him, and loved him—hit him hard. To think and know they no longer lived was more than he could comprehend at that moment.

David took the death of his parents very hard and for days moved without purpose. Raisa noticed her father's despondency and one evening cuddled next to him on the porch bench as he was reading his Bible. "Papa, will you tell me some stories about Oma and Opa who are in heaven? What was it like when you were little? What did you do for fun? I don't remember why we left there and came to America. I was too little and just don't remember much about living in Susannenthal. Why, Papa? Why don't you talk about your life and how it was back in the old country?"

David looked down at his oldest daughter. "Sweet girl, I don't talk about what is past. It is over, and there is no sense in reliving it. We should pay most attention to today and the rest of our lives. This is a better life, and it is hard to remember things that were not good when we left. Now go and play with your sisters. I am reading my Bible."

Raisa jumped back and scrunched up her face. "Papa, you need to shave tonight. Your face is all *stickery,* and it hurts when I kiss your cheek!"

David managed a smile. "Well, maybe I will do that later on while there is still light, because you know I don't want to miss any of your kisses!" True to his word, that evening after supper dishes were washed and put away, David pumped some water at the washstand and stood before the cracked mirror that hung by the front door. He lathered his face up real good and noticed out of the corner of his eye, three little spies watching him. When they crept closer, David suddenly raised his hands over his head and let out a fierce growl. He began to chase his little daughters, catching one then another as he gave them each a very messy shaving-cream kiss! They squealed and laughed so hard that Lizzie wet her pants.

"Oh, Papa, look what you made Lizzie do—you made her laugh too hard, and she went in her pants!"

That night as Raisa lay in her bed, she thought about what her father had said about the old country. *Papa says he doesn't think about the past, yet I know he is sad for Oma and Opa. I don't understand what he means. It's like he is two people, trying to be one, but he can't decide which one he is. Maybe that is why we are always moving, trying to find who he should be, what he should do. I don't understand what he is looking for. If I did, I would help him find it. Also, I don't like it when he and Mama speak mostly in German— probably so we don't know what they are saying.*

~~~~~

Several weeks after learning of the death of his parents, David announced they would be leaving Lovell. "It is no good for me here either. There aren't farms to buy, and I'm tired of working the beet fields for other farmers. They work us like slaves at the sugar beet factory." Then came the real blow; David told his family they would be moving back to Cleveland.

Sofie's mouth dropped open, and her eyes narrowed as she replied, "Cleveland? You want to leave all our friends and comforts we have here for—for Cleveland? The girls and I are happy here in Lovell, and now you want to leave again. I no sooner get a house settled, and we begin to relax and enjoy life—then out of the blue, you decide we have to pack up and move. Do you even know what you are looking for, David? You know I hated living in Cleveland, and our daughters did not thrive in that crowded, dirty place. No, David, please not Cleveland."

However, David's mind was made up. He had convinced himself he would find opportunity in Cleveland, something to call his own. When they lived there before, he was always able to find work, and he was convinced it would be even better for them this time around. He gave notice to the landlord and sold the horses and wagon.

~~~~~

December 1909

Their good-byes were made, the trunks were packed yet again and put onto the train, and the Steiner family pulled up their shallow roots and rode the rails back to Cleveland. Raisa, Maria, and Lizzie pouted most of the way, unhappy they had to leave their friends behind. They arrived just as winter was taking a bitter grip on the city. The low temperature coupled with the ever-present humidity was brutal. David found a small house on a farm to rent on the outskirts of the city.

It was midday when David pulled the rented horse and wagon to a stop in front of a weather-beaten house at the edge of Cleveland. Sofie's heart sank when she saw where they were going to live. David hopped down from the seat, came around, and helped his wife off the wagon, and then one by one he lifted his daughters to the ground. They walked up the dirt path to the weathered front door. David unlocked the door and pushed it open. As the sunshine poured through the door, all Sofie saw was dust floating and sparkling in the light. She covered her nose as the musty odor of stale cigarette smoke, garlic, and mice hit her in the face. David walked into the kitchen and set their bags down. Because there was only one window in the room, he lit a kerosene lantern that someone had left sitting on a crude, dusty table. The feeble light attempted to illuminate the small room, making it appear even more dismal.

Raisa walked to a grimy window and looked out at the dirt yard where a pitiful tree struggled to grow. She turned back to the room and surveyed the furniture intended for the renters. A wobbly table and six mismatched chairs, along with a faded brown leather davenport with holes the size of baseballs in the seats, occupied one room. Filthy limp curtains hung pathetically at the front window. Frustration and disappointment consumed Sofie, as she fought back the tears.

Sofie turned to David. "Is this the best you could find? It's going to take me weeks to get this place in shape." Sofie placed her secondhand valise on the filthy wood table; she dug around, and finding her apron, she pulled it from the bag and tied it around her middle. "Let's get busy; we've got a lot of work to do to get this house ready for the evening meal and sleeping." She turned to David. "I need water, lots of water, first thing—and a fire in that old stove!" She pushed up her sleeves as she declared, "Raisa, help your papa unload the wagon. I'll keep the little ones in here with me for now. At least it's so cold out that we don't have to worry about bedbugs yet!" She paused a moment to look out at the backyard and was happy to see a nice patch for a large garden, a small fenced chicken coop along with a fairly new outhouse.

While the water heated on the stove, Sofie opened the back door. Armed with a broom, a bucket of tepid water, and lye soap, she marched to the outhouse. She flung open the door as three or four mice scurried past her feet and a couple of sparrows flew from under the eaves. Sofie shrieked with fright then laughed as she stood in the doorway, waiting for other creatures to make their getaway. Holding the broom over her head, she proceeded to sweep a collection of spider webs from the ceiling and corners of the outhouse. Satisfied she had reduced the number of insects and rodents from the structure, she approached the bench where two holes were cut. She scrubbed the weathered wood bench and the floor with the lye soap and water. She poured the remaining soapy water down the holes!

Sofie walked through the back door and nearly collided with her three oldest daughters, all bundled up in coats and scarves. "Daddy said we could go out in the yard and swing on that old tire that is hanging from the tree. It's boring in here, and it's pretty nice outside. I will watch Maria and Lizzie, Mama, don't worry. We promise to stay inside the fence."

David and Sofie worked the rest of the afternoon, sweeping, scrubbing, and chasing vermin out into the cold. David carried the mattresses outside and draped them over the clotheslines to air out; he even beat them with a splayed iron rug bat. Regardless of all their good intentions, they all woke with red, itching bedbug bites the next morning. Sofie complained, "I guess they were just burrowed down in the warmth of the mattresses, waiting for us to arrive with their dinner!"

After breakfast, Sofie made a list of things they needed and sent David to the nearest store for supplies including kerosene and new straw mattresses. That night the legs of their beds sat inside cans of the stove fuel; the room reeked of kerosene and lye soap. Raisa complained, "It stinks in here. I can't sleep because I can't breathe. It's just disgusting."

On the third day, David hitched the horse to the wagon and drove back into town to look for work. He had noticed a poster in the grocery store yesterday, advertising that the railroad was hiring "gang" workers.

David got a job and had worked for the railroad just short of three months when his appendix burst, and he was rushed to the hospital. He fought repeated bouts of infection and almost lost his battle to live. Sofie visited him in the hospital when she could find friends or neighbors to watch their four daughters. However, her main concern was where their next meal was going to come from. She had mouths to feed and a sick husband with no money coming in.

To supplement their nonexistent income, Sofie took matters into her own hands and began to make hats in the evening by the dim glow from the kerosene lamp. She had brought some straw and grass with them from Lovell, along with a bag of colorful chicken feathers, fancy fabrics, and ribbons. One day, Sofie asked a neighbor to watch her four daughters while she hitched a ride into Cleveland with a friend. Agreeing to meet back at the grocery store in two hours, Sofie turned, and carrying the bag of hats, she quickly walked down the city street to a hat shop she had spotted some weeks ago.

The bell on the door rang cheerfully as Sofie entered Edith's Millinery. She walked confidently up to the counter where a matronly looking woman was busy helping another customer. Sofie took four hats from her cloth bundle and laid them on the counter. The customer noticed the hats immediately and hurried over to inspect them. "Are these lovely hats for sale, miss?"

Sofie looked shyly at the store owner. "I brought them in for the owner to look at, hoping she might want to sell them in her shop. I expect we should ask her if she is interested in them first."

The shopkeeper called to the back of the shop, "Herman, I need you out front. There's a woman here selling hats. Come take a look at them." A portly man of about fifty parted the calico curtains and ambled over to the counter, giving Sofie the once-over as he walked. "I take care of all suppliers—name is Herman Goldstern. Let's see what you have here."

He picked up one of the hats and inspected it carefully. It was a narrow brim straw fedora, dyed black, with one side of the brim turned up in a jaunty manner. Sofie had fastened a gray ribbon to the base of the crown. Under the ribbon she secured fiery red, gold-tipped feathers from her prize Brown/Red Cubalaya rooster. After examining the rest of the equally impressive hats, a smile crossed Herman's ruddy face as he eagerly accepted Sofie's hats, all of them. "Did you have a price in mind, madam?"

Sofie stammered her reply. "I—I don't know. That was—it was something I thought we might discuss. I have put many hours into the weaving and adorning. What do you think you could sell them for so we both make a nice profit?

Motioning to the back of the store, Mr. Goldstern said, "Let's move to the rear of the shop where we can talk—ahhh, price." Sofie flinched as he laid a thick hand on her waist, steering her to the back of the store. Purposely, she moved ahead of him so his hand left her waist and then kept her distance.

After jotting some numbers on a pad, the owner was overly complimentary and equally as generous in what he offered Sofie for her hats. Obviously, he was trying to impress her, giving her an order for an additional ten creations. With his back to his wife and her customer, he handed Sofie the payment plus a deposit on the next order.

As she reached for it, he deftly enfolded her delicate hands inside his sweaty fingers. Startled, Sofie's eyes shot up to his face as she jerked her hands away. His eyes betrayed his lustful thoughts as he smiled coyly, his tongue sliding slowly over his lower lip. Lowering his voice, he added, "There are always other ways to make money if you are willing. For now I could increase the offer for the next order from two dollars to three dollars if that would interest you?"

Sofie smiled sweetly as she gathered her samples. Her face burned with anger and embarrassment. "Mr. Goldstern, I beg your pardon. It is most improper to speak to me in such a manner, and I do not appreciate it. Perhaps I should take my hats to your competitor down the street."

Stunned by her fiery resolve, Goldstern took a step back and, while apologizing profusely, glanced nervously at his wife who was still busy with her customer. Sofie replied confidently, "Well, be that the case, we have a business deal. I will deliver the new order of hats in two weeks if that is sufficient—for three dollars each!" Lifting her chin and narrowing her green eyes, Sofie said softly and firmly, "Thank you for your time and your business, Mr. Goldstern. I am confident you will be pleased with the creations I am leaving here today, as well as the new order you just purchased."

Herman Goldstern flushed as he stammered, "Well now, perhaps I was a bit hasty in offering you that much for the second order."

Sofie tilted her head to the side as she forced a sly smile and then replied sweetly, "Do you want me to confirm the order with your wife, sir?" She took his negative head shake as a "no." "I thought not. I thank you for your business. Good day!" Sofie turned and nodded with pleasure to the man's wife as she exited the shop. Once out in the street, Sofie took a deep breath and exhaled loudly. She clutched her purse firmly in her shaking hand as she marched confidently down the street.

Sofie's thoughts were whirling in her head. She was thrilled with the shop's purchase and order. Yet her face burned with rage; she clenched her jaw as tears of indignation welled in her eyes.

She walked down the street to the market where she bought food and kerosene for the lamp. Sofie's hands were still shaking as she paid her bill. With her purchases in one bag and her purse held tightly in the other, she headed for the corner to meet her neighbor for the ride back to the edge of town.

Still upset by the owner's suggestive words, Sofie couldn't stop thinking about the profits she made that day and how she was going to continue to rebuff any future advances from the store owner. Sofie smiled to herself at the thought of Mr. Goldstein's hefty wife taking issue with her wayward husband.

~~~~~

David was released from the hospital the end of August. He was weak and noticeably despondent. That first night at the supper table, Raisa watched him as he attempted to eat the meal with the family. *Daddy's cheeks are sunken, and his eyes look empty and sad.* When one of his daughters spoke, he barely noticed. Raisa sensed his broken spirit. This wasn't the strong father she had clung to since leaving Susannenthal. This wasn't her rock, her protector. The little girl saw another side of her father, and she was scared.

That night after everyone else was asleep; Raisa lay awake in the bed she shared with her two sisters. She stared out the window at the shadowy shapes of the trees near their house. Feeling the urge to empty her bladder, she slid out from underneath the warm bedcovers. As her feet came in contact with the icy, cold floor, she let out a little squeal. Her hand flew to her mouth as she attempted to be as quiet as possible. She found the chamber pot, did her business, and then hurried back toward the bed she shared with her two sisters. Not being able to resist, she tiptoed toward the window and looked out. The full moon illuminated the snow that lay on the ground. Raisa noticed the layer of frost on the windowpane and reached to scratch across the glass; she smiled at the tracks of her fingernails, and feeling a chill, she turned back toward the bed. She pulled the covers up to her chin as she listened to the barn owl hoot from the oak tree beside the house. Raisa laid there in the dark, wondering what was going to happen to her family and why they never stayed in one place for long.

Why can't Papa find a job or a farm so we can stay put for once? I hate moving all the time, going to new schools, making new friends. Tears ran into her ears as her mind was filled with the worry of a child. She heard the mournful wail of the train whistle as it rumbled across the tracks near their house. The rhythmic beat of iron against iron was calming to Raisa as she finally closed her eyes.

~~~~~

Gradually, David healed in mind and body. One night after he had tucked his daughters in bed and listened to their evening prayers, Raisa asked, "Papa, please tell us another story about when you were a little boy in Susannenthal."

David smiled and scratched his head. "Hummm, let me think. Oh yes, this is a funny story about my older brother Carl and me. I was about your age, I think, when your Opa Phillip butchered a hog one day. As usual, he saved the bladder, which he inflated and left to dry. When it was still soft, he cut the tube end off and turned it inside out and then peeled off the inner lining. He usually soaked it in salt water for a day or two then scrubbed it again and filled it with sausage."

"Well, Carl and I got an idea, watching our father work with the hog bladder. We had longed for a ball to play with, and so we begged Opa to blow the bladder up and make a ball for us. We begged so loudly, he was forced to give in. He told us we had to help him, and we happily agreed. We were so excited at the thought of playing with a real ball.

"Opa stuck a tube in one end of the bladder and looped a cord loosely around the opening. He began to blow the 'ball' up. He told me to pull the cord tight when he signaled. He blew and blew, and the ball became very big. Suddenly, he motioned for me to pull the cord. I pulled with all my might, and to my horror, the cord broke, and all the air came out of the ball. It sputtered and fluttered around the room, coming to a heap on the floor!

"Our faces were sad thinking now we would have no ball, but Opa said he would try one more time, and he instructed me to pull the cord more gently. Opa blew and blew until his face was red and sweating. Carl and I were so excited, we could hardly stand still. Our ball grew even larger than before. Suddenly, it exploded, sending pieces in every direction. It frightened my brother and me, and we almost cried until we saw the expression on Papa's face. The force of the explosion made his hair fall down on his face, and his neat mustache was all askew. Carl and I burst out laughing. In spite of the fact we now had no ball, but we had a funny story to tell."

With a smile on his face, David continued. "Opa didn't laugh as he stood straightening his hair and mustache. Gruffly, he told us to clean up the mess, and we sobered up quick-like as he stomped off the porch muttering something about wasting half the day blowing up a silly bladder!" David laughed at the memory that filled his mind.

Raisa sat up in bed, throwing her arms around her father's neck and kissing his cheek. "That was a wonderful story, Papa. I am sorry you didn't get to play with the ball. Did you ever have another ball to play with?"

David smiled, "No, sweetheart, I didn't, but we had other things to play with."

"Like what Papa—like what?"

David tucked the cover around Raisa as he replied, "Now, Raisa, one story is enough! It is time to close your eyes like your sisters who are already asleep. Sweet dreams, *Liebling!*"

~~~~~

Recuperation took David several months. In the meantime, in order to put food on their table, Sofie continued to sell her hats and tactfully steer clear of the lecherous shop owner. One day as she was returning from making a delivery in town, she noticed a horse and buggy tied up near their front door. She gave her neighbor ten cents for the ride, hopped down from the wagon, and hurried into their house.

There at the kitchen table sat David with his cousin, Daniel, and wife, Anna. They stood as she walked into the room and approached the table. "Sofie, look who is here, they just arrived in America two weeks ago and have stopped on their journey west to visit with us." Sofie hugged Anna and shook Daniel's hand. "It is so nice of you to visit us. How was your trip over, and what news do you have of Susannenthal? Is it as bad as we have heard?" They spent over an hour catching up on news from home, eating pie, and drinking coffee. It was close to supper time when Daniel pushed back his chair and stood, preparing to leave.

"I certainly appreciate you giving us a small loan to get us started in Cleveland, cousin. I knew I could count on you to help us out when our luck was down. I'll pay it back when I can, of course."

Sofie sat at the table, dumbfounded. David was loaning them money? Where did he get money to give away when she had to sell hats to buy food and pay the rent? By the time the cousins left, she was loaded for bear! "David, sit down. We need to talk." David knew instinctively what was coming and made excuse of a chore he needed to do and attempted to make his escape.

"David, I said to sit down. There are some things we have to talk about now, and I mean *now!* I get back from town—all day, selling my hats for food for us to live on, and you are loaning money like some big-shot banker or rich man? Where did that money come from, David? I want to know now—where did you get so much money you can give it away?"

David slowly lowered himself onto the chair and looked at the faded wood of the tabletop. "I saved some money from Lovell and from working on the railroad here. My cousin needed help. How could I say no to him?"

Sofie pounded her slender fist on the table. "You saved some money and kept it from me when I needed to pay for food all those months you were in the hospital? We were down to nothing to eat, David. I went into town to sell hats so we would not starve. Are you losing your common sense? What in heaven's name is wrong with you?"

That was not the first or last time David loaned relatives and friends money he really couldn't or shouldn't loan out. Sofie had the impression that any extra money saved, was saved to buy a place of their own someday. "At this rate, David, we will never have a farm because you give everything away. I do not understand you. Do you want a farm of your own or not? Do you want to be successful and have money in the bank?"

"Sofie, the Lord helped us get to this country, and if our friends and family need help to come over here, to get out of Russia, how can I say no? What if I said no and they stayed there and died? I must do what I can to help—that is all there is to it! If the Lord means for us to have a farm of our own someday, He will make it happen." Sofie sat tall in the chair and looked her husband in the eye.

"I agree we should be grateful for what the Lord has given us, David, and that we should give back—too—ahhh, some extent! But we also have to be able to take care of ourselves and our family. Doesn't the Lord expect us to do this also? We have to find a happy middle, David. We must come to an agreement to give only so much away or we will never—have a—." Sofie struggled to find the right word that would make an impression on her husband. "We'll never have a thing to our name, much less a farm to call our own!"

She stood, rooted to the floor as tears began to run down her face. "I'm sorry to speak so, David—I—ahhh—I am so tired of

the struggle and never getting anywhere!" She ran out the screen
door, letting it slam behind her.

David remained seated at the scrubbed oilcloth-covered
table. Both hands lay flat on the surface. He was in shock. He
knew in his heart that she was right. He had to start thinking of his
family first.

~~~~~

One afternoon, in the middle of August, David drove his
wagon into the farmyard. As usual the girls came running when
they heard their father's wagon roll into the yard. Raisa, Maria, and
Lizzie stopped in their tracks when they came eye to eye with a
large, unhappy pig that was tied up in the rear of the wagon bed.

"Papa, where did you get this pig, and what are you going
to do with it?" They asked in chorus as David hopped down from
the wagon.

With a mischievous smile on his face, he replied, "I bought
him from a neighbor, and we are going to eat him!"

Horror filled the girls' faces as Lizzie began to cry. "Hush,
Lizzie. God gave us animals to use for food, and you know how
much you like bacon and the ham hocks Mama makes soup with.
Now, Raisa, take your sisters into the house, as I have work to do."
Raisa understood without being told that he was going to slaughter
the pig. They lingered for a moment on the front porch, watching
as David unloaded the pig and led him to the barn. David turned
and shouted, "Raisa, do as I said—take your sisters into the house,
now!"

David and Sofie worked for several days preparing the
meat from the hog. They found uses for almost every part, from
slow-roasted pig knuckles, pickled pig's feet, head cheese, large
pink hams, and bacon. Any parts not intended for another use were
chopped and made into liverwurst and bloodwurst sausage stuffed
inside carefully cleaned and boiled intestines.

When it was time to stuff the sections of intestine with
prepared sausage, Sofie called, "Raisa, Maria, Lizzie, you girls
come and help me." It was Raisa's job to hold the slippery
intestine open as her sisters took turns stuffing them with various
types of savory sausage. The young girls squealed and gagged as

they handled the squishy, pungent raw sausage and stuffed it in the tube. It was Raisa's job to squeeze and push the pliable meat to the knotted end until the length of the intestine was filled. When a nine-inch section of gut was filled, Raisa's small fingers tied a secure knot, and they began to fill the next section, knotting and filling until the entire length of intestine was filled and ready to hang in the cold cellar to age.

Near the end of the day, the knot at the opposite end gave loose and raw sausage oozed out, making bathroom sounds as it wormed from the broken intestine. Raisa put her hand over her mouth as she gagged and fled the room. Maria and Lizzie looked at each other and burst into laughter as they followed her out the door.

After a few minutes Raisa returned, looking a bit piqued. "I hate making sausage—it is so disgusting!" David looked up from his chair where he sat reading his Bible.

"Some of the work we do to live is not easy, but we give thanks for our food. Now be an example of strength for your sisters, Raisa."

Raisa had barely started back to school outside of Cleveland when David announced yet again that he couldn't find any work and thought they should move back to the Sandusky area of Michigan where Sofie's sister lived. Sofie couldn't pack fast enough. They moved to a small country town called Deckerville just to the north of Sandusky. They found a farm to rent and work two miles to the west of Lake Huron.

~~~~~~

One especially hot, humid Saturday night in September, David stood up and declared, "I feel like going to the lakeshore tomorrow. If we can talk your mother into frying a couple of her chickens, we could have us a picnic. Anybody want to join me?"

Sofie not only fried the two chickens David killed for her but also baked fresh bread, threw together her German potato salad, and packed plenty of dill pickles—Raisa's favorite. They spread a blanket near the water and enjoyed their picnic. Spending Sunday afternoon on the shore became a weekly occasion of relaxation and escape from the work and the heat for the Steiner family.

That fall Sofie enrolled Raisa in the local school. The self-sufficient ten-year-old got herself out of bed at the crack of dawn, prepared her own breakfast, and packed a cold sack lunch. She set out just as the sun peeked over the water to the east. She always took a coat in case it got cold on the two-mile walk to school. Raisa made friends with a little girl named Ruby Meinhall, who lived about a quarter of a mile away on the same road. When Raisa walked to school, the Meinhall's place was her first stop; when it got colder, Raisa would warm herself by the Meinhall's coal stove while Ruby got her things together, and then the two girls set off for their next stop. They walked about a mile to Dorothy Dunkle's house, where they warmed themselves beside their wood stove, and then the three of them walked on to school. Raisa never complained except when the snow was deep and the winter wind blew bitter off Lake Huron.

~~~~~

One Saturday, around the end of October, Raisa asked David if she could go with her two best friends to the woods to gather nuts. Her friend Ruby knew about a particular area where wild nuts grew and were ready to be harvested. David found an old burlap gunny sack; handing it to Raisa, he gave his permission for her to go. The girls all threw their gunny sacks over their shoulders and headed into the woods.

The Indian summer sun burned hot that day, and the cool shade of the trees was a relief as the three young girls followed a narrow path deep into the woods. Raisa stopped in her tracks and squinted her eyes. "Oh, Ruby, look over there underneath that tree! I think those are black walnuts." They giggled and scampered through the thick growth of underbrush and saplings, going from tree to tree. Soon their bags were full of walnuts, chestnuts, hazelnuts, and even a few butternuts.

Dorothy looked up at the dimming light that came through the canopy of trees. She bent over and began to gather her bags of nuts. "I don't think I can carry another bag, and besides, it is getting late. I think we should go back now—okay?"

Raisa was in the lead as they walked back down the path they came on, or at least they thought it was the same path. Suddenly, Raisa stopped and looked around. Her eyes were suddenly wide with fear. "Ruby, Dorothy, I don't think this is the right path. What do you think? Is this the way we came?"

They all stopped where they were on the path and looked around. Their faces paled as their eyes opened wide with fright. The three young girls were certain they were lost as the sun began to slide toward the horizon and the woods grew darker. Ruby began to cry as Raisa and Dorothy tried desperately to find something that looked familiar. Not succeeding, they sat together on the damp floor of the woods and tried to decide what to do. "I think we should climb up in the trees with our nuts and wait until morning, and then we might be able to find our way home."

Ruby wasn't fond of that idea, and she began to sniffle! Trying to stay calm, Dorothy said, "I think your idea is good, Raisa. We need to get away from the animals that come out at night, and if we are up in the trees, we will be safe. Perhaps when we don't come home, our fathers will come looking for us."

Ruby was really blubbering now. "But-but, what if we—we fall out of the tree, and the animals eat us? What if we have to stay out here all night? I'm afraid of the dark. I want my dad. I want to go home!"

Raisa replied, "Well, I don't know about you, Ruby, but I don't plan on falling out of this tree and finding out. So darn it, just find a good tree and shut up, okay?"

Finally, without a better plan, they each climbed a sturdy tree and found a fork in the branches where they could wedge their bodies in tight. They tied their bags of nuts to a branch and began to wait for rescue. Just as they were beginning to feel at ease with their surroundings and circumstance, a nearby barn owl began its nightly beckon of small critters with an eerie "whoo-whoo" that echoed through the darkness.

That really set Ruby off, and the level of her bawling escalated to an even higher pitch. Dorothy tried in vain to comfort her. Finally, plum out of patience, Raisa said, "Ruby, will you hush up? You are letting all the animals know exactly where we are, and then we *will* be in trouble." That seemed to do the trick. Ruby began to wipe the tears from her eyes as the thought of attracting any big animals sobered her up.

The girls continued to chatter softly in an attempt to stay awake and boost each other's spirits. Suddenly, the sultry night air was pierced with a bone chilling "yip, yip, yip, arrrroooh!" All three girls stopped talking. Their faces turned as ashen as their knuckles; they held even tighter to their respective tree branch as all three attempted to crouch into inconspicuous targets.

Dorothy was the first to speak. In a whisper she stammered, "Ra—Raisa, did you hear that? What was that noise?" The sound came again, and this time it was closer!

"Yip-yip-yipeee—arrrhooo!"

Raisa whispered loudly, "I'm not sure. It might be a wolf. Just stay quiet, and stay in your tree. I know wolves can't climb trees!" That's when she saw it—head down, nose to the ground, following their scent along the path; its gray-brown fur was all bristly as it circled their trees. Then it raised its head and peered up through the tree branches. There was a moment when all eyes met at a junction. The three little girls looked into the gleaming yellow eyes of the beast and screamed in unison.

Suddenly, gunfire flashed bright yellow from the edge of the brush as the coyote flipped and rolled onto its side. It was whining and clawing at the ground, trying to get away from the piercing pain of the bullet. Another shot rang through the night air, and the coyote lay still as several more coyotes made a quick getaway through the brush. The dark forest and everything in it was deathly quiet for only seconds before the girls yelled, "Help us! Help us! Please help us. We are up here in the trees."

It took Raisa a long time to go to sleep that night, mostly because her bottom was still sore from the spanking she got. In spite of the punishment, she was grateful her dad and the other men had come looking for them.

~~~~~

In May 1912, Sofie produced their first son. He was christened Johann, and his American nickname became Jack. Sofie immediately noticed the difference in his temperament compared to that of her daughters. Jack was full of vim and vigor from day one.

In the spring they moved to McGregor, Michigan, just to the south of Deckerville and closer to Sandusky. They were still in Sanilac County, near the cool waters of Lake Huron. David farmed, and Sofie made and sold her hats when she had a spare moment—generally in the evening after the children were in bed. She usually had a nice brood of chickens, and her earnings were hidden away in a special jar during the good times and taken out when times were lean.

Later that summer after her brother was born, Raisa noticed her mother stirring a large, boiling pot on the stove. "What are you cooking, Mama? It sure stinks!" She walked closer to the stove to get a better look as the odor became intense. Sofie put the lid on the pot and laid the wooden spoon in the dry sink. Then, taking her oldest daughter by the hand, she led her out to the front porch.

"Sit with me a moment, Raisa." Sofie reached with her apron to wipe the sweat from her full face. "You are growing up so fast, and it's time I explain a woman's life to you as my mother did to me at your age. Some things we don't speak of often, but you need to understand what is going to happen to your body someday. It does to all girls." Raisa sat up straight, her eyes wide and serious; nervously she nibbled on her lower lip. Sofie continued. "I imagine you have noticed the pail of soiled rags I keep on the porch to soak in herb and soap? Those rags I boil so they are clean to use again." She pulled a twelve-inch square of cloth from her apron pocket. "When I need to use the clean rag, I fold it into a thick rectangle, and it is ready to use."

Mystified, Raisa looked at her mother and again at the folded cloth. "What do you use it for, Mama? I've never seen you use it." Sofie smiled as she put her arm around her oldest daughter's thin shoulders.

"When a girl begins to grow into a woman, her breasts are very sore, like yours are—but as soon as they are bigger, they don't hurt anymore. Then someday when the body is ready inside, every month there will be several days when you may have a tummy ache, and you will bleed."

Raisa's face turned pale. "Bleed? I will bleed? Where does the blood come out?"

Sofie patted Raisa on the arm. "It comes from the place between your legs, Raisa. It is where babies come out, just like the animals you have seen in the barn. When you bleed, Raisa, you fold one of these clean rags like I showed you and pin it to your underwear so the blood doesn't get onto your clothes. When it's soiled, you take it off and put it in the bucket to soak, and then I boil them clean."

"Will it hurt, Mama?" Raisa's eyes were wide with concern.

"As I told you, only sometimes you might have a little stomachache. That's all. Don't worry, *Liebchen*. Now, when it first happens, you will understand that you are then a woman. Now take the basket out to the clothesline and take the dry clothes down for me, please."

Raisa stood and then stopped in the open doorway. She turned. "But Mama, does that happen to boys too?"

Sofie smiled back at her daughter. "No, it doesn't, Raisa."

Raisa stomped off. "Dumb boys, why are they so lucky?" She was out of sight, around the corner of the house, when she held the basket to her face and cried.

~~~~~

In the spring of 1914, Sofie gave birth to another son. Peter was a strong, healthy baby, and for this they were thankful. Two months later, Sofie received a letter from her parents.

May 1914
Dear Sofie and David,
It has been quite a while since we last wrote. I wish there was good news to send. More and more of our peoples are leaving the villages along the Volga; most go to Amerika like you did. Many times they leave from Germany, but some cross the borders and waters to England. The Russian government is trying to stop peoples from leaving now, so they have to use secret ways to get out of the country.

We recently received a letter from our friends who, like many others, packed a small sled with food and walked across the snow, mostly at night so no enemy would see them. Our friends had to bury their nine-month-old baby beneath the snow when she died along the way. They piled many rocks on top so the wolves wouldn't get to her. They wrote that they gave vodka to the other small children—to keep them quiet and sleeping while they pulled the sleds at night.

During the day they hid in abandoned houses, woods, or caves. Finally, she wrote, they made it to England and booked passage on a new ship called the Titanic. There were around twenty, Die Wolgadeutschen who were boarding the ship. All of their goods were stowed in the ship already. They walked up the gangplank and were stopped by a ship's officer who looked closely at the small girl they carried. She had red spots all over her face and burned with fever. The entire family was taken off the ship and told, "No, your child is sick, and you can't come on board." This was sad at the time, but the family later thanked God after hearing the Titanic sank five days later. They were able to go to Amerika after several weeks but lost all their suitcases and trunks that went to the bottom of the waters when the Titanic sank.

Our pastor tells us he believes a great war is coming soon, and it will be a dark time for us. We save everything we can and even hide food and valuables in the earth. We hear much about a group of peoples called Communists or Bolsheviks who believe all things should be shared equal by the people. That nobody owns anything of their own. There is much confusion and fear of our future.

We are happy to hear of your growing, healthy children and now you have also two sons. May God bless and keep us all.

Mama and Papa

~~~~~

The temperature dipped to fifteen degrees, and a thick fog coated the trees outside the bedroom window. Hoarfrost glimmered in the moonlight like a million diamonds. Sofie lay contented and thoughtful in the crook of David's arm. "Just listen to the silence, David. There are no children running, laughing, crying, fighting—only blessed silence. I love to hear them play, but now and then I cherish peaceful moments like this."

David propped himself up on one arm. "Sofie, I am feeling especially festive as Christmas draws near. Maybe it was inspired by the smell of your Christmas baking today." With a twinkle in his eye, he smiled down at her. "It's a good thing I slipped two of those molasses cookies in my pocket before you stored them away, since that might be my last chance with all these hungry mouths to feed."

After talking it over, they decided to make the coming Christmas a special one for their six children. When Saturday rolled around, David asked Raisa, Maria, and Lizzie to join him on a walk. "Dress warmly and bring gunny sacks and baskets— we are going to hike into the woods to gather pinecones, holly, and spruce boughs to decorate our home for Christmas."

Raisa's eyes were wide with fear. "Are—are you taking the gun, Papa—in case we see a coyote?" David crossed the floor and wrapped his daughter in his arms.

"Nothing will bother us in the daylight, *Liebchen*. Don't worry! Besides if they take one look at me, I will give them my evil eye, and they will run for the hills!"

Lizzie was all smiles. "Can we look for our Christmas tree too, Papa? Can we, please?" David assured her they would keep their eye out for a good tree as well.

Sofie kept the three younger children at home, with Emilie entertaining her baby brothers as Sofie finished her holiday baking. The small house was filled with the heady aromas of citrus, butter, cinnamon, and apple *Kuchen*. Sofie had just finished placing the buttery pound cake to soak in a brandy sauce when she heard David and the girls retuning from the woods. Their faces were rosy and glowing from the cold and excitement as they carried their baskets and sacks of aromatic pine decorations into the warmth of the house to show the family.

~~~~~

Three days before Christmas, after the children were tucked in bed and prayers said, David and Sofie decided to get started on the Christmas decorations. David went to the woodshed where they had stored the fresh evergreen. Moments later he struggled through the front door, arms filled with pine, spruce, and holly branches. David was an expert at twisting light wire around the branches to create wreaths and garlands.

Sofie took some of the decorations and laid them across the small mantel, tucking holly and berries deep in the boughs. David draped garlands over the front door and twisted some around the stair banister and railing. "Oh, David, it's wonderful. The sight and the smell are so festive. Did you find a tree today?"

David put his arms fondly around his wife's shoulders as he stood beside her. "JA, my *Liebchen,* I cut a nice, full spruce. It's out in the barn. Let me know when you want me to bring it in so the kids can decorate it. "

The next morning, Sofie took four precious oranges from the simple icebox and called the older girls into the kitchen table. "I want each of you to sit. We are going to make some more decorations for the house. Now watch carefully. Take the orange and poke a hole through the skin in one place with a toothpick. Then hold the fat end of a clove and stick the stem down in the hole—like this."

Maria looked down at the rare fruit and back again at her parents. "But...but I want to eat the orange, not stick holes in it. Isn't that wasteful?" David and Sofie assured her that they had more oranges to eat and that this would be a festive decoration. Soon the girls were laughing and making beautiful fragrant orange and clove pomander balls to place in a bowl. She watched as their fingers grew sticky with the orange juice, and they each laughed as they licked the sticky citrus-clove juice from their fingers.

"When you are finished with the oranges, I want you to take those small red apples, dip them in this fluffy egg white mixture, and then roll them in the bowl of sparkling sugar. Lay them on the cookie sheet to dry overnight, and in the morning we will have a beautiful decoration for the table."

Raisa bubbled with enthusiasm and happiness. "Mama, everything looks so amazing." Just as they finished with their project, the front door burst open and David came in, stomping the snow off his feet as he pulled their six-foot Christmas tree through the narrow doorway.

"Where do you want me to put the tree, Sofie? Over there in the corner where you have the bucket and rocks lying?" David laughed as he sat the tree in the bucket, wedged the rocks around it, and filled it with water. "There, we will let it sit here in the house overnight to open up and relax a bit. Then tomorrow we can decorate the tree. What about that, kids?"

The room erupted into cries of joy and excitement as they all went to inspect the tree and smell the wonderful spruce. The next morning after breakfast, Sofie popped the popcorn and put cranberries into a bowl. She showed the older girls how to thread a needle with strong string and make garlands of popcorn and cranberries to decorate the tree. Even little Emilie got in on the action. Two-year-old Jack had to be pulled away from the tree several times as he tried to climb up the branches and eat the popcorn and cranberry garland. "Ach, that boy, he is into everything!"

Sofie carried out a box of red ribbons and tied them on the branches as David stood on a chair and placed their pierced tin star at the top of the tree. He brought out the dozen or more candle clips, and after placing small, ivory-colored beeswax candles in them, he positioned them around on the tree. "We will light them only for a short time on Christmas Eve when we sing all of our favorite songs, especially 'Silent Night.' Okay now, you kids all get to bed, and we will hear prayers. This has been a long day, and I think this family will sleep well tonight!"

Christmas morning dawned bright and cold as the Steiner children woke at the crack of dawn to see what Santa Claus had left for them. As the little ones opened their gifts of knitted scarves, gloves, hats, long stockings, and wooden toys, Raisa gazed at the tree and basked in the happiness that filled the room. "I wish we could keep the tree in the house all winter because it makes everything smell so good and makes us all so happy!"
Sofie smiled as she watched her children enjoying the festivities. Her thoughts went to her family back on the Volga, and she wondered if they were having any kind of a Christmas at all.

Because Raisa was in school, they had given her writing paper and her own pen and ink. No sooner had she opened her gift than she scurried off to the table to sit and write. When Sofie opened her gift from David, she squealed with happiness—tortoise shell combs! She immediately wedged them into place in her thick, auburn hair. "Oh, David, the combs are so beautiful. I love them, and I love you!"

~~~~~

In 1915 Sofie gave birth to their third son, Joseph. His brothers and sisters later shortened his name to Joe. The harvest had been good that year, and they prospered. They hadn't been able to scrape enough money together to buy a place of their own, and besides, there weren't many for sale. According to local newspapers, that winter was the coldest on record as storm after storm pounded the region. Shipping on Lake Huron was big business, but a record number of shipping vessels sank because of the violent winter storms made worse by incessant fog and ice.

In the spring as soon as the weather warmed, the Steiner family eagerly packed up and traveled to the lakeshore for their traditional Sunday picnic. Sofie reminded David, "Don't forget to pack up some of my new straw beach hats. We might sell a couple."

David drove the wagon along the beach road until they came to their favorite picnic place. "Okay, now each of you kids grab something and take it down close to the water where we are going to have our picnic," David instructed as he set the brake and wound the reins around it.

Raisa had invited her best friend, Ruby, along, and they were the first off the wagon. They ran around the back, plopped down on the warm sand, and wiggled their toes in the sand. Raisa leaned over and whispered in Ruby's ear, "Are you going to roll up your pants, Ruby? We probably should so we don't get wet. Let's just leave our shoes here by the picnic. Hurry before any of the other kids are here. I hate it when they tag along with us—we never get any privacy!"

The two girls headed down the beach as Sofie warned, "Don't go any farther than that grove of trees."

Raisa turned and saw her sisters and little brother running after them. She stopped in her tracks, turned, and called back to her parents. "Ma, can you keep the kids there so Ruby and I can have some fun? They just get in the way!" David called the kids back and got them interested in building sand castles and looking for shells.

Raisa and her friend Ruby ran down the beach, skipping in and out of the surf like a couple of puppies, laughing and splashing water at each other. Every so often they stopped to pick up a special seashell or some interesting treasure. Soon their pockets were bulging.

David spread the blanket as Sofie set out the picnic. Suddenly they saw Raisa and Ruby running toward them, yelling and waving an object in the air. "Papa, Papa, we found a bottle. It's got a cork in the end, and it has a paper inside!"

Out of breath and flushed with excitement, Raisa handed the pale blue medicine bottle to her father and watched intently as he examined it. "Go over there and get me a stick, Raisa, so I can pull this paper out. Then we can see what is in it."

Raisa and Ruby found a small thin stick and hurried back to David. He fished around inside the bottle until he snagged the paper, and out it came. "Does it have writing on it? Read it, Papa. What does it say?"

Reading to himself at first, an expression of dismay washed over David's face as he turned to Sofie. "It's a note from a sailor who must have gone down with his ship over the winter. It has his name and the name of his family on the bottom. He asks whoever finds this to get in touch with his family and tell them his last thoughts were of them."

Raisa and Ruby looked at each other, eyes wide. "Wow, that is really important then, isn't it? Are we going to find the sailor's family?"

"Raisa, we could try, but maybe we should give it to the police or newspaper. They would probably know where to start looking better than we do."

The newspaper ran a couple of stories on the bottle, and even then it took two months to locate the family. They expressed in a letter how much the last words from their son meant to them.

Soon after that, the Steiner family received another letter from the Volga.

June 1916
My dear Sofie and David;
I may never know if you get our letter or not. Our life is beyond any suffering we have yet experienced. The czarist government as we knew it has been overthrown in a bloody revolution. Now a man by the name of Kerensky leads a group of people who call themselves "the White Army." They fight against "the Red Army" led by Trotsky and Lenin. They both want to control the government. We hear word that Kerensky wants to make a government like in Amerika, but Lenin and the Red Army, or Communists, want the opposite. The poor peasants believe what the Communists tell them—they will be helped, and Russia will be a strong world power. Papa says this is not true. Everything will be worse with the Bolsheviks, who have levied large taxes on our villages. Now they are taking our young men for their armies and making them to sign papers to be Communist. Most men who refuse are killed. Many young men escape across borders to other counties.

The Bolsheviks no longer allow us to go to church; prayer is banished as is even the name of God! They come into our villages and take what they want. If a man protests and says it is his, they say, "Nothing is yours! Everything now is ours!" The Polish Germans no longer own land or any property; they have been banished, most to Siberia. We fear we are next to feel the wrath of the Bolsheviks.

Peoples are afraid to work alone in the fields because of roving bands of these cruel men. If we resist, we will suffer and lose our livestock, our grain—whatever they want, they take. They have taken away four of our grandsons, who we may never see again.

In the streets of Saratov, there is constant fighting between Red and White armies, and just last week a group of Reds chased about a dozen White army men down the street. To escape, they hid in a shed. The Red Army discovered this and shot their guns into the shed until nothing moved except the blood that poured out!

We praise the Lord you and your family are safe in Amerika; for this we give thanks. It was our decision to stay behind, so do not blame yourselves for our plight. We have gone through bad times before, and we will get through this too.

Stay safe and strong in the Lord,
Mama and Papa

~~~~~

David continued to farm in McGregor for two more years. Farming there had its trials. Because of the constant humidity and cold winters, they were forced to store hay inside the barn to protect it from mold. David often complained, "This is an irritating nuisance. The grain and corn have to be stored in a dry place and turned constantly so it doesn't damp rot."

His complaints didn't fall on deaf ears. One evening after supper, the children were in bed, and David and Sofie sat in the small parlor. David was reading his Bible, and Sofie was darning a sock. She looked up from her darning. "David, I am so tired of these brutally cold, damp weathers. That winter wind off the lake cuts to the very bone, and there's so much snow this far north— more than we had in Cleveland. At least out here it is peaceful and quiet, but the children and I are always cold in the winter, and the humidity in the summer months is just plain uncomfortable. We never had anything like this back in the old country."

Two weeks after Christmas, Raisa and Lizzie came down with a persistent flu that spread through the school and community. Sofie and David took turns nursing their two daughters. For several days, both girls ran very high fevers then shook with severe chills. "David, I need you to go into town for supplies, and when you do, please put a cloth over your face as others are doing. You will find a list of things I need. Please don't forget to bring me two dozen large onions. I am going to prepare onion poultices for the girls, to draw out the fever."

When David returned from town, he reported seeing everyone with masks over their faces.

Several weeks later, they received another letter from Sofie's parents.

February 1917
Our Dearest Ones;
We wish our news was good news. Alas, it is not. Last April we had hopes that the Kerensky government would grant our request as German-Russians to be free as before. However, the government fell to Lenin and the Communists, and now we have experienced immediate repercussions. The Red Guards attacked the central village of Balzer in December. Houses were stripped of their valuables; many peoples died. Since that time, all along the Volga the German settlements are filled with roving bands of soldiers and every type of criminal who seize our food, livestock, clothing, and valuables. We live in constant fear.

I am sure you remember the village of, Katharinenstadt, which is below Susannenthal at the bend of the Volga. At five in the morning, it was overtaken by a ruthless mob of over a hundred men. They rounded up church elders, the mayor, and wealthy peoples and held them, demanding the village pay two million rubles to save them. They said they would remain until the money was paid. They tortured the men in plain sight to encourage the village peoples to pay. We aren't sure if the money they paid was the exact amount asked, but the Communists collected a large sum and went on to the next village to do the same.

Some villages have armed themselves with scythes, axes, and pitchforks since most of our guns were confiscated long ago. The local village militia drove off a band of Red Guard one night only to have a larger band revisit them a week later. They killed many peoples and burned houses and the church; they drove off the livestock and stripped the village bare. We have hidden behind locked doors and in the cellar, afraid to go into the street. If any village resists, the Bolsheviks are likely to strip them of their seed grain and livestock, as well as their men and boys.

We know of Germans who disguise themselves as Russian peasants in order to escape persecution. The people still attempt to escape the country on foot, by train, or by boat down the Volga. We have heard that our German population along the Volga has decreased by over 200,000 from leaving and killing peoples. We are doing the best as we can. We still have food to eat and a warm place to sleep.

Many families now live in the same house for safety and for cost of living. We are too old and sick to leave our home now. Pray for your papa, as he spends much time in his bed. It is not easy for me to care for him and for myself. My back gives me much pain, and there is nothing for it. Our former tsar Nicholas II, his wife, and children are being held under arrest. [19]

Pray for us as we pray for you. Mama and Papa

~~~~~~

*Maria and Raisa Steiner
in their teens*

For their two oldest daughters' birthdays that year, David agreed to let Sofie take them into town to have their photograph taken. The girls were so excited and spent hours trying on outfit after outfit. They twisted and curled their hair until they were satisfied they looked their very best. Raisa chose a white blouse with a rolled wing collar and a high-waist black serge skirt. She wound her bounty of thick, auburn hair into sleek coils and accented it with a beautiful hairpin her mother loaned her. Maria chose to wear an all-white skirt and embroidered blouse. She pulled her dark hair back into a long braid at the nape of her neck and tied a white bow around it. The girls were excited when the photographer took them into a special room and arranged them in front of a fake background.

"Now, we are ready to take your photograph, and you must appear formal and dignified—no giggling! Now, hold your bodies straight and tall!"

Raisa and Maria always loved this photo that reminded them of their life in Michigan. When Sofie first saw the photo, she was amazed at the expression Raisa had on her face. It was the same expression as the photo they had taken before they left the Volga.

Chapter Thirteen

BACK TO THE WEST

After the long winter filled with sickness and misery, Sofie found an opportunity to again mention her displeasure with where they were living. That seemed to be all the encouragement David needed, and in March of 1918, he announced they were going to pull up stakes and move—this time to Oklahoma, where he heard there was land to be had. He knew nothing more about the state, only that it was in the southwest and was hot and dry.

Sofie looked around the rooms of their small, rented house. She gazed at the furniture she had accumulated over the past several years. *Just when I start to have nice things, we decide to move again. We sell everything and start over.*

That night in bed, David and Sofie lay talking about the move. They hadn't told the children yet and were trying to decide when that should happen. Even though she wanted to get out of Michigan, Sofie still had her doubts. "How many times are we going to start over, David? We both know it is getting harder for the children to leave their friends. They are settled here and put down roots. They are not going to be happy. We need to find a place and settle once and for all."

The next day when eighteen-year-old Raisa heard the news, she was beside herself. "Why, Papa, why do we keep moving? I want to stay in one place. I've made good friends, like Ruby and Dorothy. I hate always moving so far away that I never see my friends again. I really hate it, Papa. I hate this kind of life!"

David rose quickly from his chair, knocking it backward. "Is that all you think about are your friends? Do you think about how hard I have to work to put food on our table and a roof over your heads? Do you think about all the bad luck we have had? Do you think it is easy for us to come to a strange country and learn all the ways, as well as find the best place to live? We knew nothing of this country when we came—nothing!" He turned to stalk out of the room then turned. "And, we had nothing."

Raisa never remembered hearing her father speak to her like that, and it stung! She covered her face with her hands to hide the tears as she turned and ran from the house, slamming the screen door behind her and heading deep into the solace of the woods that bordered their rented farm. She ran and ran until she could barely breathe then collapsed onto a bed of leaves at the foot of an oak tree. She let the tears come as they would. All the disappointment and resentment came bursting out.

~~~~~~

Sofie tried to understand her husband and the stress he was under to provide for them. She vowed to try whatever it took, to go where they had to go. After selling everything they could, David and Sofie packed up their seven children and most of the needed household goods. Sofie found a spot in the crowded trunks for a bag of grass, straw, and some cherished chicken feathers so she could continue making her hats. Her brother-in-law took them by wagon to the nearest train station, and they were once again riding the rails west, hoping to find their pot of gold at the end of the next rainbow.

In the middle of March, they crossed the Kansas border into the panhandle of Oklahoma. David hoped that Sofie hadn't noticed the number of abandoned homesteads obviously built for temporary inhabitation. Now they stood in silence, alone and at the mercy of the harsh environment—a victim, of bad times.

David found a farm to rent in a town called Hooker, just to the north of Guymon. He borrowed and rented machinery, as well as horses, to set up his farm. The first week, they all slept in the same room. David strung wire across the room and Sofie hung drapes of burlap bags and spare quilts to separate their sleeping area. Raisa and her sisters all slept together on the same straw mattress like they were used to doing, while the boys slept on the floor. Later in the week, Sofie found odds and ends of furniture and household goods at the secondhand store in town. The dry heat felt good to them after the humidity of Michigan—at least, at first it did.

Shortly after David planted his hardy, Turkey Red Wheat and corn, it rained for several days. "JA, this is good. The rains come now because they tell me this is 'dry-land' farming, and there is no irrigation here. We hope and pray the Lord sends more rain for the crops to grow."

In a few weeks the wheat and corn sprouts pushed their way up through the soil. Overnight the fields turned a rich emerald green. They waited for more rain, which came in spastic, short bursts, not amounting to anything near what the crops needed. They ran for the storm shelter in the cellar more than once as tornado after tornado blew through.

~~~~~

More than anything, Pete hated the outhouse, especially when he had to use it at night. Pete held onto his groin as he eased cautiously out the back door and, after scanning the yard for monsters, did a quick tippy toe run across the yard to the outhouse. It loomed dark and menacing against the moonlit sky. It was pitch black inside as he inched through the door and tried to remember exactly where the three holes were in the weathered bench. He moved from memory to the smallest hole and aimed as best he could in the dark.

Finishing his business, Pete opened the rickety outhouse door and started back toward the house at a quick trot. Suddenly, he stopped dead in his tracks as he noticed something move close to the house. He peered through the darkness, and then he heard Jack laugh. "What-cha doing Petey? Going potty in the outhouse?"

Pete's eyes opened wide with relief at the sound of his brother's voice; then he realized what his brother had been doing. "You *peed* outside the house?"

"Well, I'm not walking all the way to that creepy outhouse at night. I just took a shortcut, you might say! Hey—you'd better not tell Mom, or I'll rub your face in it, and you know I can!"

~~~~~

In late June, David walked out to a field to the west of the house. He was checking his thirsty grain when he noticed a dark cloud building to the south. He smiled with the thought of rain as he started walking back to the house. He was almost to the house when his ears picked up a buzzing sound. David couldn't tell which direction it was coming from; it was everywhere. The air grew deathly quiet as the hair on the back of his neck stood up. Just as he neared the house, he turned again and looked to the south. The black cloud was rolling across the flat land like tumbleweed, moving at ground level.

He felt something hit his cap and then saw what it was. First one, then three, then buckets of grasshoppers began to fall from the sky. It seemed the air was alive with the fluttering, clawing, chomping insects. Brushing them off his arms and body, he covered his mouth as he ran.

David yelled to his children who were playing outside under the trees. "Get to the house! Take the dog and cat. Sofie shut all the windows. Hurry, it's a grasshopper cloud; thousands of grasshoppers!"

Safe inside the house, they could hear the hoppers hitting the roof and the windows. Their little red dog whined as David tried to look outside the window, but all he could see was a seething black mass. Raisa and her sisters hid, screaming and crying under the quilts on their bed as the boys ran gleefully from window to window, taking in the gory, frightening sight.

After what seemed like an eternity, the buzzing stopped, and the sunshine warmed the earth again. David paused to put his tweed newsboy cap on, and with his family following two steps behind, he slowly walked across the dusty farmyard until they came to the edge of the once-lush field of red wheat. Not a speck of living vegetation was left standing. The hoppers had stripped the field in a matter of minutes and moved on to their next meal. Numb with disbelief, David was only slightly aware of the tears running down the faces of Sofie and his daughters.

Running from one end of the farmyard to the next, the boys were in hog heaven tearing limbs from as many grasshoppers as they could and having a good time doing it. Sofie had to smile in spite of the seriousness of the day, how boys are boys, no matter what. Jack chased Pete and Joe around the yard, stuffing the squirming hoppers down their shirts. Soon they tired of the game and followed their mother and sisters back to the house, leaving their father standing alone, stunned and staring at the destroyed crop. David needed to be alone, and they all knew this.

Squatting down to look closer at his crop, or what had been his crop, David was numb with shock as fear rolled in his belly.

After the children had gone to bed, David and Sofie sat at the kitchen table. She sat silently, patching some of the children's pants, waiting for her husband to say something, anything. With his head in his hands and barely audible, David said, "Sofie, I know you don't want to hear this again from me, but this place is no good either. I can't make a go of it here. We are done here, with no crop—it's a disaster. Maybe we should go north, to Park City, Montana. Many *Die Wolgadeutschens* from our old village have found farms to buy and are doing well in the climate. I have heard it's much like Susannenthal, and last we heard, that's where the Klinger's are."

Sofie sat for a moment, listening to and observing her husband as he tried to make some sense of what happened. His thin shoulders hung forward in defeat, and he had dark circles under his bloodshot eyes. Sofie pushed her chair back and slowly walked over to her husband. She wrapped her arms around him and gently kissed his unshaven face. "I go where you go, David. I know too we are having a bad time of it, trying to find someplace that feels like home where we can make a living. We have had much bad luck. We both know that. I admit I am growing weary of constantly trying to make a good home for our children, and just like the kids, I am tired of traveling around. We both know they need to settle down also and stay in one school. I also know we need to find a place where we can make a living." Sofie laughed at the irony of it as she continued. "But frankly, David, I am ready to leave this unbearable heat and dirt, and going north is sounding pretty good!"

Sofie walked to the front door and looked outside. "I haven't told you, but Raisa has fainted several times from the heat. I found her on the ground out by the chicken coop this morning. I think she's still weak from that flu she had last spring. I think I'm liking the idea of moving north to this town called Park City. Let's hope and pray it is where we are supposed to be. Like I said, I will go any place with you, David, but never—never—will I go back to

Cleveland." Sofie didn't laugh or smile when she said this, and David knew she meant business.

David looked at his wife and managed to smile in spite of his frustration and disappointment. "Thank you, Sofie. If it weren't for you and our seven children, I would just sit down in the road and give up. I have to keep trying, to keep hoping. And I promise we won't go back to Cleveland. Tomorrow we will pack up again, and instead of going by train, we will go by wagon, so we don't have to sell all our household goods. I will look around for another wagon to buy, and we'll head up north, across the southern plains of eastern Colorado then travel through Wyoming. I think the best way is to stay to the east of the Big Horn Mountains and up into Montana."

David smiled down at his wife. "Woman, I don't know how you do it or why you stay with me. But I'm grateful that you do. I love you, Sofie, and I am trying hard to give you a good life, an easier life, but each place I turn—it does not happen. As long as you are beside me, I won't give up. I'll keep trying to make good!

Sofie's face beamed as she cradled her husband's face in her work-worn hands. "Do you know what I feel like?" He looked up into her still-beautiful face and shook his head side to side. "I feel like a long, hot soak in the tin tub, and I don't think that is a bad idea for you either, especially after this day from hell! I'll tell you what, my dear husband, you go to the shed and bring in the tub while I pump water here at the sink and fill some pots to boil. The stove is still warm, and it won't take much to get her going again."

David returned shortly with the large tin tub in hand and a smile on his face. He placed the tub on the kitchen linoleum floor, close to the stove. He stood and looked at his wife for a moment then drew her into his arms. "Oh my, Sofie, my Sofie, what in the world would I do without you? Here we are wiped out, nearly destitute and getting ready to pack up again and move to God knows where, and all you can think of is taking a hot, soapy bath!" David threw back his head and laughed. "You are a rare jewel, my Liebchen; that you are. And you know what? That bath sounds like just the thing to ease my weary body. However, I do have another thing that I think will serve us both well on this momentous occasion. Just wait here for a moment." David hurried back out the door and just as quickly returned with a Mason jar of cool wheat beer he had retrieved from the root cellar. "We need to lighten our wagon load when we leave, don't you agree?"

It was Sofie's turn to laugh as she took two glasses from the cupboard as David poured them each a drink. While the water came to a boil, they sat on the front porch and savored the cool beer and their forever love. She leaned against her husband's shoulder as she listened to a chorus of croaking frogs from the pond and watched the glow of David's pipe as he inhaled. After a few minutes, she rose, and patted her husband on the shoulder. "Why don't you stay out here where it is cool and enjoy your beer while I soak in solitude. I will add more hot water for you when I am finished."

Sofie went back into the house, and with thick, hot pads protecting her hands, she lifted one of the pots from the stove and poured the steaming water into the tin tub. She cooled it off with a couple pitchers of water from the pump. Sofie opened the kitchen cupboard, found a metal box, and withdrew a dried sprig of rosemary. Unfolding the screen that stood in the corner, she stepped behind it and pulled the combs from her upswept knot, shaking her hair loose. She lifted her faded housedress over her head and removed her black shoes and stockings, as well as her underwear. Wrapping a thin towel around her thickening body, she tested the water with a toe then dropped the towel and slid gracefully into the tub, curling up so most of her body was submerged. With an audible sigh, she closed her eyes as the water rose to her neck, and she forgot about the day and all of the work that was ahead of them tomorrow.

After she washed her hair, she stepped out and toweled off then added the other pot of scalding water and softly called to David. Not getting a response, she padded to the screen door wrapped in a threadbare towel and looked out on the porch. His head had fallen forward onto his chest, and he was snoring loudly.

"David, David, wake up. You have to take a bath before you sleep. Come on now, it's your turn. When you are finished, just pull the tub outside here and dump it off the porch. I will be waiting for you in our bed!"

And with a sly wink of her green eyes, she slipped back into the house and hurried to their bedroom. David didn't tarry in the tub. Inspired by the twinkle in his lovely woman's eyes, he scrubbed the dirt and sweat from his rangy limbs, toweled off, and dumped the water in record time. He blew out the kerosene lamp next to their bed and crawled under the covers. David pulled back the soft curls away from Sofie's ear and whispered. "When I get a few extra dollars, Sofie, I am going to buy you a large claw-foot tin tub so you can really soak. I might even like that myself!"

~~~~~

The day before they left Oklahoma, Maria and Lizzie planned to play a trick on Jack. "He is always scaring the littler boys and us too whenever he gets a chance, so tonight we are going to give the Jack-ster some of his own medicine," Maria said. They knew Jack usually went to the outhouse to do his business right before bed, so they slipped out of the house unnoticed and hid in the brush beside the outhouse. They waited about twenty minutes before Jack swaggered out of the screen door, took a look around, and then strolled down the path to the outhouse.

Taking a quick survey of the farmyard, he began to unbutton his pants and then stepped inside. Maria and Lizzie covered their mouths as they began to silently giggle. Waiting patiently for the right moment, they were finally rewarded with sounds of Jack's grunting and talking to himself. Maria motioned for Lizzie to go to the other side of the outhouse.

Lizzie ran around and propped a board against the door so he couldn't get out and chase them. Then Maria motioned to start growling, clawing, and banging on the walls. The girls began to rock the outhouse as Jack shrieked and cussed at them. Their faces were red; they tried to hold the laughter inside as they high-tailed it back to the house and slipped into bed, pulling the covers up to their chins. Both girls had to bite down on their knuckles just listening to Jack yelling for someone to open the outhouse door.

David took his sweet time walking out to the outhouse to rescue his oldest son. He kicked the board aside and jerked the door open. At that moment, Jack was in the middle of a giant push against the door and ended up sprawled in the dirt with his pants down around his ankles. David began to laugh in spite of himself.

"Well, son, if you're gonna dish it out, then I suppose you have to expect sooner or later you're gonna get it back, huh? Probably should be watching your back from now on!"

The next morning at breakfast, Maria asked innocently, "What was that entire ruckus last night—I was almost to fall asleep when I heard a lot of noise?" David smiled and winked at her.

"Seems your brother Jack got a little of his own medicine—probably good for him! You girls wouldn't know anything about that would you?"

Lizzie and Maria looked at each other across the breakfast table with the most angelic expression they could muster and in chorus, replied, "No Papa!"

It took them five days to pack up and make arrangements to leave. This time Sofie was happy to be able to take more of the household goods she had acquired. At the back of the wagon, David packed what they'd need to camp and cook with along the way. They covered both wagons with heavy tarps and threw numerous ropes across them to hold everything in place. They crossed the Oklahoma border and entered southeastern Colorado. They were plodding along the trail south of Lamar, Colorado, when Sofie pointed to the northwest. "David, look over there at that swirling black cloud hovering above the ground. Is that a storm or more grasshoppers?"

David looked closely at the cloud and stood in the wagon seat. He looked east, then west, then south and north. He smelled the air, and Raisa noticed a grim, apprehensive expression cross over his face. In a low voice, he said to his wife, "No, Sofie, it is neither a rain storm nor grasshoppers. It is dust! We have heard that on occasion they get terrible dust storms across these flat prairie lands. When some sod busters can't make a go of it, they just up and leave the land naked and at the mercy of the wind. Now with this drought getting worse and worse, the winds pick up the dry soil and carry it wherever they blow."

Standing up in the wagon bed, David got a better look at what lay ahead. He pointed. "Look down in that draw. There's a farmhouse, and it looks abandoned. Let's make a run for it. We have to reach shelter, or we will be in for a bad time of it. Hang on, kids. We are in a hurry."

"Hah! Hah!" David pulled his Cossack whip from the holster and cracked it twice in the air over the backs of the horses. Sofie followed his lead with her wagon. The heavily packed wagons careened down the gentle curve of the southern Colorado hill as the air grew deathly still and every living, crawling creature looked for cover. David glanced back at Sofie's ashen face as she clenched the reins of her team in both hands; the loaded wagon lurched and swayed down the rut-filled road.

"Over there—let's try to get the horses and wagons inside that barn," David yelled. Both wagons slowed as they rolled into the deserted farmyard. David didn't hesitate as he drove his team straightway into the open barn and made way for Sofie's rig to follow. The wind was picking up as David instructed Sofie and the children to run for the house. He heard her voice over the rising howl of the wind. "It's locked, David. The house is locked, and we can't get in." Before David could reply, eight-year-old Jack grabbed a large branch and smashed a small window on the door; Raisa reached inside and unlocked it. They all hurried into the house as the air began to fill with choking dust.

Over the howling wind, David yelled, "Get to an inner room and close the door. Take off your coats, any clothing you can spare, or anything you find lying around. We have to plug all the holes, even under the doors and windows, to try and keep the dust out." They could hear the wind whipping tree branches against the roof and side of the house as it began to howl and pick up speed. David went to a window and attempted to look outside. "Sofie, come look at this. I have never in my life seen anything like it. It looks like some sort of beast approaching."

Sofie and the children crowded around the windows and peered out the panes at the approach of the undulating black cloud. It almost seemed tornado-like in form as it picked up tumbleweeds and branches; anything that wasn't attached to the ground became a part of the swirling beast.[20]

With tears welling in her blue eyes, Emilie asked, "Papa, we are scared. Are we going to die?"

"No, we won't die, but the next hour or so isn't going to be much fun." He pulled an old sheet off the bed and tore it into ragged squares. "Tie these around your noses and mouth. Keep your eyes closed as much as possible because the dust is going to come in whether we want it to or not. Here, let's sit on the floor and get together in a huddle, littlest ones in the middle—ready? Okay, now I am going to throw this big quilt over us, and we will play 'tent'!"

The noise and fury of the dust storm was frightening, to say the least, but no one cried. They knew they had to be brave, and, besides, Papa said it would only last a short time, which turned out to be an hour and a half. When they emerged, there was a fine layer of dust on everything, and they were all choking and coughing from breathing in the contaminated air. "You all stay in here while I check everything outside and make sure the storm is over."

"Papa, let me come with you," Emilie pleaded.

David replied firmly, "No, little Millie, you stay here. I have to see a man about a horse!"

In spite of herself, Sofie burst into laughter, and then Jack popped up. "I wanta see the horse, Papa. Let me come with you." Sofie moved to close the door before any of her children could follow their father.

Maria and Lizzie rubbed the grimy window and tried to look outside. Suddenly they began to shout, "Mama, there's an apple tree right outside, and it has apples on it. We can see them!"

As soon as David returned, they all hurried around the side of the house to where the girls saw the apple tree. It was a scraggy old tree, hanging on for dear life, and it looked to Sofie that as if sensing death, it produced a bountiful crop of dust-covered red apples. The windfall apples squished and popped under their feet, and the boys were more interested in jumping on them then picking sacks full of apples from the tree. They ate as they picked. Joe took a big bite of apple, chewed twice, stopped, and looked closely at the apple. "Hey, looka here, there's only half a worm in my apple. Where is the other half?" Raisa started laughing as she hugged her little brother.

"Joe, you ate the other half, that's where it is!" Joe looked at the apple, looked at his sister, and then spit out what was left of the apple.

After a couple hours, David clapped his hands. "Okay, we gotta get back on the road. We've wasted enough time here. I want to get out of this country. Come on—load up!" When they walked toward their wagons, they carried two gunny sacks full of crisp, red apples.

"We'll have to eat them quickly, as I don't think they will last long in this heat," Sofie instructed.

In less than half an hour, they were on the road again, urging the horses to move along the dust-covered road as fast as possible. They all wanted out of that country—the sooner the better! David looked across fields where the natural prairie grasses had been plowed and planted to wheat and then left lying fallow. "These farmers have got to stop plowing this arid prairie land. It's not meant to grow anything but that scrub grass, and there's too much wind out here. Mark my words: if they keep plowing up these grasslands, in another ten years, they are going to have real trouble down in these parts!"
There wasn't much to look at as they crossed the barren prairie. They rode past occasional farms that were still struggling to hang on. When they came upon or passed other folks on the move,

David always stopped long enough to inquire what lay ahead and to tell the folks where they had come from. Out in the middle of the Colorado prairie, they rode past swollen bodies of dead cattle. There was no water, no grass, and no life!

~~~~~

Thunder rolled across the distant mountain ranges to the west as clouds slid in to cover the midday sun. The relief from the dry, oven-like heat was welcome. Even the cold drops of rain were a blessing as the children opened their mouths wide to catch the cool, fresh water. They let it wash over their faces, taking the road dust with it. David was silently alarmed as he watched cloud fingers drop from a canopy of threatening black clouds overhead. He watched as one grew larger and touched down to the ground, spinning everything in its path upward into the sky. Jack had also spotted the strange clouds. "What's that, Pa?"

David looked up at the threatening sky again and replied, "It's a tornado like we had in Oklahoma, but it's a pretty far distance from us. Not to worry, son. It doesn't appear to be traveling this way, which is a good thing. I'll keep an eye on it, just in case."

They continued on down the road. The girls entertained themselves by reading or doing handiwork. Every time they would stop for a meal or a bathroom break, the boys would gather hats full of rocks and dirt clods and take aim at prairie dogs as they scurried from hole to hole. Raisa became irritated with this and complained to her father. "Papa, will you tell those boys to stop picking up those dirty rocks and dirt clods? They are making such a mess."

David shook his head as he smiled at his daughter. "Raisa, it's what boys do. It's a harmless way for them to entertain themselves during this long journey. Don't concern yourself with it. We have more important things to think about."

Raisa frowned as she positioned herself on her seat, ignoring Jack as he turned and stuck out his tongue at her. Raisa looked innocently to the side as she reached forward and gave the underside of his arm a sharp pinch. Jack let out a yelp and whirled to face his tormentor. Raisa smiled sweetly at him, tipped her head, and gazed serenely at the passing prairie.

~~~~~

At the end of each day, it was like an adventure to choose where they would camp that night. Some evenings there wasn't much of a choice. There were times when they were close to a city or unsafe shantytowns that had been pitched on the edge of the road or near a grove of trees. David never stopped but kept right on moving until they found a solitary place that was clean and safe.

Sofie proved to be a genius at throwing whatever they had into one pot and cooking it over an open fire. The kids always watched intently as she added some of this and some of that. "What's this called, Ma? It's real good."

Sofie would laugh and say, "It's called whatever-I-find-in-the- wagon stew!"

As soon as they could, David got them out of the eastern plains and closer to the Rocky Mountains where there was water and vegetation. They followed the mountains up through central Colorado. With subdued envy, David looked at field after field of thick, red wheat, waiting like a bride—ripe and golden. After stopping briefly for water and a few supplies in the small town of Longmont, Colorado, David discovered that there was a large population of *Die Wolgadeutschen* living in the foothills of the Rockies.

That night around their campfire, David got up the nerve to talk to his wife. "Sofie, did you notice the successful farms and good crops along the road today? At the store this afternoon, the clerk told me they belong to *Die Wolgadeutschen*. Ya, that's right. There is a large community of our people living in this place here. Do you think we should give it a try here? It looks pretty good."

Sofie gave David one of her looks, and he got the message. So the next morning they hitched the horses to the wagons and continued on their journey to Montana. After two more days of hard riding, they crossed over the border into Wyoming, and all breathed a sigh of relief as they were out of the southern plains. North out of Cheyenne, David said, "Think we'll head for the North Platte River and stay on course with that for a while. Once we hit Casper City, we'll head due north and ride along the Big Horns through Sheridan and over the Montana border."

~~~~~~

August 1918

Over the years and numerous pregnancies, Sofie had kept the baby weight on, and it was difficult to recognize whether she was pregnant or not. Her comfort came from taking a piece of homemade bread and sopping up the last of the gravy or grease in a pan of fried chicken or bacon. She also had an insatiable sweet tooth, which contributed to her escalating weight gain.

They had been settled on a farm outside of Park City, Montana, for about a month when Sofie informed her husband she was over seven months pregnant with their eighth child. David had been so busy and concerned with other things he was quite surprised when Sofie told him the news.

In the middle of October, the Spanish flu visited the Steiner house as it did almost every house in the world. Both Maria and

Jack began to complain of headaches and burning eyes. Immediately, Sofia put them to bed in a separate room and announced it was off-limits to the other children. Because David, Raisa, and Lizzie had experienced a form of the flu when they lived in Michigan, they were the main caregivers. Concerned, David said, "Sofie, I want you to stay away from the children. You haven't had the flu, and you are about to give birth. The girls and I can do what you tell us to do."

Exactly a week after the children came down with the flu, Sofie bent over to pick up a load of laundry. She stopped and looked down as a bloody puddle gathered at her feet. Suddenly her belly tightened as the first pains of labor hit her. *Ach, die lieber— not now, bitte.*

As Raisa and Lizzie bathed the heads of their ill siblings with cool cloths and administered the herbs and medicine their mother and the town doctor suggested, David acted as midwife with Maria's help. He didn't relish what he was going to have to do but knew it was up to him to help.

Sofie tied "pulling rags" to the iron bedposts. Between the pains, she instructed David to boil water and Maria to get clean rags as well as a clean flour sack to wrap the baby in. David followed her instructions to the letter, assembling scissors, twine, etc. Sofie had been in labor for only three hours when she said, "David—it's coming—get ready to catch the baby as I push." She grabbed onto the rags and, using them for leverage, she bore down!

David's face was pale, and his hands shook as he prepared to be the first to touch their eighth child. "Arghhhh, oof oofffff— arghh—ohhh here it comes!" With a little more effort, Sofie felt the baby slide from her body into the waiting hands of his father.

"It's another boy, Sofie, another son, and listen to him cry. He's a healthy one—that, he is." David gently wiped the baby and swaddled him in the clean flour sack as Sofie expelled the afterbirth. David laid their new son in his mother's waiting arms. "I would like to name him after the first man in the Bible, Adam."

Later that day, after she had cooked, cleaned up, and washed the supper dishes, Raisa peeked around the corner of her parents' bedroom. "Mama, are you awake? I brought you something." Raisa tiptoed into the dimly lit bedroom and sat a Mason jar of wildflowers on the table beside her mother's bed.

Sofie pushed herself to a sitting position as she winced with discomfort. "Oh Raisa, thank you—the flowers are so pretty. Did you have any trouble with supper, and are the kids getting their lessons done and—"

Sofie didn't get a chance to finish as Raisa interrupted her. "Mama, everything is done. Your family is fed, the little ones are down for the night, and the others are finishing up with their lessons. I handled it all, Mama. You don't have to worry about a thing. Now I want to see this new brother of mine."

Raisa walked over to the crib and gently put her hands around the tiny body to lift her brother from the crib. She held him out in front of her as she sat on the edge of the saggy bed. "Oh, Mama, he is just beautiful!" Raisa bent forward as she brought the baby up to her face and buried her nose in his newborn neck. "Have you ever smelled anything so wonderful and fresh? I love babies. I just don't think I ever want to go through having them though!"

Sofie couldn't help herself as she remarked, "I am going to remember what you just said, Raisa. The time will come when you will meet a special young man, and you will want to have his babies. You will see. It's a natural process, and you do what you have to do!"

Sofie only stayed in bed for of couple of days. She got up one morning, dressed, and announced she was fine, ready to resume her role as mother and chief bottle washer!

~~~~~

Many families lost a loved one to the dreadful flu epidemic, but the Steiner house was spared, even though some of them contracted the disease. With the addition of another child, Sofie was swamped with work. The four older girls were a great help to her. They washed, cleaned, did small outside chores, worked in the garden, and helped care for their four little brothers, who were proving to be a handful. In late spring 1919, the children were sent back to school; the Spanish flu left as suddenly as it had appeared.

Several months later David reached for his wife in bed, and when she didn't respond, he propped himself up on his elbow.

"Sofie, what is the matter? Why do you turn away from me?
Aren't you recovered enough from the birth? Do I need a bath or a
shave?"

She rolled over onto her back and looked into his soft blue
eyes. "Oh, David, David, don't you understand? It is time we stop
having babies. It is getting harder for me to carry the child in my
body, and this last birth was difficult. For me, eight children is
enough! These young boys are so different than our daughters.
They are loud, always fighting, and plain ornery. I am forty-four
years old, and you are even older. We should concentrate on
raising our family and not on making more. We have all we can
take care of. There will be days when it is safe to love, but only
then. Do you understand me?"

Disappointed by the tactful rebuke, David rolled onto his
back and stared at the ceiling. "JA, I know you speak right. But a
man needs to be a man! It is the way I show you my love. I'll do as
you say, Sofie, and wait for the time when you say it is right. Good
night, dear one." David rolled onto his side and within minutes was
snoring.

Sofie turned onto her side and stared into the darkness as
tears rolled from her eyes and into her hair. *Oh, dear Lord, I'm
sorry to turn my husband away from me. We both know I am
having troubles with these last pregnancies. I am getting too old
for it. I know all the ways to get rid of an unplanned pregnancy:
vinegar or lye douches, parsley tea, scalding baths, just plain hard
work, and, of course, the hooks and knitting needles. I've also seen
women die from these terrible methods, and besides, I know it is
against your will. Please help David to understand and forgive me.
I love him so and don't want to tell him no, but I must!* She felt
peace flow over her mind and body as she closed her eyes in sleep.

~~~~~

One afternoon, near the time she expected her children
home from school, Sofie was hanging a batch of wet clothes on the
clothesline. Suddenly she heard them running down the lane,
yelling and hollering. She stopped what she was doing and went up
on the porch and waited for them. As they neared the house, she
could see Jack in the lead, with the girls quickly bringing up the

rear. Jack confidently leaped the two steps onto the porch and stood proudly in front of Sofie, showing off his sizeable shiner. Sofie reached to inspect his eye. "Okay, what happened? You have been fighting in school? Your father will tend to you when he comes in from the field today!"

Jack swaggered back and forth, waiting for the others to catch up with him as he rubbed his bloody knuckles. Sofie took him by the shoulders as Lizzie came to his defense. "Mama, it wasn't Jack's fault. There were these boys who were calling us 'dirty German pigs—dirty Rooshins.' I told them to shut up, but they wouldn't. That's when Jack and Pete started socking 'em good. Pete got knocked on his butt right off, but Jack socked a couple of those boys hard before they got him in the eye. He made 'em cry, Mama. He sure 'nuff did. Bet they don't call us that anymore!" Lizzie looked her mother square in the eye. "Those nasty, stupid boys can just—they can just go—whistle!"

Jack and Pete were so proud of themselves they were busting buttons as they strutted up and down the porch. "Well, if that is what the ruckus was about, I suppose you had cause to give them a whooping. We'll see what your dad has to say about it though and your teachers, too," said their mother.

Jack smiled big. "Well heck, Ma, we aren't dummies. We waited till we were off the school grounds on the way home. So, the teachers don't know nothin' 'bout it!" That wasn't the first or the last time the boys got into trouble in school for some ornery or mischievous deed. For the most part they were good boys, but they never backed down from anybody, especially if their sisters were being picked on.

~~~~~

May 1919
Dear Sofie, David, and family,

The good news is we are still alive, but it becomes more of a struggle each day. After harvest last fall, the soldiers came and took everything from us that they could sell. They raided each house, shed, chicken coop, barn, even the outhouses—looking for things peoples hid. Some places they took all the peoples had and said, *"Get out!"* Even when peoples say it is their house, animals, and harvest— the soldiers of Stalin tell us, *"You own nothing!"* Some peoples are left with two or three bags of seed to plant the field with next spring. But as we starve, we eat the bags of seed so nothing remains to plant.

   More peoples and families are moving in together. They share tools, horses, wagons—whatever the soldiers haven't taken yet. Stalin's soldiers sell all our belongings and put the money in their pockets. We see them do this thing. The soldiers even stab their swords into our feather beds and thatched roofs looking for valuables! If they catch us hiding seed, or if we refuse to pay the quota, we might be shot and our bodies pushed into a waiting pit. Peoples walk over the fields picking up pieces of grain, corn— anything they can eat. Most peoples have no horses, cows, goats, or pets left, as we have eaten all that moves. Now some peoples are boiling anything that is leather for soup, throwing in grass, herbs, or pieces of grain—anything to make a hot soup.

   We see some peoples leave in the night, pulling sleds with children under blankets. This is all they take, along with what food they have. Often, they feed vodka to the children to make them quiet and help them to sleep as they travel in the night across the snow and ice to freedom. In daylight they sleep in holes, abandoned houses, caves—whatever they can find. If soldiers catch them, they are usually shot or loaded onto a cattle car and sent to Siberia where they die for sure.

   Stalin's soldiers have destroyed our crosses, churches, Bibles, icons—anything that has to do with religion, but to take our faith, they have to kill us! We don't know what the future holds; it will be what it will be. There is nothing anyone can do now. We had the opportunity to leave, and we chose not to go. Papa and I believe we had a good life. We are old, and we do not fear the end—in fact, it will be a relief compared to what we are living through now. We will all meet again in heaven. We close this letter with our love and our faith in our Lord Jesus.
   Mama and Papa

   David and Sofie were upset and thought about the letter from her parents for days. They never disclosed to their children exactly what the letter said. Sofie made up some news that would not upset or alarm the children

The family stayed in the Park City area for less than a year when they decided to make their last move, returning to Lovell, Wyoming. Finally, they agreed to put down roots in a place where they had lived before and liked. Lovell was the town where there were numerous, *Die Wolgadeutschen*, a good Lutheran church, old friends and even some family. They vowed to stay and make it, no matter what.

~~~~~

Every Sunday the first church service at the Lutheran Church was in German. David and his family made every attempt to attend faithfully. He said, "It brings me comfort to hear the Word of our Lord in our native tongue." This was the way for many German-speaking communities across America. That is until World War I began in 1919, when the German language was forbidden and German-speaking church services were abolished.

"David, I truly miss hearing the Word spoken and the familiar, old hymns sung in German. It doesn't seem the same to me and probably never will."

David looked at her for a moment, pondered her thoughts, and then replied, "JA, Sofie, I know what you mean. Everybody is afraid when there is war, and we understand when people are afraid. They need to know we are not German in our allegiance, only in our heritage. We were American from the moment we stepped off the boat. We were never Russian, even when our people lived there for over a hundred years. America took us in and gave us opportunity. This country has done so much for us—it has earned our love and our support." David hung the American flag outside their house every day from the time the United States joined in World War I.

~~~~~

1919 – Lovell, Wyoming

    David found a good farm to lease east of Lovell in an area called Sunlight, near the small town of Kane. The house wasn't much, but it was decent with plenty of room for their family. There was a good chicken coop, and one of the first things Sofie did was get a flock of chickens started again. The store in town was still in operation, and the owner remembered Sofie and her beautiful hats. He was more than eager to buy her hats and sell them as he had before.

<p style="text-align:center">~~~~~</p>

    "David, I am worried. We haven't heard from my parents in months. Is there any way to find out about them? Maybe their letters will catch up to us after we settle longer in Lovell. We've been moving around so much—I hope we'll hear something soon. By the way, when I was in town today, I heard that the Weber's lived here for several months before moving south to Longmont, Colorado, where his brother is. I heard they were doing well. It's just sad that we lost track of them and the Klinger's. It seems we all just went our separate ways once we landed in America, but that is life, I guess."

    That fall, their four daughters and two sons started school in Sunlight, leaving only two little boys at home with Sofie. When they went off to school, it was almost like a vacation. Raisa had turned nineteen in March and finished eighth grade. Shortly after her birthday, she moved off the farm; she found a job at the sugar factory and rented a room from family friends in Lovell. At first she swept floors for wages, then after a few months she was promoted to testing sugar from the evaporating tanks. Raisa spent her free time with a bunch of Lovell kids who called themselves "The Gang." When weather permitted, they took picnics to the mountains; on weekends, they found someone who played the accordion and gathered anywhere they could to dance the polka. Soon she was being courted by a nice-looking young man she introduced as Jake Kessel.

The Gang: Jake Kessel, top row center;
Raisa Steiner, bottom row second from left

~~~~~

Not many farm kids went on to high school. Most boys quit school after the sixth grade to help in the fields. They went to school when there was time free from fieldwork. When all of the Steiner family worked a sugar beet field, it was quite a crew. David and Sofie blocked the beet seedlings with a short hoe, leaving a small clump of beets every twelve inches. The kids crawled on hands and knees behind them, pulling out every beet sprout except one. It was grueling, backbreaking work, but they were experienced, and it was what they knew. Finally they were making money—good money!

Later that month, Sofie met David at the door when he came in from the fields. She took him by the hand, led him into their bedroom, and closed the door. David was alarmed by her pale, grim expression, and his heart jumped into his throat.

Sofie's breath caught in her throat as she started to speak. "Today when I was at the Ladies' Aid meeting at church, several *Die Wolgadeutschen* women were talking about letters and news they had received from the old country. They said the Volga villages also had a wonderful harvest this year, filling their barns and stomachs again. Then the Bolsheviks came and took their grain by force. They drove full wagons to the docks where ships from foreign countries bought the grain. The Bolsheviks gave our people little money in return.

"I am becoming more worried about my parents. They are old and not well. They can't bear this kind of thing. Why, oh why, didn't they all come to America when they could so now they would be safe?" David didn't say a word because there were no words for what they were feeling. Instead, they held each other in silence.

~~~~~

When all was said and done that fall, after he paid his outstanding debts, David had enough money left to buy a motorcar. He came back from Lovell one day in a used Chevy Sedan Touring car with curtains in the back window. The family saw him pull up in front of the house and couldn't believe their eyes. They all ran out to examine the car, touching it and smelling the leather seats.

Sofie opened the passenger door and sat in the seat beside her husband. "David, I didn't know you knew how to drive a car!" He leaned back onto the leather seat and smiled at her with a twinkle in his eye.

"Neither did I, but I am learning. I have to remember to step down on the brake because if I pull on the steering wheel and say, 'Whoa,' the car doesn't stop like the horses do." He was in good humor until he pulled the car into the barn and saw the mess his sons had made with his carefully stacked bales of straw.

~~~~~

David didn't take his belt off often, especially with his daughters, but his boys were another matter. It seemed like one or another was always in trouble, causing David to administer swift discipline with his leather belt.

Sofie wasn't having an easy time with them either. "David, I clean the house, and they run through it like a bunch of hooligans. They don't pick up after themselves, and they eat like a herd of pigs!

I do love to hear them laugh and cut up. They are having fun and running free on our farm with their friends. It's what children should do. I only wish they would do it with less noise!"

~~~~~

One night Jake Kessel called at the house to pick Raisa up for a date. Shortly after he arrived, another suitor showed up on the doorstep. John Moher was also sure he had a date with Raisa. David was prepared to step between the two young men as they argued over who was going to take Raisa out that night, but she settled it. After Raisa left with Jake, Sofie sat at the kitchen table with David. "JA, I was afraid of this. She is a pretty girl. The boys are collecting around her like bees to a flower!"

Sofie had taken a good look at Jake Kessel, and she liked what she saw—his sparkling blue eyes and a quick wit. Raisa had told her Jake was ambitious and such fun to be with, but she was holding him at arms' length because she thought he was a bit "fast."

Karl and Katja Kessel family: Jake, Johann, Karl, Dorothy, Christian, Katja, Eddie, Ralf, and Louise

That Christmas Jake asked Raisa to be his wife. She said yes so quickly, it shocked her. The next Sunday he took her out to meet his parents and family. Raisa immediately liked Katja, who embraced her and congratulated the couple. Jake's dad was friendly, but Raisa felt like he was watching her. Raisa crossed the room and picked up a photo Karl and Katja had taken of their family the past Christmas. She remarked, "This is a wonderful picture of your family, you must be so proud."

Karl finally smiled and replied, "Yes, you also have a large family, Ja?"

Jake and Raisa were married the first part of February 1920, in the Lutheran church in Lovell. Raisa was radiant in a pale peach chiffon dress that she made herself. She tried to keep working at the sugar beet factory, but after being married for three months, she was so ill with morning sickness she had to quit. Their daughter Beth was born late in November.

~~~~~~

Sofie knew her problem was shared by most of the women her age. They wanted to stop having children, but that would mean abstinence. David didn't come to her very often anymore, but Sophie knew it only took one time to conceive. Frustration and guilt plagued her as she tried to reason with David. "David, our granddaughter is two years younger than our last child. Do you see why we need to stop having babies now? I don't want to have children who are younger than my grandchildren! At my age, childbirth it's dangerous, and besides that I am plumb wore out. I want no more children! Do you understand me?"

Four months later, David walked into the kitchen to eat his noon meal. Sofie slid his plate in front of him as he sat at the head of the table. She turned without a word and went out the screen door and down the porch steps toward the chicken coop. David was hungry, but he was more concerned with Sofie's odd behavior. He called after her, "Sofie, wait now, just a minute— why aren't you eating the meal with me?"

He shoved back his chair and followed her outside. He pushed open the door to the coop and found her squatted down against the wall, tears running down her apple cheeks. David knelt down and put his arms around her. "Sofie, Sofie, what is the matter? Has someone died? What makes you cry so?"

In early April, Sofie gave birth to another daughter they named Edie. The midwife laid the newborn baby in Sofie's arms without saying a word as she busied herself cleaning up. Sofie looked down at her baby, expecting to see a beautiful newborn, but she knew instinctively, as she looked at the tiny face; she hadn't heard her cry. The baby's breathing was irregular, and her limbs were floppy, with little to no motor function. Sofie held her close to her heart and cried bitter tears.

After a few months had past, David called the doctor from Lovell to come out to their house. When Dr. Kraft had finished examining the baby, he slid a kitchen chair from the table and sat down. Pulling a heavy silver pocket watch from his vest, he glanced at it and returned it to the pocket.

His face grim and eyes cast down, the doctor spoke softly. "David, Sofie, I am so sorry to tell you, but I believe your baby had some serious problems. She is either what we call 'retarded' or has a condition that will limit her development. Sometimes a child's symptoms are minimal, and they can live at home and have a fairly good life. It will take time for us to know for sure how severe her problems will be. You can try and care for her yourselves for as long as you can, and of course we will do all we can as doctors to help you. There may come a time when you will know it's not possible for you to care for her anymore. I am so sorry. There is nothing we can do." 22

One evening as Sofie sat in the wooden rocker, nursing her new daughter, she looked down at the baby as she questioned softly, "David, I don't understand why she is like this—is it something I did?" Sofie bent to kiss her baby. "I'm so afraid for her, David. What kind of life is she going to have? What happens to her when we are so old we can't take care of her?"

David and Sofie were devastated but vowed to take care of their handicapped daughter for as long as they could. They didn't explain anything to their other children. They decided to wait and see how Edie matured and what she could accomplish. They figured they would know when the time was right to discuss it as a family.

~~~~

As they did every Sunday, David and Sofie went to church at the yellow clapboard Lutheran church on Shoshone Avenue. When the service was over, the people gathered outside, standing on the lawn in front of the church. This was their opportunity to visit and share town gossip or good news. The day was hot and muggy, and Sofie noticed Edie was having difficulty breathing in the humid heat. She gathered the rest of the kids, and they headed for the car. Just as Sofie was climbing in the front seat, their friend, Clara Rothardt, hurried over to the car.

"Oh goodness, I was afraid I was going to miss you, Sofie. Would it be all right if Walter and I came over this afternoon for a visit? You don't have to go to any trouble. We won't stay long." On the drive home, Sofie thought about Clara and what she had said. Something was strange about the way she looked, and her request was unusual.

Around two in the afternoon, the Rothardt car turned off the main road and rolled into the farmyard. Walter braked and cut the engine. He got out and hurried around to the passenger's side to open the door for Clara. Together they walked to the porch where David and Sofie sat in the shade. David invited their guests. "Sit down, please. Would you like a glass of fresh ice tea?" After Sofie poured the drinks for everyone, she settled back in her chair and waited for Clara to speak.

Clara smiled self-consciously and reached up to dab at the beads of sweat that had popped out on her forehead. "Goodness, it is hot today." She looked down at her hands as they lay in her lap. Then her eyes rose to meet David and Sofie; she had tears in her eyes. "Sofie, I have family news from Susannenthal. It's about your parents." David straightened abruptly in his chair as Sofie's hand flew to cover her mouth, expecting the worst.

"Sofie, I had a letter from my cousin Helmut, who continues to live in Susannenthal. He wrote me that your papa insisted on helping with the heavy fall harvest even though he hadn't been well. The third day he didn't come to the fields, so Helmut went to their house and knocked several times before your mother opened the door." Clara cleared her throat and squirmed in her seat. "I'm afraid there's no easy way to tell you this, Sofie.

Your father has passed. He apparently had heart failure in his sleep.

Your mother told Helmut she had held him in her arms through the night, not knowing for sure if he was gone or not."

Sofie's face contorted as tears ran from her green eyes, and she wrung her hands. Clara moved her chair closer to Sofie's, resting her hand on her friend's back. "I'm afraid that isn't all of the news. Your mother, Sofie—your mother died the very next day, struck down with terrible pain in her head and paralyzed.

"They were buried together. Since the pastor is no longer there, the Lutheran schoolmaster said prayers over them. They didn't have the formal burial that we were all used to, nor were the bells rung in their honor. The peoples didn't want to attract the attention of the Bolsheviks. I am so sorry to be the one to tell you this news, Sofie. I know for months you have wondered why you didn't hear from your parents."

Clara and Walter made a feeble effort at small talk, drank their ice tea, and drove back to town, giving David and Sofie the privacy they needed to mourn. "Now we know, and we worry no more about my parents. They are with God and safe. This gives me much comfort, my David, much comfort." Sofie rose from her chair and walked slowly into the house.

Chapter Fourteen

SEARCHING

In 1925, during the six years the Steiner family lived in the Lovell area, their three oldest daughters married and began families of their own. Left at home were Emilie, the four boys, and little Edie. David and Sofie had made a way for themselves, but "what-if," seemed to hover above their lives and decisions like a dark cloud.

David especially continued to be restless and question what was over the next hill—if it would be better, be easier? Sofie often looked at him and wondered if he was waiting for a sign from the Lord as a way to solve his questions. *If he doesn't make a decision soon, I may have to make one for him. We're getting too old to keep pulling up and moving.*

~~~~~

Out of the blue one day, Jack bluntly questioned his mother. "Ma, why can't Edie walk, talk, and run like the other kids? Her arms and legs just flop around, and all she does is grunt and slobber. Is there something wrong with her?" Jack wasn't the only sibling who had noticed, but he was the only one with enough moxie to question it.

Sofie stood at the kitchen sink, up to her elbows in dishwater. Jack's question hit her hard, even though she had expected the time would come for questions. Sofie took a deep breath as she wiped her hands on her apron and she turned to speak to her oldest son. "Yes, Edie has problems. I think it's time we sat you all down and told you just why she isn't like other kids, and she will never be."

After dinner that night, David asked his family to remain at the table after the meal. "There is something your mother and I want to talk to you about. We have known since she was born something was wrong with Edie. The doctors told us she would have problems learning. They said if we work with her, she may learn to walk, but they don't think she will ever learn to talk. Your sister is what the doctor calls 'retarded.' She wasn't born with all the abilities you were, and she can't learn the way you learn. She isn't the only child in the world like this. There are thousands. Most families take care of their own. However, if the child comes to have too many problems, some families send them away to a special school. We have decided to keep Edie with us for as long as we can. Right now, we want you all to try to work with her, to help her learn to walk. Do I have your word that you will all try to help her learn new things while she is still with us?"

Pete raised his hand, like he was in school. "Dad, are you going to keep her at home so she won't go to school with us? It's already hard because some of the kids make fun of her and call her an idiot. That makes me real mad, Dad. I know she can't help how she is."

David and Sofie looked around the table at their five children. David laid his large calloused hands beside his plate and looked across the oilcloth-covered table. "We understand that it is a difficult situation for you to deal with. But that doesn't excuse any of us. We all need to protect and stand up for Edie because she can't do it for herself."

Jack stood up and declared, "If anybody makes fun of her again, I'm gonna sock 'em good, and they'll know better next time!"

Understanding his oldest son's protectiveness, David replied, "Now, Jack, I don't want to hear of you doing something like that. There are other ways. I want to tell you of another decision your mother and I have made. We are moving back east again. This time, we are going to Fisher, Minnesota!"

Jack stood up so fast, his ladder-back chair tipped and crashed to the floor. His face was red, and his fists were clenched tight. "*No!* Why, Dad, why keep moving? We've got it pretty good here, and we're making lots of friends. Where in the heck is Fisher, Minnesota and why is it so much better than where we are right now?"

David looked down at the scrubbed and fading red-checked oilcloth Sofie had tacked to the kitchen table. He paused a moment. "Jack, I'm sorry if this decision doesn't fit into your plans, but your mother and I think it is a good opportunity for us to make some decent money. Just think of it as another great family adventure. It's my duty to put food on the table and a roof over your heads; this is the best way I can see to do this." David stood up, supporting himself by placing his large, calloused hands on the table, he said, "Try to understand and bear with us, son. We are doing the best we can. Someday, you will see how hard it is to make a decent living. Someday you will know!"

~~~~~

They drove to Minnesota in the Ford Model A sedan pulling a long, tarp-covered trailer heaped with household goods and small implements. Along the way they stayed at camps, pitching a tent most nights. Emilie didn't like sleeping on the ground, so she put her bag on the roof of the car.

The next morning when they pulled up at a country gas station, the attendant came out to the car and leaned in the window. "Can I gas this car up for you and check the oil?" David never got a chance to reply before the attendant moved back and staring at Edie, he said, "Whoa, it looks like you got yourself an idiot in there. How did she get that way?"

David didn't say a word, but rolled up the window and shifted into first gear as he drove out of the station, leaving the attendant standing by the gas pump, staring after them. Nobody said a word until David said, "Didn't like that gas station, I'll bet cha there is another one down the road here without an ignorant attendant." David chuckled, and then asked, "Is he still standing back there eating my dust?"

Two months after David and Sofie moved to Fisher, Raisa and her two young children Beth and Arnold made the trip by train from Port Huron, Michigan, for a visit. Two years prior, Jake and Raisa had moved to Michigan and Raisa was lonesome for her folks.

They had been there for several days when eight-year-old Adam asked Beth if she wanted to go with him looking for pop bottles along the side of the road. "When we find some, we can take them to the store. We'll get a penny for each one and buy some candy. Come on, little Beth. It'll be fun."

They spent the entire morning scouring the drain ditch alongside the road for pop bottles people had thrown out of their car windows. Adam carried a gunny sack over his shoulder as they scoured the borrow pit. After a couple of hours, Beth was getting tired; they sat under the shade of a tree and counted their loot. They had about fifteen bottles, so they decided to head for the small country grocery store and cash them in.

Proudly, the two kids dragged the gunny sack through the front door and presented their findings to the grocer. He counted out fifteen bottles and handed them fifteen pennies. Elated, Beth and Adam began to browse the candy section, carefully making their selections. Adam noticed the grocer took their bottles and went out the back door with them. He was back inside in a moment. Beth and Adam laid their candy on the counter along with the fifteen pennies. They stuffed half the candy in their pockets and the other half in their mouths as they headed for the door.

Once outside, Adam said, "Just a minute. Let's go around the back of the store. I want to see something." The two rounded the corner of the grocery, and there was a bounty of empty pop bottles all in crates, stacked against the wall, waiting to be picked up by the distributor.

Biding their time, they waited for about an hour then walked back into the grocery store with another twenty empty pop bottles. "Hi, Mr. Winterholler, we found some more bottles and want to trade them for candy." The grocer took a look at the kids and a look at the bottles, paused a moment, then counted them and handed Adam twenty cents. He took the bottles back and sat them beside the back door.

After the kids bought their candy, the grocer opened the back door just a crack so he could watch the pile of pop bottles. Sure enough, there they were, loading their gunny sack with more of his empty bottles. He jumped out of the door and yelled, "Got ya!" Adam dropped the gunny sack and took off running, followed by Beth who was bawling and screaming for him to wait for her. When they got home, Raisa asked them if they found any bottles, and Adam piped up before Beth could say anything because he could tell she was about to cry. "Yeah, we found about fifteen and traded them for some penny candy. It was sure fun." Adam knew Beth was looking at him, grateful he had offered an explanation to the question. The two mischief-makers high-tailed it out of the room before they incriminated themselves!

~~~~~

Things hadn't been that bad in Fisher. David and Sofie were there for a year, raising sweet corn, sugar beets, and ten head of dairy cattle. They made enough for David to buy his first truck to haul crops in. "Sure as heck beats harnessing up a team every day, and that old truck doesn't eat as much as those Percheron horses do!" David and the boys liked working with Holstein dairy cattle and did well selling milk and cream year around.

David and sugar beet truck

One Friday after the holidays, David came in the kitchen door, stomped the snow from his boots, hung his coat on the peg, and commenced to wash up for dinner. He sat down at the table as Sofie dished up the steaming chicken and noodles. After a couple of spoonsful of the hot soup, David stopped eating, put his spoon down, and with disbelief ringing through his words, he shared what he had just learned. "Sofie, do you know what I just learned today? These Lutherans here don't believe in dancing the polka! Have you ever heard of anything so crazy—not dancing the polka? I don't think this is going to work here either, Sofie, if we can't have a little polka dancing once in a while. These just aren't our kind of folks!" Shaking his head in disbelief, he continued, "Them not dancing the polka pretty much does it for me, that and the long winters!"

It was a long trip back west this time—back to the Big Horn Basin, back to Basin, Wyoming. Again, David found a farm to rent, and they raised more sugar beets, beans, and grain. They spent four years farming and raising the black-and-white Holstein dairy cattle near the outskirts of Basin. The cows were good milk producers, and of course, word got out, which is just what David wanted. He made some good money, not only selling milk and cream but also the calves. Buyers came from miles around to bargain and trade for the calves. Most didn't cherish the idea of trading with David Steiner, as he had the reputation of being a tough nut to crack.

~~~~~

The Steiner boys were getting older now; and as sons do from time to time, they got into trouble—some worse than others. One Saturday night, Jack went into town with his buddies, fooled around, and got into some mischief. Around midnight David heard someone rapping at the front door. He got out of bed and went to the door. Jack's friend Ed Rafferty stood there with his hat in his hands. "Uh—evening, Mr. Steiner—uh—we had some trouble at the pool hall, and Jack's in jail. He wanted me to stop by and see if you'd go down there and get him out. I would done got him myself, out 'cepting I ain't got me no money left."

David looked at the young man in disbelief. He rubbed his day-old growth of whiskers, obviously thinking of what to say. "Well, tell you what, Ed, it's after one in the morning. Jack got his-self into that jail, and Jack will have to sit it out until they unlock that door because I don't have any money for that kind of nonsense either. Now you go on home. I'm going back to bed. Thanks for comin' by and telling us about the problem."

When Jack finally came home, David told him in no uncertain terms, "You missed two days of field work around here 'cause of your orneriness. That two days' pay is comin' out of your part of the profits at the end of harvest. Now think about that the next time you decide to get out of line!"

They stayed on the farm in Basin until David heard of a large farm in the Lovell area that he could rent. In 1930 he and two of the older boys rode horseback, driving thirty head of dairy cattle across the sagebrush-covered hills to the west and then around the tip of Sheep Mountain and on north to Lovell. They had rented two hundred acres; eighty acres were already planted in row crops, and the other hundred was planted in alfalfa and grain. Their dairy business continued to flourish and became a gold mine. Their family was growing up, and the boys were a big help with the fieldwork. Emilie had married and left home when they lived in Basin, so it was just the four boys and Edie at home.

~~~~~

Sofie woke one morning to see David standing by their bedroom window. "David, are you sick? Why are you standing by the window like that—is someone out there?" He turned as a gleeful smile crinkled the corners of his eyes.

"I was looking at the Big Horns—how fast can you get a picnic together?"

Later that afternoon David hobbled the horses as the boys took off exploring the rocks and woods and doing a little fishing in the creek. They had made arrangements with a neighbor to take care of Edie for a couple of days while they made a much-anticipated trip to the mountains. After a long, hot, bumpy ride up the mountain, they arrived at a campground. Together, David and Sofie spread their blanket over a flat, grassy spot, shaded by three towering spruce trees and a hardy stand of aspens. They dropped to their knees, and Sofie curled her legs under her dress as she sat near David, who chose to lie on his back—hands supporting his head. They remained that way for a few minutes, simply basking in the fresh mountain air and leisure time.

David closed his eyes and let the sunshine warm his face. "Aw, Sofie, my love, listen to the twitter of the finches. I believe I love their song almost as much as the ones from the morning doves. It's hard to believe that in another couple of months, those aspen leaves will look like golden coins, and soon after, the snow will start to fall again.

Sofie looked up at the dollar-sized leaves on the aspen trees. "They are so beautiful, especially in the fall when they turn golden. There is something about the way those leaves flutter so gently with the slightest breeze that I love to see. They are like hundreds of wiggling circles! Look at them, moving without a sound until the breeze increases, and they give off a soft rustling sound!"

David reached for her then, pulling her down to lay beside him. Sofie bristled. "David, what will the boys think,—us lying together on the blanket?" David laughed a deep, throaty laugh.

"Oh, my Sofie, they will probably think I have myself a nice soft pillow." David covered his head as Sofie smacked him a good one. "Really, my Liebchen, our sons have seen us sleeping in our bedroom, and I'm pretty sure they know about the birds and the bees. Is—is that how you say that?" He laughed deeply as he said, "Just relax and let's listen to the birds and the wind in the trees; look up at that incredible blue sky that our Lord has given us today. I swear it's the color of a robin's egg!"

David closed his eyes for a moment then said, "I suppose we should be back at the farm right now, getting ready for haying that lower field, but when I got up this morning, I just thought the Lord would like for us all to take a day off and enjoy what He has given us!"

Sofie smiled and planted a kiss on her husband's cheek. "I am so glad that you thought of this trip—it is wonderful. Where do you think we should pitch our tent? I like this spot right here— and over there in those rocks is perfect for our cook fire. We'll let the boys decide where they want to pitch their own tent."

David winked at his wife. "JA—and I hope it is far away from ours!"

Sofie turned and, with faked shock on her face, took a playful swing at him. "I guess I'm like you, thinking about all the work that I could be doing at home, but this is lovely—just lying here beside you, gazing up at the sky and the trees, feeling the gentle mountain breeze flow over my skin. I love that about you,

David— that you think of enjoying life, rather than working all the time!"

David turned on his side to look at his wife. "Sofie, I've been wondering. Do you miss making your hats now that most women order them from the catalogs or drive to Billings to purchase store-bought hats?"

"Not really, David. It was a lot of work to find the right grass and straw. I enjoyed it while I did it, and it earned us some money, but I have enough to keep me busy these days with my chickens, the cream, and of course Edie."

Sofie took a deep breath, exhaling slowly. "You know what I do miss is being a midwife. Since we live so close to town, more women use the doctor, and even more are having their babies at the hospital. I loved being the first person to lay my hands on a newborn baby—it was such a special gift. But times change, and we're older now and need to start slowing down a bit, I suppose. Nothing ever stays the same, and we have to accept that!"

David replied, "I've been thinking, Sofie, of how the Lord first gave us four daughters, and by the time the four boys came along, you had them girls to help take care of the boys. Lord knows those boys are a handful! But ya know I am glad it worked out that way, 'cause now that I'm getting on in years, the boys help me farm."

David cleared his throat and blinked as his blue eyes brimmed over with tears. "Sofie, I know I haven't said it often enough. We have moved so many times and, and—I know you weren't always happy to pick up and leave again, to go where I thought we should go, time and time again. Thank you, Sofie, for believing in me, for sticking it out, and for making the best of it all. Without you by my side, I probably would have wandered forever!"

Sofie drew in a deep breath as the birds twittered in the treetops. Propping herself up on one elbow, she reached with the other hand to touch her husband's face. "There was nowhere else on this earth I would rather be than at your side. Our travels have certainly made our life interesting, I have to say that!"

That evening, after Sofie put away the supper dishes, they sat around the campfire and sang old German songs. The next morning at the crack of dawn, David and the boys grabbed their fishing poles and went down to the nearby creek. Before long, they delivered over a dozen wriggling brook trout to Sofie's hot frying pan.

After breakfast David and the boys took down the tents, doused the campfire, and loaded the truck before heading back to the farm and the work that waited. On the ride down the mountain, Sofie laid her chapped hand on David's arm. "Oh, David, what a splendid idea that was—and we didn't even plan it. That was the best part!"

~~~~~

Edie was eight years old, all arms and legs, almost as tall as her twelve-year-old brother. She had never learned to speak, but with the help of her siblings, she managed to walk with a stumbling gait. She seemed happy, never gloomy or aware of her disabilities. Sofie was thankful her retarded daughter was not a difficult child, but it continued to break her heart to watch her struggle with living. She often thought of what Edie could have been and worried about her future.

And then there was, Adam, who was at the age where he didn't fit into the big plans his three older brothers were always cookin' up. It never bothered him much; he was pretty good at entertaining himself. Adam recently made friends with Mac Porter, who belonged to the family that moved in just down the road. Adam and Mac spent their free time doing what most twelve-year-olds do—getting in and out of trouble! Early one morning toward the end of September, Mac knocked on the weather-beaten screen door. "Hey, Adam, can you come out and take a walk with me? I sure got something swell to show ya!"

Adam had just finished stacking the wood beside the cook stove. "Dang, Mac—you're up early!" Adam peered through the screen door. 'I gotta finish with my chores, and then I'll be out. You can just wait out here." Soon Adam bounded out the door and the two took off down the road. "Well, ya gonna make me wait all day? What's so important that ya gotta show me?"

Mac grabbed Adam's sleeve and pulled him behind an old wagon that sat on two wheels beside the pasture where David's prized Holstein cows were grazing. He stuck his hand in his pocket and pulled out a tiny tin box. "Looka here; see what I borrowed from my dad's coat pocket last night."

Adam looked down at Mac's outstretched hand and reached to get a closer look. Mac pulled back. "Oh no you don't—not gonna let you touch this prize. Looka here, watch close now—I'll show you what this nifty little box has inside." Adam moved it closer for a better look as Mac pulled on the inside of the box. Like magic, it slid open. Adam gasped at what he saw—stick matches!

Mac stuck out his chest. "That's right, my friend—stick matches and, boy, do they light fast. Watch this!" Mac selected a match from the box and slid it along the side of the tin. The match flashed and was burning in a split second.

"Wow, can I try that?" Adam asked as he reached again for a second try at getting a match. "Sure, go ahead. What are friends for?" Adam took a match and lit it like his buddy had. Remembering how his older brothers talked, he said, "Boy, is this the cat's meow! Sure glad you came over this morning, Mac."

The boys lit match after match, flipping their wrists to extinguish them just like the grown-ups did. When the flame went out, they threw the matches on the ground, not giving a lot of thought to where the matches landed. Adam exclaimed, "Wow, sure glad you came over today! This is really fun, huh, Mac?"

When the matches were all gone, they triumphantly slapped each other's back as they headed across the barnyard to the house. Before they had rounded the barn, Adam stopped in his tracks and sniffed the air. "Mac, do you smell smoke?"

Mac lifted his nose to the air. "Naw, it's just your imagination— probably the smoke from the matches that got on your clothes."

They were almost to the house when Mac happened to turn to speak to Adam, and he caught a glimpse of something: smoke! It was coming from behind the barn. Mac grabbed Adam's shirt and pointed toward the plume of smoke. "Gol damn—run, Adam. We gotta put it out—grab that bucket by the pump!"

The two boys ran like the wind, around the barn to where they had been lighting matches by the old wagon. The wagon was completely engulfed in fire, and it looked like it was spreading to the dry weeds along the ditch bank. Adam threw his bucket of water on the fire. "Well, hell's bells—that's about like spittin' on it! What are we gonna do, Mac? My Dad is going to kill us, and that ain't kiddin'!"

That's when they spotted Jack on the tractor tearing across the pasture toward them; about the same time, they heard David's truck roaring down the lane and skidding to a stop a few feet from where the boys stood. "Get some gunny sacks out of the barn and start beating the fire—get a move on!" David yelled instructions as he began to use his shovel on the fire to create a break. Jack had a two-row plow on the back of the tractor and immediately began to plow a fire break around the perimeter of the blaze.

After about an hour, the danger had passed, but a new danger was waiting as Adam took one look at his father's face and knew he was in a ton of trouble. Mac didn't need any prompting as he high-tailed it home, leaving his friend to take the brunt of the punishment.

Adam took his medicine after he apologized to his father. He didn't walk real well for a few days while his back end healed up from the thrashing he got.

~~~~~~

After a couple of years on the Kraft place, they moved back to Sunlight. They were beginning to feel the worldwide depression like everybody else, but David kept on plugging. The ground on the new farm they were renting was pretty rocky, but David had an idea about some of it. That night out on the front porch, he sat his sons down and made them a deal. "You can have five acres for your own if you clear the rocks and plant it. I'll give you the bean seed. Let's see what you boys can do." For the first few weeks, they worked their butts off, hauling three or four wagonloads of rock off the field a day, and then they planted the beans.

One morning, midsummer, Sofie had been out to the chicken coop to gather the eggs when she heard a ruckus in the barn. She opened the door and what she saw took the very breath from her; she turned and ran for the house. "David, David, come quick— Jack and Joe are fighting in the barn, and they look like they are going to kill each other. Hurry, David, please!"

David hooked his suspenders over his shoulders and crossed the gravel farmyard in lengthy, angry strides. He reached the barn door and flung it open. There they were, Jack and Joe circling and circling. Their fists were clenched and bleeding. Jack had a bloody nose, and Joe's right cheek was raw and already bruising. Their clothes were torn, and they were covered with dirt, straw, and sweat.

Joe taunted his older brother. "Come on, you big cheese. You're not as hard-boiled as you'd like people to think, are ya? You think you're the cat's meow, don't ya? You hit like a girl!" They didn't even notice their father standing in the doorway of the barn.

David reached to the right and removed his Cossack whip from the wall where it hung. He circled it once over the heads of his sons then landed it expertly across the back of his oldest son Jack—*crack!* Before either son could respond, the whip cracked again and this time opened Joe's shoulder.

Pain screamed into the brains of the two young warriors as they lifted their heads simultaneously to see their father standing in the open door. Silhouetted against the morning sun, his legs spread as he balanced his weight-- David was an ominous sight with whip in hand! "Stop this fighting *now!* You two act like animals, not like brothers. This is not the way we've raised you— to strike and hurt your brother. Now you both git up to the house, clean up, and then git on out to the field and don't come home until the sun sets. This will be a day you won't forget!"

David turned his back on his sons, slammed the barn door, and angrily stomped back to the house. He was shaking as he stashed the Cossack whip in the closet and slumped down into his chair. "That was not good, Sofie, not good. I whipped 'em— only way to get 'em to stop and teach them a lesson. They'll be in here soon for you to fix 'em up. I'm sorry I lost my temper with them, but there are times when they push me too far!"

After that day, David never had to use his whip on his sons again, and if there were any disagreements or fights, they made sure it wasn't anywhere near their father and his Cossack whip!

~~~~~~

That fall, each son took his cut of $150, and they were satisfied their Great Northern beans came in at thirty sacks to the acre.

When David handed out the profits, he said, "I'm proud of you boys. You worked plenty hard out in that field, and now you have money in your pockets. Don't go blowin' it. Spend it wisely because it wasn't easy to come by."

The next morning they all came running when Sofie hollered, "Breakfast is ready!" David sat at the head of the table, and the boys and Edie took their places. Being half awake and forgetting his manners, Joe took his fork and reached across the table to spear a couple pieces of bacon. Before his fork reached the bacon, he felt the breeze of David's knife blow past his hand; instantly awake, he stared at the big knife stuck in the wood table.

David bellowed, "You know better than that. When you're eatin' at my table, you say thanks for the food first, and then you eat. Now bow your heads—all of you." David said the traditional prayer in German like he always did. As soon as he finished, he nodded his head, and forks flew! Neither loud talk nor arguing was ever allowed at the table. David always told them, "When we are at the table, we eat. Talking is for later."

After each meal, Edie rose with difficulty and eagerly began to attend to her job of clearing the silverware and things that wouldn't break from the table; she carried them proudly to the dishpan. Adam and Joe took turns carrying the plates and stacking them on the side table as Sofie filled a large pan with hot water and soap; another pan held the rinse water. Edie dried the unbreakable things with a big dish towel made out of an old flour sack. The rest of the dishes were stacked in a wooden drainer to dry.

~~~~~

The end always comes to particular events and lifestyles. So it was for the Steiner family's constant search for a place of their own. One warm fall day, David made another decision. "You know, this seems to be where we belong. We keep coming back to Lovell. We've got a little money saved, and I think I'll ask around in town if anyone is selling out. This may or may not be the best time to buy, with the depression and all, but I think we can handle it, and I was never one to do things like the rest of the folks do anyway!"

Regardless of whether David lost the quest for his dream, the pot of gold at the end of the rainbow, or was simply physically wearing down, they made their last move in 1933. They bought a place of their own just south of Lovell. David found a house in foreclosure from the bank, and they moved it onto the farm. There were several good sheds and a decent barn already there.

Jack looked around the place then questioned, "Dad, why wasn't there a house on the farm? Looks like there might have been one over there by those trees, but all I see now is a big black place on the ground along with some burnt pots and pans."

"Well, Jack, you're right bout that. The house sat right over there, but you see with this depression, lots of folks are losing their farms and such. The man who used to own this farm burned his house down so as the bank wouldn't get it. It's desperate times. Sometimes a man can't take losing something he loves, and he doesn't want anybody else gittin' it either."

Sofie took pride in making curtains and fixing up her home. No more packing and traveling across the country. This was it! David and the boys even put up a windmill so they could have electricity in the house. It was a special treat to have electric lights and to be able to listen to the small electric Philco radio in the evening after chores.

~~~~~

The four boys were expected to get up at the crack of dawn every morning. Sofie was usually up before that, setting the percolator on the coal stove to make coffee and frying a whole pan of bacon. While the bacon was popping and sizzling on the stove, she would whip up a batch of biscuits and pop them in the oven. When the bacon was fried, she would dice some potatoes and green onions, letting them brown in the bacon grease. Finally, she cracked about a dozen fresh eggs and stirred it up. Turning down the heat, she let the mixture simmer until the kitchen filled with big appetites.

As their four boys learned and grew in their knowledge of farming, David loosened the reins, giving them each an equal number of acres; he took a percentage of their crops as landowner. They all worked hard, sweating and tending the business during the week, but the weekends were another story.

One Saturday night, Jack and Pete asked for the car and went into Lovell; they stayed out dancing and carousing all weekend, finally getting home around 2:00 a.m. Monday morning. When the rest of the family gathered at the breakfast table the next morning, two chairs were empty. David went to the foot of the pull-down stairs and called up to his oldest boys. "You get on down here. Nights are for sleeping and days for working! If you aren't down here in five minutes, I'll be up there with a pot of cold water!"

A couple weeks later at Friday morning breakfast, Pete asked, "Hey, Dad, can I have the car tonight? I have a big date with this ritzy dame." Before David could answer, Jack had something to say about that.

"Ahh, you're all wet, Pete. Ya think I'm a pushover or something? You already had the car once this week, and it's my night to drag Main and romance the dames! Joe and I have big plans, so scram, if ya know what I mean, brother. We could drop you off, and you could hang around on Main like some drugstore cowboy and put your peepers on every broad that walks on by!" Joe and Adam laughed so hard that Joe fell off his chair.

Pete didn't take kindly to a little friendly competition. "I'll tell ya what I see, a couple of wise guys out on the town lookin' for whoopee with the first dumb Dora that looks your way! You two think you're the big cheese. Too bad the dames you guys attract are usually flat tires!"

Looking at his sons, David looked perplexed as he smiled and shook his head, not understanding much of what that conversation was about. "You boys better remember something—the way it usually goes in this world is that, one guy has the money and the other the purse! So work something out and get along with what you have. I better not hear of any more foolishness from any of you."

That's pretty much the way the Steiner boys lived, working hard all week and going out on the town on Friday and Saturday nights. There was always a dance somewhere close, and if there was one thing they liked better than dames, it was dancing with them! One weekend Joe had pretty much had his fill of Jack and his swashbuckling attitude. He had heard him ask their dad for the car that night, and Joe had plans of his own with a real sweet gal. So he came up with a swell little plan.

Jack was at the kitchen wash basin, washing up and slicking back his black hair just the way the gals all liked. Suddenly he heard the car start up out in the yard; he made it to the screen door just in time to see his brother, Joe, barreling down the lane toward the county road. "Well, son of a b—"

Jack didn't get the chance to finish his sentence as he felt the business end of his mother's broom across his broad back.

"Ma, whatcha do that for? I just spent ten minutes getting every hair in place, and now look! I was supposed to have the car tonight and Joe done gone and took the keys and the car!" He stomped up the stairs to the loft he shared with his brothers and started looking for his brand-new, two-toned, Zoot-suit Spats. They were the hottest shoe from coast to coast, and Jack had recently splurged and bought himself a pair. He couldn't find them anywhere, and the box he kept them in was empty. Then a light bulb went off in his head. That damn Joe had not only made off with the car, but he was also wearing his new Spats, to boot!

It took Jack a long time to forgive Joe for doing what he did. After that little incident, the brothers gave him the nickname "Spatz," which stuck for over a lifetime!

~~~~~

Toward the middle of the summer, David was sitting out on the front porch enjoying the cool evening air and reading his Bible. Jack, Pete, and Joe came out of the house dressed to the nines, hair slicked back, and reeking of cologne. Jack pushed opened the screen door and playfully slapped his father on the back. "Hey, Dad, we're gonna go into town to the movies. Have you ever been to the movies?" It took some doing, but they got their father to put on a clean shirt, and the four of them set off to town.

They found a place to park and walked a short distance to the new movie theatre on Lovell's Main Street. David sat in the darkened theatre with arms crossed and watched as the world news came on first, followed by a cartoon. He seemed to be enjoying the experience until the featured movie, *Laurel and Hardy*. His sons kept sneaking glances at him, but he just sat stone-faced, arms still crossed. Suddenly David got up, and without a word, he walked out. The next morning at the breakfast table he said, "Movies are for fools. It is ridiculous—grown-up people making fools of themselves for all to see!" David never set foot in a movie theatre again.

When their niece, Beth, turned sixteen in 1936, the three younger Steiner boys decided it was up to them to teach her how to dance and watch out for the wise guys. On dance night it was a standing date for one or the other or even all three to stop by her house in Cowley and pick her up. Joe liked to tease her the most because she always blushed.

"Hey, kid, you're getting to be quite the dish! You got a "fave" guy yet, or are you just checking 'em out? Are ya carrying a torch for anyone special—are ya, huh?"

Beth liked it when her uncles called her "kid." It made her feel special. She didn't mind their teasing; she was used to being teased by her kid brother, Arnold. She liked the attention her uncles gave her, and they always made her laugh. Most of all, she loved going to dances with them; she knew they would protect her if some guy got fresh or something.

She was especially close to her uncle Adam, who was eighteen, just two years older than she was. He never let her sit alone at a dance. If she wasn't out on that dance floor, Adam walked up to her and twirled her out onto the floor. He was the one who taught her to dance the new "swing"! Joe was really a great dancer, but he knew it too. He would only ask the gals to dance who knew the moves he knew, but he too took the time to teach Beth a few steps.

"Thanks, Joe, you're the best. You always have something new to teach me. But, Joe, I don't want you throwing me over your shoulder anymore. That scared me to death!" she said, laughing.

Joe put his arm around her shoulder and tweaked her nose. "Listen, kid, if any of these goons try to lay their line on you, just tell them to take it on the heel and toe, know what I mean? If they don't, you come get me, and I will help the situation along!" Beth beamed as she giggled at the thought of guys actually fighting over her, even if a couple of them were her uncles.

On the way home one night, Joe mentioned to Beth, "I noticed that Haggard guy hanging around you most of the night. Did he ask to take you home?"

Beth blushed and laughed. "Well, yeah, he did, but I told him I always go home with the one who brought me."

"Way to go, kid, way to go. Let 'em know they have to ask you out on a date to take you home, 'specially when you have your three personal bodyguards around! If they don't behave, we'll give 'em a knuckle sandwich! Just watch who you hang around. Stay away from those hard-boiled swells—they ain't no good!"

~~~~~

David and Sofie stayed on the farm south of Lovell through the Great Depression years. Like everyone else, they wore cardboard in their shoes. Sofie made dresses and shirts out of flour sacks and hand-me-downs. She put in huge gardens and made the boys help her work them. They even picked and carried in the vegetables for her when it was time to can. Everybody pitched in because when Sofie was on her feet a lot or it was hot outside, her feet swelled up like melons.

Sofie's hat business had dropped off to the point she was lucky if she sold one a month. She used to get anywhere from $2 to $3 for a fancy hat; now, all that was selling in the stores were straw field hats. It was true that they brought in a few dollars, but there was no challenge or special design to weaving them. Still saving the small chicken and goose feathers, especially the down feathers, Sofie now made pillows and feather ticks from them.

David made a few dollars from half-soling shoes. Few people could buy new shoes and brought their old broken down shoes to David to repair. He put the shoe on a metal lay and cut the size of sole he needed from cowhides he had cured in the smokehouse. He spent hours cutting, gluing, and nailing the soles to shoes just to bring in a little money.

David continued to farm. He had one tractor but wasn't as comfortable on it as he was driving horses across his fields. He did admit to his wife he was beginning to slow down, but he forgot to mention the chest pains.

On those days when David and Sofie went into town to shop or run an errand, they stopped by to visit with Raisa and the kids. They enjoyed sitting around the kitchen table, drinking coffee, and talking in German even though the children didn't understand what they were saying. Arnold often stood beside his grandfather as they talked. He would look from one to the other as they spoke. "Hey, I don't understand that German talk. Why don't you talk English so I can know what you are saying?"

David stood up. "Do you know what? I think I forgot to give you a nickel today, didn't I?" He reached into his pocket and handed Arnold a shiny nickel. "Now, you run on down to the corner grocery and buy a candy. And—we speak in German so little ears don't know what we say. Not all of our talk is your business!"

It was a Saturday morning ritual to drive into town and sell the fresh cream and eggs. During the Depression, they felt fortunate if they could find buyers! Toward the end of the depression years, there were days and weeks when even the grocer wasn't buying their produce. Nobody had any money to buy anything. Often they traded their produce for something they needed.

Whatever money they made, David put a dollar or two in his pocket and gave the rest to Sofie to buy the supplies they needed. What was leftover was put into a jar for emergencies or entertainment, whichever came first. "You are better with the money than I am, Sofie, so you keep charge of the household money."

When the boys were low on their own cash and wanted to go to a movie or a dance, they would have to ask their mother for the ten-cent admission. More than once they considered looking for her hiding place and helping themselves to the money, but they knew their mother counted every penny and decided it probably wasn't a good idea. They all had experience getting on the wrong side of her; they knew she'd give them a whack and ask questions later. For their own entertainment, David and Sofie occasionally invited neighbors over on a Saturday night to play a few hands of pinochle, enjoy a glass of homemade beer or wine, and visit. David kept a good bunch of hops growing alongside the barn to put in his wheat beer. Everyone had his own way of getting his hands on liquor if he wanted it. Most people learned how to live with Prohibition laws, and in defense of the German love of beer, David often said, "We are German. We have to have a good glass of beer now and then. There is nothing wrong with that!"

When he and Sofie didn't have something planned on a Saturday night, David went to town alone, had one drink in the back room of the saloon (during Prohibition), lit up a big cigar, and went outside to stand on the street corner. He enjoyed making conversations with different farmers and men who passed his way. When he finished the cigar, he walked down the street to his car and drove home or asked one of his sons to take him home.

One balmy summer evening, David and Sofie were sitting on the front porch after finishing supper and evening chores, David with his Bible and Sofie with her fancy work and crocheting. Edie was playing by herself on the swing to the side of the house. Sofie laid her mending in her lap as she watched their challenged daughter.

"David, I didn't tell you this, but the other day when I took Edie to the grocery on Main Street, there were kids in the store who made fun of her, mocking her slobbering and grunting. It was horrible, David. Thank God, Edie doesn't realize when people are staring or making stupid comments. I have been thinking perhaps we should keep her out here on the farm now, not take her to church or into town where people stare and say hurtful things. I'm not ashamed of her. I want to protect her and, I guess, protect us as well. What do you think?"

David thoughtfully looked out over the emerald field of corn. He marked his place in the Bible and closed it on his lap. "I've had the same experience—people and their callous remarks about our girl. She is happy on the farm, gathering the eggs and helping in the garden. So for now, I agree we should keep her away from cruel comments. I believe, like the doctors told us, the time is coming when we will have to take her to the special school. She is getting to be a big girl and is more than we can handle at times. The other problem is that we are both getting on in our years and can't do all the things we used to do. I'll have my sixty-fifth birthday soon and have been thinking about cutting back and giving more of the farming to the boys. We don't need much." His mind filled with thoughts as he watched Edie for a moment then turned back to his Bible.

Sofie nodded her head in agreement as she returned to her sewing. She wished she could talk to Edie. With her older girls gone and married, she was lonesome for female conversation, but Edie had never learned to speak. Occasionally, she would look at her mother and make grunting sounds, but only she knew what they meant.

It was late one Sunday afternoon when they were relaxing on the front porch and were both surprised to see Raisa and Jake's car turn into the lane. The car pulled up in front of the house; the engine died, the car door opened, and their firstborn daughter stepped from the car. David and Sofie could tell right away that something was wrong.

"Dad, do you have a moment? I really need to talk to you. Jake and I are having some problems, and I don't know what to do." She pulled up a chair beside her father and started crying.

David put a protective arm across her shoulders. "I don't know what is going on with you and Jake, but all couples go through rough spots in the road. It's tough times, Raisa, and I know Jake struggles to farm and find work. Most folks are just tryin' to make ends meet. I hear you've been taking on some work in the laundry and cleaning houses to help out, is that right?"

Raisa wiped her nose and put the handkerchief in her front pocket. With eyes cast to the rough, unpainted porch floor, she explained, "Yeah, Dad, I know times are tough. I want to get off the farm. I hate it, Dad—I just hate it and all the work in the hot fields. I can't take it anymore. I had to quit the laundry too because I passed out from the heat. My kids need shoes and decent food, so I am cleaning houses. The problem is—Jake is spending a lot of time at the pool hall, playing cards and drinking some, when he should be home or out trying to find more work." Raisa stood up

and began to pace the weathered porch. She stopped at the edge
and looked off into the distant fields.

"We are fighting, seems like all the time. I resent working
all day cleaning houses while he's sitting in the pool hall. I wonder
if I would be better off on my own, like Emilie. Did you know she
is moving to San Francisco, California? Frank beat her up
something bad, and she packed up and left him. In the letter I just
got, she said she was taking their little boy with her."

David continued to sit and smoke his pipe. "I didn't know
Emilie left him. What is she going to do all by herself in such a big
city and with a child to take care of?"

Raisa sat back down on the bench. "Well, she has her
teaching degree from normal school, and she has experience
teaching, so I don't know if she is going to teach or what. In her
letter she mentioned she found a job already, and her landlady was
going to take care of her son during the day.

"But, Dad, that isn't the only trouble. Lizzie called the
other night. George was drunk and pounding on her again. Jake
went over there and locked him out of their place so he couldn't
hurt her anymore. I think she probably let him back in now.

"Jake has gotten a little rough with me sometimes, Dad, but
he never hit me. I don't know what I would do. I don't think I
could stay with a man who hit me. I'm real worried about Lizzie.
She believes everything that bum tells her. She thinks she loves
him. Of course, he tells her he beats her up because *she* makes him
mad! Have you ever heard of anything so stupid? Like it's her fault
he punches her! And then there are the kids. It really scares them
when their folks fight."

David took off his dusty straw hat and slapped it hard
against his thigh. "It says in the Bible divorce is not a good thing,
but I don't go along with a man hitting a woman either. I don't
care what she says to him. Maybe it's time I have a talk with
George to let him know I don't take to him beating my daughter."

He never got his chance to have a talk with George because
that next afternoon, David was out in the field on the tractor when
he noticed a car pull up and stop on the road beside his field. He
was too far away to see who it was. David stopped the tractor at
the end of the row just in time to see Lizzie stumbled across the
uneven field toward him. She was bleeding from her nose; one eye

was already black, and there was a raw bruise on her left cheek where George's fist had connected. Her gauze print dress was torn, and her brown hair was a mess. David slammed the tractor into neutral gear as he stomped on the brake. He switched the engine off and jumped from the tractor; he ran to his daughter. Gently, he held her against his chest as she sobbed.

~~~~~~

When Jake came home from work that day, Raisa met him at the door. "He's done it again, and this time she needed stitches. Lizzie is out at the folk's place. She is going to divorce him, Jake. He's a mean, nasty brute. Dad has filed the papers for her and called the sheriff to go pick him up at his job tomorrow." That was about all Raisa got out before Jake grabbed his hat, turned heel, and slammed out the door. He jumped in their black Ford and spun gravel as he backed down the driveway. Raisa stood on the porch as she watched him leave the lane in a cloud of dust. He hit the main road, fishtailed as he made the corner, and headed for town.

Jake knew where George Rimmer was, and that was exactly where he was going! He pulled into a parking spot in front of the pool hall, shifted into neutral, set the parking brake, and jumped out of the Ford. Slamming the door hard, he crossed the sidewalk and burst through the front door of the pool hall. Jake was plenty worked up and loaded for bear. "Where is that son of a bitch?" His eyes scanned the dim interior of the pool hall as several guys playing poker looked up. The bartender came around the bar, wiping his hands on his week-old apron.

"Who ya lookin for, Jake? Hope it's not me!"

Jake spotted George Rimmer near the rear of the pool hall shooting pool with a couple other guys. Like a matador's bull, Jake saw red! He crossed the worn plank floor to where George was about to make a shot and grabbed the pool cue out of George's hand. Jake twisted it to the left and brought it up hard against his brother-in-law's jaw. The whole room heard the crack as bone gave in to the wooden cue. When George attempted to turn away from his attacker, Jake brought the end of the cue down across his brother-in-law's back, sending him to the floor.

Jake tossed the pool cue aside as he pulled George to his feet and sneered. "You son of a bitch—nothing I hate more than a woman beater, especially when the woman is my sister-in-law." Jake brought his fist up under George's other jaw and gave a final blow to the belly for good measure. That's when Jake felt hands on him, pulling him off George. "Hey now, Jake, think he's had enough. What did he do? You say he beat up his wife again?"

Jake wiped his skinned fists against his pants. "Yeah, that's right, and it's the last time he's going to do it. The law is after him. In fact, you might call the sheriff and tell him he can pick this sorry SOB up right now!"

The bartender looked around at the crowd that had gathered. "Anyone here see who did this to George?" Everyone shook their heads in the negative and headed back to their games. George was not the most popular guy around Lovell at that point, nor had he ever been. The sheriff picked up his man, and Lizzie proceeded with the divorce. She and her kids moved in with David and Sofie until George got out of jail and left town.

~~~~~

David and Sofie went on with their life and did what they had to do to survive the depression and the divorces of two of their daughters. David prayed for forgiveness for his former sons-in-law but made it known they weren't welcome on the home place.

Over the years, they received a few letters from relatives and friends who had survived and escaped the eradication of the Volga Germans during the revolution.[23] News from Germany and Europe was alarming. It was 1940, and things were heating up, especially in Germany.

Sofie had thought about their life on the Volga all that morning as she worked in the garden. Finished with her hoeing, she balanced the old hoe against the fence, gathered up her vegetables and headed for the house. She felt the sun fall warm on her back as she walked across the rut-filled farmyard. Smiling with satisfaction, she looked down at her calico apron filled with potatoes, carrots, and tomatoes. Suddenly, Sofie's head snapped up as she heard a car turn into their lane. She hurried into the house and dumped the vegetables into the chipped porcelain sink. Wiping her hands on her apron, she swept the stray, damp tendrils from the back of her neck up into her top knot and went out the screen door onto the porch.

Sofie smiled as she watched Jack pull up in a shiny black Chevy. He hopped out and took the porch steps two at a time and threw his arms around his mother. "Where's Dad? Is he out in the field?"

Sofie pointed to the barn. "No, he's down working in the barn." David heard a car drive into the yard, and setting aside his work, he peered out of the barn door. Spotting the new black car sitting in front of the house, he decided to see for himself who was visiting this time of morning. He walked into the kitchen just as Jack was sitting down at the table with a big bowl of cool, pickled watermelon.

In between bites, Jack said, "Mom and Dad, I wanted you both to be the first to know about my big job. I'm going to Wake Island in the Philippines with my construction crew. We're gonna build military airfields there. We have a hell of a contract with the government. The scuttlebutt is they're expecting trouble over there and want an airfield on that particular island, so your oldest son volunteered to make the trip—for a nice wad of dough, I might add. My wife is taking little Kathy and moving back in with her folks in Thermop till I get home. It shouldn't take longer than a year, maybe less."

Jack pushed back his chair and prepared to leave. He picked Sofie up and swung her around until she squealed for him to put her down. He shook his dad's hand and then embraced him; Jack felt David hold on a bit longer than he was expecting. Before Jack headed back out the door, he went over to Edie. "Hey there, Edie, how are you doing? Getting prettier every day, yes you are! Got a boyfriend yet?" She looked up at her oldest brother with dull eyes and started to cry. Sofie hurried to her side, calming her and talking softly to her.

Jack backed away, smoothing back his head of black hair with a quick swipe of his hand. Recovering quickly from his sister's reaction, he moved closer to his father. "Dad, don't you think it's time you and Ma took Edie down to Lander to that school? It is getting too much for you to be takin' care of her. She is a woman now, or she has the body of a woman and G—." Jack stopped himself before taking the name of the Lord in vain in front of his father. "Hell, dad, the docs told you someday you would have to take her down there. I can see how things are. Do you want me to help you with that before I leave? I sure will, Dad, if you need me."

Declining his son's offer, David slapped Jack on the back as he headed for the door. "Love you, Ma. Take care of yourself. See you in 'bout a year, and save some of that pickled watermelon and chicken and dumplings for me, okay?"

David walked Jack out the front door. "Son, we want you to be careful over there. The news reports aren't sounding very good. If things start falling apart, get yourself out of there. You don't want to mess around with those Japanese."

Jack swaggered down the path to his car, climbed in, and turned the motor over as David took a step back. "Dad, I don't want you worryin' about this man. I'm a slick son of a gun, and it's the Japs that should worry about messing with me!"

David laughed in spite of his concern. "And don't worry about Edie. We have been talking, your ma and me. We know it's time. It's just so darn hard, Jack. She won't understand it, but we have to leave it in the hands of the Lord and have faith the doctors and people know how to take care of her better than we do. Watch your back, Jack. God bless and keep you, son. Go with our love and prayers—and don't forget to write!"

Jack stuck his arm out the car window, giving a jaunty two-finger salute as he swung the car around and headed down the lane. "Love you, Ma and Dad. I'll be back before you know it." And he was gone in a cloud of dust.

As Jack drove his car down the dirt road, he was surprised at the emotion that surfaced. *What the hell is this? Crying, because I'm leaving home? It's just that I—I don't know when I'll be back for sure and if I will see them again. I know they are gettn' old and aren't in the best of health. But I gotta do what I gotta do, and this is a hell of an opportunity!*

The next week, Jake and Raisa drove David, Sofie, and Edie down to Lander to the Children's Home for the Mentally Retarded. It was an impressive place with numerous brick buildings that looked brand-spanking new and clean, but there was an eerie feeling about the place just the same. They pulled to a stop and got out of the car. Jake and Raisa took Edie off and walked her around the grounds, showing her the flowers and the swings, while David and Sofie were inside signing the papers. The doctors assured them Edie would be placed in a building with other persons who suffered from the same type of affliction. Every attempt would be made to keep her busy and happy.

When it came time to leave, Sofie and David gave their daughter a hug and kiss good-bye. Sofie began to tear up, so Raisa took her outside. Jake and David waved good-bye to Edie as a staff member took her by the arm, guiding her into the dining room for an ice cream cone. Edie waved good-bye to them without any indication or expression of fear or remorse. David called after her, "You be a good girl now Edie and we will see you soon. She never turned around.

The ride back to Lovell was long and hard, as both David and Sofie were overcome with guilt and emotion. It was close to eight that night when they pulled into the farmyard in Lovell— the same time that Jack's plane took off from San Francisco for Hawaii, headed for Wake Island, Philippines.

~~~~~

The first weeks and then months after they left Edie at the school, Sofie wasn't herself. One evening as she and David sat on their front porch, Sofie said, "David, I am filled with guilt that we left our daughter in that place. I miss her so much and worry if she's happy and if she realizes we aren't there anymore. I feel like I am in a constant state of worry, what with Edie, Jack somewhere in the Pacific Ocean, and now Joe signed up in the army. I pray that he is right when he says he will be stationed on the West Coast with the National Guard."

David looked up from his Bible. "Oh, Sofie. My sweet Sofie. Of course, I miss our baby girl too, but I trust we did the right thing for her and for us. The reports from the school say she is doing well, and we'll continue to drive down to see her. She seems no different, and she is adjusting to life there. I think we need to keep busy and give our worries to the Lord. He'll watch over our Edie as well as Joe and Jack—wherever the government sends them. By the way, you know that fancy car Jack was driving the last time we saw him? Raisa told me that the police found the car on fire at the Greybull, Lovell, Emblem junction. They said there was no one around. They thought the engine had probably overheated and caught fire. As far as I can tell, this happened right before Jack left for Wake Island." David put his head down so Sofie wouldn't see him smile.

Sofie replied, "Well, mercy me, I wonder if someone stole his car before he left? Do you think he knows about this, David? I don't know what he would have done with a car while he was gone anyway, so maybe it's for the best!"

~~~~~~

Sofie tried to do as David suggested and keep busy to pass the time and keep her mind occupied with other things than her worries. There was always housework, and she enjoyed visiting her daughters. Her favorite pastime was spent tending to her chickens. She especially loved caring for the tender, fluffy baby chicks. David noticed more than once when she filled her apron with the fuzzy little balls and carried them to the shade of their porch where she sat in her rocking chair and watched them explore the corners and crevices of the porch.

Sofie and her chickens

Chapter Fifteen

The Brothers: March 19, 1941

It had been just a short while since Joe had burst through the front door with the news that he and the Wyoming National Guard, horse cavalry, had been nationalized and were being sent to guard the upper West Coast. Two days later they left on a troop train. Throughout the next four years, Jack/Spatz, Joe/Glocka— or Glogga Watz, and Adam/Mook wrote letters to each other and to their parents. It was a way to keep in touch with what was happening on the home front, in the service, and with their aging parents. Letter writing was not a favorite pastime for any of the brothers except perhaps Joe, who had stayed in school longer and had a knack for book-learning. Most of David and Sofie's children left school after the sixth grade. Pete didn't have a lot of time to write letters to his brothers; it wasn't high on his list since he had a serious girlfriend, Millie.

~~~~~

As Sofie walked down the rut-filled dirt lane to the mailbox, she thought about all that had happened in the last few months. First Edie, then Jack, and now Joe had all left; she was thankful that three of her four daughters lived around Lovell, as well two of her sons, Pete and Adam. She reached into the metal mailbox at the side of the dusty side road and pulled out a few pieces of mail.

She thumbed through it as she walked slowly back up the lane to their unpainted farmhouse. She pulled a white envelope out and stared at the return address. She hurried to the front porch and sank heavily into her wooden rocking chair as she tore the end off the envelope and unfolded the letter.

Dayton, Oregon
March 29, 1941
Dear Mother, Dad, and Brothers—
We got here yesterday at 12:30 after having a swell trip. We had to pass through one tunnel on the continental divide, one mile long, but that wasn't anything! Out here, when we had to cross the mountains close to Mt. Rainier, we went through a tunnel three miles long. The train got full of cinders and soot. All the engines on this N. Pacific line burn coal and are the biggest damn things I ever saw. On all the uphill grades with the long tunnels, we had to have helper engines hooked on. Once they had three hooked on, and all were working hard. We moved along at a good speed. We had a special train for us!

When we passed through Tacoma, I saw my first big boat. It was a freighter, so they told me. The train passed right along the shore, and the boat was about a mile away. This is one hell of a place as far as goin' to town is concerned; the bus station is three miles away, and the nearest town is Tacoma, and that is about ten. I wish I had left my suits at home. I don't see how I'm ever going to get to use them here. There are about 40,000 other soldiers around here in competition for the girls.

Well today we did not have to drill, but we really had to put in a day of hard work cleaning up the barracks. One nice thing about it is that we are all off by ourselves right on the edge of the woods, nice big pine trees standing as high as a hundred feet straight in the air. And speaking of air, there is always an airplane flying overhead. I saw one big four-engine plane fly overhead; there is a small balloon thing here too. It's always flying around, and it's called a blimp. It is used for observation purposes.

This sure is a funny country; you can't see more than a mile or so, and it isn't fog either. It's just some sort of mist or something like it. Write soon.

Love, Joe

~~~~~

David, Pete, and their youngest son, Adam, had been busy with the final harvest. When that was done, it was time to start the fall plowing before the first snow came. They had received several letters from Joe but no word from Jack until November 28th when he wrote to his brother Joe, who sent the letter on to their parents. None of them claimed to be prize English students, but they knew enough to get the job done. Joe claimed, "I tried to teach those bone-heads proper English and spelling, but that was like pouring water through a strainer!"

~~~~~

Wake Island, Philippines November 28, 1941
Dear Glocka (Watz), [24]
 Was very much surprised and glad to hear from you just because we don't get along so good is no sign I don't like you, and I admire you very much for what you are doing for your country and for yourself. (Are we patriotic?) You're now serving good old Uncle Sam in the Army, and me on a Defense Job.
 I would certainly have written to you sooner but didn't know your address until I got your letter the other day. Now, I'll try to answer some of your questions. The reason I came to Wake Island was to make money and to save it, as we can't spend any of it here. I have been here since the 11th of November. I signed a contract to stay nine months on the island—I plan to leave here with $4,000 bucks! The island is 4500 miles from the mainland (see your map), about eight miles long, and averages about one-half mile across; it's composed entirely of coral sand and hotter than hell! If the Japs give us any trouble, it will probably be hotter than that. There are about 1200 men on this defense job, also several hundred marines and sailors, but absolutely no women or liquor! Certainly feel envious of you and all your gal friends, but I have a sweet little wife waiting for me when I get back (I hope). Going to buy us a home and settle down, no more chasing around for me; do you think I can do it?
 You wanted to know how long it took to get here and how we sailed. We left from San Francisco on Oct. 10th and arrived in Honolulu the 19th. Waited there for two weeks for a boat and arrived here November 11th. You didn't ask, but I did get seasick—it's an awful feeling, but I got over it after a couple of days at sea. (Don't laugh.)

By the way, if I was out with a good-looking gal, I think I could find a more romantic subject than cows to talk about. She must be very silly as well as innocent; but women are a queer sort of animal, ain't they? And, they are very unpredictable, like mail service to Wake Island. I don't know when you will get this, but when you do, answer pronto! It only costs thirty-five cents to send a letter here; I ought to be worth that much. Well take it cool, and I hope to see you when I get back.

As ever, your big brother, Spatz

~~~~~

Joe received another letter that week from his younger brother, Adam, or, as he liked to refer to him, Mook, who remained back on the farm in Lovell. He had received a special exclusion from the service because his parents were dependent upon him and his farming their land. It stuck in his craw, but in the long run, he felt like he was doing what he could for his parents and his country by farming and raising food for the troops. One way for Mook to stay in the loop and feel like he wasn't skipping out of the war was to write to his brothers who were actively serving.

~~~~~

Lovell, Wyoming Dec. 5, 1941 Dear Watz—

I have received your letter of Dec. 22 and was very glad to hear that everything is okay and that your moral is so high, that's more than I can say of myself.

I guess your determined that I should remain at home, at least in your last letter to me you were vary definite as to how I should consider this business of joining the Army—well I have given the matter a lot of thought and have made a decision—the answer is (I will not). As you know Dad and Mother cannot earn there own live hood, and I just could not think of seeing the folks taking in washing or something like that, I think I owe my loyalty to the folks at least until the government drafts me. I do wish I were there with you in the Army I bet we could have a lot of fun.

You wanted to know more about me and my love— Anne. This is the way it stands I guess I always did love her but never did admit it to myself or anyone. It was it the only fair thing to do, so I just went up and told her that I loved her. Up to this date Anne has not given me an answer as to whether or not she loves me, and if she says that she does love me I plan to ask her to be my wife. If she says no, I still won't give up trying to make her love me tell I die. When I get an answer I tell you first as we all ways did confide in each other and too, you and me have lot in common. I did give her a Christmas present it was some real expencive perfume it was cald Indiscreet and it cost me five dollars for just a little bottle.

Now, for the folks—mother's hay fever is not so bad any more. Dad is better, still gets a little sick once in a while. They seem to think that you spend too much money and so do I. What do you do with all of that money? I am combining beans this week— the price is pretty darn good at $5.10 a bag.

We sent you Xmas package—did you receive it? We all sent you Christmas cards too. No more word has been received from Johannes. Keep on sending letters to us as they make Mom feel a lot better and that goes for the rest of us too. Well so long for now, I got to go and get the horses, I'll write more the next time.

Love, Mook

~~~~~

Adam threw on his heaviest winter coat, pulled a knit hat over his ears, and grabbed the snow shovel as he went out the front door. *I might as well start digging a path through this last snowstorm. Gotta get out to the barn and milk those bawling cows. I know if I don't do it, then Dad will get out here, and that ain't good for his heart—digging and all. Sure will be glad when my brothers get back and I don't have to do all the work myself. Actually, I feel sort left out of the action, stuck out here on the farm like this. But I guess it's up to me to take care of things for the folks. I sure like hearing from Joe, sounds like he's having himself one good time out there in Oregon.*

~~~~~

Dayton, Oregon Dec. 30, 1941
Dear Folks:

This has been some day, but I'm in the army now—I didn't do much today and that's how it is some days. It's like this, we had a dance last Friday night and of course I got my line to working. Met a gal from the University of Oregon, which is not far from here. Today I took her horseback riding and she can really ride, I have another date with her this Tuesday that is if we are still here. I'm having a wonderful time wish Mook was here. No! I don't either. Mook, you stay home and take care of Dad and Mom. You are doing your part by staying home and farming; got to stay home as long as you can. I volunteered that's enough, let them draft you. Stay home, Please!

But let me tell you more about my new girlfriend. Oh, yes, she doesn't smoke—I don't know if she drinks or not. Her name is Katie Reily, light brunette, and ask anyone— she is stunning. She's got a line too. I know it!

I went into town last night, got my hair cut, and a shave, then happened in at a dance and the gals here in Oregon dance just like the gals in Lovell only a little more advanced. The first gal I danced with followed me as good as any gal in Lovell. I hope we stay here for the duration but I know we won't.

We've been in Oregon for about two weeks now and I have seen the sun only once. It's been raining all the time. Keep writing me, I like the letters and let me know if you hear from Jack.

Love, Watz

~~~~~

Wake Island, December 1, 1941

As tension mounted in the Pacific, Jack's construction company was working on a contract to build another strategically located airfield for US aircraft. They were assigned to Wake Island, which was located right smack-dab in between the Japanese-held Marshall Islands to the south and the Marianas to the west. Jack Steiner and his construction company arrived on the tiny 2.5-square mile coral atoll around the middle of October 1941 and got right to work on the airfield.

Jack often complained, "Can't stand to stay on this 'postage stamp' much longer—am getting cabin fever. Gotta get out and stretch my legs some." On a rare day off, or on Sundays, Jack and a couple of his buddies liked to hike around the island. Sometimes they crossed over to Peale and Wilkes Islands, which lay like severed limbs off Wake.

One Sunday he and his buddy, Frank, crossed over to Wilkes in a canoe. "Hell, Jack, we coulda swam across that stretch of water, 'cept we woulda had to watch out for that gott-damn corral. That stuff will cut your legs and feet to ribbons in a second." They beached the canoe and walked down the beach for a ways then cut up through the jungle on a path that materialized out of nowhere. Suddenly, they came upon a palm-covered hut nestled back in the dense cover of the trees. It was built up on stilts with a wide, screened-in porch and a galvanized steel roof that sloped into strategically positioned rain barrels. The two men stopped in their tracks and silently surveyed the premises. Part of Jack was interested in finding out who lived in the hut, and part of him didn't care; curiosity got the best of him as he called out, "Hello, anybody around? Hello!"

The screen door slid to the side as a slightly built Japanese man stepped cautiously out onto the porch. Jack could see a woman and a handful of kids peeking out of the door and windows.

"Speak-a Eng-lish?" Jack said slowly, hoping the man understood.

The Japanese man walked slowly down the steps, and as he came near, he said in perfect English, "Yes, sir, I do speaka English. What are you boys doing out in the jungle on a hot day like this?" After recovering from the shock of 'one of them' speaking perfect English, Jack explained who they were and what they were doing. Before he knew it, they had been invited inside for a drink of plum wine and sweet cakes.

Hiro Tohama and his children were lightly dressed in a form of loincloth-looking diaper, while his wife wore a thin, sleeveless cotton shift; they sat cross-legged on floor mats across a low square table. Mr. Tohama smiled proudly. "I spent four years in the United States, going to school in San Francisco in the 1930s. It took me awhile to learn English, and out here I don't have much opportunity to speak it these days. Of course, with the tension between Japan and the United States, I never speak English when I am around my countrymen. I'm somewhat fond of my head!" They all laughed and continued talking about the mainland and Wake Island, as well as the airfield the Americans were building over there.

Jack looked around the room. "So, Mr. Tohama, what do you and your family do in this remote place, or is that a personal question?"

Mr. Tohama smiled slyly as he explained, "You might say we are hiding out—we are surviving. The Japanese military strongly encouraged me to join the army. My wife and I didn't like that idea very much. We told everyone we were going on vacation one day, and we disappeared here into the jungle. I became familiar with these islands when I worked on Clark Field on Bataan a few years back. My family was with me, and we liked to hike around the different islands. On one of the hikes, we spotted this area and another place in the jungle a few miles to the west of Clark Field on Bataan.

"If things heat up on Wake, I think we will move to the other place where we have better access to fresh water. That is becoming a real problem here. Bataan or Luzon will probably be a safer place to wait out the war because it is more secluded, and we can go farther into the jungle. I don't suppose I am telling you something you don't already know, I mean about the coming war between the United States and Japan?"

"Yeah, Mr. Tohama, we are feeling the push and seeing the signs as well. We hope to hell it doesn't happen, hope the Japanese government realizes what a hornet's nest they will be opening up if they do strike at us. But time will tell—I'm sure. Well, I suppose we had better be getting back to the base. Is there anything we can help you out with or something we might have on base that you need?"

Mr. Tohama looked at his wife and children. "That is very generous. There are a few supplies we would be grateful to have if it could be arranged. I don't have any dollars to pay you, but I could give you some fresh vegetables once in a while when we have extra."

Jack affectionately slapped the man on the back and laughed. "Sure, Mr. Tohama, that would work. What can we bring you next time we venture out this way?"

Over the next few months, Frank and Jack made several trips across the narrow inlet to Wilkes Island. First on Mr. Tohama's list was a box of water purification tablets. Jack also managed to make off with an extra charcoal filtering device to help purify stagnant rainwater. Since there was no fresh water on any of the coral atolls, fresh water was always a problem. They brought a bolt of fabric, nails, bolts, screen, a few garden implements, and a case of American beer in exchange for fresh vegetables.

Mr. Tohama was grateful. "Oh thank you, thank you very much. It is very good of you to show such kindness. If there is ever anything we can do more for you, please call on us. I think this will be the last time you see us here. We have decided to move our family up through Manila Bay and resettle at our other place in the jungle. Our door is always open, Jack-san, remember that—just in case! Here, take this map of our location."

On the way back to Wake that day, Jack commented, "He sure is a nice fella, and I hope we never have to take him up on his offer of further hospitality—if and when we need it!" Jack patted his pocket where Hiro's map was stuffed.

Jack and the rest of the guys were relieved when the 1st Marine Airborne Defense Battalion, four hundred strong, arrived on Wake. Even though the airstrip was not completed, one runway was finished. Twelve Grumman F4F-3 Wildcat planes from Marine squad VMF-211 landed on December 4th. They parked the planes in the open at the edge of the single landing strip, which was located at the northwest end of the tiny island. The barracks, hospital, and a golf course (if you could call that pile of rocks a course) were about two miles away at the east end of the island.
Jack slapped his thigh with his cap. "Damn, I don't like seeing those planes sittin' out there with their panties down! Old HoJo could send some of his bombers from Marshall over here and knock the hell out of them. Maybe we should cover 'em up with camouflaged netting for now!" Jack and his crew worked until late in the night, trying to hide the American planes with netting

plugged with palm fronds. "Shit, I sure do hate this damn place," said Jack. "Sure, it's warmer than Wyoming right now, but this humidity and foot rot is getting to me. Not used to this kinda crap!" They were all in the same boat and just wanted to get their job done and get the hell back home. "Wish they would get our damn radar over here from Pearl—would be sort of nice to know what's comin' through those clouds before the sons-a-bitches are dropping their fifty-pound bombs on our doorstep!"

~~~~~

Because of the International Dateline, it was Sunday, December 7, 1941, on the Hawaiian Islands and Monday, December 8, 1941, on Wake Island. At 6:55 Monday morning, the radio controllers on Wake Island received a warning from Pearl Harbor; they had been attacked by Jap fighters, and half of the Pacific fleet was at the bottom of the harbor. Commander Cunningham ordered four Wildcats into the air to take a look-see. "You boys stay up there for a couple of hours just in case any uninvited Jap fighters swing past here on their way home."

If Pearl Harbor had shipped the new radar when they should have, the men on Wake Island would have spotted the eight Jap fighters coming in from the Marshall Islands. Instead, the unseen fighters broke through cloud cover just after noon on December 8th. As luck would have it, the Marines didn't have a chance in hell of stopping them from wiping out half of the American fighters that sat on the tarmac like sleeping birds.

Jack had been working with a dozer on the far end of a second runway when the fighters flew low and fast over the tiny island. He stopped the dozer and jumped underneath as all hell broke loose from the Marine garrison. After the fighters dropped their bombs and the smoke settled, the Marines had lost twenty-three men, and a dozen or more were wounded. The next day, the Japs came back—and the day after that. They were also intent on beefing up their fleet by moving a couple of destroyers offshore. Their bombardment was relentless, but the Americans held out.

Jack said, "I was damn proud of the Marines and the rest of the guys today. We showed 'em we still have teeth, and we bit those Japs in the ass but good!"

A cheer went up when a gun battery on Pense Point hit the lead ship and forced it to pull back with its tail between its legs.

Before the Japanese could withdraw, the battery on Wilkes actually sank a Jap destroyer which was the "numero uno enemy sink" of the war. Several other ships took direct hits, and at the end of the day, the score was Japs minus 750 men and the Americans with four wounded and no fatalities. Spirits were high that night, but the Americans on Wake weren't kidding themselves. They all knew they were outgunned, outmanned, and out of time.

Jack's heart sank in his chest when he saw they only had two Wildcats left. They celebrated that night when they heard reinforcements were on the way from Hawaii. They expected them to arrive at any time. What arrived on December 11 was Admiral Kajioka and his invasion fleet—uninvited, of course. They seemed pretty sure of themselves as they sat offshore, taking their sweet time finishing up the job on Wake. Radio messages from Hawaii informed Wake Island that their relief force had been ordered back to Pearl.

When Jack heard the news, he just shook his head in disbelief and said to himself, "Well, those SOBs are just hanging us out to dry—must think we're a lost cause, and they don't want to chance losing any more of their men. Now, ain't that just a great feeling? Looks to me like the Japs are waiting until sunrise to take this damn hellhole with a one-two punch; and just when we got that airfield all nice and level for em'."

Jack looked out over the bay at the daunting collection of Jap warships, all flying their flag with the solo red sun. He felt the hair on the back of his neck stand up. "Now that sight would give any one a good case of the heebie-jeebies!"

~~~~~

On December 12, after several hours of desperate fighting, the American commander read the writing on the wall and surrendered Wake Island Airfield to the Imperial Japanese Army.

When Jack heard the news, he felt fear crawl up his back He didn't know a lot about the Japs, but what he did know wasn't good.

Jack took a good look around and began to assess the situation. He remembered what his dad had told him about staying out of the hands of the Japs. He figured things were going down the tube fast. They were running out of options. Jack had no allegiance to the military and was free to do whatever he wanted as a civilian. *These guys are my friends, and I can't with good conscience leave my buddies to face this alone.*

~~~~~

Admiral Kajioka, the Japs' "big cheese," wasn't fooling around this time, and it looked like they would wait until daybreak to deliver the goods! Every American on that island, military and civilian as well, knew they were fried. They could end up dead or prisoners of war. Neither option was especially attractive to any of them, especially to the civilian workers like Jack Steiner who hadn't volunteered to fight in a war.

Regardless of why they were there, they banded together and put up a fight; but to tell the truth, it didn't last long, and at the end of the day, those who were left standing and those wounded were all prisoners of the Japanese.[25] Jack noticed right off how the Jap officers were separating the civilian workers from the enlisted men. He got a funny feeling that perhaps they didn't feel a lot of responsibility toward the civilians—toward taking them as prisoners and feeding them. There was noticeable confusion as what to do with this many prisoners, and Jack figured the Japs were going to start thinning them out to alleviate the problem.

Inspired by a gut feeling, Jack bent over and pulled a khaki work cap and the dog tags from a dead soldier's body. He moved closer in, blending with a group of soldiers and Marines. He got a gut spasm when he saw ten Jap soldiers march fifty or so civilian workers to a spot and ordered them to dig a hole. At the same time, the group of military he was with was prodded by bayonets to march to the harbor and board one of the ships. "We take you to Corregidor—we have no place to put you here—island too small and no water." Just before they reached the ships, Jack heard a burst of machine gunfire. When he turned to look, the civilian workers were no longer digging the hole; they were in it! His face turned ashen, and he began to shake. *That could have been me.* 26

The prisoners spent only a couple of weeks in a makeshift pen on Corregidor until the Japs decided to march them over to Camp O'Donnell to join the other prisoners who had survived the Bataan Death March. Jack noticed the Japs were taking names of the prisoners from their dog tags. He nonchalantly dropped the one that hung around his neck in the drink and told the Japs he had lost his tags. He gave them his name so they could add it to the prisoner-of-war list.

When they arrived on Bataan, Jack could barely believe the condition of the "death march" prisoners. They looked like skeletons and were dropping like flies. That's when he spotted who he thought was Johnny Kessel from Lovell. *Hell, I knew he was over here but never would have thought he would surrender. Bet Jake and Raisa are half sick with worry. He always was a wild son of a gun, but he is Jake's brother.* He managed to say a few words to Johnny on rare occasions, but they were in different barracks and on different work details.

~~~~~

The Steiner Farm House

Salem, Oregon March 29, 1942
Dear Mook,

Your last letter was pretty short, but keep em coming as I am always glad to get letters. I keep them in my brief case for a few weeks then send them home. Are they arriving and are you putting them away as I asked you to? Thanks.

The picture I have here is of the folk's house before it was painted. Be sure to take another shot of them in front of the house after you get some paint on it, and then send me the new photo. Did I hear you say you were going to build an addition to the porch so it runs across the front of the house? That will be swell, seeing as how they like to sit on the front porch!

I'm really home sick tonight; went out to dinner with some friends from McMinnville and they treated me swell. There is this gal I met in church in Oregon; I think I will ask her to marry me when the war is over with because we have so much in common. Her Mom and I get along just perfect; she will sit beside me, we will talk a little German, and then she will put her arm around my shoulder and call me Joey. Really though, Mook, I don't think I could love this gal like I ought to, but if I remember Shaftesbury's advice such a marriage is much more apt to be successful than one that's based on mere physical attraction. Look some of this up and advise me.

The General was down on an inspection tour last week. He found everything in good condition so he let 50% of the troop go to town on one night on passes. He also expressed his belief that we were the best looking Cavalry regiment he has seen in many a day. Naturally we felt swell because we are working hard. Did I tell you we have all black horses in our troop now? Also, there is a latrine rumor that we are going to be made into a tank outfit soon. Sometimes I want to be in a tank outfit, then again I don't.

Yes, I'm still very much in the groove as far as my dancing is concerned. Every week I meet a new gal and each one is better than the last. This last dame I met can dance just as good as Dot Hall, and I quarrel with her just as I did with Hall. An example; there was a 'ladies tag dance' called, as I was dancing with her she suggested that we move over in the corner and dance, I said "I don't blame you. If I was you I would hang on to me, because you don't get guys that can dance as good as I can every day." Of course that set us to going. You see I have developed a new rhythm copied after some of the Washington dancers. I can't describe it but it's really swell. If I get a gal that can follow me she really goes for it. I just don't seem to be able to get rid of them unless I up and leave them. But of course I don't want to get rid of them if they can follow me, right? Any more, I just pick out a good dancer and dance with her all night. There are at least three girls to every soldier.

Got a letter from our brother Stute (Pete) the other day and he sent me a picture of him on his horse—swell looking horse. Also, a picture of Millie and himself; he said they are getting married. That will sure settle him down. How are you going to share the machinery when he gets his own farm? By the way, I think you had better quit chasing around and getting drunk; settle down to a summer of hard work. You can't drink and be efficient with your duties. I haven't been drunk since September and I weigh 176 pounds and still gaining; Yes, I'm in the pink of condition!

Tell Mom and Dad I'm getting along alright and read in my Bible every now and then. I haven't memorized the verse Mom sent as yet but I will. Be sure to keep me informed if Dad gets sick again by airmail or telegram.

Answer soon—Love Watz

PS: Say hello to the relatives. Let them know I'm still thinking of them and not sore about anything as they might misinterpret my silence.

~~~~~

Lovell, Wyoming—June 15, 1942

Sofie and David were sitting on the front porch relaxing after supper that spring evening while their youngest son, Adam, was in the barn milking the cows. They both looked up as a black sedan turned off the country road and into their lane, slowing as it approached their house. Neither spoke as they recognized the government car. Their faces spoke volumes as fear held their breath and caused them both to scoot to the front of their chairs. David removed his glasses, slipped them into his front pocket, and rose to his feet. Sofie struggled to rise from her chair and went to stand beside her husband, and they waited there on the front porch.

The government official turned off the motor and climbed out of the car. He cleared his throat and walked stiffly to the porch where the two elderly folks stood waiting. The man walked up the steps, tipped his hat, and then held it in his hand while he handed David a telegram. "Mr. Steiner, this Western Union message just came in. It's addressed to your youngest son, Adam, but it concerns your family. It's about your son Johannes."

David opened the telegram and read:

Washington, DC, 9:58 a.m., June 15, 1942
Stop. Adam Steiner, Lovell, Wyo. Stop. Am today advised by provost Marshall General War Department your brother Johann Steiner prisoner of war Stop. Held by Japanese at Camp O-Donnell Philippines. Stop. S.H. Schwartz
U.S.S. Stop.

David looked out into the distance then back at the floor of the porch, trying to retain his composure before he turned to Sofie, who sat rigid with her hands clenched in her lap waiting. "Sofie, it is our Johannes—he is alive but is a prisoner of the Japanese in the Philippines, same as Raisa's brother-in-law, Johnny." David stood and walked over to his wife and pulled her to her feet. They stood there in each other's arms as anguished tears rolled uncontrollably down their faces.

Adam hadn't heard the car pull into the farmyard, but it was the first thing he saw when he walked from the barn, carrying the pails of fresh cows' milk. He saw his parents holding each other and crying; that's when he dropped the buckets and ran for the house. "Ma, Dad—what has happened? Tell me, what's the matter?"

David released Sofie but held tightly to her hand. "It's Jack. He's been taken prisoner of war in the Philippines—but he is alive, son, he is alive. This is what we have to hold on to and pray that the Lord watches over him." David turned to the government man. "Thank you for bringing the telegram out to us personally. We appreciate it."

The man offered his condolences without further words because there were none; he turned and climbed back into his car and headed back to town. Several months later, they received a letter from their son, Jack, from the prisoner-of-war camp in the Philippines.

~~~~~

Camp O'Donnell, Prisoner's Camp September 3, 1942
Mrs. David Steiner
Lovell, Wyoming, USA
Dearest Mother, Father, and all:

I received a letter from sister Raisa about a month ago and was very glad to get it. She tells me you are all well and getting along fine.

I certainly hope that you all have a merry Christmas and will have a happy new year. Through the kind permission of the Japanese Authorities of this camp we will be allowed to celebrate Christmas in our own way. The American-British Relief Association will send us a nice dinner consisting of a big turkey for every five men, dressing and cranberry sauce. The Japanese promise to give us permission to have a fire in the stoves all day. Of course we plan to sing Christmas carols and have a nice time considering. We have also been receiving packages from the American and Canadian Red Cross. We have received four so far and they consist of various edibles and cigarettes and are very much appreciated. I certainly hope that I will be able to spend next Christmas at home with you and go to Church on Christmas Eve with Momma and Poppa like when I was a kid.

Well thanks again to Raisa and all for the nice letters. Lack of space forces me to cut this short. I'll come driving up the lane again as before and I won't be in any hurry to leave this time. Please write to me.

My love to all,
Johann Steiner
Barracks No. 3 Section No. 7

~~~~~

"Oh, David, this letter doesn't even sound like our Jack. He is so formal, and he didn't even tell us about where he is or how he is doing."

David gathered Sofie in his arms and gently stroked her back. "I know, my *Liebchen*. He probably had Japanese soldiers watching and reading everything he wrote to us, or they wouldn't have let him write the letter. At least we know he is alive, and we have to keep praying that the good Lord watches over him and brings him home to us when this is all over."

Chapter Sixteen

Day after Day

David and Sofie, as well as the rest of their family, continued to write to Jack and to Joe, who was still stationed on the West Coast. Letters received from Jack were few and far between, then they stopped coming. They had received no further information from the government since he was first taken prisoner. These were tough times; nobody knew for certain what was happening except that men were killing each other. David and Sofie looked forward to the weekly letters from Joe and tried to focus on their family and each other.

~~~~~

Lovell, Wyoming Sept. 5, 1942
Dear Watz—
Well so you are back to good old Fort Lewis, that's where I thought you were moving because you didn't write.
Dad has been pirty sick now for about a month and still is sick. He went to a Powell doctor and got a comleat exray of hims self. They found it to be a tomer that is almost cancer in his left intestine. Dad is taking some medson now and if that don't help they are going to operate. I will keep you informed from time to time.
I sure had a lot of fun this week and Friday night I had a date with my Basin gal. We went to the Greybull Prom. I took her to the Basin Prom too. Saterday night I took Ruth Adams to the Elks Perpel Buble Ball in Cody but after I got there I met my dream gal so I ditched the Adams gal. Joan Miller, that's my new dream gal—I kept her out for 18 strat hours I think maby I'm in love again.
I'm signing off for this time maby I'll write more next time. I'm getting to hate to write letters and I don't know why either,

sorry. Oh, I almost forgot to tell you that our niece Beth popped out her first baby. It's a girl!
With Love from—Mook

~~~~~

Lovell, Wyoming Sept. 13, 1942
Dear Watz—

I received your last letter sence you have been back in Ft. Lewis. You sertenly like to tell me off—don't you? Keep it up I can take it! I all ways could any way, and I still know I can too. (See)

Watz! I have to ask your advice. Really what is your opinon of me? In regard to me not being in the uniform – I sure feel like a slaker. Please give me your onist opinon and the vewis of all the men there. I went down the other day and past all the test at the Marine Recruiting place, they would put me in the parishute division any time I feel like it. They pay good too—$50 a month.

I'm still in the Home Guard. I was a Cpl. for a while but got busted again, down to a Pvt. I am just too dam ornery and went A.W.O.L. and they cut me. I sent a photo of me in my uniform— keep it for a while and send it back, it's the only one I have.

Now I'll tell you a little about my night life and all the fun I'm having. Sat. night, Bob Olson, Joe Korell and me sure did get around. First we went to the Junior-Senior Prom at Laural and it let out at 1:30 so after, we went to Holleys and danced until 3 or four. Sunday night Bob and I went to Cody to see our little gals— we go see them about once a week. I have only got three gals up there now.

The first and the best was a little blond with long hair and she had them in ringlets, she had blue eyes and a very light and clear complection and all so she is vary rich and can she neck. Her name is Mary Hart. The next best is a Irish girl; she has dark hair gray eyes and has 50 freckles on her nose all so good at necking. The way Bob and I work it is we keep one girl for a while, then take her home and then get the next one.

Neather dad or mom is feeling vary good today, they are bothe in bed. Dad is going to the doctor in Powell again to see if the mediceen he has been taking is helping, if not he will proply have to be operated on. Mac Johnson and Chris Daley are home on ferlogh and they sure look good. They are due to be shipped out in about a month; they think they are going to Europe.

That's all—Mook

~~~~~

Lovell, Wyoming September 29th, 1942
 Dear Watz:

I saw Phil Cotten the other day and see he is a sergeant. I also hear that you were made sergeant—congratulations. Indeed you have done very well and you have received a lot of cridet for all your work. Oh yeah, I asked Phil if you had been a good boy and he said 'hell no'! (My My Watz)

Dad is feeling better and the crops look real swell, espeshly the beets. It has been a little to cold for the beans, but it sure was hot here over the summer. Last Sat. night the Elks in Cody had their annual dance and it was a good dance. Guess who I saw there—none other then your old gal—Sue McLeary. I danced with her and we had a long talk. She asked about you—she looked—not bad!

This week we painted on the last coat of paint on the farm house and it sure does look rich. They are going to move in about 10,000 Japs into the Heart Mountain project. Maybe they will send the Lovell Home Guard up to help the army guard them. I would like something like that.

Couple of weeks ago was opening night at the Star Lit Garden at Byron. I really had lots of fun—wish you could have been there. I go to Cody every Sat. I have a different girl every time I go up there. By the way, I saw Babs Casey. Boy she sure is a good looker and is going to be married in a few weeks. I can see why you went with her. Marty left for nurses training in California, guess she is out of my life for good. I have to quit now and go to work. Please write soon and be good.

Love Mook

~~~~~

Camp O'Donnell, Philippines: Jack had spent the last ten months working the fields and gardens at Camp O'Donnell. There was word the healthy prisoners were going to be put on a bunch of rusty freighters and taken to Japan to work the mines. That's when Jack started making his plan of escape.

Jack timed his escape with opportunity and precision. One morning as he was working in a vegetable field surrounded by jungle, he decided that was the day! It wasn't like he had to pack for the move. Bent over and weeding, slowly and cautiously he purposefully moved closer and closer to the jungle. It must have been around noon and 110 degrees in the shade, when he looked over his shoulder at the guard tower; the guard was changing.

Crouching, with one fluid movement, Jack stepped silently and quickly into the dense undergrowth and began moving away from captivity.

Jack ran when he could and walked or crept through the thick undergrowth when he had to. As the day wore on, Jack moved cautiously, stopping every so often to listen for trackers—nothing. He tried to watch where he stepped, avoiding anything that would make noise. Always keeping his direction in mind, he used the sun as a guide when he could see it. Jack never ventured into a clearing but kept hidden in the cover of the jungle, going around any opening until he was headed in the right direction again.

I don't hear anyone following me. Man, I'm not real fond of walking through the jungle in the dark. If I hate anything, it's spiders. They're almost as bad as the rats. Jack had personally witnessed at least three different kinds of rats. The ones he feared the most were the huge Norway rats that were as big as a tomcat. Jack had watched the rats pull down a stand of bamboo and tear apart a gecko or skink that happened to be passing by. He shivered as he continued cautiously through the blackness of the jungle.

Jack walked for five days, sleeping in trees when he had to rest and always watching and listening for trackers. He felt lucky to find an occasional pool of fresh water and was glad he had stuffed his pockets with vegetables before he left the field. He especially liked the coconuts he found; they were full of milky liquid and stuff he could chew on. On the sixth day, Jack woke to the spectacular orange glow of the rising tropical sun as it bathed the South Pacific sky in a mélange of coral, mauve, gold, red, and peach. He stood quietly at the edge of the clearing; cautiously surveying what he hoped was the home of his friend, Hiro Tohama. He waited, hidden in the shade of the jungle, until Hiro came out of the house and began to work inside one of his small fenced vegetable patches. When he got close to where Jack was hiding, he called softly, "Mr. Tohama, Mr. Tohama, it's me, Jack—Jack Steiner.

Without indicating he had heard someone speak, Hiro Tohama walked to the edge of the jungle, acting like he was going to relieve himself. Going through the motions, he looked at the ground in front of him as he spoke softly, "I have been waiting for you, Jack-san. I didn't know if you were in the prisoner camp, but if you were, I knew you would try and escape. I have already thought of what I would do when you showed up. I will help you for as long as I can. If and when the soldiers find this place, I think it is best my wife and children do not know you are near and that I help you. It is most certain the soldiers will ask us if we have seen any Americans. I am used to lying better than my wife and children." He chuckled softly, paused a moment, and then said, "I assume that is why you are here, correct? You need a place to wait this war out? Have you thought about how long this could be?"

Jack hung back in the cover of the jungle as he replied softly, "Yes, Mr. Tohama, I need your help. I don't know how long this is going to take—this war—but if you will help me and if I get out alive and back to the States, I promise you I will send for your oldest son and educate him in an American high school when he is of age. Would this be a fair return for this favor of life I ask of you?"

That night as Jack snuggled under the porch with two of the family's Nippon Terriers, he listened to the sounds of the night in the jungle, as he had for the past week. The difference was that this night he could relax and sleep without fear in his secluded corner under the porch. He gave up a prayer of thanksgiving that night: *Dear Lord, I know I haven't always been a good and faithful servant, but you know my heart. Thanks a lot for watching over my escape and trek through the jungle. I know my escape wasn't because I'm a smart guy, but because you opened the path and guided me here. Watch after Johnny Kessel and the rest of the guys back at the camp, and end this damn war soon. If it is your will, please see that I get back home when this is all over. Also, please watch over my folks. Keep them well so I will someday see them again. Thanks, God, I owe you and hope you'll keep on watchin' my back. Amen.*

Jack remembered listening to Mr. Tohama's plan that morning and marveled at the cleverness of it all. "I also have a plan where I stash you so soldiers and my family not know. Throughout the jungle, I have hidden small vegetable patches. At one there is a tiny hut with a porch. Some of my dogs sleep under that porch when not guarding gardens. You will sleep with them, hidden out of sight where soldiers think is place only for dogs. It's not large space, but clean and dry. You will be safe there—dogs chase rats away." He had laughed wickedly, as he knew of Jack's hate for the creatures. "They will also bark if soldiers approach, giving you time to hide farther under porch."

Smiling with pride at his clever plan, Mr. Tohama had continued. "This way, wife and children don't know you here. I want for you to cut hair very short like mine. I have spare clothes like mine for you to wear and coolie hat when you not under porch. You are almost same brown as me from working under island sun. That is a good thing. White skin send bad message to soldiers!" He laughed.

"Okay, Jack-san, go into jungle, find hut, clothes, and also blanket and straw mat for sleeping. One more thing: please call me Hiro-san. It may be a long friendship we have together— no need for so formal. I'll bring you food when I can. There is rainwater barrel beside hut for drink and wash. Good-bye for now. Remember, if we unfortunate and soldiers come to my house and request to see my gardens, I will call loudly dog names, so you may hear and hide. I tell soldiers I call dogs so they no bite soldiers. Hee-hee."

The next morning, Mr. Tohama made an early call on his new guest. "I come to see if you still alive after first night under porch with my dogs. I see you okay!"

Jack asked, "Mr. Toha—Hiro-san, I have been wondering why you keep those dogs inside the fenced vegetable patches day and night. I have counted your dogs, and I think you have at least six." Mr. Tohama smiled as he looked up at Jack.

"First, these are tenacious little dogs for their eight pounds— small, maybe twelve, fourteen inches. They don't eat too much. We don't have much food to spare, so this is important. I admire the Akita and Tosa dogs of our country, but they too big and eat too much for purpose I keep dogs here."

"I think I have figured out what the purpose is but wanna ask you just the same. What do the dogs—why do you keep them inside the gardens?" Jack questioned.

Smiling, Hiro replied, "You for sure remember our large Norway rats on the islands? Have you not also noted what destruction they can make? They very fond of my vegetables; they dig under the fence or chew through netting to get to food. Terriers are normally happy dogs but not so happy when they see rats. They swift and deadly in their pursuit, and many times they save my vegetable patch while reducing the number of rats. I don't like to keep them penned up all the time, so you will have different dogs sleeping with you under the porch each night. Also, because they are there, you do not have to worry about rat chewing off your finger!" Hiro laughed and laughed at the expression on Jack's face. "Jack-san, you afraid of geckos or skinks? They good to have as friends. They eat many mosquitoes and flies—they also might like to sleep in your pockets!" It was obvious to Jack, Hiro got quite a kick out of tormenting him with the possibility or reality of little critters crawling over him.

Jack quickly adjusted to his life sleeping under the porch, and, when the coast was clear, working for short periods in the vegetable patches. Mr. Tohama had a few books in English, which he gave to Jack to read to help pass the time. They both realized the danger they were in and took great pains to camouflage the hut and vegetable patches so low-flying planes wouldn't spot them. Constant vigilance was imperative. Jack had no idea what had happened to the rest of the men in Camp O'Donnell. He thought often of Johnny Kessel and wondered if he was still alive.

Jack lay awake at night thinking about home and his folks. *I expect the War Department sent them notice that I was in a prisoner- of-war camp, and I wrote them a couple of letters, but that was a long time ago. Don't know if anyone gets through to the mainland with news about the prisoners at this stage of the war. I hope and pray that they are still alive if and when I get out of here and this damn war is over.*

~~~~~

During World War II, men who had a physical disability and/or men who worked the farms were exempt from military service. Pete had a farm of his own and was about to get married. Adam had stayed on the home place after Joe was called up with the Lovell National Guard; they agreed that one of them had to help their father with his farm because of his ill health.

One evening after they finished supper and dishes were washed, they moved out onto the front porch as usual. Sofie said, "David, I see the flags with different colored stars hanging in people's windows all over town. Do you know what this means?"

David looked up from his Bible. "JA, Sofie, you are talking about the red-bordered white flags, I think? If it has a blue star, it means a son or father of that house is in the service. If the star has a gold Greek cross in the middle, it means the soldier has been wounded. If there is a red star, it means he is captured or missing in action. A gold star with a blue border and a laurel wreath means he died in service."

Sargent Joe Steiner

Sofie sat for a moment, listening to the news on the radio. "David, I want to get two of those flags. I want one of those flags with a blue star for Joe and a red star for Jack."

Sofie went into Lovell the next day and purchased two war flags to hang in their front window; she also found an inexpensive store-bought picture frame for the photo Joe gave them before he left for the service. She placed it on the cabinet in the front room and stood for a long time just looking at his face.

~~~~~

November 1, 1942:

Sofie had just finished cleaning up the lunch dishes and sweeping the kitchen floor when she spotted the black government car maneuvering through the snow and slush on the muddy county road. It slowed as it came to their lane and turned the corner. Eyes wide, jaw clenched, Sofie didn't realize she was holding her breath until she heard the engine cough and watched the government car roll to a stop in the yard. Fear took its time crawling up Sofie's back. She felt paralyzed, and her ears rang when the two government men climbed out of the car and walked toward the house. Her heart sounded like a drum in her chest as she moved robotically across the kitchen floor toward the door.

After lunch, David had driven the Allis Chalmers tractor out into the fields to check on the haystacks and the livestock. It was late afternoon when he finally headed back to the house. Finished, he parked the tractor on the south side of the barn and cut the engine. Climbing down, he tucked his shirt into his bib overalls and headed for the house, head down, watching where he stepped. He removed his newsboy cap and slapped it against his thigh and then lifted his head as he took the first step onto the front porch. David stopped in his tracks when he noticed Sofie sitting on the front porch, hands in her lap, rocking robotically back and forth in her wooden chair. Her face was ashen and blank as she stared out into the fields to the north. David crossed the porch in long strides to where she sat. He reached down and gently enclosed her hand in his. "Sofie, *vhat ist unrecht?*"

She stopped rocking and lifted her tearstained face to him. "David, its Johann—they can't find our Johann." David felt panic rise in his throat as he squatted down beside the rocker. "Sofie, who is 'they,' and what do you mean they can't find him?"

"It was the government men in the black car. They came here today. They said, 'We are sorry to tell you that Johann Steiner is missing from the prisoner-of-war camp. His name no longer appears on the camp roster.' They said there is very little information that comes through, but the last list didn't include our Johann's name as it did at first. They also said the list didn't say he had died, just missing!"

David pulled his wife to her feet, and the two of them stood in an embrace of shock and confusion for several minutes. "Sofie, we must pray. There is nothing more we can do. They will look for Jack when they can. There are so many men over there that it must be hard to keep track of them all. The Lord will reveal what has happened to our son when he is ready to do so."

Chapter Seventeen

When Will It End?

Around the middle of November, Mook sent Watz a letter to let him know that they got word that Jack wasn't on the prisoner-of-war list any more. So they didn't know if he was dead or alive. Mook wrote: *We've been drilling with a new rifle, the L903, its three inches longer than the Spring Field Rifle, and heavier too. Ma is working too hard, taking in washing to make a few dollars. You know how stubborn she can be.*

~~~~~

Corporal Joseph Steiner Troop A, 115th Cavalry Fort Lewis, Washington Nov. 29, 1942
Dear Mook—
That is the worst news about Spats—I will try on my end to write to the army brass and see if they can tell me more about why his name isn't on the list anymore. Let me know if you hear anything else. Tell the folks that he probably escaped and is fine somewhere so they won't worry so much.
I'm over my yellow Jaundice now and am beginning to get all of my old vigor back again. Your skin turns yellow as well as your eyes. It can get pretty awful and took me down several notches. While I was in bed, I read a German army manual. My German isn't that good and it was hard in places but I thought it might be a handy thing to know. I'm sure you could get a job out here if you come out after the beets are out. But who would be at home with Dad and Mom? As much as I would like to see you, I would much rather feel that Dad and Mom were not left at home alone. Mook, I'm telling you again that you and I owe a lot to them and now that they are getting older it gives us a chance to make them feel good by letting them know that they raised some good men. And don't get too het up when I tell you that by the sound of your letters you are not helping them much. I expect to get a

furlough within the next two months, then I'll be home and we can talk and make plans.

Well, can't write anymore tonight as a bunch of us got passes and are going into a big dance in town. Should be a humdinger!!

Answer soon—Love, Watz

~~~~~

That Thursday, the Steiner address outside of Lovell got another telegram. This time it came from Fort Lewis, Washington. It was short; bad news is always short. It said:

*Corporal Joseph Steiner, hit by car while crossing street. **Stop**. When off base a week ago, Saturday night. **Stop**. He has two broken legs. **Stop**. Because of the severe extent of his injuries. **Stop**. Sending Corp. Steiner to Fitzsimmons Military Hospital in Denver. **Stop***

Lovell, Wyoming December 13th 1942
Dear Watz:

You should be in Denver by now. Your Capt. Wilson sent Dad the address of the hospital, that's how I happen to know where you are at. How fast was that car going when it hit you crossing the street? Were you too drunk to look to see if a car was coming? I can't imagine how it feels to have both legs broken. Guess you won't be going to dances for a while—what are all those dames gonna do with out crazy legs Joe?

I don't want to spend another winter in Lovell; man is it boring around here. The crops are all harvested in fine shape and so I'm leaving soon. Well, Watz—you be a good boy!

Love, Mook

~~~~~

The middle of February, Mook got another letter from Joe, telling him that he got the casts off his legs but the right one hadn't healed properly, and so he had another month of limping around with a cast. Joe said he was spending his time studying psychology and was going to get five credits from the University of

Washington. "I met this one nurse here, she is swell. Her name is Anna and she takes real good care of me. I gave her a box of chocolates for Valentine's Day. I'll let you know when I'm getting out of here and coming home for my three week furlough."

The first part of March, Joe came back to Lovell on furlough. He struggled with his legs, as they were still weak and recovering. He spent most of the time with his folks and family, basking in all the love and attention he got; then before he knew it, he was back on a train, heading back to Ft. Lewis.

United States Army May 29, 1943
Dear Folks –
    Your letter got to me when I was down in Ft. Lewis going to gas school. The first day they made some of the fellows run an obstacle course with their gas masks on. I did not have to do that, but had to run quite far with my mask on too. Man oh man, was I ever tired. Now I'll be a qualified instructor in the defense of a gas attack. That takes in gas mask drill, first aid, decontamination. They put some mustard gas on my arm, in two places, then on one spot they did not put any protective ointment and I got a small blister. I always thought the stuff burned but it doesn't, it just makes blisters and doesn't hurt when it gets on your skin but Lewisite does, it will burn right through to your bone. Mustard only goes through to the muscle. They put us through some real drills and it was pretty darn scary.
    Well, I'm all through with that now and back with the outfit again, next letter you get from me will be from a different place, not far from here. They tell us the allotment will start sometime in June so we'll see what that is about. I'm getting along swell and do regular duty now, or almost.
    Love, Joe

~~~~~

Joe kept a daily journal through the years when he was in the service and on the 28th of June made this entry:

On the night of June 27th, I met Marilyn Gunther. She was born in Tacoma, Washington; she is blond, and very pleasingly, plump—my type, and is German too. I think this is my first real love experience; I'm not kidding you, I feel swell when I am around her. She is a stenographer and a very efficient one—wears brown a lot, and well, too. My feelings for her are growing and very different than any other girl I've been with. I have taken her to lunch a couple of times and she had me over for dinner. Possibilities!

Joe went home on furlough in September to help with the harvest, much to Mook's delight. "I'm taking that forty dollars I wired you to come home on out of your pay after the crop is in. Don't think you're getting something for nothing 'round here!" Mook informed Joe. They had some good times out in the fields, just like the old days when they were younger. David stayed out of the fields for several weeks, as he was having another spell of illness; he didn't leave the house for much of anything.

"Hey, Watz, do you think they are going to send you overseas?" Adam asked as he rubbed the sweat from his face, stuck the pitchfork in the ground, and looked at his brother. Joe looked up.

"Well, things are humming plenty around the base. There's definitely something in the wind! We are getting ready for some sort of action, but the brass hasn't let us know anything yet. I sure don't think I want to get in the middle of all that. I got wind of just how bad it might be, and to tell you the truth, it scares the hell out of me!"

The two brothers spent the rest of Joe's furlough together, working and spending the nights dragging Main and picking up dames. Adam noticed that Watz talked a lot about this new gal of his, and one night when they were out on the town, he decided he was going to get to the bottom of it. "So, Watz, tell me more about this blonde gal, Marilyn. It sounds like you might be getting pretty serious about her. Is that right?"

Joe took a swig of beer and wiped the foam from his mouth. "Well, yeah—she is a terrific gal, but she's the type that wants her cake and eats it too, if you know what I mean? The closer I come to getting married, the more I think I don't really want to yet. I just know I feel swell when I am with her, and she treats me like a prince. Her folks are sure swell too, and they like talking German to me when they have me over to the house. I guess time will tell what's in the cards for ole, Watz!"

Joe left for Washington around the middle of October and got back in the swing of things right quick. They had drills and war games almost every day, and the tension on base was so thick, you could cut it with a knife! He spent Christmas with Marilyn and her family but had to work New Year's Eve. When he got back to the barracks after being gone for a couple of days on duty, there were several letters waiting for him. He opened the one from his sister Raisa first.

~~~~~

Lovell, Wyoming Dec. 27th, 1943
Dear Joe:

I hope this letter finds you well and enjoying the holidays. We were invited over to Emblem to spend Christmas with Arnold, Beth, and their little girl, Karlie. She certainly is a little sweetheart and takes my mind off all my worries, what with my brothers and son in the war. Beth lets us take her home with us every so often, which helps to keep me busy.

I have some bad news to tell you and hope you can speak to your commanding officer to see if he will let you come home for a while. Adam and some friends were coming back from a big dance over in Basin one night last week, and they hit black ice on Unterzuber's Bridge right outside of Greybull. They rolled their Ford four times, and Adam has a broken back. The other three guys have broken legs, arms, and stuff like that, but Adam's injuries are the worst. He is in pretty bad shape, Joe, and of course that sort of injury will take a long time to heal. Momma and Dad are worried about who is going to take care of the animals and get the fields ready for spring planting. Dad does what he can, but you know how that is. Jake is busy in the oil fields and the rest of the men that are left here are too busy with their own work to help out much.

Take care of yourself and please talk to your commander about this situation at home. Jake said that sometimes they release a guy if the circumstances at home are such as he is needed—as you are.

Our Love and Prayers—Raisa and Jake

~~~~~

Lovell, Wyoming
12 January 1944 —
Subject: Request for Discharge
To: Commanding Officer, 129th Cavalry Reconnaissance G Squadron, Fort Lewis, Washington
1.   The reason I find it necessary to request a discharge from the Army at this time is in regard to the farm my brother has been operating, until his recent accident in which he suffered a broken back. He will now be under a doctor's care for a year or more. This leaves the farm I have a fifty-percent interest in without an operator. My father who has the remaining fifty-percent interest is unable to operate the farm due to his age and failing health.
2.   This farm consists of eighty acres, sixty-five of which is under cultivation and the remaining acreage is pasture. The pasture is used by our eight head of milk stock and two work horses. We also have equipment enough to farm an additional eighty acres of rented land. This land we own and the afore-mentioned farm machinery will remain idle due to a shortage of farm operators in this community if I am not discharged from the Army.
Joseph Steiner
Cpl Tr 129th Cav Rcn Sq

Marilyn quit her job in Washington and moved to Lovell the first part of January. She found a small apartment in Lizzie's boardinghouse and got a job as a telephone operator. She made numerous trips out to the farm to see Joe's folks and then went around introducing herself to his brothers and sisters who lived in the area. Everybody took to her right off and wrote Joe to tell him so.

Joe got a special-request furlough, and on January 20, he and Marilyn drove to Billings and were married by a Lutheran minister. Just for good measure, Sofie, Lizzie, and Raisa drove up to represent the family. After the ceremony, they drove back to Lovell, leaving the newlyweds to themselves in Billings for a couple of days.

Joe had to report back to Fort Lewis, Washington, as his discharge still hadn't gone through. The family all assured him they would take good care of his wife. Since Marilyn had to work, Mook drove Joe to the train station. "Well, old boy, you certainly got yourself married, didn't you? Guess you can say good-bye to the good, old times you had taking out all those dames and dancing till dawn!" Mook slapped his brother on the back. 'Just want you to know that'll I'll take up where you left off, if you know what I mean!"

Mook laughed. "Hell, Watz, time you settled down anyways, and she's a keeper in my book—probably gonna give you a dozen kids! Can't believe it—the famous 'mover and shaker' is now a married man! Who would have guessed?"

Joe was discharged just in time for spring planting. He did most of the hard work while Mook did what he could and enjoyed bossing his older brother around.

Chapter Eighteen

Endurance

During the three-and-a-half years Jack hid from the Japanese army under Hiro Tohama's porch, he had more than several close calls. Frequently, Jack suggested to Hiro that he should disappear into the jungles and cease putting the Tohama family in jeopardy.

"Jack-san, speak no more of going into the jungle to hide. The soldiers would find you easier there. Where you hide now is under their nose where they do not think to look or suspect. Our plan is good and will work for as long as it takes. Remember, we stay quiet, and we stay safe."

There were spells when Jack grew impatient and despondent. *I feel like I am still living as a prisoner and wonder how long this damn war is going to last. I don't know what's going on in the world except what Hiro tells me.* Several months after the Japanese took Wake Island, Hiro informed Jack of what he heard had happened to the prisoners. "When I take vegetables to town, I hear news for you. There is talk the Americans are getting closer and winning more island battles. The officers at the camp are sending more of their healthiest prisoners on cargo freighters to Japan to work in the mines. They leave the sick and dying on the island in hope many will die so they don't have to feed them. I see some soldiers in town. They don't know where I live—they think I live in town. They laugh when they tell me some prisoners from camp escape into the jungles, thinking to escape. Soldiers brag they find most of them and shoot them where they hide. Some jungles are too thick for soldiers, and they forget about prisoners. Probably die anyway because no water except rain and also no food. So, I think they forget about Jack-san. Good—good thing they forget you."

For Jack, that night was filled with thoughts of home. There was no indication of when and if he would ever see his parents again, if he would ever walk down the streets of Lovell, or if he would ever go out on the town with his brothers. There were no guarantees he would make it out of this place alive. Exhausted, Jack fell asleep.

~~~~~

He was walking into the barn in the early morning, a milk bucket in each hand. He stopped for a moment, breathing in the mingled earthy smells of sweet, moldy hay, freshly combined grain in the storage room, and the pungent aroma of urine mixed with manure. He saw the first rays of sunlight sift through the cracks in the barn's weathered boards and play with the silky spider webs that hung from the rafters. "Come boss. Come boss." He reached to touch the velvet moistness of the cow's nose as he fingered her forelock then secured her neck in the stall.

As he sat in the cool shade of the front porch, he looked down at his hands and feet. "When had they healed—no more sign of the cracked and oozing fungus-filled nails—no cuts that had refused to heal in the constant humidity of that damn jungle. His nostrils filled with the scent of his mother's flowers—the lilacs, sweet alyssum, and wild roses. He opened the weathered screen door and walked into the familiar kitchen. The table was set for five people, and the aroma from bowls of steaming soup filled the kitchen. He pulled out a chair and sat and then picked up a spoon; he dipped it into the bowl and slowly moved it to his lips; he blew, then sipped, then blew again. He spooned it into his mouth, rolling it around and around. The ingredients—important to identify each one—important—cabbage, garlic, carrots, potatoes, parsley, beef, barley, dill—so good, so good! Tears fell from his eyes. Someone was pulling his arm, pulling him away from the table, pulling, pulling—no, no!

~~~~~

"Jack-san! Jack-san! Wake up! You must hide; soldiers!"

~~~~~

Spring1944:

David hadn't felt good for several months, and the doctor had been out to the farm a couple of times to check him over. "Mr. Steiner, I'm sorry to tell you I think it's your heart. Your breathing is not good either. Your lungs are filling with fluid. I would recommend that you sell out and move into town. I know your sons are doing most of the work, but I also know you are out in those fields when you feel like it. I want you to stay in bed for a week or more, and only get up to go to the bathroom and eat."

Reluctantly, David did what the doctor told him. Sensing the end was near, he asked Sofie to get in touch with all of their children, including the ones who lived nearby, asking them to come to the house on Sunday afternoon. He wanted to talk to each of them.

Sofie cooked a big dinner for her family; one by one she watched them drive into the yard and walk solemnly into the house. They were all there, daughters, sons, grandchildren—all, that is, except Edie, who was in Lander, Emilie, who lived far away in San Francisco, and of course Jack, who was still missing in the Pacific.

David asked them to come into his bedroom, in order of their birth; he kissed and hugged them. He shook the hand of each of his sons, telling them he wanted to say good-bye now and wanted each of them to know how much he loved them. "I don't know how much longer I have, and I want all my affairs settled if my death comes quickly. I have been blessed in so many ways all of my life—and this life we've had in this free country has been good. If we had stayed in the old country, we would have died. All of us would have died."

After their family had all left that evening, David and Sofie went out to sit on their front porch; Sofie noticed that David seemed pensive. "David, what is on your mind?

Are you troubled about something? Do you want to talk about it?"

David stopped rocking in his chair; he took a deep breath and released it as he ran his hand through his thinning hair. "JA, my Sofie, these days I have much time to think about my life and all of the directions it has gone. I think about the day my pregnant, unmarried mother arrived on the Volga and about being adopted by my parents and raised as their own. I had a good life, Sofie—as good as any boy. I was greatly blessed. Now that I can look back over my life, I think I see where I made a wrong turn. Sofie, it was when I decided to try and be a farmer like my father."

David stood and began pacing the weathered, wooden porch. "I think you probably already know this Sofie, but I should have been a pastor, not a farmer. My heart is in the Bible, in the Word—not in the field. I have been a failure in the fields, but I think I could have been a good pastor. It is what I love to do— help others understand God's Word and ways. I could have been of help to so many peoples with their lives and troubles. But to do that, I would have had to go to seminary, and I already had responsibilities as a husband and father.

"Now there is no more chance to realize my dreams, to do something that I would be successful at. I know I have done what I had to do to make a living for my family. We have been blessed with our family. The Lord has taken us many places, hoping I would find what I needed, and all the time it was right under my nose—the Good Book!"

Sofie sat with her hands in her lap, looking out over their fields as the sun sank lower in the west. "Oh, David, David, please don't put yourself down so. We made do with what we had. You always found a way to take care of us. It might not have been grand or rich, but it was enough, and we raised our family in the Christian way. And, my David, I always had you—a faithful, loving husband that I could count on. These are the important things, my *Liebchen*. You are also right in that I suspected long ago that you weren't cut out to be a farmer. Your true vocation was probably in the Bible, in counseling those who needed to hear God's Word and promise. But it was never to be that way for us, for you, and it is all right because we live free and safe in America."

David turned to look at his wife. "Sofie, are you ever sorry we left the Volga? Do you ever miss the old times we had growing up there and wish our children could have known more of the old ways?"

She smiled as she looked off into the setting sun. "JA, David, there are times when I miss what we knew growing up. I think what I miss the most is the evening singing and storytelling. We didn't have radio, so we made our own entertainment."

Sofie stood and stiffly crossed the porch to where her husband sat and looked down at him. "Do you remember how we used to sit around the stove in the winters and tell our family stories and sing our folk songs—such nice melodies, so sweet? Some could certainly sing better than others, but we all sang our hearts out."

David laughed, remembering his own family. "JA, we heard some good stories, not all true I am thinking! Those stories grew in drama and length each time they were told. I don't think I remember any of the stories, just that they were good and I loved them the most!"

David stood then, and they embraced. They stayed there in each other's arms on their front porch, watching the sun set on their lives.

~~~~~

August 1944

It had been several months since David's close call, and gradually he seemed to recover; at least, he had more good days than bad. He had tried to take it easy, and Sofie watched him like a hawk.

"Sofie, I can't stand this laying around and taking it easy. I am worth nothing if I can't go out to my fields and tend to my livestock." Most of his farm was leased out since his sons were all married and had jobs of their own.

Just like a thousand mornings before, that morning in August, David and Sofie were up at daybreak; old habits were hard to break. David walked into the kitchen dressed in his worn wool pants. He had his favorite pair of suspenders on and no belt; his hair was damp and slicked back as usual; he slowly pulled a chair out from the table. Sofie placed a cup of coffee in front of him. "I already added your cream and sugar, just the way you like it, so don't go adding any more. You know it's not good for you." She looked at him and added, "It's a good thing you have those old suspenders to hold your pants up. You are getting too skinny, David. I am going to have to fatten you up a little, so you fill out your clothes better—like me!" Sofie laughed as she bent to kiss her husband on his unshaven face.

David smiled and picked up the blue speckled cup, holding it in his leathery hand for a moment, savoring the heat and aroma. Slowly he tipped the cup and took a healthy sip. "Ahhh, you make the best coffee of anyone I know, my Sofie—that you do!"

Sofie smiled as she filled his plate with two eggs over easy and two pieces of bacon along with wheat toast—no butter, just the way he liked it. She returned to the stove, filled her own plate, and sat down to eat breakfast with her husband as they had done for fifty-four years.

David stopped eating and watched Sofie. "Sofie, what is it? Something is bothering you. Let us do what we have always done, share it. Then the problem is not so big. Come on now and tell me what is on your mind."

Sofie looked up at David; there were tears in her eyes. "I had a dream about Jack last night. He was sitting at this table and I was cooking for him. He was laughing and so happy to be home. " Sofie put her apron up to her eyes to wipe at the tears. "Oh, David—do you think our oldest son is still alive? When is this all going to be over? "

David pushed back his chair and rounded the table to place his hands on Sofie's shoulders. "There, there my Sofie. We have to ask God for patience in our waiting. We have to trust that God is watching over him and will bring him back in time." He pulled her to her feet and wrapped his arms around her plump body. "Sofie, I think the news of Raisa's brother-in-law, Johnny Kessel has probably upset both of us more than we think. At least they know now, that Johnny won't be coming home, that he is dead. But we have to sit and wonder and wait; that is also very hard, JA?"

After breakfast, Sofie headed for the chicken house as David walked slowly to the barn. Sofie spent most of her mornings caring for her fuzzy, new baby chicks. They were a comfort and distraction for her. Reaching down, she gently picked one up and held it close to her face, feeling the soft down feathers and listening to the sweet sound of its chirping. She reached into a pocket of her apron and scattered feed to the adult chickens. After finding their nests in the straw, she filled her apron with fresh eggs and started back to the house. She thought about the photo Jake and Raisa had taken of her and David in front of the summer kitchen just last Sunday when they came to visit. *I should get a copy and send it to Jack.* Then she stopped and remembered that they didn't know where Jack was!

Sofie smiled in spite of her thoughts about Jack. She fingered her apron as she walked across the farm yard. She was content and smiling as the warm spring sun fell over her face; she was careful to choose her path across the rocky farmyard as she thought. *It is getting harder for me to walk. My feet and legs swell and hurt every day. David must still be in the barn milking the cows. He takes his time these days like I do.* She smiled to herself, thinking about how things had changed for them—how life had settled, and they had finally put down roots. She welcomed the cool breeze that dried the perspiration on her neck. She tipped back her head and let the breeze blow the tendrils that had escaped from her gray topknot.

David took his time walking to the barn that morning; his shoulders slumped as the empty milk buckets clanked against his

legs. He reached out and pulled open the weathered barn door, inhaling the musty odor of cow manure and urine in union with the heavy smell of decaying hay. Once inside the hazy interior, he took a moment to lean over the fenced pen and stroke the silky head of a new calf. David leaned heavily against the frame of the barn door as he called into the pasture for his milk cows. "Come boss. Come boss."

The cows recognized the call and headed for the barn, eager to be relieved of the weight in their udders. David locked both cows into their stalls then bent over and placed the wooden T-bar stool beside the first cow. He balanced his body on the crude stool as he squatted down. Putting his forehead against the belly of the cow, he proceeded to squeeze and pull, squeeze and pull until the bucket was full of warm, fresh milk. Setting the full bucket to the side, he picked up the second bucket, and moving on to the second cow, he repeated the milking process. When the two buckets were full of milk, David stood, walked to the head of the stall, and released the cows, giving them a slap on the rump as they ambled out of the barn into the pasture. He felt a sudden wave of nausea and dizziness roll over him as he grabbed onto the door frame of the barn to steady himself. David stood there for a moment, trying to catch his breath while feeling disoriented. Recovering, he released the calf from the pen inside the barn and watched it eagerly scamper out into the corral to take what milk was left in its mother's udder.

David turned and slowly walked back inside the barn, his gait was a labored, side to side motion as he stopped, leaned over, and picked up the buckets of milk, one in each hand. He kicked open the barn door and headed for the house. A sudden, breathtaking jolt of pain sliced down his neck and left arm; he felt a viselike pressure across his chest. David stumbled and fell to his knees, dropping the buckets of milk. He didn't notice or care that the precious milk was quickly absorbed into the dry dirt.

Conscious only of the pain—the consuming pain that was spreading through his chest like a crushing wave—David felt like something was squeezing the breath from his body. He tried in vain to calm himself. *Breathe, slow. Breathe—can't get air, can't stand.* He lifted his head in the direction of the house, of Sofie, of help; all he saw was the blinding orb of the sun. Sweat beaded on his forehead as his hat fell to the ground. Everything around him began to fade and float. The second round of pain knocked him forward, face down in the dirt. With final effort, David lifted his head and turned his face to the right; he felt his cheek scrape across the gritty farmyard.

~~~~~~

When Sofie opened the screen door to go out and sit in the shade of the front porch, she saw him lying on the ground, the milk buckets turned over beside him. Her mending fell to the porch as a scream rose from her throat. She bustled down the steps; her arms were waving through the morning air in an effort to move her heavy, aging body faster across the yard.

Sofie reached her husband's side. Drops of perspiration beaded on her forehead, and her breathing was ragged as she dropped to her knees; she didn't feel the rocks dig into her puffy legs. "*Ach net*, Da-vid! *Ach Bitte Gott,* oh please God, *Mein Liebschen.* What has happened to you?" The answer exploded in her mind. "*Grosser Gott in Himmel;* not now, not yet. Don't leave me, David, *nein!*" She ran her weathered hands over his face, his hair, trying in vain to get some reaction. "David, please—please open your eyes, please wake up!"

Sofie tore the apron from around her waist and gently turned him over onto his back as she pushed the wadded-up apron under his head. Frantically, she unbuttoned his work shirt and loosened his pants. David's eyes were closed; he was deathly pale, and his face felt so cold. Sofie saw beads of sweat on his forehead. She put her ear to his mouth; he was barely breathing.

I need help. I've got to have help. If only we had a phone. I can't get him into the car by myself. I kept telling him we needed to have a phone out here, and now this. She lifted her head and saw a dust cloud about a mile down the road. She pushed herself upright and began to hurry up the lane to the road, hoping to stop the car. Sweaty, damp tendrils escaped from her topknot and clung to her neck; her breath came in audible gasps as she struggled to move as fast as she could. Sofie waved both arms wildly in the air until the car slowed and turned into their lane. Not waiting for the driver, she rushed back across the yard and back to David's side.

David didn't realize Sofie had found him and had gone for help. He was floating, and there was a woman—she looked familiar—a beautiful, young woman dressed in a long, blue gown; she held a gold crucifix in her hand. She reached for his hand as she hovered above him. Behind her he saw a brilliant tunnel of light and at the far end stood his Lord, waiting with outstretched arms. He looked back and saw his body lying on the ground and without thought or effort, he moved toward the light with his mother at his side.

~~~~~

By the time Sofie managed to flag the car down and had returned to David's side, he was already dead. John Moore's car skidded to a stop in the farmyard; he pulled the brake on the black Ford, cut the engine, and flung the door open. Sofie was kneeling in the dirt next to David, frantically trying to revive him. John hurried to where Sofie knelt on the gravel beside her husband; he pressed his finger against David's neck. He slowly closed his own eyes in defeat, and then he rose to his feet. John turned to Sofie. "I can't find a pulse. He's gone, Sofie—there is nothing we can do."

John pulled Sofie to her feet and held her in his arms, letting her cry onto his blue chambray shirt. When she finally pulled away and wiped her eyes with a corner of her apron, John asked, "Can you help me lift David into my car, and I'll take him on in to the hospital? I know the docs will want to take a look at him. I'll call Raisa and Jake to come out and pick you up, if that's okay with you. Will you be okay if I leave you here?"

"Yes, John, you go ahead and take my David to the hospital. Please, call Jake and Raisa to come out. JA, I need my Raisa. I need my girl!" Seemingly in a daze, she spoke to no one in particular. "I will go up to the house, wash my face, and straighten my hair. I can't go into town looking like this." After helping John get David's body into the car, John took her by the arm and walked her to the porch. Sofie turned and laid her hand on John's shoulder and thanked him for stopping, for trying to help her and David.

Sofie stood alone on the covered porch of their farmhouse. She felt frozen with shock and disbelief as she watched John drive off down the dusty road toward Lovell. She felt like she was having a bad dream; none of it seemed real. She remembered when one of David's shoes had fallen off as she and John were loading his body into the car. *The shoe is still there, lying in the yard. I have to get his shoe. He needs two shoes!*

As the tears came again, Sofie let them roll over her apple cheeks and drop onto the dusty farmyard. She moved slowly down the steps and shuffled across the yard to where the shoe laid, all by itself. Sofie bent over and picked David's shoe up. She held it in her hand and stared at it; it was as if she had not seen it before. Sofie turned and moved zombielike toward the house. She forgot about the black Ford that was taking David's body to the hospital as she grabbed onto the porch railing and pulled herself up the two weathered, wooden steps onto the porch.

Sofie stood for a moment in the shade of the porch, staring at David's rocking chair as it rocked gently in the breeze. Then it all came back to her as she fell to her knees and buried her face in the faded cotton seat pad. Wracking sobs came from deep within her as her body shook with grief. Sofie didn't know how long she had cried; she really didn't care. Suddenly, she was aware of hands pulling her to her feet as Jake and Raisa walked her into the cool, dim interior of the old farmhouse.

Later that day, at the hospital, Sofie asked Jake to call the rest of the family to come to the hospital. He called Emilie in California, and of course Edie was not able to make the trip; Jack was still considered a missing prisoner of war, as they had received no further information about him.

Jake and Raisa took Sofie home with them that night. She was in no shape to be alone out on the farm. After putting her mother to bed, Raisa sat by her side, reading from the Bible until she fell asleep. She gently brushed her hand across her mother's pale cheek as she leaned over and kissed her softly then tiptoed from the room, closing the door behind her.

~~~~~

The Steiner family and friends gathered five days later to bury their husband, father, grandfather, and friend. David was dearly loved and respected, a gentle, loving man who lived his life according to his faith. After the funeral they had a family gathering.

Beth sat at a table with her parents. "Mom, do you remember how Grandpa always fished around in his pocket for a penny or a nickel to give us kids when we came to visit?" She laughed as fond memories of her grandfather filled her mind.

"Yeah, he made sure we stood there, waiting for our surprise, while he pretended to search for a coin. He was the best grandfather. I loved him so much and know I'm gonna miss him."

~~~~~

Sofie went back to live on the farm after the funeral but only for a short while. She was extremely lonely out there by herself with only her memories as company. After conferring with her children, they put the farm up for sale, and in three months, it was sold.

A few weeks before Christmas, Adam, Joe, and Pete pulled up in front of the farmhouse. Sofie met them at the door in her familiar faded-print housedress covered by a bib apron. She wiped her hands on the apron as she invited her sons in for a bite of lunch. Adam gave her a big hug and said, "Only if you open a jar of your pickled watermelon, and don't tell me you don't have any because I saw you putting them up right before Dad died." Sofie laughed and hurried off to the pantry where she kept the jars of their family favorite.

As the three of them ate lunch, Pete announced, "We want to show you a nice little house in Lovell, and if you like it, it's yours! You need someplace to live now that you've sold the farm, and we think you will like this house. You'll still have a place of your own, and the great thing is that it is three blocks from Raisa and Jake's, and its four blocks from Adam and Ellen's. So while Joe and I get these dishes washed up, you go on in and change your dress. Put on one of your famous hats too—we can't wait to show you this place."

Sofie loved the little house. It had two bedrooms, a large front room, and a sunny, spacious kitchen with all the latest appliances. She walked through the house, reverently touching the appliances and opening closets. Finally, she walked out on the south-facing porch. "It's perfect, just as you said, even with this porch where I can sit evenings and watch the world go by. Now, how much is it? Can I afford this nice house? I have to say, it is the best house I have ever had, and to think I might live here, is like— is like a dream!"

In addition to the profits from the farm sale, Sofie's children each pitched in some extra money so the house would be mortgage-free. Sofie lived in peace and comfort. She never drove a car but always found someone to take her where she needed to go. She especially enjoyed inviting the older Volga German women from church over for tea, her luscious desserts, and conversation about the old country.

Raisa stopped by often for coffee and a piece of her mother's *Kuchen*. One day they were sitting out on the front porch, and Sofie was in a pensive mood. "Raisa, I have never asked you if you remember anything about the old country, about your grandparents and where we lived behind our store. Do you remember any of it? It was all so long ago—like another life." Before Raisa could respond, Sofie continued. "We were quite well off and had it much better in Susannenthal than we did here in America. We were prosperous, well-respected, and could buy almost anything we needed. We were so happy, and your dad was very successful." She lowered her head, and her memories flooded her mind.

"I know we would not have survived the revolution as Volga Germans. We most probably would have died like my parents, either there along the Volga or in Siberia. It was a terrible ending to a beautiful community of people and a life they built from nothing. But it was also hard here in America. Your papa never knew success again at making money. It was very hard for him to adapt to this way of life, but I know he did the best he could, and so I stayed with him. I stayed because I loved him and because there was no other thing for me to do."

Raisa stood and walked over to her mother. Squatting down, she wrapped her arms around Sofie and held her in her arms. "No, Mama, I don't remember very much. It is all so hazy what memories I have of Oma and Opa. One thing I do remember is the train ride through Russia, especially when we came to Moscow, I think it was. It was a big city, at night, and people were sleeping along the station platform, and small fires were burning to keep warm while they waited for the train. There were so many people, people crying and arms reaching for the train, but the train didn't stop. I remember asking Papa why they didn't stop for those people, and he just looked down and didn't answer. I know now why the train didn't stop—it was all so horrible, so sad for those poor, poor people! I am very grateful you and Papa made the decision you did, to leave the Volga and come to America—it meant our life, Mama, our life!"

~~~~~

It was a late November afternoon in 1945. Sofie thought she heard a car drive up outside and a car door slam. Before she could make it to the door, it burst open, and there stood her Johann. In shock, Sofie's hand flew to cover her mouth as she reached for the door frame to steady herself. Jack stepped through the door and in three long strides was across the front room, wrapping his arms around his mother. They stood there for a long time, mother and son together, hugging as tears of joy slid down Sofie's apple cheeks.

Sofie turned finally and hobbled across the room; she sat heavily in her chair. Jack hurried to her side. "Sorry, Ma didn't mean to give you a shock. Didn't you get the telegram the government sent, that I was on my way home? I called Raisa from the train station, and she told me you had moved into town. Mighty nice little house, Ma. Looks like you and Dad are comfortable here— off that farm and away from all the work!"

Sofie covered her face with her wrinkled hands as she began to sob; finally she took out her handkerchief and wiped her eyes. Jack knelt on the carpeted floor in front of his mother's chair. "Come on, Ma—no more crying. I'm home. Now where is that old man of mine? I sure want to see him too."

Sofie leaned forward, cradling Jack's weathered face in her hands. She didn't speak for a moment, trying to find the right words. After a few moments, she reached down and took Jack's hands in hers. "Jack, there is something I have to tell you. First, no, Jack, we didn't get any word that you were coming home. Maybe they sent it out to the farm. I couldn't stand it out there, all alone, after your papa passed away."

It was Jack's turn to be shocked as his mother's words registered in his brain. Shock fell over his tanned face, and his eyes grew wide and then filled with tears. His face lost the swaggering confidence and devil-may-care smile. "What—what did you say? Papa passed away? My father died, while I was gone? Oh, Ma, oh, Mama—no—no, don't tell me that. I wanted to see him again. I have so many stories to tell him about how I survived the war. Now you are telling me I won't have that chance. When did he die? What happened?"

Sofie told Jack all about David's heart attack, and even though he had been sick for months, the end came suddenly. "He told me that the only thing he regretted was not seeing you again. He never believed you were dead, Jack. No, sir, he always thought you would come home one day, and he was right!"

Sofie rose stiffly from her rocking chair and motioned for Jack to follow her into the kitchen. "Here, my son, sit, and I will get you some of your favorite apple *Kuchen* and maybe some of my pickled watermelon, huh? I need to fatten you up a bit. You are so skinny, but you are alive! You are alive, and I give thanks to the Lord for bringing you back home to me!"

~~~~~

Jack waited until he had a sizeable audience of his brothers and sisters before he told them how he had survived the war, how he escaped from the prison camp right under the noses of the Jap guards, and how he hid under the porch of a compassionate Japanese family for the rest of the war. "I promised Hiro that when his son was fourteen, I would bring him to America and send him to high school, and I am going to keep that promise. If it weren't for Hiro and his plan to keep me out of the hands of those Jap soldiers, I probably wouldn't have made it. I owe him big time!" 27

Later in the week, Jack slipped out to the cemetery and sat in front of his father's gravestone. With tears sliding down his lean face, he told his dad about the past four years.

~~~~~

Sofie lived in her new house in Lovell for six years; with a little effort, she found ways to enjoy her life without her husband. She still loved sitting out on the front porch in the evenings just as she and David did so often when he was alive.

Sofie stood up as dusk turned to darkness. The street lamps came on, illuminating the deepening shadows. She looked down at her feet; her shoes felt tight, and her feet tingled. It took her a moment to move her legs and feet. *Maybe it's the heat.*

She painfully hobbled into the kitchen where she ran the faucet until it was cold. Sofie drank two glasses of water before she was sated; she turned and painfully made her way into her bedroom to prepare for bed. She sat heavily on the edge of the bed and bent forward to untie her shoes. After the shoes and stockings were off, Sofie looked down at her feet. They were swollen and red; she reached down and attempted to rub one of her feet. Her big toe felt like it was filled with pins and needles; she couldn't feel the other toes at all. She frowned. *Maybe tomorrow I call Raisa and make a doctor appointment.* Sofie lay awake for a long time that night, thinking and listening to the mournful cry of the freight train whistle as it passed through Lovell.

~~~~~

Raisa and Sofie sat waiting in Dr. Helsey's office after he examined Sofie. "Until the tests come back, I can't tell for sure, Mrs. Steiner, but it is my educated guess you are suffering from diabetes. You are overweight, urinate frequently, are excessively thirsty, and have experienced severe swelling and numbness in your feet and legs. Until I see the results, I want you to follow this diet and see if you notice any change. I realize you have a sweet tooth, so I imagine you aren't going to be fond of this diet, but it's for your own good. I should have the tests back in ten days. I'll have my nurse give you a call when the results are in. Take care of yourself now. Good-bye."

Two weeks later, around the first of October, Sofie was told that she indeed was suffering from acute sugar diabetes. Dr. Helsey gave her some pills and instructed her to stay on the limiting diet. Sofie struggled with the diet but noticed further relief when the weather cooled.

~~~~~

Early Spring 1952

Sofie woke in the middle of the night to excruciating pain in her right leg and foot. The leg felt numb, like it was asleep. She had to go to the bathroom but knew she couldn't get out of bed without some help. Sofie looked at the clock beside her bed. *Oh mercy me, it is two o'clock in the morning. Do I call Raisa or the ambulance? I hate to bother anyone at this hour. Perhaps it's best just to call the hospital.*

The ambulance pulled up out front of Sofie's house about ten minutes after the phone call. Raisa and Jake were right behind them. The hospital had called Raisa as she had requested if anything happened to her mother. Besides, she had a key to the door, and if it was as bad as the hospital said, her mother couldn't answer the door or unlock it. They let themselves in, and Raisa ran to the bedroom where she found her mother flushed and in tears. "I'm sorry, Raisa and Jake, to get you out of your bed, but I am in big troubles, I think." They pulled back the covers, and Raisa gasped as she saw her mother's foot; it was black.

Jake and Raisa sat in the waiting room, along with Adam and his wife. Sofie had been in the hospital for two days undergoing treatment to try and save her leg. Earlier in the day, Dr. Helsey had explained to them it was because of the diabetes and an obliterated major artery in her right knee; her foot had actually begun to decay. In other words, Sofie had gangrene. There was only one remedy for the situation; they would have to take the foot to save her leg.

Raisa was so restless; she paced the floor, chewing her fingernails, leafing through countless magazines. "Raisa, if you don't sit down and relax, I am going to have to teach you how to smoke!" Jake teased as he took her hand in his. "Do you want me to take a walk around the block with you?"

"No, Jake, we might miss the doctor. The nurses said they were about finished with the surgery."

Sofie was in the hospital for three weeks and suffered greatly with the pain of her stump. Because of her advanced age and overweight condition, she couldn't manage crutches or therapy. That left no other means of mobility except a wheelchair, which she hated. When she was finally able to go back home, her family hired a full-time nurse to stay with her.

~~~~~

One day when Raisa was spending time with her mother, cleaning and cooking for her, she went out on the front porch to see how she was doing and if she needed anything. Sofie was just sitting in her wheelchair, staring out at the street, not looking at anything in particular. "Mama, are you all right? Is there anything I can get for you? Are you in pain?"

Tears began to roll down Sofie's face as she turned to her firstborn. "Oh, Raisa, Raisa, you don't know what this is like. Why is my Lord Jesus making me to suffer so? I have been a faithful Christian all of my life, and now I have this trial. I feel like He has abandoned me, left me here alone without my David, to suffer living my last years."

Raisa knelt beside her mother and put her arm across Sofie's shoulders. Raisa laid her head on her mother's shoulder. "Oh, Mama, I wish there was something I could do to help you. I wish I had an answer for you as to why you have to suffer so. I suppose the pastor would tell you that just because you are a faithful Christian doesn't exempt you from having suffering in your life. But you need to remember that the Lord hears your prayers, and He walks with you through this darkness." Raisa wiped her own eyes and blew her nose in her linen handkerchief. "You know your children are here for you and are praying for you too. You are deeply loved, Mama."

Sofie sat for a minute or two then said, "I think my time is near. I have been dreaming of your father. My dreams are so clear—it's as if I could reach out and touch him. I want to go to him, Raisa. I want to be with your papa. So when I die, don't cry over me. We had a good life here in America.

"I often think of what if we had stayed in Russia. We would have all died, most surely. Your papa was right in getting us out of there, even though I didn't want to leave. I only wish my parents could have come with us. It pains me deeply to think of their last days.

"I have been thinking of something else. It's time I make out a will. I don't have much, but I have this house and a few things that you children might want. Will you call an attorney for me?"

~~~~~

Sofie Steiner died in the spring of 1952 at the age of seventy-four years from a blood clot in her heart. The family buried her beside David in the Lovell cemetery, in the earth of the country that gave them a new life of freedom and opportunity—America!

Epilogue

This book owes its very existence to those determined and courageous people who first emigrated from all parts of Europe, especially southwestern Germany to settle the Volga River land granted by Catherine the Great. My grandmother, Raisa, was born in the Lutheran village of Susannenthal, on the Wiesensite or Meadow side of the Volga River. After World War II it was renamed Winkelmann; it is currently called Sosnowka. The villages were separated by religion—Catholic, Lutheran, or Mennonite. That's the way they preferred it. While living along the Volga, they held fast to their German customs and different religions.

As I researched the history and story of these extraordinary people, *Die Wolgadeutschen,* the more I learned, the more I yearned to know. In the latter part of the nineteenth century as the Volga Germans began to experience continuous threats and ensuing violation of the Russian government's promises, they chose to emigrate yet again to a better, safer life - most chose America. After the first immigrants were settled in eastern cities and states of America, they wrote letters back to the Volga, encouraging friends and family members to follow. Each year the number of emigrants leaving the Volga increased as their life in Russia became harder and more threatened.

Like other immigrants, the Volga Germans chose to live in ethnic neighborhoods where they felt comfortable. At first they chose particular areas of large cities in Michigan, Minnesota, Ohio, and Wisconsin. Often these areas were also destination points where some settled, and some merely rested before moving on to the Midwest and Great Plains. As they had in Russia, they held fast to religious beliefs and customs. Even when taunted by the name *Rooshian,* they embraced their newly found freedom and country, learning the language and becoming citizens. There was good farmland to be had. States like Montana, Nebraska, Colorado, North and South Dakota, Wyoming, and Kansas welcomed these experienced and hardworking settlers who could grow their red wheat and sugar beets in less than good conditions. Their payment for thinning the beets, hoeing them twice after thinning, and topping them after they were pulled by hand was around $20 per acre—for the entire summer's work!

As Americans, the Volga Germans were extremely pious. They lived by their religion as they had living along the Volga. They had a difficult time accepting particular American customs, especially the human consumption of corn on the cob. Along the Volga, corn was fed to the pigs! The children of the Volga Germans learned the new language easily, contrary to their parents who found it difficult and a waste of time. For this reason, worship services were usually held in two sessions: the first service in German and the second in English. Frequently (according to custom), the men sat on the opposite side from their wives and children.

Most immigrants encouraged their children to become educated, as they now understood the value of a good education. Nearly half of rural America was settled by people of German heritage.

David and Sofie lived their final years in peace on a farm they owned. I remember visiting them when I was very little. My great-grandmother always smelled like chicken soup and lavender soap. She had a soft lap and endless love for her family! As I said, I know of this story because Raisa, their oldest daughter, was my beloved grandmother.

*Generations: Raisa Kessel, Sofie Steiner,
Karen Wamhoff, Beth Wamhoff*

Endnotes

1 – The Thirty Years' War (1618 – 1648) occurred as the teachings of Martin Luther and the reformation spread through Germany. Fear, hatred, prejudice, and finally war were the results. Consumed with blind hate and narrow-minded theology, a ferocious and enduring conflict erupted between Catholics and protestant Lutherans. It spread like the plague, like a cloud of locusts throughout Germany and other European countries. The majority of the war was fought on German soil.

As each town or village was conquered time and again by marauding soldiers and princes, the religion of the village was changed to the religion of the conqueror. Even the village of Kemel, where our ancestors are buried, had originally been Lutheran but changed religion seven times. From 1701 to 1745, the War of the Spanish Succession, the Silesian Wars, and finally the Seven Years' War ravaged Germany.

Driven by pure greed and the intensifying wish to stop escalating harassment from Austria, Frederick the Great of Prussia sent his well-equipped troops against Maria Theresa, empress of Austria. It all began over the small area called Silesia. Other European countries then formed alliances with either Prussia or Austria; smelling blood and riches, they sent their own troops marching across German borders. Russian Cossacks invaded the border to the north as battle-hardened troops of the insatiable French King Louis XIV poured across the southern border. Again, they chose for their battlefields the forests and farmland of southwestern Germany.

2 - Pronunciation: Saw-ROT-off.

3 - Pronunciation: Sus-zan-net-tall

4 - There was complete devastation, followed by years of the Silesian Wars which was followed by an even more disastrous war: the Seven Years' War (1756 to 1763). This war left village after village in complete devastation and utter ruin. People had no choice but to leave to search for food and work. Extreme poverty lay everywhere, which made people desperate and ripe for the

promises Catherine the Great of Russia made in her Manifesto of 1763. However, she helped and yet misled her native countrymen because she had the opportunity!

5 - Over 30,000 Germans initially left their homes and families yearning for a better life. None could have imagined what awaited them on the Russian steppes.

6 - Filzstiefel boots were made from leather or felted wool. Long sheepskin coats and the babushka (grandmother) scarves kept the German emigrants warm. Food items like Russian borsch soup and vodka took their place with traditional German fare. They adopted particular items from the Russians which helped them live more comfortably in the brutal land. They also adapted their medicinal remedies to include local herbs, roots, foliage, and bark, which were available and gathered routinely from the Volga riverbanks and the *steppe* or upper grassland.

7 - Susannenthal was predominately inhabited by Lutherans and Mennonites. Most villages were either Catholic or Lutheran. Because of the terrible Thirty Years' War in Germany and a long-lived religious prejudice that persisted, the two major and conflicting faiths still chose to live in separate villages. The presiding forefathers had quickly set down laws that forbade any mingling of the two groups.

8 - The newly arrived German colonists spent their first winter like animals in quickly constructed dugouts burrowed into soft, exposed riverbanks. They constructed their houses with limbs, twigs, and brush, which were then plastered over with dried grass and mud from the river. The roofs consisted of thin limbs pulled from a sparse collection of scrawny trees, piling on more brush, twigs, and dirt until the meager hut threatened to collapse.

9 - Translated: *bed drape*.

10 - Camels were often used to farm the fields instead of horses. On occasion Die Wolgadeutschen would use small Kalmuck horses, but camels were strong and adapted to the harsh conditions. The German settlers also used wool from the camels for warm winter clothing.

11 - When the Russian government decided to draft Germans to serve in their armies, it was rumored that Bismarck (Germany's leader) demanded that the Czar grant all German settlers a ten-year period to leave Russia if they so desired because the *ukaz*

(promise/ agreement) was no longer in force. This was a period of heavy emigration; many Germans left Russian soil most immigrated to America. Hundreds of families left the Volga from the major river port of Saratov.

12 - The term of a Cossack's military service was for twenty years beginning when males turned eighteen. At the end of service, the Russian government granted them land. For three years they endured intense training, and only the "cream of the crop advanced. During the following twelve years, they traveled, raided, and fought wars that were theirs and wears that were not theirs. They supplied their own uniforms (some were opulent), equipment, and horses; the government supplied their arms if needed. They had a reputation for making and enforcing their own laws, as well as a history of brutal and reckless attacks throughout the continent. Cossacks were especially known for their expertise as horsemen and prowess with the whip!

13 - Translated: *cabbage cake*

14 - Translated: *potato dumplings*

15 - Translated: *berry cake*

16 - The majority of Volga Germans were quite supportive of Czar Nicholas and his German-born wife, Alexandra. She was born in Grand Duchy of Hesse-Darmstadt of a royal family. Her grandmother was Queen Victoria of England, and Alexandra was raised as a Lutheran, which made her extremely popular with most Volga Germans.

17 - When a person or a family emigrated from a tightly knit community on the Volga, it was looked upon as a death. Those who stayed behind were most confident they would never see the person or people again on this earth. They were considered dead

18 - The *S.S. Main* was built in 1900 and was a 10,200 gross-ton ship, measuring 501 feet in length and 58.1 feet across the beam. It had a speed of fourteen knots and could accommodate 2,865 steerage- class, 217 second-class, and 369 first-class passengers. The *S.S. Main* made the trip across the Atlantic from Hamburg to New York and/or Baltimore for fourteen years, carrying emigrants toward their dreams of freedom and a new beginning. As records indicate, approximately 75 percent of their passengers were *Die Wolgadeutschen. The* ship's manifest recorded many Russian/

German emigrants with names like Steiner, Klinger, Meinhard, Werner, Felk, Langolf, Steiner, Straube, Honstein, Lauck, Roth, Winterholler, Fink, Ennis, Spiecker, Stenzel, Schmidt, Ungefug, Lehmann, Runck, Wasmuth, Leonhardt, Doerr, Link, Preis, and Wegner.

19 - Russian Tsar Nicholas II, the Tsarina, and their five children were kidnapped and held hostage for months. They were eventually murdered by the Communist regime.

20 - These frequent dust storms were only a precursor to the terrible years of what was known as the Great Dust Bowl that plagued the open prairie states of southeastern Colorado, western Kansas, the panhandles of Oklahoma and Texas, and the eastern border of New Mexico. During the decade of the thirties, the intensity of the storms worsened. Roads and tent parks were filled with carloads and caravans of dispossessed farmers and homeless people driven from their homes by rolling walls of swirling, powder-like black dust.

21 - The Spanish flu infected the entire world and was more like a plague, as it killed over half a million Americans and twenty-five to forty million people worldwide. It ended the same time as World War I, which only took nine million lives. Worldwide, bodies were stacked like cordwood. Even remote villages in Alaska and the islands of the Pacific and Atlantic were not spared. There was a shortage of health workers, medicine, coffins, and gravediggers. The final moments before death were horrible to witness, as the victims suffocated and drowned in their bloody phlegm.

22 - It is highly likely their daughter, Edie, suffered from a form of cerebral palsy. She died at the age of twenty-eight in the Lander, Wyoming School for Mentally Retarded Children.

23 - After the bumper harvest of 1919, the rest was downhill for the remaining Germans who lived along the Volga. Because of droughts, grasshoppers, and Communists, there was nothing left in the once-thriving villages. Many pastors and priests were sent to Siberia, along with thousands of other people. Some of those who were arrested and packed in cattle cars scribbled notes to family on bits of paper and threw them out the cracks to those who lined the tracks. Most notes contained one word: "Siberia"! To survive the next decade, they cooked old hides, boiled and ate corn husks, and scavenged fields looking for potatoes, carrots, or cabbage. Finally

after eating what livestock were left, they ate their cats and dogs. They dug up their valuables to sell or trade for anything to eat. Small children could be heard crying in the night and only quieted when they crawled into a corner to die. *Die Wolgadeutschen* were driven from their beds in the dark of night and watched as their homes and villages were set on fire. If they weren't packed into cattle cars, they were rounded up and marched at gunpoint to Siberia. Those who fell along the road were never seen again. Even if they made it to Siberia, only a small number survived. Foreign correspondents were banned from Russia during the Revolution, so the rest of the world had little knowledge of their plight and torture.

24 - The Steiner brothers had nicknames for each other. Jack was known as "Spatz"; Pete (the first of the brothers to marry) was called "Stute." Joe was called "Watz" (Jack also called him "Glocka"); Adam was known as "Mook." How they got these names remains a mystery, although it's fun to imagine several scenarios. During the war the brothers wrote to each other and to their parents on a regular basis. Joe fell in love and married his sweetheart. A special thanks to Joe's children and his brother's children, who lent the actual historical letters to me for use in the content of this novel. The letters appear in their original form. The irregular and misspelling of some words is because, like most farm boys, they only went to school until the fifth or sixth grade.

25 - On December 22, 1941, two Japanese fleet carriers loaded with fighters escorted by two destroyers and over 1,600 men began bombing the tiny, strategically located island of Wake. The Americans fought for as long as they could inflicting as much damage as possible. However, on the morning of December 23, they saw the writing on the wall and surrendered.

26 - After the Japanese army took Wake Island, about fifty recognized civilian prisoners out of over two thousand who had contracted to build the airfields were separated from the military prisoners and told to dig a long trench. The Japanese guards lined them up and machine-gunned them, pushing them back into the trench they had dug.

27 - Two years after Jack came home from the war, he sent for the oldest son of, Hiro Tohama. As he promised, the boy lived with

him and attended high school in Greybull, Wyoming. When he graduated, Jack helped send him on to college. When asked, Jack would say it was a small debt to pay for his own life. Prior to the war, Jack had been married and fathered a daughter who still lives in the Big Horn Basin of Wyoming.

Historical, Period Notes

In 1907, America offered a better way of life than most immigrants had known. The average life expectancy was forty-seven. Fourteen percent of homes had a bathtub, and only 8 percent had a telephone. The average wage was twenty-five cents an hour and the average worker made between $300 and $430 a year. Only 7 percent of Americans graduated from high school. Baths were on Saturday nights, and church was on Sunday. Women usually washed their hair once a month with a mixture of Borax, herbs, and egg yolk followed with a vinegar/rainwater rinse. There were approximately nine thousand automobiles in the entire country, and the flag held only forty-five stars.

Emigration from the Volga to the United States had all but ended by the Russian Revolution in 1917. Only a handful of Volga Germans escaped the increasing persecution and procurements by the Bolsheviks. During World War II, after the invasion of Russian territory by brutal German troops, the cruelty of the Communist government reached a climax when they rounded up the once-prosperous Volga Germans and marched or transported them by wooden boxcar to Siberia and near-certain death.

In the United States, during World War I and continuing through World War II, people of German heritage were victims of relentless persecution and questioning. Many of their previous privileges were taken away, and there were even situations of Germans being stoned as they walked down a street. Most German immigrants rose to the occasion and proudly declared their American allegiance. Many journeyed to their county seats and applied for citizenship or signed up to serve in the armed forces.

The initial attack on Wake Island by Japanese invaders was the only attack stopped by land-based guns during the war in the Pacific. It was a much-needed boost to the morale of the Allied forces in early 1942. Once the Americans surrendered in December of 1942, the island was in Japanese hands until September 4, 1945.

Sources

Susannenthal Newsletter by Kerry Thompson (editor) *Given Up for Dead* by Bill Sloan

Wake Island by Calton Lewis

The Volga Germans by Fred C. Koch

Wir Wollen Deutsche Bleiben by George J. Walters

Photo of Germans on Camels—permission granted by The American Historical Society of Germans from Russia (AHSGR)

King James Bible Personal Family Letters

About the Author

Karen Wamhoff Schutte was born in, Lovell, Wyoming and raised on a farm in Emblem, homesteaded by her paternal grandparents John and Mary Wamhoff. For the first eight years of her education she attended the two-room, gyp-block schoolhouse in the German-Lutheran farming community. She then traveled eighteen miles by bus to high school in Greybull, Wyoming. Ms. Schutte is the oldest of four daughters born to Beata and the late Arnold Wamhoff.

After graduating from high school, she studied at the University of Wyoming for two years, married, and then spent over twenty years raising her four sons. Returning to the University of Wyoming to complete her college education, she graduated with a bachelor's degree in design/marketing in 1987 and established Interiors by Karen. She practiced her chosen field for twenty-five years as a member the American Society of Interior Designers.

"At the time, I believed I was doing what I was born to do— after raising four rambunctious sons, that is. But I was wrong. It wasn't my plan or even dream to become a published author, but it was God's plan. Why is it that *His* plans are always better than ours? I truly believe *He* wanted me to experience life---its joys and sorrows—before I was ready to sit down and breathe life into these family stories!"

After retirement, Karen has pursued a longtime passion for historical fiction and writing, developing a burning passion for everything her new career embraces. "My greatest tool is that I visualize the characters, the scenes—I am in the story, experiencing what is happening. At that point, I paint a physical picture of the story with carefully chosen, descriptive words, so those who read what I have written may also experience the journey. I love what I do, and it certainly has presented new challenges and purpose to my life. Sometimes we are given gifts we didn't ask for or think about, and those are the best of all, because they open up totally unexpected windows of opportunity and adventure!"

Schutte has written for the past fifteen years, completing (not published) an all-encompassing "beginning-to-end" teaching explanation of interior design for everybody. All in all, writing for Karen Schutte is a journey in expressing her thoughts, her faith, and her energy in a purposeful manner. "I've always wanted to leave my mark in this world. Now, I believe I am doing just that."

The Ticket (2010) is the first book in her historical fiction series revolving around, true family stories of immigration and sacrifice. *Seed of the Volga* is the second historical novel in the trilogy. Karen is currently working on the final book of the trilogy,

Flesh on the Bone and declares that it won't be the end of her writing, as she has plans for three additional novels! Schutte is a member of the Rocky Mountain Fiction Writers, Wyoming Historical Society, and American Historical Society of Germans from Russia.

Karen and her husband, Mike, have four sons and nine grandchildren. They live in Fort Collins, Colorado.

CPSIA information can be obtained
at www.ICGtesting.com
Printed in the USA
FSOW01n2305130715
8751FS